THE Reaper's VOW

DEDICATION

For the voices in my head, who refused to shut up until I
gave them fangs, trauma, and terrible coping
mechanisms.
May you all finally rest now.
(But probably not.)

TRIGGER WARNINGS

Welcome to the world of fangs, bullets, and bad decisions. This story contains wolves with territorial issues, mobsters with anger problems, and characters who think "communication" means growling louder.

If you came here looking for morally sound behavior, healthy relationships, or people who use their words instead of claws and knives—you may have wandered into the wrong story.

Expect violence, obsession, and the kind of love that probably requires therapy. This is not a safe, soft romance. It's a bloodstained, claw-marked mess with too many alpha egos and not enough impulse control.

Content Warnings / Triggers include:
- Forced mating
- Abduction

- Non-consensual sexual situations
- Stalking
- Tracking devices
- Death and murder (including patricide)
- Misogyny
- Violence and gore (including torture, blood, and graphic depictions of injury)
- Possessive and obsessive behavior
- Captivity and imprisonment
- Public humiliation and degradation
- Drug and alcohol use
- Hunting scenes and animal death
- Animal cruelty
- Biting (often in the context of a mate bond)
- Breeding kink or pressure to become pregnant
- Parental separation or death

PLAY LIST

The Summoning - Sleep Token
Big Bad Wolf - In This Moment
Another Life - Motionless In White
Hurricane - I Prevail
I Miss The Misery - Hailstorm
Forsaken - Korn
Dance Macabre - Ghost
The Night Does Not Belong To God - Sleep Token
Death Dance - Lady Gaga
Villain - K/DA ft. Madison Beer & Kim Petras
Spooky Scary Skeletons – Andrew Gold

Karina

The monster inside me doesn't growl when Travis dumps his cheap cologne into a cardboard box—it purrs.

"You sure you want me gone, babe?" Travis's voice slithers across the apartment, wrapping around my throat like it has for the past eighteen months. He sets down the box and stretches, making sure his t-shirt rides up just enough to show the abs he spends more time admiring than I ever did. "We had some good times."

I fold my arms across my chest, keeping my distance near the kitchen counter, "Come on, Karina." He steps closer, and I catch the scent, arousal mixed with desperation. My heightened senses make it impossible to miss. "One last time for the road?"

"I'll pass."

His smile falters, then returns with an edge. "Still playing the ice queen? That's why we're done, you know. You're always so...distant." He runs a hand through his perfectly styled hair. "Except in bed. That was the only time you seemed alive."

The monster inside me stirs, not with desire but with rage. If he knew what lived beneath my skin, what prowled beneath the surface on full moon nights, he'd be clawing his way out the door.

"I said no." I flick a glance at my watch, "You've got thirty more minutes before my lunch break ends."

Travis snorts and grabs another box, shoving his gaming console inside with far too much force. "You've been saying 'no' a lot lately. Disappearing in the middle of the night. Coming back smelling like the woods." His jaw tightens, suspicion hanging heavy in the air. "Who is he, Karina?"

"There's no one." The lie slips out easily, familiar on my tongue. Not because I'm unfaithful, but because my entire life has been built on half-truths.

"Bullshit." He slams the box down. "Normal people don't just vanish at 2 AM."

I bite back the response that burns in my throat. I'm not normal. I'll never be normal.

"I have insomnia," I say instead, the same excuse I've used a hundred times. "I go for walks."

"In the fucking forest? In the middle of the night?"

He laughs, but there's no humor in it. "You expect me to believe that?"

The monster inside me paces restlessly. Three days until the full moon. Three days until I have no choice but to let it out again. My skin already feels too tight, like I'm wearing clothes a size too small.

"Believe whatever you want, Travis. It doesn't matter anymore."

He moves toward me suddenly, and I tense. Not out of fear—though I've learned to act afraid when appropriate—but to keep the wolf at bay. She doesn't like sudden movements, especially from men who reek of anger and testosterone.

"You know what?" Travis takes another step closer, invading my space. "I think you've been lying to me this whole time. I think there's a lot you haven't told me."

If he only knew how right he is.

"Back up, Travis."

"Or what?" He cocks his head. "You gonna call the station and report me to my sergeant? Who do you think they'll believe?"

The monster inside me is fully awake now, clawing at my ribs. She wants out. She wants to show him exactly what happens when you corner a wolf.

"Three minutes," I say, forcing my breathing to slow. "Then I'm calling someone to remove you."

He laughs but takes a half-step back. "Who? Your mystery man?"

"The property manager. I've already spoken with him."

Something in my tone must finally get through to him. Travis's expression shifts, the facade of confidence cracking just enough to reveal the insecurity beneath.

"You'll regret this," he mutters, turning back to his boxes. "When you're alone in this place at night, you'll miss me."

I almost laugh. I'd rather face a thousand lonely nights than one more with him. But I keep that thought locked behind my teeth as I watch him pack. The air in the apartment feels charged, like the moments before a thunderstorm breaks. I've become good at weathering storms.

"You'll call," Travis says with the certainty of someone who's never been told no. "When you're done playing hard to get, you'll call."

"I won't," I say simply.

He slams the last box shut, tape screeching across cardboard. The sound hurts my sensitive ears, but I don't flinch. I've learned to hide the little tells that might give me away.

"You know what your problem is, Karina?" Travis hoists the box, biceps flexing obscenely. "You're afraid of letting people in. Of letting yourself feel something real."

The irony nearly makes me smile. If I truly let him in—if I showed him what lives beneath my skin—he'd run screaming. The real me would terrify him more than any ghost story.

"Maybe," I concede, just to speed things along. "Or maybe I'm just tired of pretending."

He doesn't catch my meaning, of course. Travis only hears what he wants to hear, sees what he wants to see. Travis stops at the door, balancing the box against his hip. For a moment, I think he might actually leave without another word. Then he turns back, that familiar smirk playing at his lips.

"You know what? I'm glad we're done." His tone carries that particular brand of cruelty men deploy when they can't get what they want. "Whatever freak you're hiding in the woods can have you. I can do better than an ice queen like you."

The words should sting. A year ago, they would have. But now they bounce off me like rain on glass. The monster inside me has gone still, almost amused. She knows what real power looks like, and it isn't this.

"Goodbye, Travis."

He wants a reaction. I can see it in the way he lingers, the way his shoulders tense with expectation. But I give him nothing.

"Fucking weirdo," he mutters, and finally—finally— he's gone.

The door clicks shut behind him, and I slide the deadbolt home with shaking fingers. The apartment already feels different, like I can breathe more deeply. The wolf inside me stretches luxuriously, no longer cramped by his presence.

I lean against the door and close my eyes. For the first time in eighteen months, I'm truly alone.

I push away from the door and walk to the living room window, pulling back the curtain just enough to make sure Travis's Camaro is leaving the parking lot. My shoulders relax as the red taillights disappear around the corner.

I move through the apartment, throwing open windows to remove the stale air, Travis's cologne dissipating bit by bit. My phone buzzes on the counter—a patient needs help finding transportation to their dialysis appointment.

I straighten, slipping into my work. Calls, confirmations, arrangements. The jagged remnants of Travis fade behind the professional mask of competent, composed Karina. The one who never snarls, never bares her teeth. The one the human world trusts to keep everything running smoothly.

If only they knew.

By the time I finish, the afternoon sun has shifted, casting long shadows across my living room floor. I should eat something. The closer we get to the full moon, the more ravenous my wolf becomes. I open the refrigerator and stare at the contents—mostly vegetables, some yogurt, a package of raw steaks I'd been saving.

My mouth waters at the sight of the red meat. I grab the steaks and set them on the counter, my fingers lingering on the packaging. The wolf inside me whines softly, wanting me to tear into the plastic and devour them raw.

"Cook them like a human," I remind myself, but I only sear them for a minute on each side. The center stays bloody, the way both parts of me prefer.

I eat standing at the counter, savoring the taste of iron on my tongue. The protein settles something restless in my chest, and for the first time today, I feel almost normal. Whatever passes for normal when you're a monster pretending to be human.

My laptop chimes with another work email, but I ignore it. My lunch break ended twenty minutes ago, but I can't bring myself to care. Today feels like a turning point, like I'm finally stepping out of a cage I didn't even realize I'd locked myself into.

The afternoon stretches ahead of me, empty and full of possibility. No Travis coming home early to complain about my "weird" eating habits. No need to explain why I'm restless, why I keep checking the moon phase app on my phone, why I sometimes pause mid-conversation to listen to sounds only I can hear.

I finish the steak and lick my fingers clean, not caring that it's undignified. The wolf approves, settling deeper into my bones with satisfaction.

A sharp knock at the door makes me freeze in the middle of cleaning up. My heart rate spikes instantly, and the wolf bristles beneath my skin, hackles raised.

Travis?

My body goes still, senses heightening as I catch a

trace of scent seeping through the doorframe. Not Travis's usual cologne or that stale note of resentment. This is softer—coconut shampoo, vanilla, and a whisper of nail polish in the air.

Britney.

My shoulders relax as I wipe my hands on a dish towel and head toward the door. I unlock it and pull it open to find my neighbor standing there in yoga pants and an oversized sweatshirt, her blonde hair piled into a messy bun.

"Hey girl!" she chirps, already sliding past me into the apartment without waiting for an invitation. "I saw Officer Douchebag loading up his car earlier. Please tell me he's actually gone this time."

I close the door behind her, inhaling the cloud of scented products that constantly surrounds her. To human noses, it probably smells pleasant. To me, it's overwhelming, but still preferable to Travis's lingering presence.

"Yeah, he's gone," I confirm, watching as Britney makes herself at home on my couch, kicking her feet up on the coffee table. She's been in my apartment maybe five times total, but she always acts like we've been best friends since childhood.

"Thank God," Britney says, reaching for the TV remote like it's her own. "That guy gave me the creeps. Always staring at my ass when I'd check my mail."

I settle into the armchair across from her. I'm not

entirely comfortable with how she makes herself at home.

"So..." Britney wiggles her eyebrows at me. "This calls for a celebration, right? Please tell me you're not just going to sit in this apartment all weekend eating ice cream and watching Netflix."

I smile thinly. "That was exactly my plan."

She groans dramatically, throwing her head back against my couch cushions. "Karina! You're free now! You need to get out there and remind yourself what fun feels like."

"I'm not really the *going out* type," I say, the same excuse I've used countless times in the past when she has asked.

"Which is exactly why you should come with me tonight." She sits up straighter, excitement practically radiating off her. "Look, I know we're not, like, besties or whatever. But I've lived next door to you for almost a year, and you never leave. It's time to expand your horizons, babe. Explore your newfound freedom."

"I appreciate that, but that's not really my style—"

"I've got an idea," Britney cuts in, leaning forward, her grin sharp enough to set my wolf on edge. "I work at this exclusive club called the Crimson Howl. It's members-only, but I can get you in tonight."

"A club?" I try not to grimace. "I'm not really in a partying mood, Britney."

She waves her hand dismissively. "Not just any club. It's a sex club."

I nearly choke on air. "A what?"

"A sex club," she repeats, completely unfazed. "Look, before you say no—which I can see you're about to—just hear me out." She slides closer on the couch. "You've spent the last year with an absolute asshole who didn't treat you right."

My wolf bristles at the assessment, not because it's wrong, but because someone else noticed.

"That doesn't mean that I need to jump from one bad situation to another," I say carefully.

"That's exactly my point!" Britney's eyes light up. "There's absolutely no pressure at Crimson Howl. Everyone wears masks—it's mandatory. You can...watch. Observe. Remember what desire looks like when it's not wrapped up in someone else's control issues."

I feel heat rise to my cheeks. "I don't know..."

"Just come out with me."

"Britney, I appreciate the offer, but—"

"No buts!" She springs from the couch with a dancer's grace and grabs my hands. "I've got this incredible black dress that would look amazing on you."

I try to pull away, but Britney holds tight. The wolf inside me twitches, not threatening, just uncomfortable with the physical contact. I'm not used to people touching me so freely.

"I don't have the right shoes for a club," I offer weakly.

"Size eight, right? I've got these killer stilettos that'll make your calves look spectacular. And don't worry about makeup. I'll do it for you. I used to work at Sephora before the club."

"I really don't think—"

"Look. I get it. Breaking up sucks, even when the guy is garbage. But sitting alone in this apartment is not going to help. If you hate it, we leave. I promise. No questions asked."

The monster inside me is curious now. She's been caged for so long—not just by Travis, but by my own fear of discovery. A night out, wearing a mask no less, might be the closest thing to freedom we'll get before the full moon.

"You promise we can leave whenever I want?" I ask.

"Cross my heart." She makes an exaggerated X over her chest. "But I'm telling you, you'll love it. The atmosphere is...intoxicating."

I study her face, looking for any sign of deception. My enhanced senses pick up only excitement and genuine concern. No malice, no hidden agenda. Just a lonely neighbor who wants a friend to play with.

"What kind of masks?" I hear myself asking.

Britney's grin widens. "Gorgeous ones. Leather, lace, feathers—whatever matches your outfit. The club provides them." She bounces on her toes. "Oh, this is going to be so good for you. I can feel it."

The wolf inside me stretches, intrigued despite my reservations. A place where everyone hides their identity. It appeals to the predator in me more than I want to admit.

"I've never been to a place like that," I say slowly.

"Even better! First-timer's luck." She's already heading toward the door. "I'll grab the dress and shoes. We'll start getting ready around eight—the club doesn't really get going until after ten anyway."

"Britney, wait—"

But she's already gone, the door swinging shut behind her with a soft click. I stare at the empty space where she stood, wondering what I just agreed to.

Damien

The night whispers death, and I am its messenger. My knuckles whiten against the steering wheel as I navigate the winding road through the redwoods.

"You know, Dom, if you grip that wheel any tighter, you'll snap it in half," Elias says from the passenger seat. "Lighten up. It's just another job."

I grunt in response. The heir to the Bellandi empire shouldn't be here. His father would skin me alive if he knew I let his precious son accompany me on a hit. But Elias has a way of wearing people down, even me. The moment his father called me into his office and to issue orders, I knew that I'd find Elias waiting in my car. Fucker never misses a chance to pop by Crimson Howl to get a taste. It's not as if he doesn't have females falling at his feet. Eligible heir status tends to draw them in. Not that I would know about that even though I am an heir myself. The females always seem to give me a wide berth. Maybe it is the fact my father loaned me out to the Bellandi family, or, according to Elias, my not so cheery disposition. Either way, I haven't gotten my dick wet in months while the jackass next to me can barely shove a she-wolf out his bedroom door before the next one is coming in. Fucking prick.

"You shouldn't be here."

Elias grins, his blue eyes gleaming with mischief behind the half-mask he's already donned. "What, and miss all the fun?"

Fun. Of course he sees this as fun. He may very well be the only heir who has never gotten his claws bloody. Alpha Anselm, his father, likes to out source that out to his enforcers. Mostly me. Growth and learning opportunities, he likes to call them, but it's really a punishment from my father. My penance for allowing my sister to get kidnapped by one of my his rivals. Despite getting her back when his own enforcers failed, it was my job to protect her.

"You know what will happen to me if you lose so much as a single hair?"

"My father will gut you and hang you for all to see like a prized buck?"

"Something like that." I downshift as we approach

the turnoff that leads deeper into my current alpha's territory. "Your father doesn't make idle threats."

"Neither does yours, from what I hear." Elias leans back in his seat, studying me with that calculating look he gets sometimes. The one that reminds me he's not just some spoiled prince playing dress-up. "Tell me, Dom—when's the last time you talked to your father? Not through intermediaries. Not through my father. Actually talked."

My jaw clenches.

"That's what I thought." He pulls out his phone, scrolling through messages. "You know, there's a rumor going around that—"

"I don't give a shit about rumors."

"This one you might." His voice drops, losing that playful edge. "Word is your sister has been asking questions about why her big brother disappeared right after saving her ass."

My foot eases off the accelerator without my permission. I haven't spoken to her in eight months. Haven't been allowed to, more like. Part of my punishment—complete severance from pack ties.

"Bullshit."

"Is it?" Elias pockets his phone and turns to face me fully. "Maybe she's finally figured out that Daddy dearest threw you under the bus to save his precious reputation."

He isn't wrong, but I will never admit that out loud, even amongst a wolf I consider a friend.

"Drop it, Elias." The words come out sharper than intended, my wolf stirring restlessly beneath my skin. The beast doesn't like being cornered, and right now that's exactly what this conversation feels like.

"Fine." He raises his hands in mock surrender, but I catch the satisfied smirk on his face. The bastard is under my skin, and he knows it. "But when this whole enforcer gig gets old, you've got options. My father respects you more than half his own blood."

I don't respond because there's nothing to say. Options. Like I have any real choice in the matter.

Finally, Crimson Howl comes into view. "Speaking of options," Elias continues, seemingly oblivious to my darkening mood, "there's this new girl at the club. Redhead. Curves that could make a saint sin. She's been asking about you."

"I'm not interested."

"When's the last time you were interested in anything besides work?" He studies me with that calculating look again. "You're wound tighter than a fucking spring, Dom. One of these days you're going to snap."

Maybe. But not tonight. Tonight, I have a job to do, and dwelling on things I can't change won't help anyone —least of all me.

I pull into the designated parking area behind Crimson Howl. The club's rear entrance looms before us, darkened by the shadows. Music pulses through the walls, a steady heartbeat promising sin and secrecy. I kill the engine and sit for a moment, gathering myself.

"Let's be clear," I say, turning to Elias. "You stay in the VIP section. You don't interfere. You don't draw attention. This isn't a fucking field trip."

Elias rolls his eyes but nods. "Yes, sir, Reaper, sir." He adjusts his mask, a sleek black affair that sharpens his already aristocratic features. "Though I'd think you'd appreciate the backup."

"I don't need backup to put down a rat."

Tonight's target is simple. A low-ranking were who thought skimming from the books was a smart career move. I'll find him among the writhing bodies inside, drag him to one of the back rooms, and make an example of him. Clean. Efficient. The way Anselm likes it.

We exit the car and approach the door. The bouncer—a hulking were named Diesel—inclines his head at the sight of me, his posture stiffening when he notices Elias.

"Sir," he says, inclining his head respectfully. "We weren't expecting—"

"Just observing," Elias cuts in smoothly. "Pretend I'm not here."

Diesel's gaze flicks to me, and I give him a slight nod. "Tell Viktor to make sure the black room is open for me."

He gives a curt nod, stepping aside to let us enter, "Of course. I'll radio him now. It will be ready whenever you need it."

The heavy door swings open, and the scent hits me immediately—sweat, sex, alcohol, and beneath it all, the unmistakable musk of wolves. The Crimson Howl lives up to its name tonight, packed wall to wall with bodies moving to the pulsing beat. Masks always hide faces, but they can't disguise scents. My nose picks out at least three rival packs mingling, everyone playing nice under the club's sacred neutrality.

I scan the crowd, searching for my target. Marco Ruiz. A wolf with expensive tastes that his income can't support. I smelled his scent on the safe myself. He's dipping his hands into the Bellandi money pot and not even trying to hide it. The idiot didn't think the first person we'd check was the accountant.

"I'll be upstairs," Elias murmurs, already drifting toward the VIP staircase. "Don't have too much fun without me."

"Stay put," I growl, but he's already gone, swallowed by the crowd. One of these days, he'll learn how to fucking listen.

I push through the mass of bodies, ignoring the inviting looks from various females. My focus narrows, senses heightening as I track the familiar scent. The wolf in me stirs, eager for the hunt. For the kill. I tamp it down. Not yet.

I spot him near the main stage, a glass of top-shelf whiskey in his hand as he watches two she-wolves put on a show for the crowd. His scent is stronger now—nervous sweat mixed with expensive cologne and the bitter tang of guilt.

Marco notices me across the room, and I see the exact

moment recognition hits. His face goes pale beneath his mask, and he starts pushing through the crowd toward the back exit. He knows why I'm here. They always do. Amateur. Does he really think he can outrun me in a building I know better than even Elias?

I follow at a leisurely pace, letting him think he has a chance. The crowd parts around me without conscious thought. Something about my presence makes even the most dominant wolves step aside. It's a useful trait in this line of work.

Marco reaches the hallway leading to the private rooms, glancing back to see how close I am. The panic in his movements sends a thrill through my wolf.

"Going somewhere, Marco?" I call out over the pounding music.

He spins around, backing against the wall. "Look, Reaper, I can explain—"

"Save it." I close the distance between us in three long strides. "You've been skimming from the Bellandi accounts. We have proof."

"It was just a few thousand here and there. Nothing that would hurt—"

My hand shoots out, gripping his throat and lifting him off his feet. His expensive shoes scrabble against the wall as I pin him there.

"Nothing that would hurt?" I repeat. "You stole from the Bellandi family. That hurts their reputation. Their trust. And when you hurt them, you hurt me."

Marco's hands claw at my wrist, but he might as well be trying to bend steel. "Please, I have a family—"

"Should have thought of that before you decided to bite the hand that feeds you." I lean closer, letting him smell the predator on my breath. "Alpha Anselm doesn't tolerate thieves. Neither do I."

I drag him toward the black room, his feet barely touching the ground. The hallway empties as other club patrons sense the violence about to unfold. Smart. They know better than to witness what happens when the Reaper comes calling.

The black room door swings open at my approach—Viktor must have unlocked it remotely. The space beyond is soundproof, windowless, and designed for one purpose. The walls are lined with disposable plastic, and drain grates dot the concrete floor. Everything necessary for cleanup.

"Wait, wait!" Marco's voice cracks as I haul him inside. "I can pay it back. Triple what I took. I have connections, information—"

"Information?" I pause, my hand still wrapped around his throat. This could be useful. "What kind of information?"

His eyes dart around the room. The smell of his fear spikes, acrid and sharp.

Normally this room is used for blood play. Easier to clean up when the room comes with drains, and a sanitizing system installed in the ceiling. Plus, it comes in handy when you have to put down a wolf. Dual-purpose room, so to speak.

"The Lockhart pack," he gasps out. "They're planning a move against your territory."

I tighten my grip slightly. "Be more specific."

"They've been recruiting. Offering protection to businesses that pay tribute to Anselm. Undercutting your rates by thirty percent." His words come out in a rush now, desperation making him talkative. "They think with you busy playing enforcer, the family's spread too thin to retaliate."

Interesting. The Lockharts have been testing boundaries for months, but this is the first I'm hearing of organized recruitment. Alpha Anselm will want to know about this.

"Who's leading the recruitment?"

"Thomas Lockhart. He's been making the rounds personally, promising better terms and less...violent collection methods."

I almost smile at that. Less violent. They have no idea what violence looks like when it's truly unleashed.

"What else?"

Marco's breathing becomes more labored as my grip remains constant. "There's a meeting. Tomorrow night. Warehouse district, the old Kellerman building. Thomas is supposed to finalize deals with at least six businesses."

Now we're getting somewhere. I release his throat, and he collapses against the wall, gasping. But I'm not done with him yet.

"Information doesn't erase your debt," I remind him, moving closer.

"But—but I told you everything I know!"

"Did you?" I grab him by his shirt collar and slam him against the wall. The impact makes his mask slip, revealing the sweaty, terrified face beneath. "Because I'm starting to think you're holding out on me."

I lean in close. "You said Thomas is finalizing deals with six businesses. Name them."

"I—I don't know all of them," Marco stammers.

My fist connects with the wall beside his head, leaving an impression in the concrete despite the sheet of plastic acting as a barrier. "Try again."

"The Golden Paw Brewery," he blurts out. "Redwood Apothecary. Sierra Supply Co." His words tumble over each other as he struggles to remember. "Blackridge Auto Shop. Um...Moonlight Diner."

"You're still one short."

Marco's throat works as he swallows. "The last one...it's new. Not a business, exactly."

"Explain."

"It's a person. Someone inside the Bellandi organization. Thomas has been bragging that he's got a big fish on the line."

"A name, Marco," I demand, my patience wearing thin. "Give me the name."

He hesitates, scanning the room as if searching for an escape that doesn't exist. Sweat beads along his hairline, sliding beneath the edge of his mask.

"I—I don't know for sure," he stammers. "Thomas never said specifically, just that it was someone close to Anselm."

My wolf stirs, catching the lie. His pulse hammers, the sour tang of fear laced with deception bleeding into the air.

"Bullshit," I growl.

"I swear, I don't—"

In one fluid motion, I draw my gun and press the cold barrel to his temple. The dull thunk of metal against bone makes him flinch.

"Tell me, or you die now." My words are flat, stripped of emotion. Pure fact. "I'm not asking again."

Marco freezes, pupils blown wide with panic. The stench of urine fills the air as a stain spreads across his tailored pants.

"Jesus Christ, please," he whimpers. "They'll kill me if I tell you."

"I'll kill you if you don't," I counter, snapping off the safety. "And I promise my way will hurt more."

His mouth opens, then shuts again. His throat bobs as he swallows hard, torn between two terrors—the brutal certainty of me, and the looming shadow of Anselm's wrath.

But in the end, he makes the wrong choice.

"I can't. You don't know what they'll—"

"You should've been more afraid of me," I say, and pull the trigger.

The shot rings out like a final judgment. Marco's

body jerks, a red bloom spreading across his temple as he drops to the floor with a lifeless thud. Blood pools beneath him, seeping into the cracks of the drain like a stain the house will never forget.

I stare down at what's left of him, no flicker of remorse in my chest. He chose silence. I chose death. A more peaceful end than anyone in his position deserves.

Karina

The black dress feels painted onto my skin, like a second coat I can't shed when the moon calls. Britney's stilettos—torture devices she swears are totally comfortable after the first hour—make me tower over her even more than usual, bringing my wolf uncomfortably close to the surface.

"You look fucking incredible. I knew that dress would work on you. It's like it was made for those hips."

I tug at the hemline, trying to coax it lower on my thighs. "It's a bit...revealing."

"That's the whole point!" She laughs, the sound bright against the midnight backdrop of redwoods. "God, I can't believe you've been hiding that body under those baggy clothes all this time. Those legs should be illegal."

I swallow hard, feeling exposed in more ways than one. "I'm not used to showing this much skin."

"That's exactly why you needed this." She loops her arm through mine, steadying me on the borrowed stilettos as we walk toward what looks like an abandoned mill nestled among towering redwoods. "Travis kept you hidden away like some dirty secret. Time to remind yourself you're a goddamn goddess."

My wolf preens at the compliment, even as anxiety churns in my stomach. I'm walking into a sex club filled with humans when my control is at its weakest. Stupid. Reckless.

"So, the bartender I mentioned—Axel—he's got these arms that should be in a museum." Britney chatters as we approach the unassuming entrance, her words tumbling out faster as her excitement builds. "And he makes this drink called a Silver Bullet that will change your life. One is enough to knock me on my ass, so maybe don't get that to start off."

Silver Bullet? My steps falter as the name of the club comes into full view, illuminated by subtle red lighting against the old timber facade.

Crimson Howl.

My heart stops.

Howl. Crimson. Like blood. Like pack.

This isn't just any sex club. It's a were club. It has to be.

Shit.

"Britney," I manage through suddenly dry lips, "how long have you worked here?"

She doesn't notice my panic, too busy digging through her clutch for our invitations. "About six months. Best job I've ever had. The owners are loaded—some rich family that owns half the town. Super private people, but the pay is amazing."

My mind races. Does Britney know what I am? Is this some elaborate trap? But no—her heartbeat is steady, her scent unchanged. There's no trace of deception. She genuinely thinks she's just bringing her repressed neighbor to a kinky human club.

"You okay?" Britney's looking at me now, head tilted. "You are like super pale. I promise no one's going to make you do anything you don't want to do. Consent is like the number one rule here."

"Fine," I say, forcing a smile. "Just a little nervous. I've never been to a place like this."

Inside, I'm spiraling. I have to get out of here. Now. But my feet won't move. The pounding of my heart must be audible to everyone within a mile radius. My palms are sweaty, and I'm struggling to maintain my composure.

"That's totally normal," Britney says, patting my arm. "First-time jitters. Trust me, after one drink, you'll be fine."

One drink won't solve the fact that I'm in a literal wolf's den. The moment I step through those doors, every wolf in that club will catch my scent.

"Maybe we should go somewhere else," I suggest, trying to sound casual. "Get a drink at a regular bar first?"

Britney laughs. "No way! Do you know how hard it was to get these invitations? They never let us come in to play on our days off. Come on, it'll be fun."

She practically drags me toward the entrance. I could break free easily—my strength would send her stumbling —but not without revealing myself.

A large man in an impeccably tailored suit stands at the door. Human, from the smell of him, but every movement radiates the calm alertness of someone who knows exactly what he's guarding.

"Good evening, Miss Carr," he greets, "And you must be the guest."

His attention lingers on me a beat too long before he finally steps aside and gestures toward the heavy wooden doors behind him.

"Do you need my ID?" I ask, fingers fumbling through the small, chained purse I insisted Britney let me bring to hold my phone and small wallet.

He shakes his head at me. "No names are used here. Special invitations only. Masks are mandatory once you cross the threshold," he explains, producing two elegant pieces from a velvet-lined box. "They remain on for the duration of your visit."

The mask he offers me is a black leather mask with ears. Metal studs line the outline of the ears and the brow bones. It's a cat mask.

I stare at the mask in his hands, my throat closing up. The universe has a sick sense of humor—dressing the predator as prey. But I can't refuse without drawing attention, so I take it with trembling fingers.

"Thank you," I manage.

Britney gets a sleek black bunny mask with silver whiskers. She slips it on with practiced ease, transforming into someone mysterious and confident. The mask suits her perfectly.

"Your turn," she says, her voice slightly muffled but still cheerful.

I lift the mask to my face, the leather cool against my heated skin. The moment it settles into place, something shifts. The anonymity should be comforting, but instead, it feels like I'm walking into a trap, wearing a sign that says, *eat me*.

"Perfect," the doorman says, but there's something in his tone that makes my wolf's hackles rise. "Enjoy your evening, ladies."

The doors swing open, and the scent hits me. Pack. Multiple packs. The air is thick with werewolf musk, arousal, and power. Ancient, territorial power that makes my wolf want to both submit and run. I freeze in the doorway, every instinct screaming at me to run. But Britney's already pulling me forward, her excitement palpable as she leads me deeper into what I now realize is enemy territory.

The interior is all wood, shadows dancing in the amber light from wrought-iron fixtures. A bar dominates one wall, bottles of expensive liquor gleaming like jewels. The main floor opens into a larger space where I can see figures moving—some watching and some participating in activities that make my cheeks burn even through the mask.

But it's not the sight that overwhelms me. It's the scents. Layer upon layer of werewolf pheromones, so thick I can barely breathe.

"Isn't this place amazing?" Britney beams, completely oblivious to my internal crisis.

The air practically crackles with supernatural energy. I count at least a dozen different werewolf scents, maybe more. All male. All dominant. All now aware that a female has just entered their territory.

A low growl rumbles from somewhere to my left, and I turn to see a man in a wolf mask watching me from the bar. Even from this distance, I can feel his stare. My wolf whimpers, caught between attraction and terror.

"Let's go to the bar. I'll introduce you to Axel." Britney starts toward the bar, but I catch her arm.

"Actually, can you get me something? I need a minute to...take this all in."

She studies my face through the mask, and I pray she can't see how badly I'm shaking. "Of course! What do you want?"

"Something strong. Not the Silver Bullet— just...whatever you think is good."

"I'll be right back," she promises, squeezing my hand before disappearing into the crowd.

The moment she's gone, I press my back against the nearest wall, trying to steady my breathing. This was a mistake. A catastrophic, potentially life-threatening mistake. I need to text Britney some excuse and get out of here before—

"You smell like moonlight and honey, baby."

The voice comes from directly beside me, low and rough with barely contained power. I turn to find a man in an elaborate wolf mask leaning against the wall, his towering presence radiating the kind of dominance that makes my wolf want to bare her throat.

"I'm sorry?" I manage, though my voice comes out breathier than I intended.

"Your scent." He pushes away from the wall, moving closer. "It's...intoxicating. I caught it the moment you walked in."

My heart hammers against my ribs. Panic floods my system. He can smell what I am. Of course he can. I'm broadcasting my scent like a neon sign to every wolf in this place.

"I don't know what you mean," I lie, taking a step back only to find myself pressed more firmly against the wall.

He follows, closing the distance between us with predatory grace. "Don't you?" His head tilts, studying me. "You meeting someone here?"

My mouth goes dry. "I'm here with my friend. She works here."

"Britney." It's not a question. "Sweet girl." He leans

closer, and I catch his scent—tobacco and whiskey. "But you aren't sweet, are you, baby?"

I can't breathe. Can't think. The space between us crackles with tension, and I'm hyperaware of how the black dress clings to my skin, how exposed I am in this den of predators.

"I should go," I stutter.

"Should you?" His voice drops lower, and I feel the rumble of it in my chest. "Tell me, little wolf, what pack do you belong to?"

"I think you've confused me with someone else."

When I try to slide past him, his hand catches my wrist, not roughly, but with unmistakable strength. Warmth radiates from his touch, a jolt of electricity shooting up my arm that makes my wolf whine.

"You didn't answer my question." His voice drops an octave, the kind of tone that makes lesser wolves submit instantly. "What pack?"

"Let go of me."

"What fucking pack are you from?"

I press myself harder against the wall, desperately scanning the room for Britney.

"None." The word slips out before I can stop it, and I watch his entire body go rigid. "I don't belong to any pack."

The silence stretches between us. Even through the mask, I can feel the intensity of his stare boring into me. Around us, the club continues its rhythm, but it feels like we're trapped in a bubble of tension.

"Impossible." His grip on my wrist tightens slightly. "Every she-wolf belongs to a pack. Especially one like you."

"One like me?"

He sniffs me again, smiling wide, "Fuck. Are you a desperate little wolf slut looking to be bred, baby?"

My blood turns to ice. Shit. I hadn't noticed. I've been with a human so long that I didn't even think about it much anymore. Travis was never the wiser when my cycle started. He only cared that our active sex life went into overdrive.

I have to get out of here.

"Let. Go," I say through gritted teeth, struggling to keep my claws from extending.

"Do you honestly think I am about to let you slip through my fingers so easily? Coming here was a mistake," he growls, his voice dropping even lower as he leans in so close I can feel his breath through the eyeholes of my mask. "Not one male will let you walk out of here smelling so fucking good. Not until you're bred."

My heart hammers against my ribs. I try to pull away again, but his grip remains firm. Not painful, but immovable.

"I can smell him on you," he continues, disgust evident in his tone. "A human male. His scent clings to you like a disease." He leans closer, inhaling deeply near my neck. "I could teach you what it's like to be with a real wolf. What it's like to be fucked properly."

"I don't need to be fucked by anyone," I hiss, finding my courage. "Least of all you."

"You have no idea who you're talking to."

"I don't care if you're the king. Let. Go."

His grip tightens around my wrist, and before I can fight back, he's pulling me away from the wall, dragging me toward a dimly lit hallway at the back of the club. I dig my heels in, but these ridiculous stilettos offer zero traction on the polished floor.

"You're not going anywhere," he snarls low enough that only I can hear. "Not until we figure out exactly what to do with a rogue she-wolf in heat."

I struggle against his hold, careful not to use my full strength with so many human witnesses around. "Let me go. You have no right—"

"I have every right," he cuts me off, voice dropping to a growl that makes my wolf whimper despite my anger. "As an alpha, I can take whatever the fuck I want."

Two men materialize on either side of us, their expensive suits and blank expressions marking them as security. They flank us as the masked wolf continues dragging me down the hallway, away from the main floor and any chance of Britney seeing what's happening.

"My friend will look for me," I warn, desperation creeping into my voice.

"Your human friend will be told you left with a handsome stranger," he says dismissively. "It happens here all the time."

The hallway stretches before us, doors lining both

sides. He reaches for a door handle, and I see my chance. I twist my wrist sharply, using a technique my father taught me years ago—one quick jerk with all my strength. His grip loosens just enough, and I wrench free.

"Fucking bitch!" he snarls, lunging for me.

I kick off the ridiculous stilettos and bolt down the hallway, my bare feet silent against the polished floors. Behind me, I hear shouting and the thunder of footsteps. My heart pounds in my ears as I race past door after door, testing handles as I go. Locked. Locked. Locked.

"Stop her!"

I glance over my shoulder to see the security guards giving chase, their human speed no match for my wolf-enhanced legs. But the wolf moves faster, gaining on me with every stride.

The next door handle gives under my desperate grip, and I throw myself inside, slamming it shut behind me. I fumble for a lock, but there isn't one. Panic rises in my throat as I back away from the door, searching for something to barricade it with.

That's when the smell hits me—copper and iron, hot and fresh. Blood. So much blood.

I turn slowly, my senses overwhelmed by the metallic tang filling the small room, and freeze.

A man stands with his back to me, and another on the ground before me, unmoving, with blood pooling around his body.

Damien

I'm still staring at Marco's body when the door flies open, slamming against the wall with enough force to crack the hinges. The gunshot must have been louder than I thought, despite the room's soundproofing.

My head snaps up to find a woman frozen in the doorway, her face obscured by an elaborate cat mask. Her eyes wide underneath it with a pair of cherry red lips parting in shock. She's not supposed to be here. No one is.

For one charged heartbeat, we face each other, and then her attention drops to the corpse at my feet, the still smoking gun in my hand. Her breath hitches, a small, strangled sound that slices through the silence.

Fuck.

Before I can move, she bolts, turning on her heel with the fluid grace of prey that knows it's been spotted by a predator. I lunge forward, but I'm too late. She's already halfway down the corridor.

"Stop!" I roar, my voice reverberating off the walls.

She doesn't even slow down. Smart girl.

I'm about to give chase when a familiar figure appears behind her—Thomas Lockhart himself. Of all the goddamn wolves who could have shown up tonight. He blocks the hallway and her escape.

I slam the door shut behind me, cutting off any view of Marco's body. Lockhart doesn't need to see my handiwork, not when he's been trying to undermine the Bellandi family for months. The last thing I need is to give him ammunition.

My back presses against the door as I take a steadying breath. The woman in the cat mask is an immediate problem—a witness. But Lockhart's presence here is the bigger threat. What the hell is he doing at Crimson Howl tonight of all nights?

The woman in the cat mask freezes between us, trapped in the narrow hallway with two apex predators. Her scent reaches me even through the club's miasma of sex and liquor.

"Well, well," Lockhart drawls, his attention sliding from the woman to me. "If it isn't the Reaper himself. Busy night?"

I hold steady, though my wolf thrashes beneath my

skin, snarling for blood. "Nothing that concerns you, Lockhart."

He steps closer to the woman, and something inside me detonates. My wolf lunges against the cage of my ribs, clawing, howling, violent in a way that steals my breath. Possessive. Mine. Not his.

I force myself to remain outwardly still while my beast batters against me, desperate to strike. What the hell? I don't even know this woman. But my wolf doesn't care. Lockhart's predatory lean toward her sets every territorial instinct ablaze.

"You seem tense, Reaper," Lockhart taunts, his lips curling in a mockery of a smile. He edges closer to the masked woman, and my muscles tighten, drawn taut as bowstrings. "Something troubling you?"

"Step away from her."

Lockhart raises an eyebrow. "I wasn't aware the Bellandi's attack dog had developed a soft spot for club patrons." He reaches out, fingers hovering near the woman's arm. "Unfortunately, she's off the menu for someone like you, pup. She and I were about to get better acquainted. Weren't we, pussy cat?"

The word lights a white-hot fury under my skin. My wolf rakes at whatever is holding him back, a single brutal need to rip Lockhart apart for that look. The intensity blinds me; this hunger is unlike anything I've ever known.

"I said, step away." The words come out as a growl,

my wolf bleeding through despite my attempts to contain it.

The woman's head jerks between us, her breathing shallow and uneven. She flattens herself against the wall, trying to make her frame smaller, but there's nowhere left to retreat. The hallway seems to close in, the air heavy with tension and barely restrained violence.

Lockhart chuckles, a sound like gravel grinding. "Protective, aren't we? How fascinating." His hand drops to rest on the woman's shoulder, and I see red.

I'm moving before conscious thought kicks in, crossing the distance between us in two strides. My hand shoots out, wrapping around Lockhart's wrist with enough force to snap bone. His smug expression falters as I squeeze.

"Touch her again and I'll break every bone in your hand," I snarl.

"Damien." A familiar voice cuts through the haze of rage. Elias appears at the far end of the hallway, his mask pushed up on his forehead.

"What the hell is going on here?" Elias demands, his voice carrying the authority of his bloodline despite his youth.

Lockhart's lips curl into a cold smile. "Just having a conversation with your pet about boundaries." He tries to twist his wrist free, but I tighten my grip until I feel the bones creak. "Perhaps you should keep him on a shorter leash."

"Let him go, Dom." Elias's voice is steady, but I catch the warning beneath it. "Now."

I release Lockhart with a shove that sends him stumbling back a step. He flexes his fingers, testing for damage. The woman remains pressed against the wall, her chest rising and falling rapidly.

"This isn't over, Reaper," Lockhart says, straightening his jacket. "Keep overstepping your place, pup, and you will find out what happens when you cross a real Alpha."

"Is that a threat?" I ask, my hand drifting toward my gun.

"It's a promise." Lockhart's gaze shifts to the woman, and my wolf snarls again. "Until next time, pussy cat."

He turns and walks away, his footsteps echoing down the hallway. I watch until he disappears around the corner, every instinct screaming at me to follow him and finish what we started.

The woman seizes her chance the moment Lockhart is out of sight. Like a cornered animal finally spotting an escape route, she bolts, ducking under my arm and sprinting toward the exit opposite from where Elias stands. The sudden movement catches me off guard—her speed impressive even by werewolf standards.

"Shit!" I lunge after her, but she's already gained ground, her heels clicking frantically against the floor as she runs.

"Dom, what the hell?" Elias calls after me, but I'm

already in pursuit, my wolf surging forward with an urgency I don't understand.

I follow her through the maze of Crimson Howl's back corridors, past startled staff members and private rooms where masks turn in our direction. She moves like she knows the layout, taking turns without hesitation, pushing through doors that should be locked.

"Stop!" I shout, but she only runs faster.

She bursts through the fire exit, an alarm blaring as she hits the cool night air. The sound pierces my sensitive ears, but I don't slow down. The door slams back against the wall as I follow her into the parking lot, my longer strides closing the distance between us.

"I'm not going to hurt you," I call out, though I know how hollow those words must sound coming from a man she just saw murder someone.

She doesn't look back, doesn't hesitate. Her cat mask flies off as she runs, dislodging in her frantic escape. I lunge forward and snatch the mask from the ground, the leather still warm from her skin. The scent of vanilla and honey clings to it, filling my nostrils and sending a jolt through my system. My fingers tighten around the intricate feline design.

I could track her by scent alone, but something stops me. The mask in my hand feels heavy with significance. A witness. A liability. But my wolf whines, pushing against my consciousness with an urgency I've never felt before.

The distant sound of car tires screeching tells me she's found her escape. I turn the mask over in my hands, examining it in the harsh glow of the parking lot lights. Black leather molded to the shape of a cat's face, with delicate silver detailing around the eyes and whiskers. Custom work.

"Dom!" Elias's voice cuts through the night as he jogs toward me. "What the fuck was that about? And why are you holding a mask?"

I slip the mask into my jacket pocket before he can get a good look at it. "She saw Marco."

Elias stops short, "Shit. Are you sure?"

"Dead sure." I glance back at the club's fire exit, the alarm still blaring inside. "She walked in right after I pulled the trigger."

"Fuck." Elias seethes. "Perfect. Just fucking perfect."

My wolf is still agitated, pacing beneath my skin like a caged animal. The scent of honeyed vanilla lingers in the air, taunting me. I should be focusing on the threat she poses, the danger of leaving a witness alive. Instead, all I can think about is the way she looked at me. Not with the revulsion I expected, but with something else. Something I can't name.

"We need to find her."

"We?" Elias catches my arm. "Dom, think about this. She's a witness to a murder. You know what that means."

"I know what it means," I snap, jerking my arm free from his grip. "But I need to know who she is first."

"Why? So you can have a nice chat before you put a bullet in her head?" Elias follows me as I stalk toward the main floor. "This isn't like you, Dom. You're usually more...clinical about these things."

He's right, and that pisses me off even more. I've never hesitated before, never questioned an order. Find the threat, eliminate it, move on. That's what I do. It's why they call me the Reaper. But something about this woman has gotten under my skin, burrowed deep where I can't dig it out.

"Think she came here with Lockhart? If she talks to him—"

"Then we're fucked," Elias finishes for me. "I get it. But you need to think with your head, not your...other parts."

I whirl on him, a growl building in my throat. "That's not what this is about."

"If you say so."

I ignore him, turning on my heels and heading back to the club. My wolf is frantic now, desperate to find her. I fling open the door and step back inside.

"We need to check the exits," I say, already moving toward the front of the club. "Security cameras. Invitations."

"We'll need Viktor to pull them." Elias grabs my arm, tugging me toward the security room. "And we need to be discreet about it. My father can't know about this."

"No shit, Sherlock."

"Let me handle Viktor. If I tell him it's for me, he'll be less likely to run straight to my father."

I tear my arm free from his grip. "I don't need your help."

"Clearly you do, because you're acting like a lovesick teenager instead of the Reaper. Get your shit together, Dom."

I take a deep breath, forcing my wolf to heel. He's right. I'm compromised, and I don't understand why. One woman in a cat mask shouldn't have this effect on me.

"Fine," I mutter, following him toward the back of the club.

Viktor, the club's head of security, is stationed by the VIP entrance, his stature intimidating even to the wolves who approach. He straightens when he sees us coming.

"Sir," he says, nodding to Elias. "Is everything alright?"

"Did you see a woman in a cat mask come in? She a regular?"

"I wasn't working the front door. Bobby was. Why?"

"I need to talk to Bobby," I growl, already moving toward the front entrance.

Elias falls into step beside me, his presence a constant reminder that I'm not handling this situation the way I should. The Reaper doesn't get rattled. The Reaper doesn't lose control. But here I am, practically running through the club to find a woman whose face I haven't even seen.

Bobby's manning the front door, checking IDs and

scanning the invitations of those entering the club. He straightens when he sees us approaching.

"Mr. Bellandi," he says, nodding respectfully to Elias before turning to me with considerably more caution. "What can I do for you?"

"Woman in a black cat mask," I say without preamble. "When did she come in? Was she alone?"

Bobby's brow furrows beneath his crew cut. "Cat mask? There've been a few tonight, sir."

"This one would have been memorable," I press, leaning closer. "Black cat mask, cherry red lips. Came in within the last two hours."

Recognition flickers in Bobby's eyes. "Oh, her. Yeah, she came in about an hour ago with Britney. Friend, I think. Never seen her before."

"Britney?" Elias perks up beside me. "The redhead who works here?"

"That's the one," Bobby confirms. "They came in together, but I haven't seen either of them leave."

My wolf stirs with renewed interest. If she came with Britney, then she's not some random club patron. She's connected to someone who works for the family, even if Britney doesn't know it.

"Where does Britney live?"

"I...I don't know her address, sir."

I turn from him. Fucking useless human. Elias is hot on my heels.

"Tell Viktor to pull the employment records. Find the fuck out where she lives."

"Dom," Elias catches my arm again. "What's your plan here? Show up at her apartment and what, interrogate her?"

I shake off his grip, my patience finally snapping. "My plan is to find the woman who saw me put a bullet in Marco's head before she decides to share that information with the wrong people."

"And if she's already shared it?"

If she's already talking, then it's too late for damage control. But my wolf refuses to accept that possibility, snarling at the mere thought of her betraying us.

"Then I'll handle it. Like I always do."

Elias studies me for a long moment. He knows me well enough to recognize when I've made up my mind. Finally, he sighs and pulls out his phone.

"I'll call Nate in HR. He'll have Britney's address." He steps away to make the call, leaving me alone with my thoughts and my increasingly agitated wolf.

I pace the small area near the entrance, every muscle in my body tense. The woman in the cat mask shouldn't matter this much. She's just another loose end to tie up, another potential threat to eliminate. So why does the thought of putting a bullet in her head make my stomach twist?

Karina

The taste of blood and terror floods my mouth as I streak through the forest, my paws barely touching the damp earth. The night air burns in my lungs, my heartbeat thundering like a war drum against my ribs. I am nothing instinct now, vanishing between ancient redwoods.

I shouldn't have gone to that club. Shouldn't have let Britney talk me into it. Shouldn't have lost her in the crowd. Shouldn't have opened that door even if the alternative was far, far worse.

But I did. A man with eyes like liquid mercury. A corpse with a hole where a face should be. A gun still smoking in the killer's hand.

The monster inside me—the wolf I've spent my

entire life hating—saved me tonight. The irony isn't lost on me, even as I push my four legs harder, faster, desperate to put miles between myself and Crimson Howl.

My muscles scream in protest as I approach the edges of Blackridge, where the forest thins and civilization begins. I slow my pace, ears swiveling to catch any sounds of pursuit. Nothing but the typical night chorus—owls, insects, the distant hum of the occasional car.

I've never been more grateful for the tiny garden shed behind my apartment building. Slipping inside, I force my body to shift back to human form, the transformation sending waves of agony through my body. Bones crack and reshape, fur recedes into skin, and I collapse onto the dirt floor, naked and shaking.

Every shift is torture—a reminder of what I am—a reminder of what I've spent twenty-seven years trying to forget.

I reach for my handbag with trembling fingers, fumbling for the spare key to the shed where I keep emergency clothes. My teeth chatter uncontrollably as I pull on sweatpants and a hoodie, the fabric rough against my hypersensitive skin.

"Breathe," I order myself, pressing my back against the wooden wall. "Just breathe."

But the images won't stop flashing behind my eyelids —the silver-eyed killer, the dead man's face, the way that other wolf had looked at me like I was prey. And worst of all, the inexplicable way my wolf had responded to the killer. Like it recognized something in him that I couldn't see.

It has to be my heat cycle. That's the only explanation. It has to be.

My phone buzzes inside my bag—Britney, calling for the fifth time. I silence it without answering. What would I even say? Sorry, I disappeared. I was busy witnessing a murder and then turning into a monster.

I force myself to my feet, legs still wobbly from the shift. I need to get inside my apartment, lock the doors, and figure out what the hell I'm going to do. Every survival instinct roars at me to run—to pack a bag and disappear before they find me. Because they will find me. Men like that always do.

I slip out of the shed, scanning the yard before dashing toward the back entrance of my building. The key trembles in my hand as I unlock the door, slipping inside and taking the stairs two at a time.

Once inside, I slam the door shut, engaging every lock before sliding down against it. My legs finally give out, and I wrap my arms around my knees, trying to stop the violent shaking that's overtaken my body.

"Think, Karina," I whisper to myself. "Think."

My options are limited. I could run—I have enough savings to disappear for a while. But how long before they track me down? And where would I even go? I've spent my entire life hiding what I am. I have no pack, no connections to the wolf world. Just the curse I've carried since birth.

My phone buzzes again. This time, I answer.

"Oh my God, Karina!" Britney's voice pierces my ear. "Where the hell did you go?"

"I just...I wasn't feeling well. I went home."

"Without telling me? I've been looking everywhere for you!"

Because I went out as a wolf through the back exit, I think grimly. "Look, I'm sorry, okay? I just needed to get out of there."

There's a pause, and I can practically hear her frowning. "You sound weird. Are you sure you're okay?"

No. I'm the furthest thing from okay. I witnessed a murder, nearly got cornered by some alpha asshole, and my wolf is still pacing restlessly under my skin like it's searching for something. Or someone.

"I'm fine, Britt. Just tired. Can we talk tomorrow?"

"I guess..." She doesn't sound convinced. "But you're buying me coffee and explaining why you bailed on me."

I end the call and toss my phone aside, burying my face in my hands. The normalcy of Britney's concern feels surreal after what I've just experienced. She has no idea that the club she works at is a front for monsters. That her employers are killers who execute people in sound-proof rooms.

I should shower. Wash the scent of the club off my skin, try to scrub away the memory of what I saw. But my legs feel like jelly, and I can't bring myself to move from this spot against the door.

The wolf inside me is still restless, pacing like a caged

animal. She's been more active tonight than she's been in months, and I hate it.

A sound from the hallway makes me freeze. Footsteps. Heavy, deliberate. They pause outside my door.

My heart hammers against my ribs as I press my ear to the wood. The footsteps continue past, and I hear Mrs. Chen's door open and close. Just my elderly neighbor coming home from her late shift at the hospital.

I'm paranoid. Jumping at shadows. But can I really blame myself? I've never been exposed to that world before—the world of wolves who embrace what they are instead of hiding from it. The world where violence is currency and death is just another business transaction.

My phone buzzes with a text from Britney.

Why is my boss asking about you?
Please tell me you didn't do
something to jeopardize my job. I
really need it.

Oh fuck. No. No. No.
I type back a quick response:

What did he ask?

My fingers hover over the screen, waiting for her response. The three dots appear and disappear several times before her next message comes through.

> He asked for your name, and where you lived? Did you leave something behind?

My handbag is sitting right here on the floor beside me, everything accounted for. This is a lie—a way to get information about me. I type back quickly.

> What did you tell him?

> Just that you were my friend and it was your first time here. Why are you being so weird about this?

I stare at the screen, my blood turning to ice. They know I was with Britney. They know it was my first time at the club. How long before they connect the dots and figure out exactly who I am?

> I'm not being weird. I swear I didn't do anything. Talk tomorrow?

I power off my phone before she can respond, my hands shaking so badly I nearly drop it. They're already looking for me. Already asking questions. How long before they show up at my door?

I need to leave. Tonight. Pack a bag and disappear before they—

A knock at my door freezes the blood in my veins. Three sharp raps.

I force myself to my feet. My wolf paces beneath my skin, alert and agitated. She can sense something I can't—or won't acknowledge.

Another knock. More insistent this time.

"Karina?" A voice calls through the door. Male. Deep. Unfamiliar.

My blood turns to ice. They know where I live. I back away from the door, my bare feet silent on the hardwood floor.

"I know you're in there," the voice continues, calm and patient. "I can hear your heartbeat."

Enhanced hearing. Wolf senses. Of course.

I press myself against the wall beside my window, mind racing through escape routes. Fire escape. But it's on the other side of the apartment, and the floorboards creak. He'd hear me moving.

"I'm not here to hurt you. I just want to talk."

Like hell. Men who "just want to talk" don't show up at your apartment at two in the morning after you've witnessed them commit murder.

"I don't know what you're talking about," I call out, surprised by how steady my voice sounds. "You have the wrong apartment."

A low chuckle filters through the door. "We both know that's not true. How about you open the door?"

"No." My wolf is pacing frantically now, torn between fight and flight. "Go away or I'm calling the police."

"The police?" There's genuine amusement in his voice now. "And tell them what, exactly?"

My stomach drops. He's right, and we both know it. What would I tell them? That I saw a murder at an underground sex club while I was trespassing in a room I had no business entering? That I'm a werewolf who shifted to escape? They'd either laugh me out of the station or lock me up for psychiatric evaluation.

"Karina." He says my name like he's testing how it sounds. "That is your name, isn't it? Karina Greene. Now, are you going to open this door, or do I need to rip it off its fucking hinges? Don't make this more difficult than it needs to be."

My wolf whimpers. My blood runs cold. I've spent my whole life hiding in plain sight, and in one night, he's unraveled my carefully constructed normalcy.

"So you can put a bullet in my head like you did to that man?" The words escape before I can stop them. "No thanks."

There's a pause, then a soft sound that might be a sigh. "If I wanted you dead, I wouldn't be standing at your door asking to come in."

He has a point, but I'm not about to admit it.

"Open the fucking door."

There's no scenario where opening that door ends well for me.

A horrible splintering sound makes me jump away from the wall. He wasn't joking.

"Jesus Christ!" I gasp as I watch one of my door

hinges pop free, metal screws flying across my apartment floor like confetti. Claws—actual fucking claws—are visible through the gap where the hinge used to be.

"Don't make this difficult," his voice rumbles through the damaged door.

Another hinge groans as his claws work at it. I've never seen a wolf strong enough to do this—to tear through metal like it's paper. My parents certainly couldn't. Neither can I.

"Stop!" I lunge for the door, fumbling with the locks with trembling fingers. "I'm opening it, just stop destroying my door!"

The claws pause, withdrawing slightly. I take a deep breath, steeling myself as I unlock the deadbolt and chain. My hand hovers over the knob for one last second before I pull the door open.

The Reaper fills my doorway, blocking my escape. He's even more imposing up close, towering over me at what must be six and a half feet, shoulders broad enough to cast a shadow across my entire entryway.

I stumble backward, my heart hammering against my ribs like a caged bird. Up close, he's even more terrifying. His shaggy black hair falls across his forehead, shadowing features that radiate an unnerving intensity, as if nothing about me is hidden from him.

His nostrils flare as he inhales deeply, his expression shifting from threatening to stunned in an instant. He goes still...and utters a single word.

"Mate."

My breath catches in my throat as his pupils expand, swallowing the silver until only a thin ring of mercury remains.

"You're my fucking mate."

Damien

The moment my wolf identifies her, my world splinters.

Her scent slams into me—honeyed vanilla and sharp fear— buried underneath something feral. Something mine. Every cell in my body responds, bones humming, skin stretching too tight. The recognition is instant, undeniable.

Not here. Not now. Not her.

She's backed against the kitchen counter, breathing hard, eyes locked on mine like she expects me to tear her throat out. And maybe I was about to. I'd come here to silence a witness. She saw too much at the club. Saw me.

"What did you just say?"

I don't answer.

I step farther into the apartment, letting the door swing shut behind me. The place is wrong. Wrong in ways that make my skin crawl.

Everything is pristine. Air-freshener clean. A plug-in hums faintly in the wall, pumping out artificial lavender and something citrusy, cloying and sharp. It's an attempt to hide what she is. A poor one.

Wolves don't live like this.

The walls are lined with curated, meaningless art. Generic photos in generic frames—smiling people at parties, someone's arm around her shoulders. I don't know who. I don't care.

Then I smell him. Human. Male. Recently here.

I freeze mid-step, nostrils flaring. The scent coils in my lungs like acid. Cheap cologne. Sweat. Skin.

He was close. On the couch. On her. His scent clings to the blanket like a fucking claim. My muscles tense as a savage growl tears from my chest.

She flinches, pressing herself further into the counter like she could disappear into it.

"I can smell the human," I snarl. "The male scent all over this apartment."

She says nothing, but I can see it—her pulse fluttering in her throat, her hands clenched into fists at her sides.

My wolf is furious.

Rage burns through me, sharp and irrational. My vision blurs at the edges. I taste copper. My claws threaten to burst through my skin. The idea of another man, a human, this close to her, touching her, breathing her in...

It sends my instincts spiraling into something feral. Possessive. He tainted her space. Left his scent where it doesn't belong.

My wolf is howling, pacing inside me, demanding we track him down and rip him apart for daring to come near what's ours.

"Who is he?" I demand, stalking closer. Every step feels like wading through molten lava, my composure fraying with each heartbeat. "Tell me his name."

"What?" She looks genuinely confused, her attention flicking between my face and my hands, where my claws have partially extended. "I don't—"

"The human who's been here," I growl, gesturing toward the couch. "His stink is all over this place. All over you."

Her features harden, submission burning off until only defiance remains. "That's none of your business."

Wrong answer.

I'm across the room before she can blink, caging her against the counter with my arms on either side of her. She gasps, shrinking back, but there's nowhere to go. I lower my head until our faces are inches apart, breathing in that intoxicating scent beneath her artificial perfumes.

"It became my business the moment my wolf recognized you. So, I'll ask again. Who is he?"

"My boyfriend," she lies, chin lifting slightly despite her obvious terror. "And he'll be here any minute, so—"

I laugh, the sound harsh and cutting. "No, he won't. You're lying. Your heartbeat gives you away."

I can hear the rapid flutter of her pulse, smell the acrid scent of adrenaline seeping through her pores. "You're not a very good liar, Karina."

Her name tastes like honey on my tongue. I want to say it again. Want to growl it against her skin.

"Who the fuck is he?"

"My ex," she seethes. "But that is none of your business."

Good. One less fucking human to kill for even breathing in her presence. My wolf settles slightly at the admission, but the rage still simmers beneath my skin. Ex or not, his scent is too recent, too strong. The thought of him here, in her space, touching what belongs to me, drives me mad.

"Why does that matter. You're here to kill me, right? To hunt me down for what I saw."

The question hangs between us, and for a moment, I don't know how to answer. Because she's right—that's exactly why I came here. To eliminate the witness. To clean up the mess. It's what I do, what I've always done.

But now, with her scent flooding my senses and my wolf clawing at my insides, the thought of putting a bullet in her head makes me physically sick.

"I should," I admit with a shrug. "Any other night, with any other witness, I would have already pulled the trigger."

Her breath hitches, but she doesn't look away.

Doesn't back down. There's a steel in her spine that I didn't expect.

"But you're not any other witness," I continue, leaning closer until the warmth radiating off her skin brushes against me. "You're mine."

"I'm not your anything," she snaps, shoving at my chest. Her hands are too small, too weak to move me. "I don't even know what that means."

She doesn't know. Of course she doesn't—living like this, masking what she is, drowning her scent in artificial bullshit. Raised human. No pack. No guidance. No idea of the blood running in her veins.

"It means you belong to me," I growl, my wolf clawing forward at her denial. "The only one who'll ever carry my mark. The only one who could ever carry my children."

"That's—That's insane," she stammers. "We don't even know each other. You're a murderer. I saw you kill someone."

"And yet your wolf recognizes mine," I counter, inhaling deep. "I can smell it on you. The way your body reacts to me, even while your mind tries to fight."

Color blooms across her cheeks, spilling down her throat in a flush that makes my mouth water. I want to follow that trail with my tongue, taste the burn of her skin.

"I don't have a wolf," she hisses. "You've got the wrong person."

The lie is so blatant it nearly makes me laugh. "I can

smell you, Karina. Beneath all this—" I gesture at the air fresheners, "—manufactured bullshit."

Her flush deepens, crimson with embarrassment and anger. "Get out of my apartment."

"I'm not leaving you unprotected," I snap. "Not when Lockhart saw you. Not when your cycle is this close. Do you have any fucking idea what that means? What danger you are in?"

"I've handled my cycles for ten years without your help," she fires back, her brown eyes flashing with defiance. "I don't need your protection. I don't need you calling me your mate like I'm some...some possession."

"You think this is about possession?" I let out a short, bitter laugh. "It's about keeping you *alive*."

"The man who grabbed you tonight? That was Thomas Lockhart. One of the most dangerous alphas in this territory. He's not going to forget your face," I continue. "He'll come for you just for brushing off his advances. And, if he discovers your connection to me, he will use you for far more than breeding purposes."

I pause, jaw clenched.

"I am not your mate!" she shouts, shoving at my chest again. "Stop saying that. I don't even know your name."

I capture her wrists in one hand, pinning them against the counter. My patience is fraying, thread by thread, with every denial that leaves her lips.

"Damien Marek," I say, stepping into her space until

there's barely a breath between us. "You'd better remember it, kitten."

She stiffens, jaw tight, but I can feel her body react—tense, alert, alive.

She opens her mouth, but I cut her off before the first word forms.

"Mate isn't some label I'm throwing around. It's what you are. What we *are*." I let the pause drag, just long enough for the reality of it to sink in. "The sooner you accept that, the sooner I stop worrying about keeping you alive...and start thinking about what I'm going to do with you."

She struggles against my grip, her strength impressive for someone her size, but nothing compared to mine. Her scent shifts to something hotter, angrier. My wolf responds instantly, surging forward with a need that obliterates rational thought. I'm drowning in her—the scent of her skin, the defiance in her eyes, the pulse hammering in her throat.

I crash my mouth against hers.

The kiss is brutal, desperate. Her lips are soft beneath mine, parting on a gasp that I swallow hungrily. I release her wrists to cup her face, fingers tangling in her curls as I angle her head to deepen the kiss. My tongue sweeps into her mouth, tasting her, devouring her. She tastes like cinnamon and wine and something wild that makes my blood sing.

Her hands fly to my shoulders, nails digging in through my shirt. For one glorious moment, she kisses me back. Her body arching into mine and a soft moan vibrating against my lips that nearly brings me to my knees.

Then her hands flatten against my chest, and she shoves hard, breaking the kiss with a force that surprises me. I stumble back a step, my wolf howling in protest at the sudden distance.

"Don't," she pants, wiping her mouth with the back of her hand. Her pupils are blown wide, lips swollen from my kiss. "Don't you dare touch me like that again."

Her defiance only makes me want her more. The way she stands there, chest heaving, fury radiating off her—it's intoxicating. My wolf vibrates beneath my skin, demanding I take what's rightfully mine.

But the fear beneath her anger stops me cold. I can smell it, cutting through her sweet scent. She's terrified of me. Of what I am. What I represent.

And she should be.

I drag a hand through my hair, fighting to pull myself together. "You felt it too. When I kissed you. Your wolf responded."

"I don't have a wolf," she repeats, but her voice lacks conviction now. Her fingers touch her lips unconsciously, and I catch the way her breathing hasn't quite steadied.

"Stop lying to yourself." I step back, giving her room, though every instinct pulls at me to close the gap again. "You shifted tonight. That's how you escaped the club so quickly. I can still smell the forest on you, the earth clinging to your skin."

Her face goes pale. She glances down at her hands, and I see dirt caked beneath her fingernails—evidence of running wild through the redwoods.

"I don't understand what's happening," she admits, a hint of vulnerability cracking through her defiance. "I've spent my whole life hiding what I am."

I draw in a slow breath, holding my wolf at bay even as he snarls for her. Understanding cuts deep—she's lived among humans, smothering the creature inside her, taught to see her own blood as something dangerous.

"Look, I don't know your story," I say, softening my tone slightly. "But we have time for all that. Time for me to teach you what it means to be a wolf. A real one. Not one pretending to be human."

Her eyes flash with indignation. "I'm not pretending—"

"Yes, you are," I cut her off. "These air fresheners. The way you've scrubbed this place of any natural scent. The way you're fighting against what your body clearly wants right now." I gesture between us. "This isn't living, Karina. It's hiding."

She crosses her arms protectively over her chest. "You don't know anything about me."

"I know enough," I counter. "Living alone without pack protection in a territory crawling with predators who'd tear you apart if they knew of your existence."

"I've been fine so far," she says, but there's a hint uncertainty in her voice now.

"By pure fucking luck," I growl. "Luck that ran out tonight."

"You don't get to just barge in here and—"

My phone vibrates in my pocket, cutting her off mid-sentence. I pull it out, ready to silence whoever's interrupting, but Elias's name flashes on the screen. I answer with a snarl.

"What?"

"Where the fuck are you?" Elias's voice is tight with urgency.

"I found the female. It's being handled."

"Well, handle it faster," he hisses. "I tracked your phone. Don't give me that look. Lockhart left the club not long after you did. I managed to put a tracker on his vehicle. He's headed straight for you."

"Fuck." The word rips from my throat as I move to the window, peering through the blinds. Sure enough, a black SUV idles at the intersection, its tinted windows revealing nothing of who's inside, but I know.

"How the hell did he find her so quickly?" I demand, already scanning the apartment for anything Karina might need.

"Same way we did, I'm guessing. He must have people at the club who recognized her with Britney."

Karina's face drains of color as she picks up snippets of the conversation. "What's happening?"

I cover the phone. "Lockhart is on his way here. I need to get you out of here."

"What? No. I'm not going anywhere with you." Karina backs away, her hands raise defensively.

I pocket my phone and close the distance between us in two strides. "This isn't a fucking debate. Lockhart will tear you apart when he realizes what you are to me."

"I'm not—"

"Stop." I grip her shoulders, forcing her to look at me. "You can deny this all you want later, but right now, you need to trust me. He's here for you, and he won't be as gentle as I've been."

She glances towards the window, then back to me. The fear rolling off her in waves makes my wolf howl with protective rage. She may not accept me yet, but her safety is non-negotiable.

"Pack a bag," I order, releasing her. "Five minutes. Clothes, toiletries, anything you can't live without. You won't be coming back here."

To my surprise, she doesn't argue further. Something in my tone must have gotten through to her. She disappears into her bedroom, and I hear drawers opening and closing in rapid succession.

I use the time to check my weapon and scan the apartment for escape routes. The building's old—probably built in the sixties—with thin walls and creaky floors. Not ideal for a firefight, but the fire escape outside her bedroom window could work if we move fast enough.

My phone buzzes again. I pull it out to read Elias's text.

Almost there.

"Fuck!" I shove the phone back in my pocket and stalk toward her bedroom. No more time for niceties.

She crams clothes into a small duffel, every motion sharp with desperation. The change in her scent hits me, sharp, frantic, cutting through the haze of her cycle that's had my wolf on edge since I walked in.

"Time's up," I growl, grabbing her arm.

"Wait!" She yanks free, lunging for her laptop on the desk. "I need this. And my purse."

I'm about to argue when I hear car doors slamming outside. My wolf's hearing picks up footsteps—multiple sets—entering the building downstairs.

"Move," I snarl, seizing her wrist and pulling her toward the door. She clutches her laptop and purse to her chest with her free hand, stumbling as I drag her from the bedroom.

We burst into the hallway just as heavy footfalls echo up the stairwell. Three, maybe four men. Lockhart isn't taking chances.

"Fire escape," I mutter, changing direction and hauling her back toward the bedroom window. My claws extend with a painful prick as adrenaline floods my system.

She doesn't fight me now. I slam the bedroom door

behind us, twisting the lock. She drops her laptop on the bed and rushes to the window while I drag her dresser in front of the door. It won't stop them, but it'll buy us precious seconds.

"It's stuck," she hisses, straining against the window frame.

I shoulder her aside and drive my fist through the glass. Shards rain down on the fire escape as I clear the jagged edges with my jacket sleeve.

"Go," I order, boosting her through the opening. She lands hard on the metal grating outside, her bag tumbling from her shoulder.

Heavy footsteps thunder down the hallway outside her door. They've found us.

I grab her laptop and shove it into her arms before following her through the window. The fire escape groans under our combined weight as we start our descent, but the old metal holds.

"Faster," I growl, taking the stairs three at a time.

Above us, something crashes against her apartment door—probably a shoulder or boot. Wood splinters, and I hear the dresser scraping across the floor.

Shouts echo from inside her apartment, followed by the distinctive sound of furniture being overturned.

"Where are they?" Lockhart's voice carries through the shattered window.

"Not here," one of his men responds. "Looks like they went out the window."

I press Karina against the brick wall of the adjacent

building, my hand covering her mouth as footsteps thunder above us. My heart pounds against my ribs like a caged animal, but I force my breathing to remain steady.

"Stay quiet," I whisper against her ear, my lips brushing the shell of it. She shivers, and I catch the subtle shift in her scent. Even now, even terrified and running for her life, her body responds to mine.

The fire escape above us groans as Lockhart's men climb out onto it. I can hear them moving, their heavy boots clanging against the metal grating.

"Check the alley," Lockhart's voice drifts down to us. "I can smell her. She hasn't gone far. "

I wait until the sounds fade before releasing Karina. She sags against the wall, clutching her laptop like a lifeline. Her scent lingers in the air, sharp and impossible to miss. Lockhart will smell her if he's close, and we're running out of time. I need to move her before he gets the chance.

"My car is two blocks over. Can you run?"

She nods, her voice unsteady. "I think so."

"Think isn't good enough." I grip her chin, tilting her face up to mine. "I need to know you can keep up. If you fall behind—"

"I won't fall behind," she insists, straightening her spine. "I know these streets better than they do."

My mate isn't just beautiful, she's fierce too, even if she doesn't know it yet.

"Follow me. Stay close." I release her chin and grab her hand instead, threading our fingers together. The contact sends a jolt of electricity up my arm, my wolf howling with satisfaction at the simple touch.

We run through the alley, our footsteps swallowed by the night. Lockhart has already ordered his men to check this route, and their lights slash through the darkness behind us, sweeping closer. There's no time to hide. The air burns in my lungs as I push Karina ahead, faster, keeping her within reach but out of sightlines. We have seconds before they spot us, and I'm not letting him have her.

Karina matches my stride, breathing measured though I can feel the unease coming off her in waves. Her fingers clutch mine hard enough to sting when footsteps sound up the road.

I pull her into a narrow space between two dumpsters that smell like roadkill and rotten eggs, pressing her against the brick wall with my body, hoping the smell from the dumpster will mask her scent long enough for them to move on. My arm braces above her head as I lean down, my lips nearly touching her ear. "Don't move."

She freezes, her chest rising and falling rapidly against mine. Her heartbeat pulses, her breath coming in short, panicked gasps that brush my neck. The closeness is torture. I want nothing more than to bury my face in her neck, to taste her skin, to mark her as mine where everyone can see it.

But now is not the time.

Heavy footsteps approach, boots scraping against asphalt. I press Karina deeper into the shadows, shielding her with my body. One of Lockhart's men passes within feet of us, whistling like he's at a fucking summer camp sing-a-long and not hunting a female. My fucking female. My lip curls in a silent snarl. He's enjoying this.

I'll kill him for that alone.

The footsteps pause. He's scenting the air, trying to catch our trail. My muscles coil, ready to spring if he gets any closer. Karina must sense the change in me because her fingers tighten around mine, a silent plea to stay hidden.

Smart girl.

After what feels like an eternity, the footsteps move on. Thank fuck for smelly dumpsters. That was too goddamn close. I wait until they fade completely before pulling back slightly, just enough to look down at her.

"My car is just around the corner."

She nods. Despite everything, there's a quiet steel in her expression that catches me off guard. This isn't some fragile human in need of coddling. There's a strong wolf in her, buried deep but unmistakably there.

"Let's go." I take her hand in mine as we slip from our hiding spot, moving like ghosts through the maze of back alleys. My car sits where I left it. I unlock it remotely, the soft beep making Karina flinch.

"Get in," I order, scanning the street one last time. "Stay low."

She slips into the passenger seat, pulling the door shut as I round the hood and slide into the driver's side. The engine hums to life with a low growl, but I keep the headlights off, easing out of the parking space under the cover of darkness.

"Where are we going?" she asks quietly.

I don't answer.

Not yet.

My eyes are locked on the rearview mirror, scanning for signs of pursuit. No headlights. No movement. But that doesn't mean we're safe.

Not by a long shot.

I make a sharp turn onto a back road and press the gas a little harder.

"It's the last place I want to take you," I mutter. "But it's the closest—and the only place I know you'll be safe until I figure this out."

She's quiet, but I can feel her staring, waiting for more. I don't offer it.

I grip the wheel tighter, jaw clenched, every muscle wound tight. My wolf is restless beneath my skin, prowling. Angry. *Possessive.*

The thought of walking her into that compound makes something violent rise in me. My wolf doesn't want her there. He wants her away from all of them. Hidden. Guarded. *Claimed.*

I should keep driving. Past the compound. Out of the city. Into the woods. Somewhere no one can find her but me. Somewhere I can keep her locked away until I figure out what the hell the universe is playing at, throwing a mate into my path in the middle of a blood-soaked night.

But there's no time. No plan. No safe house.

Her apartment is compromised.

And I can't exactly book us a room at the goddamn Holiday Inn while Lockhart's wolves are combing the city for her scent.

So I drive.

Toward the last place I should be taking her. The last place she belongs.

Better the devil you know, I tell myself, knowing how much a fucking lie it is.

Karina

I hate him.

I hate how calm he looks dragging me out of my apartment as if it is just a typical day for him.

I hate how he smells like cedar and smoke and something that curls around my throat and makes it hard to breathe.

And I really hate how my wolf responds.

She's alert now, ears perked. Pleased. Like she's finally found what she's been waiting for.

Most infuriating of all is how she reacts to his rough handling. As if being yanked through the stairwell like a damn sack of potatoes is some kind of affection.

I can't even blame him for being what he is. It's not like I didn't know about wolves. My parents made sure I knew. They spent my entire childhood drilling one rule into me—stay out of the were world. Hide what you are. Blend in. Keep your head down. Don't shift unless it's a full moon and do it far away from home. Don't sniff the air in public. Don't lose control.

And I listened.

Until tonight.

And now I'm trapped in a car with a stranger who makes my wolf roll over like a lovesick mutt.

"Where are we going?" I demand again, sharper this time.

Still, no answer.

His focus stays fixed on the rearview mirror, scanning the road behind us as if headlights might appear at any moment. His jaw is clenched so tight I'm surprised his teeth haven't cracked.

I could scream. I want to scream.

Because I'm not just angry, I'm humiliated. Exposed. My apartment, my life, all of it is gone. Every piece of the normal I worked so hard to build just burned to the ground the second this man showed up.

And what's worse?

Part of me. Some wild, stupid part of me doesn't care.

Because my wolf is pacing now. Eager. Interested. Claiming him with every breath I take.

I turn away from him and stare out the window, blinking hard.

I hate him.

But not nearly as much as I hate the part of me that already wants to follow him.

We've been driving for maybe ten minutes, and I can't take the silence anymore. The hum of the road beneath the tires, the low growl of the engine, his tense profile bathed in the dull orange glow of passing street-lights—it's all starting to wear on me.

I cross my arms tightly over my chest.

"So, you're just going to keep driving in silence like I'm not owed any kind of explanation?"

He doesn't flinch, doesn't look at me.

I stare at him, waiting. Nothing.

"Where are we going?"

A beat. Then finally, with a sigh, like it physically pains him to speak.

"Bellandi territory."

I blink. "What?"

His jaw ticks. "You heard me."

The name still means nothing to me. I shift in my seat, staring hard at Damien's profile. "I've never heard of them."

He doesn't react at first, but I can feel the tension in him spike. His knuckles flex around the wheel. "Of course you haven't," he mutters.

I bristle. "So enlighten me, since you've already dragged me into this nightmare. Who are they?"

"They're one of the oldest and most powerful packs on the West Coast," he says finally. "They rule most of central California—territorially, politically, economically. No one moves against them without bleeding for it."

I blink at him. "They run California?"

"In the ways that matter, yes." He glances at me briefly, expression unreadable. "You don't grow that big and last this long without making enemies. And crushing them."

I sit back, stunned. This is way bigger than I thought.

"And you work for them?"

He hesitates, then mutters, "I'm on loan."

"Loan?" I scoff. "Like...a library book?"

He doesn't smile.

"I'm an enforcer," he says tightly. "Temporarily. I belong to another pack."

"So, you work for a crime syndicate?"

He smirks, just barely. "In a manner of speaking, yes."

My stomach twists. This wasn't supposed to happen. I was supposed to go out, have a drink with my neighbor, and put Travis behind me. Not end up in a muscle car with a killer at the wheel being taken to the heart of werewolf mafia central.

The road stretches on, twisting deeper into the trees. The city is long gone now, swallowed by black hills and thick forest. I try to keep my breathing steady, but every mile we put between us and my apartment makes the reality of this situation worse.

I don't know where I am. I don't know who these

people are. I don't even know if I'll survive whatever this is.

"What happens when we get there?" I ask, not bothering to hide the edge in my voice. "Do I just get handed off to someone else? Locked up?"

Damien doesn't answer right away. His hands tighten around the steering wheel, the only sign that I've actually gotten under his skin.

"You'll stay in my quarters," he says, low and clipped. "Until I speak with the Alpha."

I stare at him. "Your...quarters."

He nods once. "You'll stay out of sight. No one touches you. No one talks to you. Not until I've secured your safety with Anselm."

I swallow hard, turning my face to the window and trying to ignore the way my stomach twists. My wolf doesn't help. She's practically curled up in the back of my mind like she's settling in for a nap, smug and content, like the idea of being in *his* space is the best thing that has happened to her in years.

"Don't get comfortable," I mutter under my breath.

She huffs a little, stretching. *Traitor.*

"You'll stay in my space," Damien says again, as if repeating it makes it more acceptable. "No one will come near you. Not without going through me." There's something brutal in the way he says it, something final. Like a warning, or a promise. Maybe both.

"And if I say no?" I ask.

"Then I'll carry you."

My mouth goes dry. As much as I want to fight him, scream at him, throw open the door and launch myself into the forest, we both know I won't.

Because if half of what he's said is true...then the only thing more dangerous than staying with Damien is *not* staying with him.

"How long have you known?"

"Known what?"

"About...this." I gesture vaguely between us, unable to say the words aloud.

He's silent for so long I think he won't answer. When he finally speaks, his voice is rougher than before. "My whole life. It's pack knowledge. Something every wolf grows up understanding."

Of course. Another thing my parents kept from me in their desperate attempt to make me normal. "My parents never told me."

"They did you a disservice." His jaw clenches. "Leaving you unprepared for what you are."

"They were protecting me." The defense comes automatically, even though part of me has always wondered if he's right.

"From what? Your own nature?" He takes a sharp turn, tires gripping the asphalt. "Look how well that worked out."

I want to argue, but the words stick in my throat because he's not wrong. Twenty-seven years of suppressing my wolf, of pretending to be human, and where has it gotten me? Sitting in a killer's car and being dragged to a compound filled with more wolves.

"They tried their best," I say finally, though the words taste hollow.

"Their best left you defenseless. Ignorant." His voice drops lower, more intimate. "Tell me kitten, how many times have you felt like something was missing? Like you were only living half a life?"

The question hits too close to home. I press my lips together, refusing to give him the satisfaction of an answer. But he doesn't need one, my silence is confirmation enough.

"That's what I thought." He reaches over, his fingers brushing against mine where they rest on my thigh. The contact sends fire racing through my veins, and I jerk my hand away. "Your wolf's been starving, hasn't she? Locked away, denied everything she needs."

"Stop." My voice cracks despite my best efforts to stay composed. "You don't know anything about my life."

"I know enough. We have the rest of our lives to dive into the details. First, I need to secure your safety without killing every single male on that fucking compound. Your cycle complicates it even more."

My cheeks burn with humiliation. Living amongst humans made this part of my life so much easier. They can't smell it.

"That's none of your business," I snap, pressing thighs together.

"It becomes my business when I'm taking you to a compound full of wolves." His hands tighten on the steering wheel until I hear it creak under the pressure. "Fuck. This is the last thing we need right now."

"I have suppressants in my bag," I say, though I know they're not strong enough to mask it completely. Just enough to take the edge off until it passes.

"Suppressants won't do shit in a wolf compound." He's grinding his teeth now, the muscle in his jaw working overtime. "Every male will smell you the moment we arrive."

"Take me back." I grab the door handle, though I know it's useless. We're moving too fast, and even if I could jump out, where would I go? "This is a sign from the universe that this is a terrible idea."

His laugh is humorless. "The universe doesn't give signs, kitten. It gives consequences."

"Don't call me that." I wrap my arms around myself. "My name is Karina."

"Karina," he says, and something about the way my name rolls off his tongue makes my wolf stir again. "Your cycle complicates things, but it doesn't change my decision. You're coming with me."

"You don't understand. I can't—" I swallow hard, embarrassment making it difficult to form words. "I've never been around other wolves. I don't know what will happen."

"I know exactly what will happen, and I'll kill anyone who gets too close."

The casual way he talks about murder sends a chill down my spine. "That's not reassuring."

"It wasn't meant to be." He takes a sharp turn onto a narrow road that disappears into the forest. "It was meant to be honest."

"Well, it didn't come off that way."

You really don't understand, do you?"

"What?" I shift uncomfortably.

"Female werewolves are rare, Karina. Extremely rare." He glances at me before returning his eyes to the winding road. "Wolf matings typically produce males. Maybe one in twenty births results in a female. And those females are guarded like crown jewels."

I stare at him, processing this information. Another thing my parents never told me. "That can't be right. My mother—"

"Was one of the lucky few," he cuts in. "Which is probably why your father took her and ran. Pack politics around females can get...intense."

"So, I'm what, some kind of endangered species?" The thought makes my skin crawl.

"In a manner of speaking." His voice drops lower. "Most females are kept under lock and key by their alphas until they're properly mated. Protected from other packs who might try to claim them."

I recoil against the door. "That's barbaric."

"Not barbaric. Practical. Females are the future of any pack. The ability to produce pups is...valuable."

"This is insane. All of it."

"Welcome to wolf politics, kitten." His nostrils flare again, and I know he can smell the changes in my scent. "Your parents sheltered you from this world, but they couldn't keep you from it forever."

I turn away, unwilling to let him see how his words affect me. The trees outside continue to grow denser, the road narrower.

"How much longer?" I ask, desperate to change the subject.

"Ten minutes." He shifts gears as we climb a steep incline. "When we arrive, stay close to me. Don't look at anyone else. Don't speak unless spoken to. And whatever you do, don't let them know you're afraid."

"I'm not afraid," I lie, though my racing heartbeat probably gives me away.

"You should be. Fear keeps you alive in places like this."

The compound emerges like something out of a nightmare, all timber and stone, designed to blend seamlessly with the forest while projecting an aura of barely contained power. Security lights illuminate a gate flanked by guards who straighten as our car approaches.

My wolf whimpers as we slow to a stop, her earlier confidence dissolving beneath the sheer intensity of so much concentrated dominance. The guards are wolves—I can sense it even through the car windows. Their attention locks onto us with a steady, unsettling focus that makes my skin crawl.

"Reaper," the guard greets, respectful but wary.

"Alpha Anselm is waiting for you in his office. He's not pleased."

"When is he ever? I'll report directly to him."

The guard's attention slides toward me, nostrils flaring as my scent reaches him. His pupils expand, a growl rumbling low in his chest before he can smother it.

"Who's this?" he demands, leaning closer, intent locked on me.

Damien's arm snaps out, pressing me back against the seat as he shifts his body into a shield between us. "None of your fucking business, Kenny."

The comment makes my wolf purr even as I bristle at being handled like property. Kenny raises his hands in mock surrender, but the way he studies me carries a sharpness that leaves my skin crawling.

"Just asking," he says, backing away slightly. "Alpha might want to know why you're bringing an unknown female into his territory."

"Alpha can ask me himself. Now open the gate before I decide to use your face as the key."

Kenny hesitates for a fraction of a second before nodding to someone I can't see. The iron gates swing open with a groan of the metal, revealing a winding driveway that leads deeper into the compound.

As we pull forward, I catch Kenny speaking into a radio. Reporting our arrival.

"Fuck," Damien mutters under his breath. "He's already spreading the word."

My stomach clenches as the implications hit me. "What does that mean?"

"It means we need to get you somewhere safe before they start showing up at my door with flowers and poetry." His jaw ticks. "Wolves aren't exactly subtle when they're courting."

"Courting?" The word comes out strangled. "I thought you said I was your mate."

"You are. But they don't know that yet." He parks in front of a building that looks like a cross between a luxury cabin and a fortress. "And even if they did, some of them might be stupid enough to challenge me for you."

The burn under my skin spikes at his words, and I press my thighs together harder. My wolf preens at the idea of males fighting over us. I want to strangle her.

"This keeps getting better and better," I mutter, unbuckling my seatbelt.

Damien's out of the car before I can blink, moving around to my side. He opens the back door, retrieves my bag, then steps closer and extends his hand. I stare at it like it might bite me.

"Come on, kitten. Standing here in the open isn't helping."

I reluctantly take it, hating the way my skin tingles at the contact. His palm is rough and callused, his grip firm yet careful as he helps me out of the car. The moment I'm standing, he tugs me against his side, an arm locking around my waist.

"What are you doing?" I hiss, trying to push space between us.

"Making it clear you're spoken for. Your scent's getting stronger."

"This is mortifying," I groan as he guides me toward the entrance of what I assume are his quarters.

"Better mortified than mauled." His hold tightens as a group of men emerge from a nearby building, their attention snapping toward us like predators catching wind of prey. "Eyes down, kitten."

I obey without thinking, some instinct warning me against challenging dominant males in this state. My wolf goes quiet, unnervingly submissive.

The men change course angling straight for us. I count five. Damien's arm tightens around me protectively as they approach. My heartbeat spikes, sweat beading at my brow. The pheromones I'm giving off must be a beacon to them.

"Reaper," the tallest one calls out, his voice deceptively casual. "Didn't know you were bringing company home tonight."

"Not company. Mine," Damien growls, the vibration of his chest against my side sending unwelcome tingles down my spine. "Keep walking, Jackson."

Jackson's nostrils flare as he inhales deeply. "She doesn't smell claimed to me."

"That's because your nose is too far up your own ass to smell properly," Damien retorts.

The men laugh, but there's no humor in it, just

tension and something predatory that makes my skin crawl. They're circling us now, not close enough to touch but near enough that I can smell their interest—musky and sharp.

"Alpha Anselm will want to meet her," says another, a stocky wolf with a scar bisecting his left eyebrow. "She's a pretty little wolf. What's your name, sweetheart?"

I don't get a chance to answer. Damien drops my bag on the ground next to my feet. His now free hand moves to his waistband, and suddenly there's a gun pointed directly at the scarred wolf's forehead.

"The next person who speaks to her dies," he says conversationally, like he's commenting on the weather instead of threatening murder. "She's under my protection, which means she's under Bellandi protection. Touch her, look at her wrong, even think about her, and I'll paint these grounds with your blood."

The wolves freeze, their casual predatory stance shifting to something more wary. I can smell the sudden spike of adrenaline and aggression rolling off them in waves. My wolf whimpers, pressing closer to Damien's warmth despite my mind's protests.

"Easy, Reaper," Jackson says, hands raised in mock surrender. "We're just being friendly."

"Your version of friendly looks a lot like stalking prey. Back off. Now."

I hold my breath, acutely aware of how quickly this could turn violent. The scarred wolf's hand twitches toward his own weapon, and I know we're seconds away from bloodshed.

"Is there a problem here?"

The new voice cuts through the standoff like a blade. All eyes turn toward the compound's main building, where a tall figure emerges from the shadows. Even in the dim lighting, I can see the authority radiating from him.

"I'm sure you all of you have somewhere else to be."

The wolves hesitate, clearly torn between their interest in me and their respect for the pack hierarchy. My wolf shrinks further into herself, overwhelmed by the competing dominance displays surrounding us.

"We were just welcoming the Reaper's...guest."

"How thoughtful. I'm sure she appreciates the warm reception. Now fuck off before my father decides you're all expendable."

The mention of his father has the desired effect. The wolves back away reluctantly, but I can still feel their attention burning into my skin as they retreat. My legs weaken with relief.

"Thanks," Damien mutters.

"Don't thank me yet. My father wants to see you. Immediately." Elias pauses, his attention sliding to me, taking in the way I'm pressed against Damien's side. "Though I think he may be more interested in her than in murder. I'm Elias, by the way, since Dom hasn't bothered to introduce us." He extends a hand but freezes mid-motion when Damien stiffens beside me. "Nevermind..."

"How did you get back here so fast?"

"Shifted." He shrugs. "Not like I can call a car service to bring me back to the compound after you abandoned me at Crimson Howl. Though... I had some fun while I waited. You know, passed the time while you ran for your life. Looks like you won't be spending your night alone either, brother."

"I need you to do me a favor. Watch her while I deal with your father." Damien lowers his weapon, sliding it back into his waistband, then retrieves my discarded bag and hands it to me.

Elias arches a brow, studying the space between us. "And why exactly would I do that?"

"She's my mate." The declaration leaves no room for argument.

"You left to commit your second murder of the night, and you come home with a mate? I never thought you'd be so full of surprises, Dom." He steps closer, but Damien moves to block him. Elias takes a sniff and smiles, understanding dawns on his face. "Well, that explains the welcoming committee."

"I need her safe, Elias. Take her to my quarters and keep everyone else away. Everyone."

I bristle at being discussed like I'm not standing right here. "I don't need a babysitter."

Both men ignore me completely.

"Fine," Elias sighs, running a hand through his blond hair. "But you owe me. Big time."

"Consider it payment for all the times I've saved your ass." Damien's arm finally releases me, though he doesn't step away. "Don't let anyone near her. Not even your brothers."

"Yes, Mom. Anything else?"

Damien's hand shoots out, grabbing Elias by the collar and yanking him close enough that their faces are inches apart. The sudden violence makes me flinch.

"This isn't a joke," he growls. "If anyone—and I mean anyone—touches her while I'm gone, I'll rip their fucking throat out. Starting with yours. Your balls will be next."

Elias doesn't seem fazed by the threat, but I see the subtle way his body tenses. "Relax, Dom. I'll guard her with my life. No one gets past me."

"They better not." Damien's attention flicks to me. "I'll be back as soon as I can."

Before I can respond, he's striding toward the main building, his shoulders set in a rigid line. I watch him go, hating the way my wolf whines at his departure, like she's being abandoned.

"Well," Elias says beside me. "That was intense. Even for Dom."

I wrap my arms around myself, suddenly feeling exposed without Damien's presence. The night air feels cooler, and my skin prickles with awareness of how vulnerable I am in this unfamiliar territory.

"Is he always like that?"

"Like what? Homicidal? Overprotective? Brooding? Yeah, pretty much." Elias grins, but there's something cautious in his expression as he studies me. "Though I've never seen him claim anyone before. That's new."

"He hasn't claimed me," I snap, though my cheeks burn with embarrassment.

He turns to look behind him, shaking his head with a quiet laugh. "And now I know why Dom threatened me."

"What's that supposed to mean?" I ask, glaring at Elias as he leads me toward a cabin at the edge of the compound. His cryptic smile only irritates me further.

"It means you're spicy. I like it." He unlocks the door with a key from his pocket. "Most women who encounter Dom either run screaming or fall at his feet. You're doing neither."

"I tried the running part. Didn't work out so well."

He chuckles, pushing the door open and gesturing for me to enter. "Ladies first."

I hesitate at the threshold, my wolf suddenly alert and wary. This is Damien's space—his den. Entering it feels like crossing a line I can't uncross.

"It's just a cabin," Elias says, misreading my hesitation. "Dom keeps it clean, I promise."

Taking a deep breath, I step inside. Damien's scent hits me immediately — pine, smoke, and something darkly male that curls through the air and wraps around me. My wolf stirs beneath my skin, restless and alert. The warmth that's been simmering inside me surges, and I have to lock my knees to keep from swaying.

The cabin is sparse but inviting, the kind of space

that feels lived in without ever being cluttered. An open kitchen lines one wall; the opposite side holds a sitting area furnished in dark wood and soft leather. A single door at the back likely leads to the bedroom, though I don't dare look too long in that direction.

"Make yourself at home," Elias says, shutting the door behind him and turning the lock with a quiet, deliberate click.

The sound makes my pulse jump. The air feels thicker here, saturated with Damien's scent until it's almost tangible. Each breath drags more of it into my lungs, clouding my thoughts, quickening my heartbeat.

"So," Elias drawls, sinking into one of the armchairs like he owns the place. "Want to tell me how you managed to almost mate yourself to the most antisocial wolf in Northern California?"

If only I knew that answer myself.

Damien

Anselm's eyes burn into me. The temperature in his office seems to drop twenty degrees as he leans forward, palms flat against his mahogany desk.

"Explain to me," he says, each word a carefully measured threat, "why I had to hear about Marco's death from Viktor? He's the head of my club's fucking security, not your clean up crew."

I stand at rigid attention, my face a careful mask despite the storm tearing through me. Every part of me aches to get back to Karina, to make sure Elias is keeping his word. My wolf prowls beneath my skin, restless and unsettled by the distance between us.

"I was handling a witness, Alpha." No point lying to

him, his senses are too sharp, his experience too vast to be fooled.

"A witness." He repeats the words slowly. "And this witness was more important than reporting directly to me after executing one of my orders?"

The air thickens with his displeasure. At fifty-three, Alpha Anselm Bellandi is still a force of nature—six-foot-five of pure muscle and ruthless intelligence. The scar across his left brow twitches as he waits for my response.

"The witness saw everything. I had to contain the situation."

"An interesting choice of words for someone who left a corpse in my club and a witness running free." Alpha Anselm rounds his desk, closing the distance between us until I can smell the scotch on his breath. "Viktor tells me that Thomas Lockhart claims you threatened him over some female. Is that true?"

My jaw clenches. "He was harassing her."

"Harassing." Anselm's laugh is cold, mirthless. "He says you nearly broke his wrist over some masked bitch then disappeared."

My hands curl into fists at his description of Karina. "Lockhart exaggerates."

"Does he?" Anselm stops directly in front of me, his height allowing him to look down at me despite my own considerable stature. "Would this be the same female that Kenny reported as your guest?

"She's under my protection."

"Your protection?" Anselm's eyebrows rise. "Not the family's protection? Interesting distinction."

He's testing me, looking for cracks in my composure. I've survived eight months under his scrutiny by keeping my emotions locked down tight. But tonight, with Karina's scent still clinging to my clothes and my wolf howling for her, my restrain feels paper-thin.

"She witnessed Marco's execution," I explain, choosing my words with precision. "I couldn't risk her talking."

"So, you brought her here?" Anselm shakes his head, disappointment etched in the lines of his face. "That's not like you, Damien. You don't bring problems home, you eliminate them."

The casual way he suggests killing Karina makes my blood boil. I clench my jaw so hard I hear my teeth creak.

"The situation is more complicated than that."

"Enlighten me." He settles into the leather chair behind his desk, the effortless confidence of a man long accustomed to being obeyed.

I weigh my options, knowing that half-truths will serve me better than outright lies.

"She's my mate."

Anselm goes perfectly still, his attention sharpening on my face with renewed interest. I can almost feel the calculations grinding behind that measured stillness—the implications, the opportunities, the potential complications.

He leans back in his chair, fingers steepled beneath his chin. "Go on."

"I tracked her down with every intention of tying up loose ends. But then Lockhart showed up at her apartment. He wasn't there by accident."

Anselm's features tighten. "Explain."

"He had a team with him. Professional extraction. They were there to take her." My wolf surges at the memory of those men approaching Karina's door. "I couldn't let that happen."

"So instead of eliminating the problem, you brought it to my doorstep."

"I brought her to safety," I correct him.

"How convenient that you discovered her right when you need to justify breaking protocol."

I wait, knowing he's not finished. Anselm never speaks without purpose, never shows his hand before he's ready to play it.

"Why would Thomas Lockhart be interested in this female? Who is her family?"

"I have no idea," I admit, holding his scrutiny without flinching. "We weren't exactly sitting down with coffee to trace her family lineage while people were trying to kidnap her."

"You expect me to believe you took this female under your protection without knowing her bloodline?" Anselm's tone is cool but laced with skepticism. "She could already be promised to someone else. For all we know, Lockhart might have laid a claim years ago."

"I find that unlikely," Damien replies, voice steady. "She's been living among humans, hidden. Lockhart isn't the type to misplace something he considers valuable."

Anselm's mouth twists into a grim smile. "Is that so? If Lockhart has been hunting her, I can see why you're suddenly so interested. Perhaps you take after your father more than you'd like to admit. Hudson always had a talent for turning other men's assets to his advantage."

"My father's ambition has nothing to do with this. She has no idea how our world works. Best guess, her parents were rogues. It would explain why she doesn't shift often and why she refers to her wolf as a monster."

"She doesn't shift?" His interest sharpens.

"Only when necessary, from what I gather. She hides what she is, even from herself."

Anselm rises, moving to the window that overlooks the estate grounds.

"You've brought an unknown variable into my territory, Damien. A wolf with no pack ties, no allegiance, and apparently no training." He turns back to me. "You know better than anyone what a liability that represents."

"I need your protection for her." I step closer to his desk, "Lockhart will have caught my scent in her apartment. He knows I interfered with whatever he had planned. He'll come after her again."

Anselm's expression remains cold, calculating. The silence stretches between us stretching like a rubber band pulled too tight.

"Your mate. Your problem." He waves his hand

dismissively, as if swatting away an annoying fly. "I didn't send you to kill Marco so you could bring home a stray."

My wolf rages at his callousness, but I keep my face neutral. "She's not a stray."

"We'll see about that, won't we? We'll put a pin in that for now. There are more pressing matters at hand. You haven't told me what information you extracted from Marco before you put a bullet in his skull."

The abrupt change of subject doesn't surprise me. It's a classic Anselm tactic—keeping me off balance, reminding me who holds the power. I clench my jaw, recognizing the game but having no choice except to play along.

I force myself to focus on the original reason I was summoned. "He confirmed Lockhart's been recruiting businesses from under us. Undercutting our protection rates by thirty percent. Six businesses are meeting with Lockhart tomorrow night at the old Kellerman building. Golden Paw Brewery, Redwood Apothecary, Sierra Supply Co, Blackridge Auto Shop, and Moonlight Diner."

"And the sixth?"

I hesitate, weighing how much to reveal. "The sixth isn't a business. It's a person. Someone inside your organization."

The temperature in the room seems to drop another ten degrees. Anselm goes perfectly still, only his eyes betraying the fury building inside him.

"A name," he demands.

"Marco didn't give one. Said Lockhart never speci-fied, just that it was someone close to you."

Anselm stares at me for a long moment. "Someone close to me," he repeats. "That narrows it down considerably."

"It could be anyone. Marco might have been lying to save his skin."

"Perhaps." Anselm moves to the liquor cabinet behind his desk, pouring himself two fingers of scotch with deliberate precision. "But Lockhart has been too well-informed lately. His timing too convenient." He downs the amber liquid in one swallow. "I want names. Possibilities."

"I'll look into it," I promise, already calculating how to use this assignment to my advantage. The sooner I resolve this issue, the sooner I can focus on Karina.

"See that you do." Anselm sets his glass down with a decisive click. "In the meantime, I want you at that meeting tomorrow night. Find out which of my busi-nesses are betraying me."

"And after I identify them?"

His smile is cold and empty. "Make an example of them. The way only the Reaper can."

I nod, accepting the assignment. "I'll make it clear what happens to those who betray your family."

"Good. Now, about this female of yours..."

My spine stiffens, every muscle in my body tensing at the mention of Karina. "What about her?"

"I want to meet her. Tomorrow morning, breakfast. My private dining room."

My wolf growls at the so-called invitation, sensing the demand beneath it. The thought of letting Anselm near Karina twists something deep in me; she's still too shaken from what happened tonight. But I can't refuse—not when I need his help to keep her safe.

"She's been through a lot tonight," I say carefully. "She might need more time to—"

"Nine o'clock sharp." Anselm's tone brooks no argument. "If you want my protection for her, you will both be present, and she will be wearing your mark. If she isn't, well, I have two sons who may be in the market for a mate."

The barb lands as he intends, but I don't flinch. "Understood."

I turn toward the door, every step feeling like I'm walking through quicksand.

"Damien."

I pause, my hand on the doorknob.

"If this female proves to be more trouble than she's worth..." He doesn't finish the threat, but he doesn't need to. The implication hangs in the air like smoke from a funeral pyre.

"She won't be," I say without turning around.

"For your sake, I hope you're right."

I walk out before I say something I'll regret. The door clicks shut behind me, but the tension stays lodged deep in my chest.

The hallway is quiet, cold. But in my blood, everything is loud.

Because no matter what I tell him, no matter what I tell myself, I don't know if Karina will survive this world.

And worse, I don't know if I'll survive what I'll become trying to protect her.

Damien

I smell Elias on her before I even open the door.

My wolf claws under my skin, snarling with territorial fury as I turn the key in the lock with more force than necessary. The door flies open, slamming against the wall with a crack that makes both occupants of my cabin jump.

Karina sits perched on the edge of my couch. Elias sprawls in the armchair across from her, posture deceptively casual, his smile a little too familiar.

"Well, that was fast," Elias says, rising with an easy grin that can't quite hide the tight coil in his shoulders. He knows he's pushing it. "Your girl here was just telling me about her life among humans. Fascinating stuff."

"Out." The word grates from my throat like broken glass.

Elias lifts his brows, glancing between us. "Is that any way to thank your faithful guard dog? I kept the wolves from your door, literally."

My fingers curl, claws threatening to break skin. "I said, out."

Karina shifts slightly, watching the standoff with wary attention. Her pulse beats fast at her throat, chest rising and falling with quickened rhythm. The sight of that delicate skin, the scent rolling off her in waves sends another surge of hunger tearing through me.

"Don't make me drag you out," I growl, the words meant for Elias even as my focus is pulled inexorably toward her.

"Jesus, Dom." Elias shakes his head but moves toward the door. "Ask nicely."

"Nicely?" I slam the door behind him with enough force to rattle the windows. The lock clicks with finality, and suddenly the cabin feels impossibly small with just the two of us inside. "Since when do I ask for anything nicely?"

Karina flinches at the violence in my tone, pressing herself deeper into the couch cushions. Her scent wraps around me like a drug, making my wolf pace frantically beneath my skin.

"You didn't have to be so rude to him. He was just keeping me company. Like you asked him to, remember?"

I move closer, unable to stop myself from prowling toward her. "Why is his scent all over you?"

Her cheeks flush pink. "We were just talking. He sat across the room the entire time."

"Talking about what?" I stop in front of the couch, towering over her seated form. This close, her scent is overwhelming, which makes my mouth water.

"Nothing important. My job, my life…" She trails off, her attention flicking to my hands where claws have begun to edge through. "Why are you so angry?"

Because another male scent clings to you. Because I can taste your arousal in the air, and it's driving me insane. Because every instinct I possess is screaming to claim you. Right here. Right fucking now.

"Because you're mine," I growl, the words ripping free before I can stop them. "And I don't share."

Her breath stutters at the declaration, her scent shifting.

"I'm not yours," she manages, but the protest trembles at the edges. "And I wasn't doing anything wrong."

I lean down, planting my hands on either side of her against the couch, caging her in. The move brings me so close I can feel the warmth radiating from her skin, close enough to catch every shiver in the air between us.

"Your scent says otherwise, kitten." My nostrils flare as I inhale deeply, drowning in the honeyed vanilla that's now sharp with arousal. "You're practically dripping."

She gasps, her cheeks flushing crimson. "That's not —I can't help—"

"Can't help what? Getting wet while talking to another male?" The words taste like poison on my tongue, but I can't stop them from coming.

"It's not like that. It doesn't mean anything."

"Doesn't mean anything?" I laugh, the sound harsh even to my own ears. "Your body responds to me. Your wolf recognizes me. And you want to tell me it doesn't mean anything?"

She shifts beneath me, her thighs pressing together in a futile attempt to ease the ache I can smell building between them. Her wolf is closer to the surface now, golden flecks dancing in her eyes as she stares up at me.

"I barely know you." Her pulse hammers at her throat, a rapid flutter that makes my mouth water with the need to press my lips there. "This is just biology. Chemistry."

"Then let's talk chemistry." I lower my face until our lips are mere inches apart, drinking in her scent like the finest whiskey. "Because right now, every molecule in my body is screaming to claim you."

Her breath hitches, the sound sending a jolt of electricity straight to my groin. "Damien..."

The way she says my name—half plea, half warning—nearly breaks my control. I pull back slightly, fighting the urge to crush my mouth against hers.

"What happened with Anselm?" she asks, clearly trying to change the subject, to diffuse the tension crackling between us.

"We aren't finished with our current discussion, kitten."

Her brow furrows. "Elias was protecting me, at your request, remember? That's all."

I let out a harsh breath, trying to cage the growl building in my chest. "My wolf doesn't care about logic."

"He didn't touch me, Damien."

"I know." The words scrape out like gravel. "But knowing doesn't stop the part of me that wants to rip out the throat of anyone who even looks at you too long."

She stares at me, chest rising and falling fast. "You think that's fair?"

"No," I admit, voice low. "It's instinct. Irrational. But when it comes to you, kitten..." I lean in, close enough to feel her breath tremble against my lips. "...my wolf doesn't understand reason."

She frowns, confusion cutting through the heat between us. "You're acting like I did something wrong. You said I shouldn't be alone while you met with the alpha here."

"I know what I said."

"Then why are you acting like I fucked your friend the second you walked out the door? I know him even less then I know you."

"Elias might be my best friend, but he's still a dominant male. His wolf would've reacted, even if he didn't mean to. And mine..." I shake my head, forcing down the growl building in my throat. "Mine didn't like it."

"You're jealous of him? Of Elias?"

I meet her gaze, no use hiding it now. "My wolf is."

She studies me for a long moment, something like understanding flickering behind her eyes. "But he didn't touch me, Damien. We talked. That's it."

"I know," I answer, running a hand down my face. "But knowing doesn't quiet him. He still sees Elias near you. Smelling you. Protecting you. It feels like a challenge, even when it's not."

Her lips curve faintly, a breath of humor slipping through the tension. "So, your wolf's an overprotective idiot."

A low sound rumbles in my chest—half laugh, half growl. "Yeah," I admit. "But he's my idiot. And right now, he's losing his mind over you."

She blinks, still catching up. "I don't understand. Why does it matter what anyone thinks if nothing happened?"

"Because it's not just about what happened," I say, forcing my voice level. "It's about how they see you. How they see us." My wolf bristles again at the thought of Anselm, the man already circling like a vulture. "And how little protection you have right now. It's the only reason why I agreed to the alpha's demands."

"What demands?"

I straighten, giving her space to breathe. "He won't extend his protection unless you're wearing my mark and he gets to meet you."

Her face drains of color. "What does that mean?"

"It means we're fucked unless I claim you...properly." The words taste like ash on my tongue, but they're the truth. "As long as you're unmated, any alpha can challenge my right to you. Anselm made that clear."

"Challenge your right?" She stands abruptly, fury flashing in her eyes. "I'm not property."

"In our world, you are." The admission hits like a gut punch, even to me. My wolf paces inside me, ears flat, tail low. He hates it. I hate it. But that doesn't change the fact that it's true. "I hate it as much as you do, but that's reality. You're free game, and he has three available sons."

"That's barbaric." She backs away, her scent spiking with distress, sour and sharp, like panic and rage tangled into one.

"Yeah," I grit out. "It is."

She's quiet for a beat. Then she shakes her head and spits words like a weapon, "Then I'll leave."

Something snaps inside me.

I move before I think, closing the space between us in two long strides. I don't touch her. Not yet. But I make sure she feels every inch of my presence pressing down.

"The only way you're leaving," I say low, my words razor-sharp, "is if I'm walking beside you—*or I'm dead.*"

She blinks, startled. I can see her wolf stir just beneath the surface, confused, hesitant.

"You don't get it," I continue, softer now, but no less intense. "You're thinking like a human. This isn't their world. You walk out of this room unclaimed, unprotected, and you won't make it past the fucking gates."

Her mouth opens, but I keep going.

"You're a wolf, Karina. Whether you want to be or not. You don't get to ignore that anymore."

Her hands are balled into fists at her sides. She's shaking. With rage. With fear. Maybe both.

I want to touch her. Pull her close. Let her feel that she's not alone in this. That I'm not the enemy. But I can't do that right now, not when she's one wrong word away from bolting.

"I'm not trying to control you," I say, quieter now. "I'm trying to *keep you alive.*"

She stays silent, jaw tight, fists curled as if holding herself together by sheer will. The struggle is clear—the human in her pushing back against the pull of the wolf. But I can also *feel* her wolf. Stirring. Restless. Curious.

I take a breath, trying to keep the edge out of my voice.

"Your wolf wants me," I continue. "I can smell it on you. I can feel it calling out to mine."

"My wolf is an idiot," she snaps, but her body betrays her. Her nipples are hard beneath her shirt, her breathing shallow and rapid.

"Is she?" I reach out slowly, telegraphing my movement so she can pull away if she wants. When she doesn't, I brush a strand of hair from her face, my knuckles grazing her heated cheek. "Or does she understand something your human half refuses to accept?"

The contact sends electricity racing through my veins. Her scent spikes with arousal, so sharp and sweet I nearly groan aloud. My wolf howls with triumph at the response.

"I won't be treated like some prize," she snaps, voice shaking with anger that only makes her scent burn hotter in the air.

"Then tell me what you do want," I rasp, the words rough against my throat. "Because everything about you is saying you want *something*, kitten."

Her eyes flutter close at the endearment, a soft sound escaping her lips that makes my cock throb painfully against my jeans. When she opens them again, the brown has darkened. I want to close the distance between us, to press her against the wall and show her exactly what she's doing to me. But something in her expression stops me—vulnerability beneath the defiance, confusion warring with desire.

"I want..." She swallows hard, her throat working in a way that makes me want to press my mouth there. "I want to understand what's happening to me. Why does my body betray me every time you're near?"

My wolf preens at her words, at the recognition that she feels the pull between us even if she doesn't understand it.

"It's the bond," I say, trying to hold my voice steady while every nerve in my body pulls me toward her. "Your wolf knows me. It's instinct, yes, but it's older than that. Something sacred. Something that's always been."

"Just because our wolves think we're compatible doesn't mean we are."

I let my hand drift from her cheek to her throat, feeling her pulse race beneath my palm. "Then explain this. Explain why your heart pounds when I touch you. Why your scent changes when I touch you. This is deeper than that, kitten. This is recognition. Soul calling to soul."

"You don't know anything about my soul."

"Don't I?" I press closer, my body caging hers against the wall. "Then why does touching you feel like coming home? Why does your wolf purr when mine gets close?"

"She doesn't purr," Karina protests, but even as she says it, I can feel the subtle shift in her energy, her wolf stretching beneath her skin, reaching for mine.

"Liar." I brush my thumb across her pulse point, feeling the rapid flutter of her heartbeat. "I can feel her right now, pressing against your skin, wanting out."

A soft whimper escapes her lips, the sound going straight to my cock. Her scent spikes again, so rich with arousal that I grip the wall behind her to keep from crushing my mouth to hers.

"This is insane." Her back arches slightly, pressing her breasts against my chest, and I bite back a groan at the contact.

"Insane would be fighting this." My other hand comes up to frame her face, my thumb tracing the curve of her bottom lip. "Insane would be pretending we don't both feel this pull."

Her pulse hammers beneath my fingers, a rapid drumbeat that matches the thunder of my own heart.

My wolf is clawing at the edges of my restraint, demanding I close the final inches between us and take what it believes is already ours. Her heat saturates the air, filling my lungs until my head swims and my body aches with need.

"Tell me to stop," I growl, the sound unrecognizable even to myself. "Tell me you don't feel it too, and I'll walk away."

Karina sits frozen, pupils blown wide, her scent betraying desire braided with unease. Her lips part soundlessly before a soft, helpless sound slips from her throat. The noise makes my body tighten painfully against my zipper.

"That's what I thought." I lean in until my breath brushes her mouth. "Your words can fight me, but your body already knows."

"I didn't ask for this. For you. For any of it."

"Neither did I." The confession grates out of me, a crack in the armor I've worn my entire life. "But here we are."

My thumb drags slowly across her bottom lip, and she shudders under the contact. Her self-control is fraying; I can sense it in every tremor of her body, in the way her wolf presses closer to the surface.

Her voice breaks the quiet, rough with confusion. "If I... let this happen," she whispers, eyes flicking up to mine, "if I give in to this thing between us... what does it mean? What happens to me?"

"There are two steps," I say, my voice rough with

need. "First is marking. We bite each other at the neck, drawing blood. It initiates the bond between us."

Her hand flies to her throat, fingers pressing against the pulse point. "You want to bite me?"

"I want to do a lot more than bite you," I growl, unable to keep the hunger from my voice. "But yes, I bite you. My teeth here—" I brush my fingers against the juncture where her neck meets her shoulder, feeling her shiver beneath my touch. "And yours on me, in the same spot."

"That's it?" She sounds almost hopeful, and my wolf snarls at her obvious relief.

"No." I lean closer, inhaling her intoxicating scent. "That's just the beginning. To make it permanent, we mate under the full moon."

"So, we have to..." She can't finish the sentence, her cheeks flushing crimson.

"Yes." I stroke my thumb along her jawline, marveling at the softness of her skin. "My cock inside of you, claiming you in the most ancient way possible," I continue, watching her pupils dilate. "Your body taking mine while the moon witnesses our union, binding us together."

"Binds us how?"

"Our wolves become one pack. We'll be able to sense each other's emotions, locations, and physical state." I watch her as the implications sink in. "We'll know when the other is hurt, afraid, aroused...it means you'll never be alone again. You'll always be connected to me."

She worries her bottom lip between her teeth, and the sight stirs a low, restless sound from deep in my chest. I crave those teeth on my skin, claiming me as fiercely as I ache to claim her.

"What if..." she begins, then falters, hesitation flickering across her face. "What if we only did the first step? The bond. But not the... rest. The full moon is only days away. That gives me time to decide."

"Decide? This isn't some trial run, Karina."

"It is for me." Her palms press against my chest—not pushing me away, but holding space between us. "I didn't ask for any of this. I didn't ask to be tied to you, to be thrown into this life of bloodlines and pack rivalries."

My grip on my restraint frays as she meets my eyes, defiance blazing through every line of her body. The thought of sharing a bond with her without sealing it fully is a torment of its own, yet the idea of forcing a union she's not ready for is worse. Even the beast inside me recoils at the thought, despite the bone-deep hunger to make her mine.

"You don't understand what you're asking," I snarl, voice rough with restraint. "To form the bond without the final act brings agony. A pain beyond imagining."

"For both of us?" she presses, searching me as if trying to catch even the smallest crack of deception.

"Yes." I press my forehead to hers, unable to keep even that distance between us. "It would be like starting a fire in your veins that nothing can put out."

She draws a shuddering breath, her scent sharp in the

air—an electric mix of panic and desire. "But it would buy me time. Time to understand what all this means. I can live with the pain. Can you?"

Can I live with the torment? To brand her as mine and endure the constant, burning hunger—the ache that will tear at me every second until we finish it?

I pull back just enough to study her face, searching for cruelty, for any sign she means this as punishment. But all I find is determination threaded through with trembling uncertainty. She's terrified and still reaching for a fragile middle ground in a world that doesn't allow one.

"You're asking me to bind us, knowing I'll live in unrelenting agony until the full moon. Knowing every instinct I have will be screaming to finish what we started."

"I'm asking you to give me a choice. Something no one else in this world seems willing to do."

My wolf howls, pacing beneath my skin, feral and restless. The thought is torment, but the idea of losing her completely is worse.

I shut my eyes, wrestling every instinct clawing inside me. When I open them again, her face is so close I can feel the tremor of her breath, hope and desperation entwined in every line of her expression.

"You have no idea what you're asking of me," I growl. Even as I say it, I know I'll give her what she wants. Because the thought of her becoming prey for every other alpha in the territory is a nightmare I won't allow.

"Fine." The word scrapes out of me, metallic on my tongue. "But you need to understand what you're asking. The second our bond is sealed, every instinct in me will drive to finish it. Thought won't matter. I'll be ruled by hunger."

Relief rolls off her in waves, a subtle tremor of it brushing against my senses. "I understand."

"No, you don't." My fingers slide under her chin, forcing her gaze up to mine. "You *think* you do, but you have no idea what you're about to unleash. The bond will twist inside you, too. Your wolf will press against your skin, demanding what comes next. Every time I'm near, you'll ache for me."

Her breath hitches, but she doesn't retreat. "I can handle it."

I laugh, a sound as rough and jagged as broken glass. "Can you? Because right now, you can barely stand being this close to me without your scent spiking with want. After the bond is forged, that craving won't just grow— it'll devour you."

"I said I can handle it." There's steel in her voice now, the same stubborn determination that drew my wolf to her in the first place.

I study her face, searching for any crack in her resolve. Finding none, I release her chin and step back, running my hands through my hair in frustration.

"When?"

"Now. Before I change my mind."

My wolf surges forward with a howl of triumph that vibrates through every cell in my body. I take a deep breath, trying to steady myself, but her scent fills my lungs and makes my head swim.

"Are you sure?" I manage to ask, though my wolf snarls at the delay. My claws have fully emerged now.

She tilts her head, exposing the smooth column of her throat in an offering. "Yes. Just...be gentle."

I can't promise that, but I nod anyway, cupping her face between my palms as I lean closer.

"It will hurt," I warn, "but only for a moment."

Her pulse leaps at her throat, a rapid flutter that draws me in like a beacon. I lower my head, nose skimming along the delicate skin there, breathing her scent in straight from the source. She trembles beneath me, a soft gasp breaking free from her parted lips.

"Damien..." My name falls from her mouth, breathless and desperate, snapping the final thread of my restraint.

"Now, kitten," I growl against her skin. "Hold onto me."

My fangs drop fully, razor-sharp canines aching with purpose. I grip her shoulders, anchoring us both as I angle my bite at the perfect spot.

She fists the fabric of my shirt, knuckles white with tension as she braces. Her fear lingers sharp in the air, but beneath it something hotter unfurls—arousal blooming like a flower straining toward sunlight. Her wolf pushes forward, flickering close to the surface, shimmering through her like fire threatening to catch.

"Together," I whisper, and sink my teeth into her flesh.

Her blood bursts across my tongue. The taste floods my system like molten gold, every nerve ending lighting up as the ancient magic takes hold. Karina cries out, her back arching as pain and pleasure war across her features.

But she doesn't pull away. Instead, her own canines extend—smaller than mine but just as sharp—and she bites down on the same spot on my neck with surprising ferocity.

The world detonates. The tether snaps into place like a rubber band pulled too tight, connecting us in ways I never thought possible.

I feel her—not just her body pressed against mine, but the storm of her emotions. Terror tangled with arousal, confusion bleeding into something deeper. Her wolf calls to mine across the new link, a song of recognition that makes my beast howl with savage satisfaction.

The taste of her blood is intoxicating, addictive enough that I want more, but I force myself to stop. My fangs retract, leaving perfect crescents that will never fade, permanent reminders of what we've begun.

Karina releases my neck with a gasp, her mouth lowering to close her own mark on me. The contact sends a jolt of raw energy down my spine, and I have to brace against the wall behind her to keep from crushing her against me.

"Oh god." Her breath hitches, shock etched across her face. "I can feel you inside my head."

"The tether," I confirm, holding myself steady while every cell hums with need. Her confusion filters through the link, but so does the calm pulse of her wolf, stretching beneath her skin even as her human mind tries to make sense of it. "It will fade if we don't finish it, but for now..."

"You'll know what I'm feeling."

"Not just know." I brush my thumb across the fresh indentations on her skin, and she flinches at the sudden spark of sensation. The reaction hits me too, a rush of warmth spreading through the bond until it settles low in my chest. "Your pleasure. Your pain. Every thought that makes your pulse race."

Her breath catches, and through the tether I feel the flutter of uncertainty melting into something softer—an ache that's half wonder, half yearning. It moves through me like a current, filling the space between every heartbeat.

I draw in a slow breath, letting the connection settle. "And I'll feel it too. Every flicker of emotion, every shift in your breathing, every tremor when the world feels too much."

Her eyes close, and for a moment we're suspended in something wordless—her warmth flowing through me, my steadiness echoing back to her. The tether hums, soft and alive, a rhythm that matches the rise and fall of her chest.

"I didn't know it would feel like this," she whispers.

"Neither did I," I admit. The truth vibrates between us, the link alive with shared breath and heartbeat, blurring the edges where one of us ends and the other begins.

For a moment, everything is still. The air feels charged, soft light spilling across her skin as I trace the faint shimmer where the tether hums strongest. Her emotions ripple through me—warmth, exhaustion, the lingering thrum of something tender that neither of us dares name.

Her fingers brush my wrist, tentative, grounding. "It doesn't hurt," she murmurs. "It feels... alive."

"It is," I say quietly. "It's us."

But then the bond flickers, just slightly, and her pulse stutters. A sharp jolt of pain echoes through the link, hitting me at the same time she gasps. I look down and see it: a thin line of blood welling along her neck, bright against her skin.

"Karina." Her name leaves me on a breath as I step closer, the metallic tang of blood already coating the back of my throat. My thumb hovers near the wound—skin torn, still too raw to touch.

Dark stains spread across the collar of her shirt where my teeth had broken through, red droplets tracing down her neck even though the injury should have begun to close. I lean in before reason can stop me. My breath ghosts over the wound, and I let my tongue pass lightly across it, once, letting instinct and nature take over.

Her breath catches. She doesn't move away.

Between us, the connection hums to life—a low, thrumming pulse that syncs with my heartbeat. The bleeding slows; the flesh knits together, smooth again within seconds, leaving only a faint flush where the skin had been torn.

When I finally pull back, her eyes are half-lidded, her pulse slowing to something calm and steady. I rest my forehead against hers, my voice barely above a whisper. "There. It's sealed."

"Did you just lick me?"

Gods, she's so fucking adorable with how little she knows about our world.

"Yeah," I shrug before I take her hand, surprised when she doesn't resist. Through our connection, I sense her exhaustion and the adrenaline crash after everything she's experienced tonight. Her legs wobble slightly as I guide her.

"Where are we going?" Her voice sounds small, uncertain.

"You need to get cleaned up." I push open the bedroom door.

My bedroom feels different with her in it. The space both too large and too small simultaneously. Her scent mingles with mine, creating something new that makes my wolf pace with satisfaction.

I lead Karina into the bathroom, my wolf still howling beneath my skin. The fluorescent lights cast harsh shadows across her face, highlighting the exhaustion in her eyes and the blood trailing from my mark on her neck. The sight sends another wave of satisfaction through me, even as I try to tamp it down.

"Sit," I tell her, gesturing to the edge of the bathtub. She obeys without argument, her movements slow and careful, like she's afraid any sudden motion might shatter what little composure I have left.

She's not wrong.

I grab a washcloth from the cabinet and wet it with warm water. Every part of me burns to press her down on the bathroom floor, to give in to what we're both fighting so hard to resist. Instead, I kneel in front of her and wipe her neck with slow, deliberate care. The blood has already dried, leaving a dark sheen across her skin.

The wound is closed—smooth now, her body already healing the damage I caused. Relief settles low in my gut, chased by something warmer when her eyes meet mine. She looks exhausted, her lashes trembling as she fights to stay awake.

"You should rest," I murmur.

She nods, barely holding herself upright. I take her hand and help her to her feet, guiding her back toward the bedroom. The light from the hall stretches across the floor, catching in her hair as she moves, slow and unsteady.

"You're not sleeping on that piece of shit couch," I tell her, my voice rougher than I intend. "Take the bed."

"Then where will you sleep?" she asks, already knowing the answer but needing to hear it anyway.

"With my mate." The words come out before I can

stop them—simple, absolute, true in a way that settles something deep inside me.

She plants her feet, trying to stand her ground even though she can barely keep her eyes open. "No. Either I take the couch, or you do."

I should argue. I should let her win this one. But she looks too pale, too drained, and I'm done pretending this is something I can detach from. So I step forward, slip an arm under her knees and another around her back, and lift her before she can say another word.

She makes a small sound of protest, but it dies against my chest. Her head falls against my shoulder as I carry her the rest of the way to the bed.

The sheets are still warm from earlier, faintly scented with soap and cedar. I set her down carefully, pulling the blanket up around her shoulders. She exhales, the tension melting from her body as she sinks into the mattress.

"Sleep," I tell her quietly.

Her hand twitches once, reaching for the edge of the blanket, then stills. Within seconds, her breathing evens out.

I stand there, watching her. The moonlight spills across her face, softening every line, and something in my chest goes still.

She's in my bed. Finally. And it makes me fucking happy.

Karina

The throb at my neck yanks me from sleep like a fishhook, pain and pleasure twisting into a single burning thread that makes me gasp. I jolt upright in Damien's bed, hand flying to the spot where his teeth broke skin last night.

The sheets are still warm, tangled around my legs, and his scent clings to the room—dense, heady, making my pulse stumble. But the space beside me is empty.

"Damien?"

Silence.

The room feels wrong without him. The air hums with the ghost of his presence, as if he's still lying beside me, though the mattress on his side has already cooled. Did he even stay? The wound at my throat pulses again, sending molten heat spiraling through my veins. My fingers trace the raised edges of the bite, tender skin thrumming beneath my touch.

I can't believe how quickly my life has unraveled. Thirty-six hours ago, the worst thing I had to face was Travis. Now I've been claimed by a man who kills for a living, marooned in a compound full of wolves who look at me like I'm some prize—and bound to a world my parents escaped before I was born.

My parents. The thought of them hollows out my chest. They tried so hard to give me a normal life, hiding me from pack politics and blood feuds. But they never prepared me for this. Never warned me about bonds that sink into bone or the way a stranger's bite could feel like home.

"You should have told me," I whisper to the empty room. "You should have explained what I was, what this meant."

Heat flares beneath my palm again, not just pain but something deeper, hungrier—a low, pulsing demand. It's a reminder of what we started but haven't finished. My cycle sharpens the ache until the sheets rasp against my skin like sandpaper, and every breath feels too heavy to take.

I need to move. Now.

The clock on the nightstand glares 7:00 AM in red digits, and my stomach twists. Two hours until I face the Alpha. Two hours until I stand in front of the most dominant wolf in the territory.

My body burns from the inside out, skin raw with sensitivity. I squeeze my thighs together, trying to ignore the slickness gathering between them.

This is bad. Really bad. My cycle has never hit like this before. Normally, I could get by with over-the-counter suppressants and stubborn willpower, locking myself away until it passed. But the mark has magnified everything and I can barely think straight.

My wolf paces restlessly beneath my skin, whimpering with need. She has a simple solution. Find Damien. Let him take care of this burning ache inside us. Let him finish what he started.

"Absolutely not," I mutter, shoving her suggestions aside. I don't need him. I can handle this myself.

I swing my legs over the side of the bed, the cool air against my overheated skin providing momentary relief. The bathroom door is closed, but I can hear water running behind it. A shower. Of course. The mental image that conjures...Damien's powerful build under the spray, water cascading over him, sends another jolt of arousal through me that I absolutely do not need right now.

I force myself to stand, my legs unsteady beneath me. The movement sends my scent spiraling through the room, rich with arousal that makes me want to crawl under the covers and hide. But hiding won't make this go away.

I need clothes. Clean clothes that don't smell like sex and desperation. My duffel bag sits on the dresser where

Damien placed it last night, looking small and out of place among his belongings. I rifle through it, grateful I packed practical items, pulling out jeans and a simple sweater.

The shower shuts off behind the bathroom door, and my wolf perks up with interest. I can practically feel her pushing against my skin, eager to be closer to Damien.

"Stop it," I hiss at her, grabbing my clothes and heading for the door. "We're not doing this."

But my wolf has other ideas. The moment my hand touches the doorknob, she floods my system with images. Damien's hands on my skin, his mouth at my throat, his body covering mine. I grip the doorknob harder, trying to push her suggestions away.

The bathroom door swings open before I can escape, and suddenly he's there—towel slung low on his hips, water droplets still clinging to his broad chest, his hair slicked back from his face. My mouth goes dry at the sight of him, my wolf practically purring with appreciation.

""Going somewhere?" His voice is rough from sleep despite the shower, a low growl that curls through the air. His gaze sweeps over my face before dropping to the fresh wound at my throat, and satisfaction rolls off him in steady, invisible waves.

"I need space," I manage, my words embarrassingly breathless. "This is... a lot."

His nostrils flare as he inhales, and I know he's tasting the heat coming off me. The bite at my neck throbs under his attention, a pulse that sends another shuddering wave spiraling through my body.

"Your heat's worsening," he says, moving closer, each step deliberate. "What I did to you sped it up."

"I'm fine," I lie, retreating until my shoulders press into the wall. "I've managed this before. For years. Alone."

"This isn't like before."

He's right, and I hate that he's right. My skin feels fevered, every nerve ending so hypersensitive the brush of air over it makes me tremble. The wound at my throat pulses with each heartbeat—a constant reminder of what we've begun but haven't finished.

"It will only get stronger," he continues, closing the distance between us. Warmth radiates from his still-damp skin, soap and pine mingling into a scent that makes my knees weak. "You've never gone through this with your mate near. Only humans." He spits the last word like a challenge.

Inside me, my wolf whimpers, clawing at my skin as though she's trying to break free. She knows who she wants. She knows what she wants.

"I can handle it," I insist, though my voice trembles. Water beads trail down his chest, and my mouth goes dry for reasons that have nothing to do with thirst. "I just need some air. Some space to think."

"Space won't help." He raises his hand, fingers hovering near the place where his teeth broke skin but not quite touching. Even that almost-contact sends electricity tearing through me. "Distance will only make the hunger worse."

"Let me help you. Take some of the edge off, I mean."

"Help me? What exactly are you suggesting?"

"Not what you think." He runs a hand through his damp hair. "But there are...other ways to ease the pressure."

A flush fills my cheeks as his meaning sinks in. "Absolutely not."

"You're in pain." He takes another step closer, close enough that I can feel the warmth radiating from his skin. "I can feel it through the bond—the ache, the need burning under your skin. Let me—"

"No." I duck under his arm, escaping to the relative safety of the main room. But there's no real escape, not when his scent clings to everything. "You said you'd give me three days to decide."

He follows me, that towel still riding low on his hips. "I am still upholding that agreement, kitten. What I am offering is relief."

"Relief." I cross my arms over my chest, trying to ignore how the movement makes my oversensitive skin spark with sensation. "You mean sexual relief."

"I mean, taking the edge off so you can function." His voice drops to that rough growl that makes my wolf stretch beneath my skin. "So you can sit across from an alpha in two hours without broadcasting your need to every wolf in the room."

The reminder of the upcoming meeting sends a fresh wave of panic through me. I can barely think straight as it is, how am I supposed to face the most dominant wolf in the territory while my body burns with unfinished need?

"There has to be another way." I pace to the window, putting distance between us that feels both necessary and torturous. "Suppressants, medication, something."

He doesn't move closer. "I've seen what happens when someone is separated from their mate during the heat cycle. It's not pretty, Karina. If you think males are feral…"

I press my forehead to the cool glass, desperate for even a moment's relief from the fire licking beneath my skin. Outside, wolves drift across the compound. Males who will scent me the instant I step beyond this room. The thought makes my stomach knot with dread.

"What you're suggesting… it wouldn't change anything between us?" I ask without turning around. "It wouldn't affect the three-day agreement?"

"No." His response is too sharp, too sure. His features remain carefully arranged, though, betraying nothing.

"You're lying." My reflection stares back from the glass—flushed, disheveled. "I can feel it. You're holding something back."

The silence stretches, heavy with everything unsaid. When he finally answers, the sound is rougher, pulled taut. "Relief won't change our agreement. But it might complicate things."

"Complicate how?" I turn toward him and regret it instantly. Hunger radiates off him like fire from a forge. The towel hangs low on his hips, and it takes everything in me to keep my focus above his shoulders.

"Because once I touch you that way, I won't want to stop." The stark honesty in his words makes my wolf purr in satisfaction. "Because your scent will be on my hands, in my mouth, and my wolf will go insane knowing I've tasted you but can't have you fully."

My cheeks burn at his bluntness, but liquid fire gathers low in my belly in response.

"And because," he adds, stepping closer, "you'll know exactly how good I can make you feel."

Air hitches in my lungs at his certainty, the raw inevitability of it sending another molten rush through me. The way he says it makes my wolf howl with anticipation.

"You're very sure of yourself," I manage, trying to sound dismissive even as my body betrays me. The scent of my arousal thickens in the air between us, impossible to hide from him.

He moves closer, prowling toward me with predatory grace that makes my heart hammer against my ribs. "I'm sure of what I smell. What I feel." His gaze drops to where my nipples have hardened beneath my thin sleep shirt. "What I see right in front of me."

I back up until I hit the window, the cool glass a stark contrast to my overheated skin. "This is...it doesn't mean anything."

"Keep telling yourself that, kitten." His hand rises, hovering near my face without touching. Even that almost-contact sends electricity skittering across my skin. "Your wolf knows better."

She does. She's practically clawing at my insides, desperate for his touch, the completion of what we started. The rational part of me—the human who values independence and choice—is rapidly losing ground to the creature inside of me.

"I need to shower and get ready to meet the alpha," I answer, grasping for any excuse I can.

"I don't fucking care."

He pounces before I can react, his body caging me against the window as his mouth crashes down on mine. The kiss is nothing like I expected—not gentle, not tentative, but consuming. Devouring. His tongue sweeps past my lips, **seizing** me with a ferocity that makes my knees buckle.

My wolf howls with triumph as I melt against him, my body betraying me completely. His hands find my waist, fingers digging into my hips with bruising force as he lifts me effortlessly. My legs wrap around him of their own accord, my core pressing against the hard ridge beneath his towel.

"Damien," I gasp when he finally breaks the kiss, his mouth trailing fire down my neck toward the **scar** he left. "We shouldn't—"

"Tell me to stop," he growls against my skin, teeth

grazing the tender flesh where his bite still throbs. "Tell me you don't want this, and I'll walk away."

I can't. The words stick in my throat as his hand slides beneath my sleep shirt, calloused fingers skimming across my ribs. Every touch sends lightning through my veins, the connection between us amplifying every sensation until I'm drowning in need.

"That's what I thought," he says, satisfaction rumbling through his chest as he carries me across the room. My back hits the mattress with enough force to knock the breath from my lungs. He looms over me like a predator **laying claim to prey**. The towel slips in our struggle, revealing hard muscle and dark tattoos.

"I want your fucking eyes on me, kitten," he orders, one hand cupping my face to hold my gaze.

I should protest. Should push him away and remember all the reasons this is a terrible idea. But my body is no longer my own—it belongs to the fire he's ignited, to the wolf prowling beneath my skin, to the **imprint** throbbing at my neck.

His mouth **takes** mine again, swallowing my gasp as his hand slides between my thighs. Even through the thin fabric of my sleep shorts, his touch sends electricity racing through my veins. My hips buck against his hand, seeking more pressure, more friction, more of everything he's offering.

"So responsive," he growls against my lips, his fingers finding the waistband of my shorts. "Already soaked for me, aren't you, kitten?"

I can't answer. Can't form words when his hand slips beneath the fabric, fingers parting my folds with devastating precision. The first touch against my center pulls a strangled cry from my throat, my back arching off the mattress.

"That's it," he encourages. "Purr for me."

I shatter.

The word he uses—that soft command—breaks something inside me. My wolf surges forward with a keening sound that's half-human, half-animal, and I realize I am purring. Actually purring like the kitten he keeps calling me, the vibration rumbling through my chest as his fingers work magic between my thighs.

His thumb finds that sensitive bundle of nerves, and I cry out, my hips bucking against his hand.

"Please," I gasp, though I'm not sure what I'm begging for. More? Less? For him to stop before I lose myself completely?

"Please, what?" His fingers slow their torturous rhythm, and I whimper at the loss. "Tell me what you want."

"I want..." I swallow hard, my cheeks burning with embarrassment. "I want you to make it stop. The ache. The need."

"This ache?" His fingers press deeper, finding that spot inside me.

"Yes," I moan, shame and need battling inside me as his fingers curl in just the right way. "That one."

He leans down, his mouth hovering inches from mine. "There's only one way to truly make it stop."

I know what he means. Completion. Our union under the full moon. My wolf howls in agreement, but the human part of me still clings to the shreds of my independence.

"You promised me three days," I remind him, my voice breaking as his thumb circles my clit with devastating precision.

"And you'll have them, but that doesn't mean I can't give you this."

Before I can respond, he slides down my body, his shoulders pushing my thighs wider as he settles between them. The sight of him there—this powerful predator positioning himself at my most vulnerable point—should terrify me. Instead, my wolf purrs more, arching toward him with shameless need.

"What are you—" My question dissolves into a strangled cry as his mouth replaces his fingers, hot and demanding against my core. My hands fly to his hair, not sure if I'm trying to push him away or pull him closer.

The first stroke of his tongue nearly undoes me.

"Damien," I gasp, my fingers tightening in his hair as another wave of pleasure crashes over me. "I can't—it's too much—"

He growls against my flesh, the vibration sending shockwaves through my core. His hands grip my thighs, holding me open for his assault as his tongue works mercilessly against my center.

The pleasure builds too quickly, a tidal wave I can't stop. My wolf is at the surface now. The purring intensifies, a primal sound I've never made before rumbling from my chest as Damien's mouth devours me.

When the orgasm hits, it's unlike anything I've ever experienced. Colors explode behind my eyelids, my back arching off the mattress as wave after wave of pleasure crashes through me. I cry out his name, my voice breaking on the syllables as my body convulses under his relentless attention.

He doesn't stop. Even as I tremble with aftershocks, his tongue continues its torturous rhythm, pushing me toward a second peak I didn't know was possible. My nails rake across his scalp as another wave builds impossibly fast, my hips bucking against his mouth.

"I can't—not again—" But even as I protest, my body betrays me, arching into his touch as the second orgasm crashes over me with brutal intensity.

He finally releases me, crawling up my body with predatory grace. His face is slick with evidence of what he's done to me. The towel is long gone, and I catch a glimpse of his arousal—thick and intimidating—before he captures my mouth in a kiss that tastes of me.

"That's just the beginning, kitten," he growls against my lips. "Just a taste of what I can give you."

I should feel embarrassed. Ashamed of how quickly I surrendered, how completely I lost control. But all I feel is a languid satisfaction mingled with a deeper hunger that hasn't been fully sated.

"Damien..." I reach for him, needing to touch him, to return some measure of what he's given me, but he catches my wrists, pinning them above my head with one hand.

"No. Not today." His body trembles with the effort, muscles coiled tight as he fights his own instincts.

"But you need—" I can see his arousal, feel his desire burning through our connection like molten metal.

"What I need is to get you ready for that meeting." He releases my wrists, rolling away from me with obvious reluctance. "And what I need is to not completely lose my fucking mind before then."

The loss of his warmth leaves me cold despite the fire still coursing through my veins. I watch him stalk toward his dresser, his movements sharp with barely contained energy. The muscles in his back flex as he yanks open drawers, and I can't help but admire the Norse tattoos that cover his shoulders and spine.

"That was..." I struggle to find words for what just happened between us. "I've never felt anything like that."

"Neither have I."

More intense is an understatement. I can still feel echoes of his pleasure mixing with mine, a phantom sensation that makes my skin tingle. The reality of what just happened settles over me as I watch him turn away. My body still hums with aftershocks. What terrifies me most isn't what he did, it's how desperately I wanted it. How completely I surrendered to a man I barely know.

Damien pauses at the bathroom door, his broad

shoulders tense. Without turning around, he says, "You should get dressed. We need to leave in an hour."

Then he's gone, the bathroom door closing behind him with a soft click. The shower turns on again seconds later.

I lie there, limbs heavy with satisfaction yet somehow still aching for more. My wolf whines, unhappy with his departure, with the unfinished nature of what just happened between us.

Then I feel it—his pleasure surging through our connection. The sensation is so unexpected, so intimate that I sit up, pressing my hand against the mark as if that could somehow block the transmission. But there's no stopping it. I can feel him touching himself. In the shower. Because of me.

My cheeks burn as I realize what's happening. Every sensation, his need, his pleasure, the roughness of his hand. I'm no longer just in my body; I'm in his too, feeling the hot water cascading down his skin, the coil of tension building in his core, the desperation driving his movements.

My wolf stretches beneath my skin, purring with satisfaction at this unexpected intimacy. I should give him privacy, but I can't tear myself from the connection. Each stroke, each tightening of his grip sends echoes of pleasure ricocheting through me until I'm pressing my thighs together again, my own need rebuilding despite his earlier attentions.

I can feel his frustration, his desperate attempt to

release the pressure without binding us together. Images flash through my mind. His hand wrapped around his length, head thrown back as water sluices down his powerful body.

When his release finally comes, it crashes through me like a tidal wave. I gasp, my back arching as phantom pleasure courses through me. For a moment, I'm both in my body and his, experiencing his release as if it were my own. The intensity leaves me breathless, trembling on the bed as the feeling slowly dims to a more manageable hum.

The shower cuts off, and I scramble to get dressed, trying to block out what I just felt, and praying to the gods that I can make it through meeting his Alpha without thinking about it.

Karina

I'm drowning in his scent with every step we take. Pine and danger wrapping around me like invisible chains, pulling me closer even as I fight to maintain distance between us.

"Don't speak unless spoken to," Damien growls, his hand at the small of my back guiding me toward the imposing main house. "Keep your eyes down, but not too down. Looking at his feet is an insult, looking him in the eye is a challenge."

"So where exactly am I supposed to look? His kneecaps?" I mutter, trying to ignore how his touch sends electricity racing through my system.

"His shoulder. Or his hands. Just not his eyes or his throat. Don't bare your neck to him."

"Why would I—"

"It's a submissive gesture. One that females use to invite attention from alphas." His fingers press harder against my back. "You're mine. Not his."

The casual claim makes my wolf purr even as I bristle. "I'm not yours. Not completely."

"Three days, kitten. Less than that now, but until then, you're still marked as mine."

I swallow hard, memories of this morning flooding back with vivid clarity—his mouth between my thighs, his fingers working me to heights I never knew existed, the way his pleasure echoed when he finished in the shower. I know he can smell the shift in my scent because his nostrils flare, pupils dilating slightly.

"Keep those thoughts in check," he mutters. "Your scent shifts when you remember."

"How am I supposed to rein in my thoughts?" I hiss back, mortified that my body betrays me so completely.

"Think about something else. Anything else."

Easy for him to say.

"Anselm is testing us," Damien says as we approach the heavy wooden doors of the main house. "He knows what a newly bonded pair goes through—the hunger, the need. He's counting on us slipping."

"Why would he want that?"

"Opportunity. He's been pressuring Elias to settle down for years."

The implication sends ice through my veins despite

the fire still burning under my skin. "You think he would—"

"Never underestimate an alpha with his kind of power, kitten. He seizes chances like a kid snatching candy on a parade route."

My stomach knots as his words settle. "So, this breakfast isn't about getting to know me. It's about weighing me as a potential match for his son."

"Among other things." Damien's hand slides up my back, settling at the nape of my neck in a quiet claim. "He's also testing my restraint—watching how far he can push before I snap."

"And if you snap?"

"Then I prove I'm not ready for the responsibility my father sent me here to learn. And you become fair game for any alpha strong enough to take you as theirs."

The doors swing open before I can respond, revealing a uniformed staff member who bows slightly at our approach. "Alpha Anselm is waiting in the private dining room," he says, his attention fixed firmly on Damien as though I don't exist. "This way, please."

We're led through a maze of corridors that reek of old money and older power. Oil portraits of stern-faced wolves line the walls, their painted expressions heavy with judgment, the kind that makes your skin prickle. The hardwood floors gleam with a polish so pristine it reflects every flicker of the chandeliers overhead—wealth carved into every board, every step.

This isn't just a house. It's a fortress, a seat of dominance that has weathered decades of politics and blood. The intimidation is deliberate, the **presence of history pressing down** until even my wolf curls tighter under my skin, uneasy beneath so much concentrated authority.

"Is this what all alpha homes look like?" I whisper, trying to distract myself from the growing anxiety churning in my stomach.

"Only the ones with something to prove," Damien answers, his breath warm against my ear. "Anselm fought his way to power. He likes reminders of what he's built."

The staff member stops before an ornate set of double doors, knocking twice before pushing them open. "Mr. Marek and his guest, Alpha."

Damien's hand tightens at my neck, his thumb brushing against the edge of his mark in a gesture that's both possessive and reassuring. The contact sends sparks racing down my spine, and I fight to keep my expression neutral as we step into the dining room.

The space is dominated by an oak table that could easily seat twenty, though only three places are set at one end. Morning sunlight streams through floor-to-ceiling windows, illuminating the man who rises from the head of the table as we enter.

The Alpha is exactly like what I expect from the ruler of a powerful wolf pack. Tall, broad-shouldered, with salt-and-pepper hair that only enhances his authority rather than diminishing it. The scar across his left brow catches the light as he studies me with pale eyes that seem to see straight through to my soul.

My wolf immediately cowers, pressing herself flat against my ribs in instinctive submission. The alpha's presence is overwhelming, a **crushing force** that makes my knees want to buckle. I force myself to focus on his hands, clasped behind his back, just as Damien instructed.

Then Anselm's lips curl into something far too close to amusement. "Before we proceed, you will meet the Luna of this pack, my Luna, Saloma."

A woman glides forward from his side, her steps soundless, her presence sharp and merciless. Her beauty is undeniable, but it carries the same chill as a blade in moonlight. Saloma focuses on me, and the intensity of her gaze pins me more effectively than any alpha command. I keep my chin lifted, though the air feels thick with warning. Whatever this is, it's not just ceremony, it's a test. And failure will cost far more than pride. Beside me, Damien stiffens, his hand steady at my nape.

"Alpha. Luna." His words come measured, respectful, but not submissive. "Allow me to introduce Karina. My mate."

The alpha steps closer, nostrils flaring as he drinks in my scent. "I see his mark on her neck, Reaper, but that hardly makes her yours."

My stomach knots as his scrutiny lingers on the bite.

"With respect, Alpha," Damien says at my side, his

words pulled tight with restraint, "the full moon is still two days away."

"I am well aware of the moon's cycle," he cuts in with a snarl. "And I am equally aware that she's little more than spoken for—for now. Until the ritual is finished, she remains untaken."

The way he says it makes my skin crawl.

"And a female in heat, no less," Saloma remarks. "How...convenient for you, Damien."

She steps closer to me, inhaling as deeply as the Alpha did.

"I can smell her from here," she continues, circling me. "Her scent is quite...potent. Most males would find such desperation irresistible."

"Saloma," Anselm's voice carries a warning, though amusement curls at the edges. "Manners."

"Of course." She settles back beside him, her smile sharp as glass. "I simply find it fascinating how biology can...cloud judgment."

The jab strikes exactly where she wanted it to. My wolf bristles under my skin, claws itching to tear through flesh, but I force myself to remain still. Damien's thumb brushes once against my nape, a grounding stroke, a reminder to hold the line.

The dining room doors slam open, breaking the taut silence. Elias strides in, followed by two younger males at his heels. My stomach knots as the trio approaches, their nostrils flaring in unison as they catch my scent.

"Father," Elias says with forced cheer, "sorry we're late."

Anselm's irritation melts into something far more calculating. He gestures toward the vacant chairs. "Not at all. You're just in time to meet our...guest."

The two who trail behind Elias can't seem to look anywhere but me. Their resemblance to him is undeniable—same patrician angles, same proud bearing. But where Elias is sunlight and golden polish, these two are shadows. Chestnut hair, amber-tinted intensity, and movements too deliberate, too hungry, as they circle the table closer to where I sit.

"Matthew, Leo, this is Karina."

"Is she for us?" asks the taller of the two young males. His nostrils flare as he inhales deeply. "Can I have her, father?"

"She's mine," Damien growls. "Touch her and lose your hand, Matthew."

Matthew smirks, unfazed by the threat. "A mark isn't a mating, Reaper. Everyone knows that."

I resist the urge to shrink behind Damien. These wolves are circling like sharks that have scented blood in the water, and I'm the bleeding seal in their midst.

"Enough," Alpha Anselm demands. "We're here to break bread, not bones. Sit."

Could have fooled me. Anselm is playing a game, and I'm the pawn.

I take the chair Damien pulls out for me, hyperaware of how every male in the room tracks my movement.

Damien takes the chair beside me, creating a barrier between me and the other wolves.

"Tell me about yourself, Karina," Anselm asks as staff members appear with platters of food. His tone is conversational, but there's steel beneath the civility. "Your background. Your family."

I glance at Damien, who gives an almost imperceptible nod. "My parents raised me in Eureka."

"Eureka." Anselm cuts into his steak with surgical precision. "And what did they tell you about your heritage?"

"Nothing." The admission tastes bitter on my tongue. "I didn't know what I was until my first shift when I was sixteen."

His eyes narrow at my admission, his fork pausing halfway to his mouth.

"Sixteen?" He sets his utensils down with deliberate care. "And they never told you what you were before that?"

I swallow hard, feeling like I've just revealed a weakness I shouldn't have. "They wanted me to have a normal childhood."

"Normal." He says the word like it's poison. "There's nothing normal about denying a wolf their heritage. Their instincts." His line of questioning shifts to Damien. "Did you know about this?"

Damien's thigh presses against mine under the table, a silent warning. "Yes."

"Interesting." Anselm takes a sip of his coffee,

studying me over the rim. "And what pack did your parents belong to before they decided to play human?"

"I don't know." Another admission that makes me feel naked under his scrutiny. "They never talked about it."

Matthew leans forward, amber glint catching in the low light. "So, you're pack-less and unmated?" Each word lands like a hammer strike. "Fascinating."

"She's mine to protect," Damien growls, his hand finding my thigh beneath the table, heat searing through denim.

"Temporarily," Leo smirks.

I feel Damien's wolf clawing at the surface, demanding blood.

"It will be completed," I hear myself say. The words spill before I can stop them, and silence crashes over the room—attention locks on me, heavy and suffocating.

"Why would he want you?" Saloma's smile is pure venom. "You're a pathetic excuse for a female."

"The only value you have is your ability to breed. Damien will be Alpha to his pack. An Alpha needs a female of worth to be his Luna. Not a stray," Leo adds, grinning like a fool who doesn't know he's already dead.

Before I can respond, Damien explodes into motion. His chair clatters to the floor as he lunges across the table, hand snapping around Matthew's throat. Claws pierce skin in a flash of crimson.

"Say that again," Damien snarls.

Chaos detonates. Leo surges upright, his wolf

surfacing with a vicious snarl. Elias grabs for his brother, struggling to restrain him as the scent of aggression thickens the room. At the head of the table, Alpha Anselm remains perfectly still, watching it all with unnerving calm, his focus never wavering.

I feel Damien's rage like molten lava—pure, consuming fury at the insult to me. His wolf has taken control, and I can sense how close he is to shifting, to letting his beast tear Matthew apart for daring to call me damaged.

"Release my son, Reaper." Alpha Anselm remains seated, his expression unreadable as he watches his son clutch his bleeding throat.

Damien's grip tightens for a heartbeat longer before he forces himself to let go. Matthew stumbles backward, hand flying to his bleeding throat as he glares at Damien with undisguised hatred. "You'll pay for that, you fucking dog."

"Will I? Because from where I'm standing, you insulted the female under my protection. That's grounds for challenge in any pack."

"Your *temporary* bond," Leo corrects. "Who just announced she intends to make it permanent. How...convenient."

Shit. I've backed myself into a corner with that impulsive declaration. But in a room full of predators, it was the only move I had.

"I said sit down." This time, there's alpha command

in Anselm's voice, the kind of dominance that compels obedience from lesser wolves.

But Damien isn't lesser. He's the son of an alpha. For a heartbeat, I think he might challenge Anselm here and now over me.

I slide closer, my fingers curling around his arm. "Please."

He looks down at me, and I see the exact moment his control reasserts itself. Damien takes his seat again, his movements stiff. His hand finds mine beneath the table, squeezing so hard it almost hurts.

Servants file in silently, breaking the tension as they place plates before each of us. The food looks incredible —eggs Benedict, fresh fruit, pastries arranged like artwork —but my stomach is too knotted to consider eating.

"Eat," Anselm commands. "Food always helps cool hot tempers."

Matthew glares at Damien from across the table, his hand still pressed to the puncture wounds on his neck. Leo watches us with interest while Elias looks like he'd rather be anywhere else.

I force myself to pick up my fork, spearing a piece of egg more to appease Anselm than from any desire to eat. Beside me, Damien doesn't touch his food.

"I spoke with your father this morning, Damien," Anselm continues conversationally, as if his son wasn't just bleeding from claw marks. "Hudson sends his regards."

"What did you tell him?"

"The truth." Anselm cuts another piece of steak, chewing slowly as if savoring Damien's discomfort. "That his son has found his mate.

A slight smirk plays at Anselm's lips as he takes another bite, watching Damien's reaction closely. "Though he seems less than enthusiastic with the match, considering how hard he's been working to secure the DeLupo girl for you. But pack magic doesn't always make the logical choice, does it?"

I freeze, my fork suspended halfway to my mouth as the implications sink in. Damien was promised to someone else? Someone his father had chosen? A political match that I apparently disrupted.

"The DeLupo pack has significant territory in Oregon. Their only daughter is quite the prize. Pure bloodlines going back centuries. Trained from birth in pack politics. The perfect Luna for a future alpha."

Each word is a knife sliding between my ribs. I set my fork down, suddenly unable to swallow past the lump in my throat. "I see."

"Do you?" Anselm's smile is thin, hollow of warmth. "I wonder if you truly understand what you've stepped into, my dear. Wolf politics aren't for the faint of heart." His attention drifts toward Elias, who has stayed silent through everything that's unfolded this morning.

"For all we know, she'll run screaming when the full moon comes," Matthew adds with a scowl.

"I meant what I said."

"Is that so? And if it isn't completed—if you change your mind—I could certainly find a place for you here with my younger sons. Matthew seems quite taken with you already, despite his...colorful language."

The room goes still. The temperature in the room drops ten degrees. Even Elias looks uncomfortable now.

"She's mine."

Before Anselm can respond, the dining room doors burst open. A wolf I don't recognize rushes in, his face flushed with urgency. He whispers something in Anselm's ear that makes the Alpha's expression harden into granite.

"Excuse me," Anselm says, rising from his seat with fluid grace that belies the tension in his shoulders. "It seems there's been an incident at the southern border. We'll continue this...discussion another time."

He leaves without another word, the messenger trailing behind him. The moment the doors close, Damien's hand clamps around my wrist.

"We're leaving. Now."

"But we haven't finished—" Matthew begins, half-rising from his chair.

"We're done here," Damien snarls, positioning his body between me and the brothers. "Touch her, look at her, even think about her, and I'll finish what I started with your throat."

I let him guide me toward the door, putting much needed distance between me and Elias's brothers.

"If you fail to seal the deal, she'll be mine for the taking," Matthew calls after us.

I feel Damien's grip tighten on my arm as he guides me through the ornate hallways. I struggle to keep pace with his long strides, practically jogging to avoid being dragged.

"Damien, slow down," I hiss, trying to wrench my arm free. "You're hurting me."

He stops so abruptly I nearly crash into his back. When he turns to face me, his face is almost unreadable.

"Did you mean it?" he demands.

I swallow hard. "I don't know. It just came out. They were looking at me like I was prey, and I—"

"Needed protection," he finishes, disappointment bleeding through our connection. "So, it was self-preservation, not desire."

Truthfully, I don't know why I said it. I know nothing about this world—or about him. But faced with the choice between Damien or one of Anselm's prick sons, I'd rather bind myself to the devil I half know than to the one who clearly wants me as a trophy to lord over Damien.

"Not entirely," I admit. The words scrape out of me like broken glass. "I meant...I don't know what I meant. But when they looked at me like that, every instinct I had screamed to choose you."

"Choose me over what? Over being tied to a stranger?" His laugh is sharp, hollow. "That's not the same as *wanting* me, kitten."

"Isn't it?" I step closer, pulled by the ache bleeding through our connection. "You think I don't feel this pull between us? You think I don't know exactly what you did to me this morning—what you made me feel?"

"Feeling good when I touch you isn't the same thing," he growls, though he doesn't retreat. If anything, he closes the distance. "Pleasure is fleeting. The bond is forever."

"You think I don't know that."

"I'm honestly not sure what you're thinking, Karina. You're hot. You're cold." He pauses with a deep breath. "Look. I know this is a lot to understand, but you're in it now, whether you like it or not. What can I do to make this better for you?"

I fall silent, weighing my options as I stare at him. My wolf paces restlessly beneath my skin, pushing me toward him even as my human half tries to maintain distance.

"If you're it for me, then we need to get to know each other."

A slow smile curves his mouth, transforming those severe, chiseled features into something devastatingly handsome. "After this morning, kitten, I'm pretty sure I know you pretty well already." The rough growl in his words vibrates through me, making my insides clench. "Every inch of you."

Need coils low in my belly. "No," I insist. "I mean about you. I didn't even know you were an alpha in the making, or that your father was arranging a mating for you."

The smile fades, replaced by a guarded wariness. "We haven't exactly had time to sit down and exchange histories," he says. "Between people trying to kidnap you, my marking you, and Anselm's little breakfast ambush, small talk hasn't exactly been a priority."

"Then that's what I want," I tell him.

"Fine. But not here." Damien's hand finds mine, his grip warm and firm, and he tugs me forward. His pace is relentless, pulling me along like a current I can't resist until we're outside, the crisp air cooling the flush in my cheeks.

He heads straight for his cabin. The moment we're inside, he shuts the door with a decisive thud and gestures toward the couch.

"Sit," he orders, the single word carrying that command-edge that makes my pulse jump. I obey, perching on the cushion while he plops into the chair across from me.

"All right, kitten. What do you want to know?"

Karina

Damien's long legs stretch out like he owns not just the room, but the ground beneath it. One arm drapes lazily over the armrest, the other resting on his thigh, and yet there's nothing casual about him.

"This was your idea, kitten," he says, his smirk slow and deliberate. "If you want to get to know me, you're the one who has to start talking. Ask me something."

I lean back against the couch cushion, crossing my legs to keep from fidgeting. What do I even ask a man like him? My mind is spinning with a thousand questions, but they all feel too invasive or too trivial. I've never been good at this—getting to know people. I'm the one who sits in the corner at parties, the one who listens rather than speaks. It's why I have avoided blind dates like the plague. Conversation starters are just not my cup of tea.

"Okay, um, tell me about your family." Jesus. That's what I start with? Why am I so awkward with this stuff?

Something flickers across his face—a tightening around his eyes, a slight clench of his jaw. "What about them?"

"Everything. Anything." I shrug, trying to appear casual when nothing about this situation is casual. "You're an alpha's son. That seems like a big deal."

"My father is Hudson Marek, Alpha of the Northern Territories. My mother, Helena, is his Luna. I have one sister, Bella."

The way he says his sister's name—softer, almost protective—catches my attention. "You're close with her?"

"Was. She was kidnapped. Under my watch."

My heart skips. "Is she—"

"She's alive." He cuts me off. "But she's not the same. None of us are."

"If she was kidnapped, why are you here instead of with your family?"

The muscle in his jaw twitches, and for a moment, I think he might not answer.

"It was my fault. All of it. I was supposed to be guarding her at a pack gathering. She wanted to slip away to meet some boy she liked." A bitter laugh escapes him. "I gave her twenty minutes. Told her I'd cover for her with our father."

"Twenty minutes turned into thirty. Then an hour. When I went to find her, all I discovered was her scent mixed with blood and strangers."

"That's not your fault," I add, leaning forward. "You couldn't have known—"

"I should have known. I'm the alpha's son. The future leader. I'm supposed to protect what's mine...I found her three days later. The guy she had met up with turned out to be a lower level alpha from a small pack. She was alive, a fresh mark on her neck. Had I been ten minutes later, he would have forced her into the full mating bond."

The realization hits me like a slap across the face.

"That's why you get so angry when I waver."

His eyes snap to mine, suddenly razor-sharp. "What?"

"You couldn't protect her from being claimed against her will," I say, the truth slotting together in my mind. "You're terrified the same thing will happen to me."

Damien goes completely still. The kind of stillness that makes prey animals freeze in terror. "Don't," he warns.

But I can't stop, not now that I see it so clearly. "Every time I question what's between us, I'm reminding you of your failure to protect her. Every time I push back, I'm—"

"Enough." He stands in one fluid motion, towering over me. "This isn't about Bella."

"Isn't it?" I stand too, refusing to be intimidated even

as my wolf cowers. "You're punishing yourself through me. Making yourself endure this because you think you deserve to suffer."

"You don't know what you're talking about." But the change in his scent betrays him, sharp and tense—instinct recoiling from what I'm stripping bare, from what he's terrified I'll expose.

"I'm right, aren't I?" I press further, emboldened by the subtle shift in his demeanor. "You see me as your redemption for your father's punishment."

"My father sent me away to learn discipline," he growls, pacing now, a caged predator with nowhere to run. "To learn the consequences of putting personal desires above pack duty."

"And what was your personal desire that day? To give your sister a moment of freedom?"

He stops pacing, his back to me, shoulders rigid. "She begged me. Said she just wanted to feel normal for once. Just twenty minutes of being a regular girl, not the alpha's daughter."

I approach him slowly, careful not to startle. "That sounds like compassion to me, not failure."

"Compassion gets wolves killed." He turns to face me, his expression hardened again. "My father made that perfectly clear."

"Is that why you became the Reaper? To prove you could be ruthless enough?"

"I became the Reaper because it was the role Anselm needed filled. The role my father assigned me."

"The role, or the punishment?"

"Does it matter?" He shrugs, but the casualness is forced. "I'm good at it."

"Too good at it. That's what scares you."

"You think you've got me all figured out after one day?"

"I think I'm starting to." I reach out, hesitating before my fingers make contact with his arm. When he doesn't pull away, I let my palm rest against his bicep. "I think you're terrified that you've become exactly what your father wanted—a weapon. The Reaper."

"You don't know what I am."

"Then tell me." I move my hand up to his shoulder, then to his face, cupping his jaw. The stubble there is rough against my palm, and I feel him tense at the contact before leaning into it slightly. "Tell me who Damien Marek is when he's not being the Reaper."

He laughs, the sound hollow, brittle, without warmth. "I don't think I remember anymore."

"I don't believe that."

"Believe what you want." The dismissal cuts, but there's something in the way his shoulders tense—something raw he can't quite cover—that makes me press harder.

"Ask me something else," he says abruptly, folding his arms tight across his chest like a shield.

I bite my lip, weighing my options. There's one question that's been burning since breakfast.

"Tell me about the DeLupo girl," I say carefully.

"The one Anselm mentioned. The one your father picked for you."

Damien goes still, the shift in his expression subtle but unmistakable. His jaw locks, a muscle ticking there, and though he schools his features into indifference, I catch the flicker of surprise before the mask settles into place.

"Selena DeLupo," he says, the name falling from his lips with practiced ease. "Daughter of the Oregon Alpha. Twenty-four. Born wolf. Trained from birth to be a Luna."

"That's her résumé," I point out. "Not who she is."

He shrugs. "I've met her exactly three times. Formal pack functions. We exchanged maybe fifty words total."

"But your father arranged the match for you?"

"Not exactly arranged. More like...strongly encouraged." His jaw tightens. "The DeLupo pack rules significant territory in the Pacific Northwest. An alliance through mating would double our combined influence."

I swallow hard, trying to ignore the knot forming in my stomach. "And now? Am I stepping on her toes if I accept our mating?"

A muscle in his jaw jumps, and he looks away. "The arrangement was never formalized. No contracts signed, no ceremonies planned. Just...expectations."

"That's not what I asked." I step closer. "Does it ruin her chances at finding someone else?"

"Selena will have no shortage of suitors," he says flatly. "She's what every pack wants for their Luna."

"But not what you wanted?"

"I never thought about what I wanted. It wasn't relevant."

"And now?"

"Now everything's different," he admits, the words rough and unsteady. "You changed everything the moment I caught your scent."

My heart hammers against my ribs at the raw honesty etched into his features. "How?"

He reaches up, covering my hand with his, where it still rests against his jaw. "Because for the first time in my life, I want something that's mine. Not my father's choice, not a political alliance, not a duty to fulfill." His thumb strokes across my knuckles. "I want something that is wholly mine."

"What if I'm not worth it?" The question escapes before I can stop it, my own fears spilling out. "What if I'm not strong enough for this world?

For a moment, I think he'll pull away, erect those walls again. Instead, he cups my face in his hands, his touch surprisingly gentle for someone who deals in death.

"Worth it?" The word escapes him like it physically pains him. "You don't understand what you are, do you?"

I try to look away, but he holds me firmly.

"Listen to me, Karina. You survived for years on your own, without a pack, without training. You built a life among humans while carrying a secret that would have destroyed you if discovered." His thumbs brush across my cheekbones. "That kind of strength isn't taught. It's born."

"But I'm not like Selena. I don't know pack politics or wolf customs. I didn't even know mates existed until I met you."

"Good." The word surprises me. "I've had enough of politics and customs to last ten lifetimes. What I need isn't another wolf who knows how to play the game. What I need is someone who reminds me there's more to life than power struggles and territory disputes."

My wolf preens at his words, stretching beneath my skin with satisfaction. But the human part of me isn't so easily convinced.

"And what happens when your father finds out you've chosen a stray over his political alliance? What happens when he calls you home?"

Damien's jaw tightens at the mention of his father, but his hands don't leave my face. "Then I deal with the consequences."

"Just like that? You'd risk everything—your pack, your birthright, your family—for me?"

"You're not just someone. You're the other half of my soul. It means that losing you would be like losing half of myself. It means that no title, no territory, no alliance is worth more than what we have." His thumbs trace my jawline. "It means I'd burn down everything I've ever known before I'd let anyone take you from me. I would rather die than live without you, Karina."

The other half of my soul.

Something inside me cracks open—something I've kept locked away my entire life. The part of me that always wanted to belong somewhere. To someone. My wolf howls with joy, pressing against my skin like she wants to break free and roll around in his declaration.

And I'm terrified because I feel the same way.

I've known this man for two days. Two. Days. I should be running for the hills, not melting at his feet. This isn't me. I'm practical. Cautious. I research minor purchases for weeks before buying. I once spent three months deciding on a coffee maker. And yet here I am, ready to bind myself eternally to a man who kills people for a living, all because my body hums when he's near?

I'm losing my mind. There's no other explanation.

But even as I think it, I know it's a lie. This feeling—this pull between us—it's more real than anything I've ever felt.

"Kitten, you still with me?"

I blink, refocusing on his face.

"Yeah," I breathe. "I'm here."

"Where did you go?" His thumb drags slowly across my bottom lip, deliberate, almost punishing in its restraint. The touch makes my body ache to lean into him. "I could feel you spiraling."

Of course he could. It's impossible to breathe, this constant exchange where my emotions bleed into his and his into mine until the edges blur and I can't tell where I end, and he begins.

"I was just... thinking." The words scrape out of me, uneven. "About how insane this is. Two days ago, I was crying over a breakup, and now I'm in your cabin, letting you touch me like I already belong to you. I'm shaking because all I want is for you to finish what you started this morning, and I hate myself for wanting it so badly. Because I'm terrified." My chest seizes, the confession spilling too fast to stop. "Terrified that I'm falling for you, and I don't know if it's this link making me crave you...or if it's real. Everything I thought I knew about myself, about what I wanted from life, is shattered into pieces. I had plans. A promotion at work. Maybe buy a house someday. Normal things."

He studies me for a long moment, his thumb still brushing against my mouth, steady as if to anchor me. "Even if we complete the ritual, I won't stop you from working, Karina. As long as I can keep you safe, I won't stop you from..."

"I work as a patient advocate for the local hospitals. From home."

"You can keep working if that makes you happy. Though truthfully, if you didn't want to work, you don't have to."

I frown at his words, something sharp cutting through me. "And what makes you think I'd ever be comfortable just living off you? I've been independent my whole life."

"Not independent," he corrects me. "Alone. There's a difference."

The observation stings because it's true. I've been calling it independence, but really, I've been isolated. Living in the shadows, hiding what I am, keeping people at arm's length.

"Besides," he continues when I don't respond, "the Marek pack has more money than anyone could spend in ten lifetimes. My father may be many things, but financially irresponsible isn't one of them."

"So, what. I'd just be your kept woman?" I cross my arms over my chest. "I don't think so."

"That's not what I meant."

"Then what did you mean?"

"I mean that you have choices." He steps back, running a hand through his hair in frustration. "Something I've never had. Something I'd never take from you."

"I'm sorry," I say, softly. "I didn't mean for it to come off that way. I am just so confused. I thought I had what I wanted in life. Now I'm wondering if I ever really wanted those things, or if I was just going through the motions because that's what humans do, pretending to be happy."

His thumb traces my cheekbone, the calluses rough against my skin. "Were you? Happy?"

The question hits me harder than it should. Was I happy before Damien crashed into my life? Certainly not the last few months with Travis. But before I knew what it felt like to have someone look at me the way he does, like I'm precious and necessary?

"I was...content or I thought I was."

Damien's eyes soften as he steps closer, his hands coming up to frame my face. "Then let me make you happy, Karina. If it's within my power to give you what you need, whatever you need, to be happy with me, I'll do it. Just tell me what you want."

"I want—" My voice catches, and I have to clear my throat. "I want to complete the bond."

His pupils dilate, his scent spiking with desire and hope so powerful I can taste it on my tongue. But I place my hand against his chest, keeping a small distance between us.

"But I need you to understand something first," I continue. "We're in this together. Equal partners. I need you to be open with me—about everything. No more surprises." I take a deep breath. "You're not the heir to some other kingdom too, are you?"

The question draws a genuine laugh from him, the sound transforming his face into something so beautiful it makes my heart ache.

"Just one as far as I know," he promises, his thumbs drawing slow, steady circles against my cheeks. "I'll be open with you. I don't want someone silent at my side. I want a partner who stands beside me, who'll call me out on my bullshit when I need it, who won't flinch at the shared responsibility of this life. Think you can handle that?"

The words hit deeper than I expect, settling heavy in my chest. A partner, not a possession. An equal, not an ornament.

Can I handle it?

My pulse stutters, caught between fear and longing. Because part of me already knows the answer...and it terrifies me.

"I don't know," I answer honestly. "I've never led anything more complicated than a book club, and even that fell apart after three meetings."

His lips quirk up at that, and I feel a flutter in my chest at making this man smile.

"But I want to try," I continue, surprising myself with how much I mean it. "I want to learn. To be what you need."

"What I need is exactly what you already are."

The warmth in his tone wraps around me, steadying the doubts still swirling in my chest. For a moment, I let myself sink into it—into him—and believe that maybe I could be this woman he sees. His thumbs still against my cheeks.

But then his expression changes as if a thought has pushed its way between us.

"That being said, I have to do something tonight for Anselm."

"Is it dangerous?"

"I'd be lying if I said it wasn't. I still have a job to do. There's a meeting. Businesses that are considering switching their allegiances." His jaw tightens. "I need to remind them why that's a bad idea."

I think of the man I saw executed at the club, the casual violence with which Damien put a bullet in his head. That's who he is—what he does—and no amount of electric chemistry between us can change that fundamental truth. He's a killer, though my discomfort with that idea isn't as black and white as it was before all this happened.

"I want you to stay here at the cabin," Damien says, leaving no room for argument. "I'm going to have Elias come stay with you."

"Elias?" I blink, surprised. "After what happened at breakfast, you trust him?"

Damien's mouth curves slightly, but it's not amusement, it's more like he's remembering the scene in detail. "That was Matthew and Leo running their mouths, not Elias. He kept quiet for a reason."

I think back to the table, the way Elias had simply watched while his brothers provoked and needled. His silence unsettling in its own way.

"I trust him more than his brothers," Damien continues, leaning back in his chair, stretching out like he's claiming every inch of space between us. "Elias won't let anything happen to you."

"And what if something happens to you?" The words slip out before I can stop them.

His head tilts, that faint smirk appearing like he's caught me in a truth I didn't mean to reveal. "Worried about me, kitten?"

"I'm worried about being stuck here if you get yourself killed. What happens to me if you don't come back?"

"I always come back."

"That's not an answer."

His smirk fades. He leans forward, resting his forearms on his knees. "You'll be protected if I don't come back. Elias is a good guy. He will get you out if it comes down to that."

I want to argue, to tell him that's not good enough—that it's not the same as him walking back through that door—but my throat feels tight. His certainty is unshakable, but I've seen enough to know that even men like Damien aren't invincible.

He must see something in my expression, because his voice softens, losing its edge. "I'm coming back to you, Karina. There is nothing in this world that would keep me from you."

God, I hope he's not wrong because I'm not sure I can survive this new world without him.

Damien

After our talk, Karina excused herself to my bedroom, exhaustion from everything, and the lack of sleep this morning finally catching up with her.

I'm pacing the small confines of my cabin like a caged animal, pausing only to check on her every few minutes. Each time I enter the bedroom, I'm hit with the intoxicating blend of our scents mingling together. My wolf purrs with satisfaction at the sight of her curled up in our bed, her curls spilling across my pillow, her face peaceful in sleep.

It's better this way. Sleep is the only reprieve she has from the constant ache that I can feel in her. The same ache that has me prowling restlessly, checking windows and doors, my senses hyper alert to any threat.

Hours pass until I can't stay any longer. The meeting with Lockhart's potential recruits is an hour. With one last look, I leave the confines of my bedroom and head back out to the living room, where my go bag is waiting for me on the kitchen table. Fuck. Leaving her like this is killing me, but violating the agreement made by my father with Alpha Anselm is non-negotiable. All I need to do is get through tonight, do my fucking job, and then maybe I can take a few days. Just long enough to get her through her cycle, the full moon, and whatever comes after that.

I reach into my bag and pull out my sidearm when a noise comes from behind me.

"You look like shit," Elias remarks from the doorway of my cabin, leaning against the frame with that casual arrogance only the heir to an empire can pull off. "Are you sure you can handle this tonight?"

I continue checking my weapons, sliding an extra magazine into my pocket without looking up. "I've killed men in worse condition."

"That's not what I meant."

I know exactly what he means. Our incomplete bond is tearing me apart from the inside out. Every part of me aches to stay with Karina, to shield her from the wolves already circling her scent. But I have a job to do—one that might keep us both alive if I play it right.

"She'll be safe with you." It's not a question because it can't be. If I allow doubt to creep in, I'll never make it out the door.

Elias steps into the cabin, closing the distance between us. "You know my brothers won't stay away for long. Matthew's pride is wounded—literally. He'll be looking to even the score."

"If he touches her—"

"He won't," Elias interrupts, his blue eyes serious for once. "I'll make sure of it. I've already told the security team that no one enters this area of the compound without my explicit permission."

I holster my weapon, eyeing him skeptically. "And your father's okay with that?"

"My father's distracted with the border issue. Some kind of territorial dispute with the Lockhart pack." He shrugs, but there's tension in his shoulders.

"More like getting your father out of town while he creeps in on his business."

"Probably, but Lockhart suspects you're with him, so there's that."

I grunt in acknowledgment, strapping a knife to my ankle. "If anything happens to her—"

"You'll tear my throat out, rip my balls off, feed me my own intestines. I know the drill." Elias's attempt at humor falls flat. "But seriously, Dom. Are you sure you're good to do this job tonight? Your control seems...tenuous at best."

My jaw tightens. "I don't have a choice."

"Everyone has choices."

"Not me. Not anymore." I check my watch, forty-five

minutes until the meeting. "If I don't show up tonight, Anselm will see it as a direct challenge to his authority. And right now, he is the only thing keeping the other alphas or your brothers from making a play for Karina."

Elias's expression softens slightly. "You really care about her."

"She's my mate."

"It's more than that. I've seen you kill for my father without blinking. I've seen you take bullets without flinching. But I've never seen you like this—ready to tear apart anyone who looks at her wrong."

I turn away, uncomfortable with his scrutiny. "I don't have time for this psychoanalysis bullshit."

"Make time. Because if you go out there half-crazed with bond sickness, you're going to get yourself killed. And then what happens to her?"

"I'll be fine," I growl, shoving the last of my equipment into my pockets. "Just keep her safe."

A soft noise from the bedroom doorway makes us both turn. Karina stands there, hair tousled from sleep, wearing one of my t-shirts that hangs to mid-thigh on her smaller frame. The sight of her in my clothes sends a wave of satisfaction through me that I struggle to restrain.

"You're leaving."

"Put some clothes on, Karina." The request spills from my lips as a demand. She flinches. Fuck. "Please."

Karina looks down, realizing how naked she is in

front of Elias, and moves to cover herself up with the door frame.

I force myself to stay where I am, knowing that if I get too close to her now, I might not leave at all. "I'll be back. Just like we talked about."

"Just be careful," she says, crossing her arms over her chest like she's holding herself together.

I nod stiffly, not trusting myself to speak. If I open my mouth now, I might tell her everything—how the thought of leaving her tears at my insides, how every cell in my body claws to stay, how I'd rather cut off my own arm than walk out that door.

"I'll be back before dawn," I manage.

With one last look at Karina—memorizing the sight of her in my shirt, her scent saturating my space—I wrench myself away and stride through the door. The night air hits my overheated skin like a slap, carrying traces of other wolves on patrol around the compound. Every part of me howls to turn back, to barricade us inside until we can complete the bond under the full moon.

Instead, I force myself toward my car, each step feeling like I'm dragging lead weights. The distance from Karina creates an immediate ache in my chest.

I slide behind the wheel, gripping it so hard it creaks under the pressure.

I fucking hate this.

Every step away from Karina feels like tearing off a piece of my own skin.

"She's fine," I mutter to myself. "Elias will keep her safe."

My wolf snarls at the thought of another male—any male—near our mate. The rational part of me knows Elias is trustworthy. He's kept my secrets before. Protected my back in situations that would have gotten us both killed if he'd hesitated.

But he's still a Bellandi. Still answerable to his father. And Anselm made his intentions clear at breakfast this morning.

Two more days. Two more fucking days until the full moon. I can get through this. I have to for her sake and for mine.

I start the car with a growl, forcing myself to focus on the mission ahead rather than the woman I'm leaving behind. The engine roars to life, vibrating beneath me as I pull away from the cabin.

Fuck Anselm. Fuck my father. Fuck this entire situation.

The road twists through the redwoods, shadows flickering across my windshield as I take the turns faster than I should. My wolf paces restlessly beneath my skin, testing the limits of my restraint with every mile that stretches between us and Karina. I roll down the window, letting the cold night air slap my face, trying to clear my head of her scent still clinging to my clothes.

I need to compartmentalize. Lock away my need to be with Karina long enough to do my job. The Reaper can't afford distractions, and tonight, I need to be the Reaper more than ever.

The old Kellerman building sits on the outskirts of Blackridge, a forgotten warehouse that's been abandoned for decades. Perfect for clandestine meetings between traitors. I park half a mile away and continue on foot.

The forest around me is alive with night sounds as I move silently between the trees. My training takes over, body shifting into predator mode despite the constant ache pulling me back toward the compound, back toward her.

Focus, damn it.

I circle the Kellerman building once, cataloging entry points, potential escape routes, and the three vehicles parked behind the structure. A black SUV with tinted windows. A mid-range sedan. A pickup truck with a gun rack—typical Blackridge business owner. All local plates.

My wolf's senses pick up five distinct scents inside. The brewery owner, the apothecary woman, the auto shop guy, and two others I can't immediately place. No sign of Lockhart himself yet, which is interesting. Either he's running late, or he's smart enough to send representatives rather than show his face.

I check my watch. Ten minutes early. Perfect.

Slipping through a broken window at the back of the building, I land soundlessly on the dusty concrete. The warehouse yawns open around me, cavernous and cold, with support columns rising like skeletal trees that offer perfect cover. I keep low, moving from shadow to shadow until I'm close enough to catch the murmur of conversation drifting from the cluster of old office rooms at the far end.

"—ridiculous protection fees," a woman complains. Sierra from the apothecary. Her voice carries the brittle edge of exhaustion. "Bellandi takes forty percent of my profits and calls it insurance. Insurance against what? His own threats?"

"Same here," a man adds, deeper timbre roughened by frustration. Richard. The mechanic. "His people came by last week demanding double what we agreed to. Said it was a market adjustment." He spits, the wet sound sharp against the silence. "More like extortion."

My jaw tightens. They think they're being squeezed now? They don't understand the real price of weakness. What Bellandi takes is steep, but it keeps predators from other packs off t doorsteps. Try explaining that to wolves who have lived in relative peace thanks to Anselm's protection, though. Might as well be lecturing calculus to toddlers.

Then another voice—one I don't know. Smooth. Persuasive. "Lockhart's offer is generous. Twenty percent instead of forty. Better security. No sudden *adjustments* to your rates."

"And what's the catch?" the brewery owner asks. His scent hits me—sweat, nerves, and the sour tang of old beer woven into the fabric of his shirt..

"No catch. Just new management."

I ease closer, using the shadows to mask my

approach. Through a gap in the wall, I can see five figures huddling around a folding table. A battery-powered lantern casts harsh shadows across their faces. The three business owners look exactly like what they are—small-town entrepreneurs in over their heads. The other two are clearly Lockhart's people, though I don't recognize either of them.

One is a thin man in an expensive suit—too polished, too clean. Outsider. His scent doesn't belong here; not pack, maybe not even wolf. The other is a blonde woman with cropped hair and an air of easy confidence. I know her face, or maybe her posture. She's pack, but not one of Lockhart's.

"What about the Reaper?" the brewery owner asks. "I heard what happened to Marco at the Crimson Howl."

My lips curl into a smile despite myself. Good. Let them be afraid. Fear is a better deterrent than any contract.

"The Reaper is just one man," the suit says dismissively. "And Lockhart has resources Bellandi can only dream of."

I've heard enough. Time to make my presence known.

I step out of the shadows, my boots deliberately heavy on the concrete floor. "Is that so?"

The reaction is immediate and satisfying. The brewery owner knocks over his chair scrambling backward. The apothecary woman freezes like prey spotting a predator. Richard from the auto shop reaches for something under his jacket, but thinks better of it when he sees my hand already resting on my sidearm.

Only Lockhart's representatives maintain some semblance of composure.

"Speak of the devil," the blonde woman says.

Now I place her—Vanessa Holt. Only daughter of the Summit Pack out Upper Plains. She's a small fish in a very big pond, playing the intermediary for Lockhart.

"Vanessa Holt. You're a long way from Summit territory. Does your father know you're playing errand girl for Thomas Lockhart?"

Her expression tightens, telling me I've hit a nerve. Good.

"The Reaper," she replies, recovering quickly. "A long way from your master's compound. Does Anselm know you're here alone?"

I step closer, enjoying how the business owners shrink back.

"I don't need backup to handle traitors. Unlike Lockhart, who sends his pets to do his dirty work."

The man in the suit steps forward, trying to appear unafraid despite the stench of terror rolling off him. "This is a private business meeting. You're trespassing."

I laugh, the sound echoing coldly through the abandoned warehouse. I turn to the business owners. "Did these two explain what happens to those who break agreements with the Bellandi family?"

"Empty threats," Vanessa cuts in. "Anselm's empire is crumbling. Everyone knows it."

"Is that what Lockhart told you?" I move closer, my hand never straying from my weapon. "Is that why he sent his lapdog instead of showing up himself? Because he's so confident?"

The business owners exchange nervous glances. It's almost amusing how little they understand the world they're playing in.

"Let me make this simple for all of you," I say, addressing the business owners directly. "You have exactly one chance to walk out of here alive. Leave now, return to your businesses, and forget this meeting ever happened. Anselm might even be merciful."

"And if we don't?" Richard challenges.

"Then I'll deliver your heads to Anselm as an example to others who might consider switching allegiances."

The brewery owner is already backing toward the door, survival instinct overriding whatever financial incentives Lockhart offered. "I'm out. This isn't worth dying over."

Smart man.

"You can't just threaten people like this," the apothecary woman protests, though she's also inching toward the exit.

"I'm not threatening anyone," I reply calmly. "I'm explaining the consequences. There's a difference."

He hesitates. "Bellandi's bleeding us dry. We can't—"

"You can't afford to die either," I cut in. "Go home, Richard. Kiss your human wife and wake up alive tomorrow."

His face pales as my words hit home. The mention of his wife—his human wife who has no idea what world her husband operates in—is the final push he needs. Without another word, he turns and follows the other business owners toward the exit.

That leaves me alone with Lockhart's representatives. The dynamic in the room shifts immediately. Vanessa straightens, her wolf finally surfacing enough that I can sense her power. She's stronger than I initially gave her credit for—not alpha material, but beta at least.

"Impressive show," she says, clapping slowly. "But empty threats won't save your boss when Lockhart makes his move."

"What move?" I step closer, noting how the suit takes an involuntary step back. "Sending shitty accountants to poach businesses? That's hardly a declaration of war."

Her eyes flash golden at the insult, canines extending slightly. Good. Angry wolves make mistakes.

"You have no idea what's coming," she snarls. "The old ways are dying, and Lockhart represents the future."

"The future?" I laugh, genuinely amused. "Thomas Lockhart is a third-generation nobody who inherited daddy's territory and thinks that makes him a player."

"He's alpha enough to take everything Anselm holds

dear," the suit interjects. "Starting with his precious heir."

My wolf surges forward with murderous intent. "What did you just say?"

Vanessa's smile turns predatory. "Did we touch a nerve? Poor Reaper, so focused on his new toy that he's missing the bigger picture."

My hand moves to my weapon, but I force myself to stop. Information first. Violence second. "Explain."

"Lockhart knows about your little mate," the suit continues, emboldened by my restraint.

Vanessa tilts her head, studying my reaction with obvious satisfaction. "Karina Greene. Lives alone in a shitty apartment in Eureka. Oh, and she's your mate."

My vision tunnels, the warehouse fading except for the two figures in front of me. They know everything. How the fuck do they know everything?

"You see, she wasn't as invisible as you think," Vanessa continues. "Lockhart has been tracking her and others like her for months. Building a database of potential...acquisitions."

The word 'acquisitions' makes my wolf howl with fury.

"You're lying," I growl, but doubt creeps in like poison. How could they know so much about her? About us?

Vanessa's smile widens. "Am I? Then why is your hand shaking, Reaper?"

I glance down, surprised to find my fingers trembling against my sidearm. I force my hand to steady.

"Whatever game you're playing, it ends now," I say, drawing my weapon in one fluid motion. "Tell me what Lockhart knows and how he knows it."

The suit raises his hands. "We're just messengers. Kill us, and you'll never get the information you need."

"I don't need both of you alive to get information." I aim directly at his head. "One will do."

Vanessa steps forward, positioning herself slightly in front of the suit. "You're making a mistake. This isn't about territory or businesses anymore. Lockhart is playing a different game—one Anselm doesn't even understand yet."

"What game?" I demand, my patience evaporating with each second that passes. Every moment I waste here is another moment Karina could be in danger.

"Genetics."

Ice floods my veins. "What are you talking about?"

Vanessa circles me slowly, confidence radiating from her in waves. "You really don't know, do you? The big bad Reaper, so focused on taking his prize that he never stopped to ask why she was worth taking in the first place."

"Stop playing games," I growl, my finger tightening on the trigger. "What does Lockhart want with Karina?"

"The same thing everyone will want once they discover what she is. Who she is," Vanessa's smile widens.

"Lockhart's just been...patient. Watching her for years while the rest of you remained oblivious."

My world tilts on its axis. Years? That can't be right. Karina was living a normal life until two days ago. She was hidden among humans, unknown to our kind.

"Why?" The question scrapes from my throat, raw with an emotion I can't name. "Why would he watch her?"

She laughs, the sound like broken glass. "All this time, you thought you found her by chance. That fate brought her to you."

"Get to the point," I snarl, my patience shredded to nothing.

"She isn't some random wolf who happened to catch your attention." Vanessa beams with malicious satisfaction. "She's the daughter of Elena Rosewood."

Every wolf on the West Coast knows the legend of Elena Rosewood—the only female alpha born in three centuries.

"That's impossible," I breathe, but even as I say it, doubt creeps into my mind.

"Is it?" Vanessa tilts her head, savoring my shock.

"Elena Rosewood disappeared in 1995."

"So she did, but did you know her mate disappeared with her? They had a daughter born the following year. A daughter they kept hidden from the supernatural world."

My mind races, connecting dots I should have seen earlier. Karina's parents' insistence on keeping her from pack life. They weren't just protecting her from pack politics. They were protecting her from wolves who would see her bloodline as the ultimate prize.

"Even if that's true, it doesn't change anything."

"The daughter of the only female alpha? It changes everything."

My blood runs cold. "Lockhart will never touch her."

"He already has someone at the compound," Vanessa says, her smile widening. "Did you think we wouldn't have allies inside Bellandi territory? People who recognize which way the wind is blowing?"

The warehouse feels smaller by the second, walls pressing in. A raw pulse drives through me—get to Karina, now. I've been baited, led off while they move against her.

"You're lying," I growl, but my wolf knows better. The constant pull I've felt all night wasn't just about protecting Karina—it was warning me of danger. Why the fuck didn't I realize that?

"It's been...what, two hours since you left her? More than enough time."

I don't hesitate. The gun barks twice in my hand, each shot precise. The suit crumples first, a clean hole drilled through his forehead. Vanessa manages half a step backward before the second round tears into her throat. She staggers, clutching at the wound as blood spills hot between her fingers, disbelief etched across her features.

I'm already moving toward the exit when her strangled voice stops me.

"You...can't...save her..."

I turn back, watching dispassionately as she slides down the wall, leaving a crimson smear in her wake. "Who's inside the compound?"

She laughs, the sound wet and gurgling. "It doesn't matter....you're...too...late." The last word slips out as she takes one last ragged breath before she goes still.

I don't wait for her body to cool before I'm sprinting back to my car. My heart hammers against my ribs like it's trying to escape my chest. Every second feels like an eternity as I tear through the forest, branches whipping my face, roots threatening to trip me. I don't feel any of it. All I feel is the mark burning on my neck and the rising tide of panic that threatens to drown me.

Elena Rosewood's daughter. The implications crash through my mind like a wrecking ball. If it's true, she's not just rare—she's practically royalty in our world. A bloodline that could birth the next female alpha, something that happens once in centuries.

No wonder her parents hid her away. No wonder they never told her what she was.

I slam into my car, fumbling with the keys, my hands slick with Vanessa's blood. The engine roars to life, and I'm already accelerating before the door fully closes. The tires screech against the asphalt as I take the first turn too fast, the back end fishtailing before I regain control.

"Fuck, fuck, fuck," I growl, pressing the accelerator to the floor. The engine whines in protest as I push it beyond its limits, but it's still not fast enough. Nothing is fast enough.

I grab my phone, dialing Elias with one hand while taking another curve at reckless speed. The call rings once, twice, three times before his voicemail kicks on."

I try calling again, the phone slipping in my blood-slicked grip as I take another turn. Nothing. Either he's not answering, or something's already happened.

The tether in my chest pulls tight, anxiety crashing through me in waves I can't tell are mine or hers. Her distress slices into me—sharp bursts of fear that set my wolf howling beneath my skin. She's in danger. Real, immediate danger.

I floor the accelerator again, the speedometer climbing past ninety as I tear down the winding mountain road. The compound is still twenty minutes away at legal speeds. I'll make it in ten.

I can only hope that I make it in time because if I lose her, I will become something much worse than the Reaper. I will scorch the fucking earth to get her back.

Karina

The pain of the incomplete mark is the worst kind of addiction. A hunger that nothing can satisfy, a fire that nothing can quench. It's only gotten worse the longer Damien is gone. An hour seems like an eternity in hell.

I sit at Damien's kitchen table, watching Elias move around the space with surprising familiarity. For the heir to a criminal empire, he seems remarkably at ease doing something as mundane as cooking pasta. The domesticity of the scene feels jarring after everything that's happened in the last forty-eight hours.

"You should eat something," Elias says, stirring what smells like garlic and herbs into a simmering pot. "Dom will kill me if I let you starve while he's out playing Reaper."

"I'm not hungry." It's a lie. I'm starving, but not for food. The fever rolling through me has sharpened to the point where even the soft cotton of my borrowed T-shirt scrapes against my skin like sandpaper.

"Cycles burn through calories fast," Elias says, ignoring my protest. "You need to keep your strength up."

I sigh. "How do you know so much about it? You're not..." I hesitate, unsure how to phrase the question.

"Mated?" He laughs, the sound surprisingly gentle. "No. But I watched my father with his current Luna. He didn't complete the bond for almost a month," Elias continues, his back to me as he drains the pasta. "It was ugly. My father was practically feral by the end."

I wrap my arms around myself, trying to contain the shivers that have nothing to do with cold. "Why would anyone put themselves through that?"

"Politics." He shrugs, as if that explains everything. In his world, maybe it does. "Her pack wanted assurances before allowing the full mating. My father agreed to their terms, thinking he could handle the wait."

"And could he?"

Elias's expression darkens as he turns to face me. "Let's just say there's a reason Matthew is...the way he is. Children born from an incomplete bond carry the strain of it."

My stomach drops. "Children?"

"Shit." He winces. "I forgot you're new to all this. It's possible to conceive, though it's rare. The offspring tend to be unstable."

Great. Another complication I hadn't considered. As if this situation needed more potential disasters.

"Has Damien told you what happens if you don't complete it?" Elias asks, setting a plate of pasta in front of me.

I nod, picking up my fork without any real intention of eating. "Pain. For both of us."

"It's more than pain." He sits across from me, placing a second plate of steaming pasta in front of him. "It gets worse the closer you are to your mate without completing it. Like an addiction where the drug is right in front of you, but you can't take it. For both of your sakes, I hope it doesn't come down to that."

"Why are you being so nice to me?" I ask, pushing the pasta around my plate.

"Because Dom is the closest thing I have to a friend in this godforsaken place."

I raise an eyebrow. "You don't have friends?"

"I have allies. Associates. People who want something from me." Elias takes a bite of his pasta, chewing thoughtfully. "Dom is different. He doesn't care about my position or my family's power. He just...is who he is. Though he's more than that now with you in the picture."

"You make it sound like caring about me is a weakness."

"In our world?" Elias laughs, but there's no humor in it. "Caring about anyone is a death sentence waiting to happen."

"Is that why you don't have a mate?"

"I don't have one because my father thinks I should marry for politics, not for love." The fork scrapes softly against the plate as he twirls the pasta with more force than necessary, jaw tight. "He's already in talks with three different packs—negotiating my hand like I'm some bargaining chip."

"That's barbaric," I blurt out before I can stop myself.

"That's pack politics." He shrugs as if it doesn't bother him, but I can see the tension in his shoulders. "The same politics you've stumbled into by catching Damien's attention."

"It's not just about politics," I say, my fork still pushing the pasta around. "It's about choice. Shouldn't we all have the right to choose who we—"

A sharp crack from outside cuts through my words. My head snaps toward the window, wolf senses immediately on alert.

Elias is on his feet in an instant, his relaxed demeanor vanishing. "Stay here," he commands. "Don't move. Don't make a sound."

Before I can respond, he's moving toward the door, his movements fluid and predatory in a way that reminds me this isn't just Damien's friendly acquaintance—this is the heir to a criminal empire, born and raised in violence.

Elias disappears outside, closing the door behind him with barely a sound. I strain my enhanced hearing, catching the soft crunch of footsteps on gravel, then silence.

My wolf paces anxiously beneath my skin. Something's wrong. The air feels charged, like the moment before lightning strikes. The scent of unfamiliar wolves drifts through the cracked window.

I should stay put. That would be the smart thing to do. But my wolf is howling now, sensing danger with an instinct that bypasses rational thought.

Rising from the chair, I move silently toward the window, my bare feet making no sound on the wooden floor.

The compound looks eerily quiet. Too quiet. Even the normal sounds of night patrol are absent, leaving only the whisper of wind through the trees. My wolf whines, pressing against my skin with increasing urgency.

A shadow moves between the cabins—too large to be Elias, too unfamiliar to be pack security. My breath catches as more shapes emerge, surrounding Damien's cabin with practiced precision. These aren't random intruders. This is a coordinated attack.

Hide. You have to hide.

The sound of footsteps circling the cabin jolts me into motion. I dart away from the window, scanning the small space for somewhere, anywhere, to hide. The bedroom will be the first place they check. The bathroom offers no escape. My attention snags on the weapons cabinet Damien opened earlier, now locked tight.

Think, Karina. Think.

The floorboards creak outside the front door. My hands shake as I back toward the kitchen, grabbing a knife from the counter. It feels pathetically inadequate against whatever's coming, but it's better than nothing.

A muffled thud from outside makes me flinch. Elias? Has something happened to him? I press my back against the wall beside the door, knife gripped in white-knuckled fingers.

The door handle turns slowly, silently. Whoever's out there isn't trying to break in—they have a key. My breath catches in my throat as the door swings open, revealing a silhouette I don't recognize.

"I know you're in here, little wolf." The voice is male, unfamiliar, with an accent I can't place. "I can smell you. Your guard dog put up quite a fight," the man continues. "Though I'm afraid he won't be joining us."

The intruder moves deeper into the cabin, his boots heavy on the wooden floor. I catch a glimpse of his profile as he passes. I don't recognize him at all.

"Lockhart sends his regards," he says, moving toward the bedroom. "He's been very eager to meet Elena Rosewood's daughter."

The knife nearly slips from my numb fingers. Elena Rosewood? I've never heard that name before, but the way he says it—like it should mean something to me— sends fresh terror racing through my veins.

"Come now, Karina," he calls from bedroom, growing more irritated when he finds it empty. "We both know you're here. Your scent is practically saturating the air, and I can hear your heart thumping."

The mark on my neck burns white-hot, I feel an echo of rage so pure it nearly knocks me to my knees.

Damien. He knows something's wrong.

The intruder's footsteps return to the main room.

My body moves before my mind processes what's happening. As he turns toward the kitchen, I lunge from my hiding spot, driving the knife into his side with all my strength.

He howls, a sound more surprised than pained, as the blade sinks between his ribs. His hands grasp at me, but I twist the knife deeper and rip it sideways. Hot blood spills over my fingers as he drops to one knee.

"You bitch," he gasps, clutching his side as blood seeps between his fingers.

I back away, knife still clutched in my trembling hand. I need a distraction, something to buy me time to escape.

"She's in here!" the man calls out strained with pain. "Get in here now!"

I hear footsteps rushing toward the cabin. I'm out of time and escape routes.

My eyes flick to the front door, my only way in or out of this cabin. There's no time for a plan, only for the simplest, stupidest thing that might point them the wrong way. I run towards the bedroom, making sure that the incapacitated wolf in front of me sees me go that way. It's my only shot, hiding in plain sight.

Blood slicks my fingers as I run, every breath tearing at my throat. I stumble down the hallway toward the bedroom, smearing the doorframe as I pass. Each touch is deliberate—bright streaks that say *this way*, leading them exactly where I want them to look. The carpet drinks my trail, uneven drops marking my path like breadcrumbs for monsters.

I shove the bedroom door open hard enough for it to slam against the wall and drag my hand down the edge, leaving one last swipe of red before darting inside. The smell of blood is strong, thick in the air. It'll pull them right in.

But I'm already backing out, breath shaking. I slip into the hall again and reach the narrow closet by the kitchen. The space is barely big enough for me to squeeze into, crammed with cleaning supplies and old coats. I duck inside, leaving the door cracked just enough to see a sliver of the hallway.

My fingers brush over a bottle of bleach on the shelf. I grab it, twist the cap off, and pour a jagged line across the threshold—just enough to let the sharp, stinging scent swallow everything else. The fumes hit instantly, burning my nose, making my eyes water. Good. Wolves hunt by scent; if I'm lucky, this will blur the trail long enough to fool them.

The front door crashes open. Heavy boots hit the floor.

"She went towards the bedroom. Lockhart wants her alive, but I don't give a shit about her condition after what she just did."

I press a hand over my mouth as they rush past, shadows slicing through the hallway, the air vibrating with growls and the scrape of furniture. The smell of bleach mixes with blood, sharp enough to make my head swim.

One of them snarls from the bedroom, "She's bleeding—she's right here!"

No, I think. I'm not.

I stay still, crouched in the dark, every muscle trembling, listening as they tear the room apart. Sheets rip. Furniture breaks. Boots scrape the floor. And then, slowly, the sounds shift—fading deeper into the house, away from me.

Now.

I push the closet door open just enough to slip through, lungs burning, eyes stinging. The hall is empty. The front door stands open just ten feet away, freedom if I can reach it without being seen.

My wolf pushes closer to the surface as she prepares to run. I feel Damien's rage building to dangerous levels. He's coming. I just have to survive until he gets here.

"She's not in the bedroom!" one of the men calls out.

The wounded man's head snaps toward my hiding spot, his nostrils flaring. "Then where the fuck—"

I don't wait for him to finish. Bursting from behind the door, I sprint toward the open entrance, knife still clutched in my blood-slicked hand. The wounded man lunges for me, his fingers grazing my arm as I twist away.

"She's running!" he shouts.

Cold night air hits my face as I clear the threshold, my bare feet slapping against the gravel path. The compound is eerily silent—no guards, no patrols. Where is everyone? What happened to Elias?

I scan the shadows, searching for any sign of him, when something catches my attention—a crumpled form near the tree line. My stomach lurches as I recognize the blond hair, now matted with blood.

No time to check. No time to help. I keep moving.

I veer away from the main buildings, aiming for the dense forest that surrounds the compound. If I can make it to the trees, I might have a chance. My wolf surges closer to the surface, lending me strength and speed I didn't know I possessed. The knife feels like an extension of my arm as I drive my legs harder, ignoring the sharp stones slicing into my bare feet.

"Cut her off!" someone shouts behind me. I hear them splitting up, trying to flank me.

The tree line is so close—fifty yards, maybe. My lungs burn as I push harder, the woods wavering in front of me like a mirage. Forty yards. Thirty. The sounds of pursuit crash through the night—boots pounding gravel, shouted commands, the rustle of bodies tearing through underbrush.

Twenty yards.

Something slams into me from the side, sending me

sprawling across the rocky ground. The knife skitters from my grip, clattering somewhere in the gloom as I roll to absorb the impact. My shoulder screams in protest, but I force myself up, scrambling on hands and knees toward where I think the blade landed.

"Got her." Heavy hands grab my arms, hauling me upright despite my struggles. "Feisty little bitch."

I twist in his grip, my wolf snarling beneath my skin, lending me strength I didn't know I possessed. My elbow connects with something soft—his solar plexus—and he doubles over with a grunt.

"Shift," I whisper to my wolf. "Please, I need you."

But she's still too close to human, too confused by years of suppression to break free completely. The partial transformation leaves me caught between forms. Stronger than human but not fully wolf, claws extending from fingertips that shake with the effort of holding the change.

The man recovers faster than I expected, backhanding me across the face with enough force to send stars exploding across my vision. I taste copper as blood fills my mouth, but the pain only makes my wolf angrier.

"Enough games," he snarls, producing a syringe from his jacket. The liquid inside glows faintly in the moonlight—something unnatural, something wrong. "Lockhart said to bring you in conscious, but he didn't say anything about cooperative."

I lash out with my partially extended claws, raking

them across his wrist. He curses, dropping the syringe as blood wells from the gouges. The glass vial shatters against the rocks, its contents hissing as they eat into the stone.

"You stupid bitch!" He grabs my hair, yanking my head back to expose my throat. "I should have just shot you."

He's close—so close I can almost smell pine on the night air.

"Hold her still." A second man emerges, carrying a rope and what appears to be a shock collar. The first man tightens his grip on my hair while the second approaches with the collar. The metal gleams dully in the moonlight, and I can smell the acrid scent of electricity crackling through its circuits. Whatever that thing is, I know I can't let them put it on me.

"This would be so much easier if you'd just cooperate," the second man says, reaching for my throat.

I don't waste breath on a response. Instead, I drive my knee up between his legs with every ounce of strength I possess. He doubles over with a strangled cry, the collar falling from his hands. The first man's grip loosens in surprise, and I tear free, leaving strands of hair in his bloody fingers.

But there's nowhere left to run. Three more figures emerge, surrounding me in a loose circle. My back hits the rough bark of an ancient redwood as they close in, their faces cast in shadow but their intent crystal clear as they close in. Five men now. I press harder against the tree, feeling the rough bark dig into my back. There's nowhere left to run.

"Just come quietly," one of them says, reaching for my arm. "Lockhart doesn't want you damaged."

"Too late for that," another laughs, gesturing to the blood on my hands and face.

A gunshot cracks through the night, so close it makes my ears ring. One of the men crumples to the ground with a strangled cry. The others whirl around, weapons appearing in their hands as they search for the source.

"Get away from her!"

Elias staggers from the shadows, blood streaming down his face from a gash across his forehead. His shirt is torn and soaked crimson, but the gun in his hand is steady as he fires again. Another man falls, clutching his thigh and howling.

"Kill him!" shouts the one who tried to collar me. "Now!"

The remaining men turn their attention to Elias, who ducks behind a tree as bullets splinter the bark around him. His eyes meet mine across the clearing, and I see the silent command in them. Run.

I don't hesitate. As gunfire erupts between Elias and my captors, I bolt toward the trees, my bare feet finding purchase on the uneven ground. The forest swallows me. The sounds of gunfire fade behind me as I push deeper into the woods, my lungs burning with each desperate breath.

I run until my legs threaten to buckle, until the mark on my neck pulses with such intensity I can barely see straight. Every step carries me farther from the compound, from Elias, from whatever fate Lockhart had planned for me. Elena Rosewood. The words echo in my mind like a foreign language. Who is she? What does it have to do with me?

Branches whip across my face as I stumble through the underbrush. My feet are torn and bleeding, but I don't slow down. Can't slow down. The night air fills my lungs in ragged gasps as I push myself harder, faster, my wolf lending me strength to keep moving.

I don't know how long I run—minutes or hours blur together in a haze of adrenaline. The forest gradually thins, and suddenly I'm breaking through the tree line onto asphalt—a road. Somewhere to my right, I hear the distant hum of an engine.

Headlights appear around the bend, blinding in their intensity. I freeze, The car skids to a violent stop mere inches from where I stand. The tires screech against the asphalt, burning rubber and sending gravel flying. I throw my arms up to shield my face, certain I'm about to be hit, when the driver's door flies open.

"Karina!"

Damien. My knees nearly buckle with relief as he unfolds from the car. Blood covers his shirt, none of it his own, from what I can tell. He rushes toward me, pulling me into his arms with such force that the breath leaves my lungs.

"You're alive," he mutters against my hair, his hands frantically checking me for injuries. "You're alive."

I cling to him, my fingers digging into his back as I breathe in his scent.

"They came for me," I gasp, the words tumbling out between ragged breaths.

Damien stiffens against me, his arms tightening possessively. "I know. Get in the car. Now."

He doesn't wait for me to respond, practically lifting me off my feet as he guides me to the passenger side.

My hands shake as I fumble with the seatbelt, adrenaline making my fingers clumsy. Damien slams the car into drive before I'm even fully seated, the engine roaring as we tear down a mountain road.

"Elias," I gasp, suddenly remembering. "He was shot. He helped me escape. We have to go back for him."

"Elias can handle himself. You're what matters now."

"Where are we going?"

Damien clenches his jaw. "Home. To my father, and the protection of my pack."

"No, I can't—"

"There's no choice, Karina. My father's territory is the only place with enough strength to protect you."

The road is a blur of shadows and headlights, the silence between us thick with everything I don't understand. He's keeping something from me. I can feel it in every clipped word, every sharp inhale. And whatever it is —it's big.

Somewhere beyond it waits his father. His pack. And answers I'm no longer sure I'm ready for.

Damien

I drive through the endless night with death riding shotgun. Not the kind I deal in but the kind that nearly stole her from me. The kind that still might.

Karina sleeps beside me, her body curled toward the door like she's ready to run even in unconsciousness. Blood still crusts beneath her fingernails. Karina fought like hell tonight. Pride swells in my chest even as rage continues to simmer beneath my skin.

I nearly lost her.

Three more hours until we reach my father's territory in Oregon. Three more hours of mountain roads and forest shadows, each mile putting distance between us and the chaos we left behind. My knuckles ache from gripping the steering wheel too tight, but I can't seem to loosen my hold. If I do, I might shatter completely.

The headlights cut through fog that clings to the asphalt like ghostly fingers. My wolf paces restlessly beneath my skin, still half-feral from her terror.

"Karina Rosewood." I test the words in the silence of the car.

Could it be true? Elena had been long gone by the time I was born. I only knew about her from the stories my father had told me. If Karina is truly her daughter...

"Fuck." The word escapes on a breath. It's the kind of revelation that will shatter our world as soon as the news gets out. Keeping her safe will be all-out war.

Karina stirs, her brow furrowing in sleep as if she can sense my turmoil.

The road narrows as we climb higher into the mountains, switchbacks hugging cliffs that drop into nothing below. My father's territory lies just beyond these peaks —the Marek pack lands that have been in our family for generations. I haven't been home in nearly a year, not since my father sent me away to learn my lesson.

Learn. As if becoming the Reaper was some kind of education.

My phone buzzes on the console between us, Elias's name flashing on the screen. I snatch it up, keeping one eye on the winding road.

"Tell me you're alive," I growl into the phone.

"Barely. They thought they finished me. Rookie mistake."

"How bad?"

"I'm not going to be running marathons anytime soon. Fuckers barely missed braining me," he coughs, the wet sound making my jaw clench. "

"Where are you now?"

"Safe house in Ferndale. My father is on his way back." There's a pause, the sound of liquid being poured. Probably whiskey if I know Elias. "Is she okay? Karina?"

I glance at her sleeping form, the blood still matting her hair, the bruise forming on her cheekbone where someone struck her. My wolf snarls beneath my skin.

"She's alive."

"Good." Another pause. "They knew what they were after, Dom. She was their target. Said something about—"

"Elena Rosewood. I know. Lockhart's people told me before I killed them."

"Fuck." Elias exhales sharply. "If that's true...shit will hit the fucking fan, my friend. You'll be enemy number one. Tell me you have a plan."

"I'm taking her to my father. If she's who they say she is, they'll come after her again. And with more firepower next time."

"No shit." Elias coughs again, and I hear the strain in his voice. "You're going to need more than your pack to protect her."

"Can I count on your pack?"

"Look, Dom. If I were Alpha, I wouldn't even hesitate to join up. But my father is a different story. He's furious about the breach, but he's also asking questions about her that make me uneasy."

"What kind of questions?"

"The kind that makes me think he might have known who she was all along." There's a pause, the sound of ice clinking against glass. "Be careful, Dom. I'm starting to think this goes deeper than Lockhart."

"I know." This isn't just about territory or business anymore—this is about power that transcends normal pack politics. "Watch your back."

"Always do."

The line goes dead before I can respond. I toss the phone onto the console.

Karina whimpers in her sleep, her body tensing as another nightmare grips her.

I pull over at the next wide spot in the road, gravel crunching under the tires as I bring the car to a stop. My hands shake as I reach for her, unable to watch her suffer through whatever hell her subconscious has conjured.

"Wake up, kitten."

Her eyes snap open, wild and unfocused. For a moment, she doesn't recognize me, her body coiled to fight or flee. Then the bond pulses between us, and recognition floods her features.

"Damien?"

"I'm here." I cup her face in my hands, thumbs stroking across her cheekbones. "You're safe."

She melts into my touch, a soft sob escaping her lips. "I keep seeing them."

"Tell me about it," I declare, pulling her closer until our foreheads touch. Her tears wet my fingers as I cradle her face. "Tell me what you see."

"Their hands." She shudders against me. "I can still feel them grabbing me, trying to put that collar on me. And Elias—there was so much blood—"

"Elias is alive," I tell her, relief washing through me when her body sags against mine. "I just spoke to him. He's hurt but safe."

She nods against my palm, her breath coming in shaky gasps that spark something raw and feral inside me. My wolf prowls closer to the surface, desperate to comfort her.

"I thought I'd never see you again," she whispers, her fingers digging into my wrists as if to anchor herself to something solid. "I thought they'd take me before you could—"

I don't let her finish. *I can't.* The thought of her slipping through my fingers—of those fuckers dragging her away, touching what's mine—detonates the last thread of restraint I have left.

My mouth crashes down on hers drinking in her gasp like it belongs to me.

Then she breaks—melts into me with a soft, sinful moan that nearly brings me to my knees. Her lips part for me, and I take everything. My tongue sweeps into her mouth, desperate and hungry, tasting her submission.

I drag her across the console without finesse, needing her closer, needing her on me. She lands on my lap with a whimper that shreds the last of my humanity. My hands roam without hesitation, over her hips, up her sides, palming the swell of her breast through her thin shirt. I squeeze hard enough to make her gasp, to remind her whose hands she's in.

"Mine," I growl against her mouth. "You fucking belong to me."

Her fingers tangle in my hair, nails scraping my scalp, and she arches into me like she needs this just as badly. Like she wants to be taken. Marked. Owned.

I slip my hand beneath her shirt, dragging it up until my palm meets bare skin. Her nipple is already tight, begging for my attention. I pinch it between my fingers, and she moans into my mouth, louder this time, shameless.

My cock throbs beneath her, straining against my jeans. She shifts her hips, and I nearly lose it, a low, guttural sound tearing from my throat.

"I should throw you in the backseat and remind you exactly what that mark on your neck means," I rasp, nipping at her lower lip hard enough to sting. "But not here. Not where anyone could take you from me again."

She shivers in my arms, her eyes heavy-lidded and lips kiss-swollen, and for a moment I forget about everything else—the danger, the blood, the war waiting just beyond the tree line.

Right now, all I know is her.

And I will tear apart the fucking world before I let anyone else touch her again.

"You deserve better than the front seat of a car on the side of a mountain road." I brush my thumb across her swollen lips, marveling at how soft they are despite everything she's been through tonight. "Because when I make you mine, it won't be while we're running for our lives."

Her breath catches, but she doesn't pull away. Her body is still pressed against mine, warm and trembling, and all I want is to bury myself in her until the rest of the world disappears. But I don't. Not yet.

Instead, I let my touch linger just a moment longer—thumb trailing down her throat to where her pulse thrums wild beneath skin that tastes like smoke and defiance. She tilts her head, exposing her neck in the smallest, most instinctive show of trust I've ever seen. My wolf growls his approval, but I force myself to still.

Not here. Not like this.

"I'll make it right. You have my word."

She swallows hard, her fingers still twisted in my shirt, and I feel her walls slowly rising again gathering the pieces of herself she had let slip for just a breath. Just enough to let me in.

I press one last kiss to the corner of her mouth, then shift her gently off my lap and back into the passenger seat. She curls into herself, silent but watching me.

The engine rumbles back to life beneath us, and I force my hands to stay on the wheel where they won't betray how close I am to turning this car around just to take her somewhere I can finish what we started.

But I don't.

I drive. The hours pass, the car ride stretching between us like a live wire. Karina hasn't spoken since our roadside encounter, her face turned toward the window as miles disappear beneath our tires. The silence should bother me, but it doesn't. My wolf understands what words can't express—the terror still clinging to her skin, the uncertainty of what lies ahead.

The first hints of dawn bleed across the horizon when I see it. My ancestral home. The Marek compound rises from the mist-shrouded forest like something from another time—stone and timber and power stretching across the mountainside. Watchtowers mark the perimeter, sentries already alerted to our approach. My father's security doesn't miss a thing.

"We're here."

Karina stirs beside me, tension radiating through her body as she takes in the imposing structure ahead. "This is where you grew up?"

"This is where I was born." The distinction matters, though I can't explain why.

The iron gates stand open, a rare sight that tells me my father received my message. He's expecting us. The knowledge sits like lead in my stomach. Hudson Marek doesn't do anything without calculation, including welcoming home his prodigal son.

I feel Karina's anxiety spike as we drive past the first checkpoint. Guards with assault rifles track our movement, their expressions giving nothing away. To them,

I'm still the Alpha's son. The Marek heir coming home at last.

"Who are all these people?" Karina whispers, shrinking into her seat as we pass groups of wolves going about their morning routines. Some stop to watch us, recognition and curiosity flickering across their faces.

"My pack," I answer, the words feeling foreign on my tongue after so long away.

I guide the car up the winding drive that leads to the main house—a sprawling structure of stone and timber that dominates the highest point of the compound. My father's pride and joy, designed to showcase the Marek power to anyone who visits. The message is clear. We see everything from up here.

"Your father lives there?"

"We all do." I park near the front steps, killing the engine but making no move to exit.

And all the danger that comes with it.

"It's time," I say, reaching for the door handle. "Knowing my father, he's already waiting for me."

The mountain air hits us like a slap as we exit the car —crisp and thin at this elevation, carrying the scents of pine and wolf and home. Karina shivers beside me. I wrap my arm around her shoulders, pulling her against my side as we ascend the stone steps. My scent will offer some protection, marking her as mine even to those who can't see the bite on her neck.

The oak doors swing open before we reach them. My father's beta, Gabriel, stands in the entryway, his expression carefully neutral as he takes in our blood-stained appearance.

"Alpha Hudson is waiting in his study."

No 'welcome home.' No questions about our condition. Just business as usual in the Marek household.

"We need to clean up first."

Gabriel hesitates, clearly weighing my request against my father's orders. "Alpha Hudson was very specific about—"

"Gabriel." My voice drops to the register I've used on men before I killed them. "Look at us. We're covered in blood. My mate needs a shower and clean clothes before she meets my father."

The word has the desired effect. Gabriel stiffens, his focus shifting back to Karina with sharpened interest. "Of course. I'll inform Alpha Hudson you'll join him within the hour."

"Make it two, and have someone bring a change of clothes for her."

His jaw tightens, but he inclines his head. "As you wish."

He steps aside, granting us entry.

I guide Karina through the grand hall, my palm steady at the small of her back. The marble floors gleam beneath our feet, immaculate despite the predawn hour. My mother's influence lingers in every detail—the tasteful artwork, the vases of fresh-cut flowers, the faint polish of lemon that can't quite smother the deeper scent of wolf.

Karina takes it all in, shoulders taut with the effort of composure. I see the house as she must, not a home, but a fortress, opulent and cold. Compared to this mausoleum, even the cabin's sparseness feels warm.

"This way," I say, guiding her toward the sweeping staircase. Pack members pause in their morning routines, nostrils flaring as they register her scent.

"Eyes down," I command as heads bow in unison.

We reach the second floor, and I guide her down the east wing toward my suite. My childhood bedroom sits exactly as I left it a year ago—if you can call a space this size a bedroom. The suite spans nearly a thousand square feet, with floor-to-ceiling windows overlooking the pack's training grounds and a sitting area that could host a small dinner party.

Karina stops just inside the doorway, her mouth falling open as she takes in the king-sized bed, the stone fireplace, the walk-in closet that's larger than her entire apartment back in Eureka.

"This is your room?" she breathes.

"Was." I close the door behind us, engaging the lock.

She drifts toward the windows, her fingers trailing across surfaces that have been dusted regularly despite my absence. My mother's orders, no doubt. Helena Marek doesn't allow anything in her house to fall into disrepair, even the room of her disappointing son.

"The bathroom's through there," I tell her, nodding toward the door on the far side of the room. "There should be everything you need."

She turns to face me, uncertainty written across her features. "What about you?"

"I'll use the guest bath down the hall." I move toward my dresser, pulling out clothes. "Take your time. My father can wait."

"Stay."

The word hangs between us, soft yet unmistakable. I turn to find Karina standing in the middle of my childhood bedroom, arms wrapped around herself, looking somehow smaller amid the grandeur of Marek wealth.

"Please. I don't...I don't want to be alone right now."

Something in my chest tightens at the vulnerability in her request. After everything she's endured—the attack, the escape, the revelation of who she might be— she's asking for me. Not safety. Not answers. Just me.

"Are you sure?" I ask, already knowing I'll give her anything she asks for. "You've been through hell tonight."

She nods, a slight tremble in her lower lip betraying her composure. "That's why I need you close...it helps. When you're near, I can breathe."

I know exactly what she means. When we're apart, it's an ache that nothing can soothe. Together, at least the pain becomes bearable.

"Okay," I say, setting down the clothes I'd gathered.

Relief washes over her features, and through our connection, I feel the knot of anxiety in her chest loosen slightly. She turns toward the bathroom, then pauses at the threshold.

"I meant...in there."

My mouth goes dry. The shower. She wants me in the shower with her. Every rational thought in my head blares that this is a terrible idea. I'm barely holding on as it is; seeing her naked under the spray of hot water will shatter what little restraint I have left.

But this isn't about seduction. It's about trust. About needing me close when the world has tried to tear her apart again.

"I don't think that's wise," I manage. The last thing I want to do is trigger her fight-or-flight response.

"I'm not asking you to touch me," she interrupts, color flooding her cheeks. "I just...I only feel safe around you."

The bathroom is larger than my cabin at the Bellandi compound, featuring all-black marble and chrome, with a walk-in shower that could comfortably fit six people. I follow Karina inside, keeping my distance as she turns on the water. Steam fills the space almost immediately, fogging the mirrors and glass shower doors.

She strips her bloody, torn clothes without hesitation, as if the act of baring herself means nothing compared to what she's endured. The fabric pools at her feet, forgotten, and she steps into the shower. Steam rises around her as the spray hits her skin, plastering her dark hair to her back, water racing over every curve.

I shed my clothes quickly, letting the bloodied pile fall beside hers, and move in after her. I keep a measured distance, though every instinct in me strains to close it. "Is this all right?"

She gives a short nod, shoulders easing at my presence.

I reach for the shampoo, working the thick gel into my palms before stepping close enough to touch. "Let me."

My fingers slide into her damp hair, gentle, careful of the bruised spot where rough hands had pulled her earlier. Dried blood loosens beneath my touch, spiraling in pink streams down the drain. She exhales softly, the sound escaping her lips with each slow stroke of my fingers over her scalp. The quiet, trusting sound slams into me, low and hot, settling hard between my legs.

I force myself to focus on the task—cleaning away the evidence of tonight's violence, washing the fear from her skin.

"Better?" I ask, rinsing the suds from her hair with cupped handfuls of water.

She turns in my arms before I can stop her, and suddenly we're chest to chest, her naked body pressed against mine under the spray. My breath catches as I feel every soft curve, every place where her skin meets mine.

"Karina." Her name comes out as a warning, a plea. Her hands come up to rest against my chest, fingers splaying over the tattoos that mark me as my father's son. I have to grip the shower wall behind her to keep from crushing her against me.

"I'm done running." It's not a plea. It's a surrender. A declaration. "When the full moon rises...I'm yours."

The animal inside me roars.

The tension I've been holding back shatters in an instant. My palm slams against the tile beside her head, the wall rattling from the impact. My body cages hers, warmth radiating between us, slick skin sliding against mine. My cock throbs where it presses against her stomach, demanding more, merciless.

"You don't fucking know what you're offering me, Karina."

She doesn't retreat. Not an inch. Her breath stutters, but her chin tips up in reckless defiance. "Then teach me."

"If you give yourself to an alpha, there's no taking it back. It's forever." My mouth brushes her ear, the words harsh and raw. "I'll drive my scent so deep into your flesh no wolf will ever dare question who you belong to."

She shivers—reckless, glorious girl. Her nipples harden against my chest, and her thighs squeeze together like she's trying to trap the fire I've set alight with nothing but words and promise.

"You want that?" I growl, dragging my hand down her body, fingers skimming over the curve of her breast, her waist, her hip. "Want me to ruin you for anyone else? Want to be my good little mate, dripping with me for days?"

She trembles, nodding. Her lips part, but nothing

comes, only a strangled gasp when my fingers slip between her legs.

"Fuck," I rasp, stroking through her slickness. "You're drenched. And it's not the damn water, is it?"

Her head shakes, her expression dazed, heavy-lidded. "No. It's you."

My free hand seizes her jaw, tilting her head so I can crush my mouth to hers. The kiss is brutal—tongue and teeth, desperation and possession. She whimpers into me, grinding against my hand, chasing every filthy stroke of my fingers.

"I want to feel you fall apart on my hand. Right here. Right now. Before I take you apart in every other way that matters."

Her hand finds my cock, wrapping around it like instinct, like she's done it a hundred times. Bold. Certain. Mine. A curse tears from me as she strokes, relentless and filthy.

"That's it," I snarl, circling her clit faster now. "Touch me, sweetheart. Use me."

Her moans spiral higher, body arching, legs shaking. "Damien—"

"Keep your focus on me," I command. "I want your eyes on me when you break for me."

Her lips part, chest rising in ragged bursts as she unravels, convulsing around my fingers, a cry ripping from her throat as release slams through her.

I don't stop. I can't. Her orgasm fuels mine—her

slickness, the grip of her hand on my cock, the sheer surrender in every trembling pulse of her body.

I jerk in her grip, teeth clenched, coming hard across her belly with a ragged growl. My muscles lock, my forehead pressed to hers as I breathe through the flood of need that still simmers under my skin.

Water pours down around us, steam rising, scent of sex and wolf thick between our bodies.

I rest my hands on either side of her head, caging her in place with my body.

"I'm going to make you scream for me, Karina. Loud enough the whole damn pack hears. And when I knot you under the moon, you'll feel it for days—my teeth in your neck, my cum dripping down your thighs. You won't need words. They'll smell it on you."

She bites her bottom lip, then lets it go slowly as her fingers drift up my chest.

"I want them to know. I want them to see."

A wicked grin pulls at my mouth as I lean in, pressing a kiss to her throat.

"Good," I murmur against her skin. "Because there's no going back now."

# 16

Karina

Water drips from my hair onto Damien's plush carpet as I stand in the middle of his childhood bedroom, wrapped in a towel that costs more than my monthly rent. The shower still steams up the bathroom behind us, evidence of promises made under hot water and desperate hands. My body hums with aftershocks, the place between my thighs still pulsing from his touch.

I'm still processing what happened in the shower when I spot something that wasn't there before. On the edge of his bed lies a neatly folded stack of clothes—a soft gray sweater and what looks like matching leggings.

"Whose clothes are these?" I ask, moving closer. As I lean in, I catch an unfamiliar female scent clinging to the fabric.

Damien glances over as he pulls a fresh shirt over his head, muscles rippling beneath tattooed skin. "My sister's."

I run my fingers over the soft material, suddenly aware of how real this all is. I'm not just in his territory, I'm being absorbed into his world.

He crosses the room to stand behind me. His chest presses against my back.

I lift the sweater and examine it more closely. It's expensive, cashmere maybe, and impossibly soft against my fingers. Nothing like the threadbare clothes I left behind. "Will I meet her soon?"

"After we see my father." His grip steadies on my hips, heat seeping through his palms. "She might keep her distance at first. After what she's endured, letting anyone close takes time."

I set the sweater down, turning in his arms. The towel shifts, and I catch it before it falls completely. "And what will you tell your family? About us?"

His focus drops to where my hands clutch the towel. "That you're mine. That anyone with a problem can take it up with me." His fingers slide over mine, prying the fabric from my grip and letting it fall in a heap at my feet. "As much as I hate to say this, get dressed, kitten. My father doesn't like to be kept waiting."

Reluctantly, I reach for the borrowed clothes. The leggings and sweater slip over my skin easily.

"There's something I need to ask you. Who is Elena Rosewood?"

Damien stills, his expression instantly guarded. "How do you know that name, kitten?"

"When they came for me, one of them said something." I swallow hard, the memory of those terrifying moments flooding back. "He said Lockhart wanted to meet her daughter."

Damien's face gives nothing away.

"Who is she?" I press.

Damien runs a hand through his damp hair. "Elena was a legend among our kind. The only female alpha to ever exist."

"Alpha?" The word feels strange on my tongue. "Like your father?"

"More powerful, some would say." He moves to the window, his back to me as he chooses his next words carefully. "She disappeared twenty-eight years ago along with her mate. Some say they were killed. Others believe they went into hiding to protect something...or someone."

The implication hangs heavy in the air between us. My mouth goes dry.

"You think I'm her daughter." It's not a question. The pieces are clicking into place with terrifying clarity.

"I think it's a possibility we need to consider." Damien turns to face me.

"That's ridiculous. My parents were normal. Ordinary. They ran a hardware store in Eureka, for god's sake. They weren't...wolves on the run."

"Did they ever talk about their past? Their families? Where they came from before Eureka?"

I open my mouth to argue, then close it again. The truth is, they didn't. My parents never talked about the past. Never mentioned grandparents, cousins, or family traditions. When I asked as a child, they'd deflect with gentle smiles and promises to tell me when I was older. A day that never came.

"They were protecting you," Damien says, reading my expression. "If you are her daughter, your bloodline makes you the most valuable female in North America. Wars have been fought over less."

My legs give out, and I sink onto the edge of his bed. The cashmere sweater suddenly feels suffocating against my skin. "I can barely manage my own life, let alone be some kind of...supernatural royalty."

"Your wolf disagrees. She's not ordinary, Karina. Neither are you."

Part of me wants to reject everything he's saying, to cling to the illusion of normalcy I've lived with for twenty-seven years. But the other part—the part that's always felt different, always struggled to contain something wild beneath my skin—recognizes the truth in his words.

Damien kneels before me, his imposing form somehow making the gesture more powerful than submissive. His hands engulf mine, warm and steady.

"If what you're saying is true..." my voice cracks, "then my entire life has been a lie."

"Not a lie," Damien says, his thumb tracing circles on my palm. "A protection. Your parents loved you enough to give up everything—their pack, their status, their very identities—to keep you safe."

Tears sting hot, threatening to spill. "And now they're gone, and I have no idea who I really am."

"You're still Karina," he says firmly. "Nothing changes that. But you're also something more."

"Will you tell your father about who my mother might be?"

Damien's expression hardens. "I have to. We need his protection, and he needs to understand exactly what we're dealing with."

He rises from his kneeling position, towering over me again as he sits beside me on the bed. The mattress dips under his weight, causing me to lean slightly into him. "There's more that you should know. Lockhart has been tracking you. When I got to the warehouse, Lockhart's people were waiting. They knew intimate details about your life, your routine." His jaw clenches. "They've been watching you, Karina. Long before you and I ever met."

I stare at Damien, his words knocking the air from my lungs. "Months? Before we met? But why? What does he want with me?"

"Elena's bloodline carries something unique—the potential to birth female alphas. In our world, that's the equivalent of having a nuclear weapon."

I wrap my arms around myself, suddenly cold despite the cashmere sweater. "So, he wants to...what? Breed me?"

Damien's growl is so deep I feel it vibrate through the

mattress. "He wants to control your bloodline. Any children you bear would strengthen his pack beyond imagination. He'd rise from a third-rate alpha to the most powerful wolf on the West Coast overnight."

The word "children" hits me like a punch to the gut. I hadn't even considered that part of the equation—that this isn't just about me, but about what my body could potentially create. The thought of Lockhart or anyone else viewing me as nothing more than a breeding vessel makes bile rise in my throat.

"I will never let that happen, kitten."

I'm about to respond when a sharp knock cuts through our conversation.

Damien's head snaps toward the door, his entire demeanor shifting instantly from intimate to guarded. "That'll be Gabriel. My father's running out of patience."

"I'm not ready for this."

Damien crosses to me in two strides, tilting my chin up with gentle fingers that belie his strength. "You were born ready for this. You just didn't know it."

The knock comes again, more insistent this time.

"Enter," Damien calls, his hand finding the small of my back as the door swings open.

Gabriel stands in the doorway, his expression carefully neutral. "Alpha Hudson requests your presence. Immediately."

"We're coming."

I follow them through the sprawling mansion, trying to memorize the route as we wind through corridors adorned with artwork that probably costs more than my entire life. Gabriel leads us to the end of a long hallway where double doors loom before us. He knocks once, then pushes them open without waiting for a response.

I hesitate at the threshold, my heart hammering against my ribs. Damien's hand presses gently against my lower back, urging me forward.

"Breathe," he whispers. "Remember who you are."

The problem is, I'm no longer sure who that is.

I step into the study, and my breath catches. The room is expansive, lined with bookshelves that stretch from floor to ceiling. A fire crackles in a stone hearth large enough to roast a small animal. But it's not the opulence that freezes me in place, it's the three figures waiting for us.

In the study, sits his father behind the desk. Alpha Hudson Marek is exactly what I'd expect from the father of a man like Damien—broad-shouldered and imposing even while seated, with gray streaks threading through dark hair that's identical to his son's. His eyes, though, are a piercing blue that seems to cut right through me.

Beside him stands a woman who must be Damien's mother, Helena. She's stunning in a cold, untouchable way—elegantly dressed in what looks like designer clothes, her dark hair swept into a perfect updo without a strand out of place. Her hand rests possessively on her husband's shoulder, and I catch a flash of diamond and platinum on her ring finger that could probably pay off my car and the damages to my apartment.

And then there's his sister, Bella. Younger than Damien by several years but carrying the same fierce presence. Her attention flicks between her brother and me with open curiosity. She's beautiful in a wild way her mother isn't—less polished, more untamed. The resemblance to Damien is immediate in the cut of her jaw and the force of her presence.

"Care to explain to me why you're here, Damien," Hudson growls. He doesn't rise from his seat. "You're exiled." His focus shifts to me, and I fight the urge to step back. The way he studies me is clinical, assessing, like I'm a horse at auction. "Who is this female?"

"This is Karina," Damien says, his hand pressing more firmly against the small of my back. "My mate."

Helena's gasp cuts through the silence, her hand flying to her throat. "You bonded without your father's approval?"

"I wasn't aware I needed permission."

"Don't be insolent," Hudson snaps, rising with a fluid grace that belies his age. He circles the desk, each step deliberate, predatory. "You were sent to Bellandi to learn discipline—not to forget your place in my pack."

I fight the urge to step back as he approaches. Up close, his power is overwhelming—an invisible pressure against my skin, demanding submission. My wolf bristles beneath the surface, refusing to cower despite the alpha's presence.

"The bond's unfinished—you haven't sealed it," Hudson murmurs, eyes gleaming.

"The full moon is tomorrow night," Damien says, his hand never leaving my back.

Hudson narrows his focus on me, the force of his scrutiny pressing like something tangible. "And does she agree to this arrangement? Or did you simply take what you wanted, as usual?"

"I'm right here," I snap before I can stop myself. "You can ask me directly."

The room goes deathly silent. Helena stiffens, her hand tightening around the edge of her chair, while Bella's mouth twitches with what might be suppressed laughter. Damien's fingers dig into my hip in warning, but I don't back down. If I'm going to be thrown to these wolves, I'm not going meekly.

Hudson's expression shifts from surprise to something more calculating. He circles me slowly, like a predator evaluating prey. "She has spirit, I'll give her that, but she's not even close to what we arranged."

"Serena DeLupo was your arrangement, not mine," Damien counters.

Hudson completes his circle, stopping directly in front of me. He's tall—not as tall as Damien but imposing in a different way. Where Damien's power is raw and physical, Hudson's is refined, honed by decades of command.

"What pack are you from?" he demands.

"I don't have a pack."

"Damien, really. You could have at least found

someone with proper lineage," Helena interjects, dripping with disdain.

I feel Damien tense beside me, but before he can respond, Bella steps forward. "Mom, don't be such a snob."

"Come here, girl."

I hesitate, glancing at Damien whose jaw has tightened to granite. His slight nod gives me permission.

I step forward, my legs trembling slightly as I move away from Damien's protective presence.

"It can't be..." Hudson leans in close enough that I can feel his breath on my neck. He inhales deeply, his nostrils flaring as he takes in my scent.

"I'll ask you once more. What pack do you belong to?"

"I told you, I don't have a pack," I repeat.

Hudson doesn't blink as he steps back, his focus following me like a shadow. Then, to my surprise, he turns toward Damien. The room goes utterly still. Even Helena stills her fidgeting, her polished composure cracking as she studies me with sharp, hungry interest.

"Why do you carry Elena Rosewood's scent?" Hudson asks.

"That's impossible," Helena breathes. She stares as though I've sprouted horns. "Elena vanished years ago. She didn't have children. You must be mistaken."

"Am I?" Hudson resumes his slow circle around me, every step deliberate. He stops directly in front of me. "Who are you?"

My throat locks. Every head in the room is turned toward me, their collective attention a crushing weight. There's no wriggling out of this. No polite deflection.

"I don't know."

"Your parents' names," Hudson presses.

I swallow hard, my hands trembling at my sides. "David and Sarah Greene."

Helena's heels strike sharp against the floor as she moves closer, manicured fingers brushing her lips in thought. "Greene?" she repeats softly. "Elena's mate was Marcus Greene."

"Describe your father," Hudson commands.

"Tall. Dark hair. Green eyes. He had a scar on his left hand from when he..." My chest tightens with the memory, sudden and raw. "From when he said he got caught in machinery at work."

Hudson exchanges a look with Helena that sends my stomach plummeting. "He earned that scar protecting Elena during the Blackrock conflict."

A ringing builds in my ears, drowning the room. The floor tilts beneath me, and I reach blindly for stability. My hand finds Damien's arm, his muscles rigid under my grasp—solid and anchoring when everything else feels like it's unraveling.

Hudson's jaw hardens with decision. He strides to his desk, movements sharp with purpose. Without a word, he reaches for the wall behind his chair, lifting down a framed photograph I hadn't noticed before. He carries it back to me with surprising care, his attention locked on me as if waiting for the final confirmation.

"Look," he commands, holding the frame out.

With trembling hands, I take it from him. The photograph is old, the colors faded with time, but the faces staring back at me are unmistakable. A group of wolves stands around a campfire, arms thrown around each other's shoulders, faces bright with laughter. And there, in the middle of the group, are my parents—younger, wilder, happier than I've ever seen them.

My mother's dark curls cascade down her back, her smile fierce and proud as she leans into the man beside her. My father. But not as the quiet hardware store owner I knew. This man stands tall, a visible aura of power radiating from him even in a decades-old photograph.

I gasp, my finger tracing their faces behind the glass. "That's my parents."

"That's Elena and Marcus," Hudson corrects. "Taken the summer before they disappeared."

My mother—Elena—stands at the center of the group, clearly its focal point. The woman in the photograph radiates power in a way that makes my knees weak. She doesn't just stand among the other wolves—she commands them. Her posture, her expression, the way the others seem to gravitate toward her...This isn't just any female wolf. This is an alpha.

There's no denying the resemblance. The same stubborn line of the jaw. The same shape in the face I've seen in the mirror all my life.

It's true. Oh god. I am Elena Rosewood's daughter.

The photograph slips from my numb fingers, hitting the floor with a sharp crack that echoes in the silence. The truth slams into me like a tidal wave, stealing the breath from my lungs. I stumble backward, hip striking Hudson's desk hard enough to jolt me, but the spinning in my head doesn't stop.

Through the haze, I register Damien moving closer, his energy bristling with alarm. I lift a shaking hand to hold him off. If he touches me now, I'll break into pieces I won't be able to put back together.

"Get out," Hudson orders. For a heartbeat, I think he means me. Then I realize his command is aimed at Helena and Bella.

"But Hudson—" Helena starts, only to wither under the sheer force of his stare.

"Out. Now."

Bella lingers a second longer, uncertainty written in the tightness of her mouth, before following her mother to the door. The heavy thud of it closing behind them feels final, like the walls have locked me into a destiny I never asked for.

Karina

Hudson doesn't speak immediately. He retrieves the fallen photograph, examining it with an expression I can't read before carefully placing it on his desk. When he finally turns to me, his eyes have lost some of their coldness.

"You truly didn't know?"

I shake my head, still struggling to breathe normally. "They never told me anything about...this."

Hudson moves to a cabinet against the wall. He pulls out a crystal decanter, pouring amber liquid into three glasses. "Elena was hunted relentlessly after she challenged the old order. Many wanted her dead. Others wanted to leash her. If her intention was to keep you away from this world, it not surprising that she kept this all from you." He hands a glass to Damien, then offers one to me. I take it with shaking fingers. "Despite how much it's stunted you and your wolf."

"Lockhart is picking up where they left off with her mother it seems," Damien remarks. "He's been hunting Karina." He pauses. "That's why we're here. They attempted to abduct her from her apartment and again last night from the Bellandi compound."

"Anselm must be getting sloppy with his security if outsiders were able to breach his walls."

"The Bellandi security protocols aren't what concern me, father. It's Lockhart's obsession with my mate."

"Wouldn't you be obsessed with such a rare female within claw's reach?" Hudson continues, settling into his chair with the glass cradled in his hands. "Lockhart wants power, and more territory. He gets both with her."

"He will *never* have Karina," Damien snarls.

The whiskey burns my throat as I take sip, but I welcome the distraction from the chaos in my mind. "So, what now? Do I spend the rest of my life running?"

"You take up your birthright."

I nearly choke on my second sip. "My what?"

"You are the rightful heir to the Rosewood pack lands—territory that's been disputed since your mother disappeared. Your uncle, Remus, was her successor, but he didn't hold it long. You may very well be the last of the true Rosewood line. Remus died childless. With the right backing, you could take back what's yours."

"I don't want territory."

"Are you rejecting my son? Because he is my heir and will inherit this pack and territory."

I feel Damien's immediate, violent rejection of that idea. His wolf snarls beneath his skin, protective and possessive.

"I'm not rejecting him."

Hudson assesses me with new interest. "So, you accept what you are? What your bloodline means?"

My head spins with too many revelations. Elena Rosewood. Female alpha. Disputed territories. I've spent my entire life running from the wolf inside me, calling her a monster, keeping her caged. What if she's been something else all along—not a curse but a birthright?

"I don't know what I accept yet," I admit, setting the whiskey glass on Hudson's desk with a soft clink. "But I know I won't keep running."

Damien moves closer, his presence steadying me even without physical contact.

"The full moon is tomorrow night," Hudson says, rising from his chair. "If you complete the bond with my son, you'll be under Marek protection. No wolf would dare challenge a pair carrying both our bloodlines."

My jaw tightens. "Is that why you're suddenly fine with me at Damien's side? Because of who my mother was?"

"Don't mistake practicality for acceptance," Hudson replies coldly. "I had plans for my son. Years of negotiations with the DeLupo pack, territory exchanges, political alliances—all of it undone because of you." His gaze pierces through me, weighing my worth against his abandoned ambitions. "But I'm not blind. A Rosewood female bound to my son? That's a power play no alpha in his right mind would turn down."

Damien bristles beside me. "You will take care in how you speak about her."

"Watch your tone," Hudson warns sharply. "I am still your Alpha." His attention snaps back to me. "Yes, this changes everything. Marek and Rosewood united could forge the strongest pack the West Coast has seen in centuries. The wolves you'll create..."

"I'm not a broodmare," I bite out. "I won't be used to churn out some super-pack just because my mother was an alpha."

"You think too small, girl. This isn't about breeding. It's about reclaiming what was stolen when your parents vanished. The Rosewood lands lie fractured, carved up by lesser alphas who fed like vultures. With you as heir, and my son by your side, we could restore the order that should have been."

"What if I don't want any of it? I want Damien, but that's it. I don't need lands or packs. None of that. Just him."

"Then you're a fool," Hudson says bluntly. "Lockhart won't stop hunting you. Neither will the others who want the Rosewood territory through you. You can run, but eventually someone will find you. The question is whether you'll face them as a victim or as the alpha you were born to be."

"I don't know how to be an alpha."

"Neither did your mother. Elena was twenty-three when she first manifested alpha traits. Younger than you are now."

My wolf perks up at this information, pressing closer to my consciousness like she's been waiting for this conversation her entire life. The sensation is so intense it makes me dizzy.

"How do you know so much about my mother?" I ask, sinking into one of the leather chairs facing his desk. My legs won't support me anymore.

Hudson exchanges a look with Damien that I can't interpret. "Because I was there when she challenged the Blackrock Alpha for territory. Watched her tear his throat out with nothing but claws and fury." His stare drifts somewhere far away. "Your mother was magnificent. And terrifying."

I try to picture the woman who made me pancakes every Sunday morning sinking her teeth into someone's throat, and the image won't come. It's like trying to merge two strangers into one body—impossible.

Across from me, Damien studies his father with sharp suspicion, the shift in his posture betraying unease. Hudson, however, seems wrapped in memories of a woman I barely recognize.

"How well did you know my mother?" The question scrapes from my throat before I can stop it.

Hudson blinks, dragged back to the present. For a flicker of a heartbeat, something fragile crosses his face, gone as quickly as it came beneath the impenetrable mask of alpha composure.

"I knew her quite well," he says finally, rolling the amber liquid in his glass before swallowing a mouthful. His next words fall like stones in a pond, rippling outward, disturbing everything I thought I knew. "Better than most. She was meant to be mine. Before your father came strolling in with his idealistic notions and pretty words. I was...sidelined."

Hudson Marek wanted my mother. Still wants her, judging by the bitterness lacing every syllable.

"Our families had an arrangement," he continues, his gaze roaming over my features like he's cataloguing every hint of Elena he can find. "The Rosewood and Marek bloodlines were to be united through marriage. The match was decided before either of us came of age."

I stare at him, the truth clicking into place. The bitterness in his words isn't about land or politics—it's about my mother. Hudson Marek loved her, and she chose someone else.

"But she didn't want you," I say before I can stop myself. "She wanted my father."

His jaw clenches, a muscle ticking hard beneath his skin. "Marcus was a nobody. A beta with pretty words and reckless ideas. He filled her head with nonsense about challenging the old ways, about females leading as equals."

The disdain in his tone makes my blood heat. I see it clearly now—the pride she wounded, the jealousy he's nurtured for decades. It's not just old politics. It's an obsession.

"Those 'reckless ideas' worked for them," I shoot back, steadier now, defending parents I barely had time to know. "They loved each other. They had me."

Hudson's composure cracks, just slightly. "And look how that ended," he snaps. "Both of them dead. Their land splintered. Their daughter raised blind to her own bloodline."

Beside me, Damien stiffens. The air shifts with him, heavy and lethal, like the seconds before a storm breaks.

"Enough." His words slice through the room, cold and final. The effect is immediate—Hudson falls silent, his authority undercut by the force of his son's fury. "You don't get to speak about her parents again."

"Watch yourself, boy—"

"No." Damien steps forward, placing himself between me and his father. "We didn't come here for your approval or your politics. We came here because Karina is being hunted, and I need to keep her safe."

My heart hammers against my ribs as I watch the standoff between father and son.

"You forget your place," Hudson snarls, rising from his chair.

"And you forget yours. She is mine to protect. Mine to defend. Not your second chance at securing a Rosewood."

Hudson's nostrils flare as he scents the challenge in the air. "You dare—"

"I dare everything for her." Damien's hand finds mine, his grip warm and steady. "We're done here."

I squeeze his hand back, drawing strength from his touch as the tension between father and son crackles like electricity in the air. For a moment, I think Hudson might actually lunge at Damien.

"You would choose her over your family? Over your pack? Over everything I've built for you?"

"Without hesitation," Damien replies.

My wolf stirs beneath my skin, recognizing and savoring his loyalty. For the first time since this nightmare began, I feel something other than dread and uncertainty. A fierce, protective joy that this man, this predator who intimidates everyone else, has chosen me above all.

"Then you're a bigger fool than her mother was," Hudson spits. "Very well. Take her to the east wing. She'll stay there until the full moon."

"She stays with me," Damien counters.

"You know our traditions. It's better for her to be sequestered. Kept under lock and key."

"I don't give a fuck about traditions." Damien's grip tightens on mine. "She doesn't leave my sight. Not with Lockhart's people still out there. Where she goes, I go. End of fucking story."

Hudson's face flushes red, his hands clenching into fists at his sides. For a heartbeat, I think he might actually strike his son. The alpha power radiating from both men makes my wolf whimper and press closer to my ribs, recognizing the danger crackling between them.

"Fine," Hudson says through gritted teeth. "But you'll both be present for the pack meeting tomorrow night. Before the full moon rises, every wolf in this territory needs to see her. To understand what we're dealing with."

My stomach drops. "Pack meeting?"

"You think we can hide who you are forever? Word will spread. It always does. Better to control the narrative from the beginning."

"She's not ready for that," Damien growls.

"She better get ready fast," Hudson snaps back. "Because whether she likes it or not, the other packs will take notice. They'll want to test her strength, challenge her right to the Rosewood territory."

"I never said I wanted—"

"It doesn't matter what you want anymore. You carry that bloodline whether you accept it or not. Others will force the issue."

Damien's hand finds the small of my back, his touch both protective and grounding. "We're done here," he tells his father.

Hudson doesn't try to stop us as Damien guides me toward the door. Just as we reach the threshold, Hudson calls out.

"Karina."

I pause, turning to face the man who might have been my father in another life.

"Your mother was the strongest wolf I've ever

known," he says. "Remember that when you face what's coming."

As we step out of his father's study, the world around me blurs into a haze. The journey back to Damien's room feels surreal, each step heavy with the weight of what I've just learned. When he finally shuts the door behind us, the soft click resonates like a final note, sealing away my old life. I stand frozen in the center of the plush carpet, its fibers warm beneath my bare feet. My arms instinctively wrap around myself, as if trying to hold together the fragments of my shattered reality. A suffocating silence envelops us, and I find myself unable to move, speak, or even draw a proper breath.

"Karina..." Damien approaches slowly, like I'm a wounded animal that might bolt. "Talk to me, kitten."

I open my mouth, but no words come. Just a small, broken sound that doesn't even sound human. My legs give out without warning, and I sink to my knees on the carpet, my entire body trembling.

The dam breaks.

"It's all a lie," I gasp between sobs that tear from my chest with such force they hurt. "My whole life. Everything I thought I knew about myself, about them—" I press my fist against my mouth, trying to hold back the tears.

But they won't stop coming. I bury my face in my hands, shoulders shaking. "They loved me enough to give up everything—their names, their pack, their power—

and I called my wolf a monster. I hated the very thing they died protecting."

Damien drops to his knees beside me, his frame folding around mine like a shield. His arms encircle me, pulling me against his chest where I can hear his heart beating steady and strong beneath my ear.

"They didn't die for nothing. They gave you twenty-seven years of safety. Twenty-seven years to grow strong enough to face this."

"I'm not strong enough." The admission scrapes from my throat, raw and broken. "I can barely handle my own wolf, let alone lead a pack or reclaim territory or whatever the hell everyone expects from me."

His arms tighten around me, firm but careful. "You survived last night. You fought off five trained wolves with nothing but a kitchen knife and instinct. That's not weakness, kitten. That's strength. That's you and your wolf refusing to die."

I pull back, blinking through the blur of tears until I can meet his eyes. "Your father was in love with my mother."

"I know," he says quietly. "I could smell it on him the moment he saw you. It wasn't just memory—it was grief. He's been carrying it for years."

"Is that why he sent your mother and sister out of the room?"

Damien's jaw flexes. "My father rarely includes them in pack business. He never has. To him—and to most of the older alphas—Lunas exist to smile at ceremonies and keep quiet while the men make decisions. My mother accepted that a long time ago. She's lived her life as an ornament, not a partner. She knows he's never loved her." His voice lowers, softer but edged with something bitter. "It's the role she was raised to play. And he was content to let her stay there."

I swallow hard. "So my mother...she threatened that."

He nods once. "Elena didn't fit the mold. She questioned, challenged, pushed. She became an alpha in her own right. Centuries of a male alphas upended by one female who dared to ascend."

My chest tightens, a strange mix of pride and sorrow twisting through me. "And now me."

His gaze finds mine again, steady, certain. "You won't be anyone's ornament either. Not mine. Not anyone's. You'll stand beside me in every decision, every fight, every breath of this life."

He says it like a vow, not of possession, but of equality. Of defiance.

And for a moment, I understand why my mother terrified men like his father. Because equality and love, in a world like ours, was the greatest rebellion of all.

"What happens now? What do I do with all of this?"

"Whatever you want."

"That's the problem. I don't know what I want anymore." I pull away slightly, needing space to think. "Yesterday, I was just trying to survive you. Now the daughter and heir to disputed territory, with an alpha who wants to breed me, and another who wants to use me to fulfill some decades-old political alliance."

"You're more than your bloodline, Karina. You always have been."

"Am I? Because it feels like that's all anyone sees now." I stand up, moving to the window that overlooks the sprawling Marek compound. Pack members move about their daily business below, unaware that their world is about to be upended by my existence. "Your father doesn't want me—he wants what I represent. The chance to finally get what he thinks he deserves."

Damien's reflection appears in the glass behind me, his large build blocking out everything else.

"I'm just a vessel to all of them. A means to power."

Damien reaches out, grasping my arm, and spinning me on my heels before pulling me against his chest. "Not to me, kitten. I marked you before I knew who you were, Karina."

I lean into his touch, desperate for the connection. "I'm scared, Damien. I don't know how to be what everyone expects."

"Then don't be. Be what you want. Take what you want. The rest will follow."

"What if what I want is just you?"

"Then take me. The rest of it—the politics, the territory, the fucking bloodlines—none of it matters if it's not what you want."

"But your father—"

"Fuck my father." His thumb traces my lower lip.

"Fuck Lockhart. Fuck all of them. I've spent my entire life being what everyone else needed me to be. The heir. The enforcer. The Reaper." His forehead presses against mine, our breath mingling in the space between us. "The only thing I want to be now is yours."

Something breaks loose inside me—a dam of uncertainty and hesitation crumbling with his words. I surge forward, capturing his mouth with mine, my hands fisting in his shirt to pull him closer. This time, I'm the one taking control. I'm the one demanding.

He responds instantly, a growl rumbling from deep in his chest as his arms encircle my waist, lifting me against him until my feet barely touch the floor. His mouth is hungry, desperate, taking everything I offer and demanding more.

"I want you," I gasp against his lips. "Just you. Nothing else."

His hands slide down to grip my thighs, hoisting me up against him as if I weigh nothing. My legs wrap around his waist instinctively, my body knowing what it wants even if my mind is still reeling from everything that's happened. His mouth moves to my neck, teeth grazing the sensitive skin where his mark already burns.

"Are you sure?" he growls against my throat. "Once I start, I won't be able to stop."

"I don't want you to stop," I whisper, arching into him as his hands tighten on my thighs. "I need this. I need you."

That's all it takes. With a sound more animal than

human, he carries me to the bed and lays me down with unexpected gentleness before lowering himself over me. His presence presses me into the mattress, a grounding force in a storm-tossed sea—the only thing keeping me from drifting away entirely.

His mouth finds mine again, hungry and demanding, as his hands slide beneath the borrowed sweater. I gasp as his calloused fingers meet bare skin, tracing patterns of fire up my sides until they reach the underside of my breasts.

"You're wearing too many clothes," I pant against his lips, tugging at his shirt with desperate fingers.

He sits back on his heels, yanking his shirt over his head in one fluid motion that makes the muscles in his abdomen ripple. My breath catches as I take in the full sight of him—the broad expanse of his chest, the intricate tattoos that cover his torso, the raw power evident in every inch of his physique. My fingers reach out of their own accord, tracing the lines of ink that swirl across his skin.

"Your turn," he growls, his hands finding the hem of my borrowed sweater.

I lift my arms, letting him pull the soft material over my head. The cool air of the bedroom kisses my bare skin, my nipples hardening instantly. I should feel vulnerable, exposed, but all I feel is wanted.

"Fucking flawless," he says, his large hands cupping my breasts with reverent possession. His thumbs circle over my nipples, pulling a gasp from my lips that melts into a moan when he replaces one thumb with his mouth.

The wet stroke of his tongue sends electricity coursing through my body. I arch into him, my fingers tangling in his dark hair as he laves and sucks at the sensitive peak. His other hand continues its exploration, tracing patterns down my ribs, across my stomach, to the waistband of the borrowed leggings.

"These need to go," he says against my skin, hooking his fingers under the elastic.

I lift my hips, helping him slide the leggings down my legs until I'm left in nothing but a pair of simple cotton panties. His attention devours me like I'm his last meal as he runs his hands up my bare thighs. I shiver under his touch, my body already responding to him in ways I can't control.

"I've dreamt of having you like this. Spread out beneath me. Mine for the taking."

"Then take me," I whisper, reaching for him. "I don't want to wait anymore."

In one swift movement, he hooks his fingers into my panties and tears them clean off me. The sound of ripping fabric fills the air as the shredded cotton lands somewhere across the room.

"Sorry," he growls, not looking sorry at all. "I'll buy you more."

I laugh breathlessly, my heart hammering against my ribs. "I think I can forgive you."

His large hands gently push my thighs further apart,

and I feel completely exposed. Instead of feeling vulnerable, I feel powerful.

"You're still wearing too much," I say, reaching for the button of his jeans.

He lets me work the button free, but when I try to hook my fingers in the waistband of his jeans, he captures my wrists, pinning them gently above my head.

"Not yet." His free hand trails down my body with deliberate slowness. "I want to taste you first."

My breath catches as his meaning becomes clear.

"Trust me," he says, pressing a kiss to the inside of my wrist where my pulse thrums wildly. "Let me worship you the way you deserve."

His mouth begins a torturous journey down my body. Kissing and nipping at my throat, lavishing attention on my breasts until I'm writhing beneath him, then moving lower across my ribs, my stomach. When he settles between my thighs, his broad shoulders force my legs wider, and I think I might die from anticipation.

The first touch of his tongue against my most sensitive flesh makes me cry out, my back arching off the mattress. He groans against me, the vibration sending shockwaves through my system.

"So fucking sweet," he growls between long, languid strokes that have me gasping his name. "I could spend hours between your thighs."

I lose myself in the sensation—his mouth working me with single-minded devotion, his hands gripping my hips to hold me steady as I writhe beneath him. The tension coiling in my core builds to an unbearable peak as his tongue works against me with devastating precision. My fingers tangle in his hair, holding him to me as waves of pleasure crash through my system.

"Damien, I can't—" My words dissolve into a broken moan as he increases the pressure, his mouth relentless in its pursuit of my release.

"Give it to me," he rasps against my thigh, his breath hot, voice low and rough like gravel dragged over velvet. "Every last fucking drop."

The demand rips through me like a live wire, and I unravel, body seizing, breath punched from my lungs as pleasure crashes into me hard and fast. My vision whites out, hips jerking against his mouth as my orgasm tears through me, fierce and unrelenting. I'm trembling, over-stimulated, and wrung out, every nerve stripped raw.

Through the haze, I feel intense satisfaction rolling off him. He licks through the aftershocks with cruelty, drawing it out until I'm a twitching mess beneath him.

When he finally pulls back, his mouth is slick, his chin wet, and his eyes burn like he just won a war. He prowls up my body. His mouth crashes against mine, tongue slick with my taste, and it makes my stomach clench all over again.

"I'm not done with you," I breathe against his lips, reaching for his jeans. My fingers find the button, and this time, he doesn't stop me. Doesn't speak. Just holds still like he wants to see how far I'll go, how desperate I'll get.

I shove the denim down his hips. He lifts, granting silent permission. The thin black briefs do nothing to disguise the sheer size of him—thick, flushed, already straining.

My mouth goes dry and he doesn't move. Just lets me take him in.

"Second thoughts?" he asks, the sound roughened by restraint.

This powerful man, this killer who terrifies entire packs, is worried about my reaction to him.

"Never," I breathe, cupping his face with both hands. "I want you, Damien. All of you."

Something breaks in his expression, raw emotion flooding his features before he crushes his mouth to mine. The kiss is desperate as if he's trying to pour everything he can't say into the connection between our lips.

I feel him position himself at my entrance, the thick head of him pressing against my slick heat. My breath catches as he begins to push forward slowly, giving my body time to adjust to his size.

"Breathe, kitten," he rasps, the tension rolling off him as if he's a breath away from losing control.

I manage a nod, focusing on the brutal, exquisite stretch as he sinks into me, inch by slow inch. It burns—in the best possible way—like my body was forged for this, for him. My wolf arches inside me, thrilled, greedy for every shard of pleasure and possession. This isn't just sex. It's a binding of flesh and soul.

When he's fully sheathed, we freeze. The air

between us crackles, thick and wild, as if the bond itself is a living thing clawing under my skin. I can *feel* his restraint, the need straining at its leash, begging to be unleashed.

"Move," I breathe, tilting my hips in invitation. The drag of him inside me rips a desperate sound from my throat.

He withdraws, slow and measured, only to thrust back with a force that steals my breath. Every stroke is precise, each one feeding my hunger but never quite satisfying it.

I want the beast.

"More," I bite out, nails raking down his back. "I'm not glass. Stop holding back."

The tension snaps. A guttural sound rumbles through his chest as his grip clamps down on my hips, holding me in place. Then he moves. Hard. Relentless. Each thrust drives me into the mattress like he's branding his presence me, like his body is the only language he needs to speak.

"You want more?" he growls, breath hot against my ear. "Then take it. Take every inch until you're too sore to stand and too full to think."

His pace turns punishing, brutal in its intensity.

"I'm going to fuck you so deep you'll still feel me tomorrow. So every step you take reminds you who owns this perfect little pussy."

The headboard slams against the wall, the sound a savage rhythm. My body sings for him, made to be used like this. Claimed. Worshipped. Broken apart and remade in his hands.

"I'll put my cum so deeply inside you, kitten," he grits, "my scent will soak into your bones."

"Oh gods," I moan.

"When you cry out kitten, the only thing I want you to praise is me. You're mine," he growls against my throat, his breath hot as sin, his teeth grazing over the tender skin. "Say it."

"Yours," I gasp, my nails digging into his shoulders hard enough to break skin as the pressure builds inside me like a live wire ready to snap. "And you're mine."

That does it. His rhythm falters, the next thrust landing deep and brutal.

"Fuck," he grits out.

The rough honesty in his voice sparks through me, setting every nerve alight. My legs lock around his hips, drawing him in, chasing the closeness like it's the only thing keeping me grounded. I want him completely. His strength, his warmth, the ache that burns in all the best ways.

The second orgasm coils tight and sharp, riding the edge of pain and pleasure. Every thrust punches a ragged sound from my throat.

"Damien—" I pant, barely holding on.

"I feel it," he snarls, fingers bruising my hips as he drives into me harder. "I feel your cunt choking on my cock, begging to be filled. So greedy."

He leans in close, teeth dragging across my jaw.

"You want to be bred, don't you? Stuffed so full you'll drip with me for days. You want the whole fucking pack to smell me on you."

I cry out, my body shattering violently around him. Fire explodes outward, and the connection—it doesn't just flare, it detonates.

He roars, teeth sinking into the mark at my neck, tearing it open with a brutal bite that sends a surge of blinding white pain-pleasure racing down my spine. His hips drive forward one last time, burying himself to the hilt as release crashes through him in hot, unrelenting waves. Each pulse sears like fire, branding me from the inside out.

His body collapses over mine, still trembling, chest heaving against my breasts, but his hold never loosens. One hand tangled in my hair. The other still gripping my hip like I might vanish if he lets go.

"Mine," he breathes again, lower this time. Fierce. Final.

And this time, I don't just say it back.

I drag my nails down his spine and *bite*.

Hard.

He freezes—just for a second. A low, stunned sound rips from his throat, half growl, half moan, and then he's moving again, like I flipped some hidden switch. His hips roll, grinding into me, and I feel him still thick and pulsing inside, not softening at all.

My body is wrecked and trembling, but the hunger hasn't faded. It's worse now—sharpened by the taste of him, the burn of his teeth still fresh in my skin, the way his cum still leaks slowly out of me.

"You're not done. I can feel it."

His head lifts, hair falling into his face as he looks down at me like a man possessed. His lips are red, and his chin is still smeared with the mess he made of me earlier. That mouth curls into a wicked grin.

He pulls out slowly, watching the way I whimper and arch without shame. Then he slides back in with one brutal thrust.

The sharp, overstimulated edge makes me cry out again—but I don't beg him to stop.

I *can't*.

"I just filled you," he growls, fucking me slow and deep now, each stroke filthy and reverent. "You feel that? That ache? That's mine. That's your body remembering who the fuck it belongs to."

"Damien," I gasp again, delirious from it. My nails claw down his back. "I want all of it. I want everything."

"Oh, kitten," he laughs, panting into my neck. "You'll get everything. Every drop. Every inch. I'll fuck you so full of me that your body forgets it ever belonged to anyone else. I'll fuck you until you forget your own damn name."

His pace picks up, wet slaps and ragged breathing filling the room. The sheets twist beneath us. The headboard slams into the wall again.

But all I can feel is *him*.

His cock pounding into me with savage intensity. My

body building toward a third orgasm, stretched thin and aching for it.

"When I take you under the full moon, I will make you take every drop until you're swollen with it. Until every wolf in the territory knows you're mine."

And gods help me...I *want that.*

Pleasure crashes through me, blinding and all-consuming. I feel his body tense, every muscle drawn tight as he spills inside me again—hot, endless, claiming me down to my soul.

His mouth is still at my neck, teeth sinking deep as he bites hard—*too* hard—and something shifts.

What the fuck?

I hear the words clearly, though Damien's mouth is still latched onto my neck, his teeth breaking skin as he marks me permanently.

"What?" I gasp, the dual sensation of his climax and the voice in my head making me dizzy.

Damien pulls back, eyes wide with shock as he stares down at me. His lips haven't moved, but I can still hear him—feel him—inside my mind.

Can you hear me?

I nod my answer.

Can you hear me?

He shakes his head, still buried deep inside me, our bodies joined in every possible way. "The mating bond," he breathes. "It's complete."

I reach up to touch the place where his teeth broke my skin. The wound burns hot, pulsing in rhythm with my heartbeat. When my fingers come away, they are streaked with blood and a silvery substance that shimmers in the light. "But you said we couldn't complete it until the full moon."

"Moon's blessing..." Damien's voice comes out rough, almost reverent. The faint glow along my fingers reflects in his eyes, silver and sharp. "It shouldn't be possible. This kind of seal, without the full moon, without the ritual, it's something out of the old stories."

I blink up at him, my pulse still wild. "What stories?"

"When I was young," he says slowly, "my grandmother used to tell me about bonds so rare the Moon Goddess herself intervened. She called them true mates. Two souls cut from the same breath of the moon. It's said their wolves recognize each other instantly, no matter rank, bloodline, or pack. But that kind of connection..." He shakes his head, half-laughing under his breath. "I thought it was a fairytale. Every wolf does."

The bond hums between us, alive, pulling tighter with each heartbeat. I can feel everything inside him. His pulse syncs with mine until I can't tell whose heart is beating faster.

"So we're..." I try to speak, but the words catch in my throat.

"Bound. Completely. This isn't just instinct or proximity. It's the Goddess's mark. No one can undo it. Not my father. Not Lockhart. Not anyone."

His thumb lingers, the glow fading slowly between us but the bond thrumming stronger, steady as breath. "I used to think true mates were just something elders said to make the bond sound holy," he admits quietly. "Now I know why they feared it. You can't control something the Goddess claims for herself."

Relief floods me so completely that it blurs my vision. In a world where everything else has been taken from me—my identity, my past, my sense of self—this connection is the one thing that cannot be stolen.

"I can feel you," I say softly, reaching up to touch his face. "Not just physically. I can feel you inside me. Your thoughts, your emotions..."

He turns his face to press a kiss against my palm.

I close my eyes, focusing on the sensation. It's like having another heartbeat alongside my own—steady, powerful, undeniable. Where before I felt his emotions as vague impressions, now they flow through me with crystal clarity. His fierce, protective love that burns so bright it almost hurts to feel it.

"I thought it would happen tomorrow," I murmur, tracing my fingers the mark on my neck. It feels different now—settled, permanent.

"So did I." Damien shifts his weight, carefully pulling out of me before gathering me against his chest. The physical separation doesn't diminish our mental connection at all. If anything, it grows stronger as he cradles me against him. "This type of bond doesn't follow normal rules. They're governed by something older than pack law."

I curl into him, my body still trembling with aftershocks. For the first time in what feels like forever, I feel more like myself than I ever have. The future is still uncertain, the danger far from over—but in his arms, I find something solid to hold onto. Something real.

We lie in silence, the kind that doesn't demand to be filled. Outside, the wind rustles through the trees, and somewhere in the distance, a wolf howls.

The sound doesn't frighten me anymore.

Because I'm not alone.

And I never will be again.

Damien

We've spent the entire day in my room. Fucking and sleeping. We've claimed each other in every sense. Karina's scent has seeped into every inch of the room—into me, too. Wolf and man both satisfied but never sated. Over and over again until her body couldn't take it anymore. She fell asleep hours ago in my arms just as the sun began to set.

For hours, I lie awake. Unable to close my eyes for even a single second for fear that she will just disappear. That the last few days were a daydream. Afraid that I will wake up and none of this was real. Even now, watching the sunrise paint gold across Karina's sleeping face, I'm unable to look away, The world could be ending around us, and I would not notice. Maybe it is.

I brush a strand of dark hair from her cheek, my fingers trembling slightly. Even this small touch sends ripples through our connection, echoing back to me in waves of contentment that aren't entirely mine. The silver mark on her neck gleams in the early light—proof that the impossible has happened. True mates.

My wolf paces beneath my skin, no longer restless but watchful, protective. He's finally at peace after a lifetime of searching for something I didn't even know was missing.

"I will burn the fucking world down before I let anyone touch you," I whisper, though she can't hear me.

But she can feel me. Even in sleep, I sense her consciousness brushing against mine—a feather-light touch that makes my chest ache with something I've never felt before. Is this what it means to be whole? This certainty that part of my soul now lives outside my body, wrapped in her skin?

Karina sighs in her sleep, turning toward me like a flower seeking the sun. The sheet slips down, revealing the curve of her shoulder, the gentle slope of her breast. My body responds instantly, hardening with want, but I make no move to wake her. She needs the rest after everything her body has endured.

A soft knock at my door breaks the morning quiet. I'm up instantly, my body moving with predatory silence as I slip from the bed without disturbing her. The knock comes again, more insistent this time.

I pull on a pair of jeans and pad barefoot to the door,

cracking it open just wide enough to see Gabriel standing in the hallway. His expression is carefully neutral, but I catch the tension in his shoulders.

"What?" I growl.

"Your father requests your presence. Immediately." Gabriel tries to peer past me into the room, but I block his view with my body. "There's been a development."

Ice floods my veins. "What kind of development?"

"Lockhart's people were spotted at the southern border an hour ago. They're requesting a meeting."

My wolf snarls beneath my skin, every protective instinct flaring to life. "Tell my father I'll be there in ten minutes."

Gabriel nods and disappears down the hallway. I close the door and turn back to find Karina awake, watching me with sleepy concern.

"What's wrong?" she asks, her voice husky from sleep.

I cross back to the bed, sitting on the edge beside her, my hand finding her bare thigh beneath the sheet.

"Lockhart's people are at our border," I tell her, watching her face carefully. "They want to meet."

"They found us."

"They found the territory. That doesn't mean they found you." I lean down, pressing my forehead against hers. Through our connection, I push waves of calm toward her, trying to ease the panic I feel building in her chest. "You're safe here. This compound has defenses Lockhart can't breach."

"Then why do you look terrified?"

Because I am. The admission sits heavy in my throat, but I can't lie to her.

"Because my father will want to use this as an opportunity," I say finally. "He'll want to parade you in front of Lockhart, show him what he can't have."

Karina sits up, the sheet pooling around her waist. I'm momentarily distracted by how beautiful she looks in the morning light.

"Maybe that's not such a bad idea," she says quietly.

My wolf snarls at the thought. "Absolutely fucking not."

"Think about it, Dam—"

I cut her off before she can finish that line of thinking, my hand sliding up to cup her face. "No. Whatever you're about to suggest, the answer is no."

"I want to help."

"You can. By staying here. By staying safe while I deal with this."

I shift away from her, trudging toward my closet. I quickly pull on a pair of pants and grab a shirt, only to return to find Karina perched on the side of the bed.

"Where are you going?"

"To tell my father that his political games end now." I pull a black shirt over my head, the fabric stretching across muscles still tender from our lovemaking. "Lockhart can request all the meetings he wants. He's not getting within a mile of you."

When I turn, she's standing beside the bed, the sheet

wrapped around her like armor. "He's here for me. I'm involved whether you like it or not." She moves toward me, her bare feet silent on the carpet. "He can't take me by force."

I want to argue, but she's right.

"That doesn't mean I'm letting you anywhere near him."

She reaches me, her free hand coming up to rest against my chest.

"You're not *letting* me do anything," she says quietly. "I'm choosing."

My wolf rages against her idea, desperate to lock her away somewhere safe where no one can find her. The dormant alpha inside of her is waking up. Gods help me.

"This isn't about being allowed. This is about keeping you safe."

"I know." Her fingers trace the tattoo peeking from beneath my collar. "But I can't hide forever, Damien. Not from who I am. Not from what I am."

"I need to get dressed," she says, glancing down at the sheet wrapped around her body.

"Wear something of mine." The possessive request slips out before I can stop it. I want Lockhart's people to see her draped in my scent.

She nods, understanding the strategy without me having to explain. The sheet falls away as she moves toward my closet, and I force myself to look away. If I watch her naked form any longer, we won't make it to my father's office, and Lockhart's people will be the least of our problems.

"Ten minutes," I remind her. "I'll be back to escort you."

I slip out before she can respond, closing the door firmly behind me. The hallway feels cold after the warmth of her presence. My wolf hates every step that takes me away from her.

The compound buzzes with activity as I make my way toward my father's study. Pack members move with purpose, weapons visible at their sides. My father's elite guard stands at attention near every entrance, their faces grim with anticipation. Word travels fast in wolf packs—everyone knows something is about to happen.

Gabriel waits outside my father's door, his expression carefully neutral as I approach. "He's been asking for you."

I shove through the heavy oak doors without waiting for permission. My father sits behind his desk, maps spread across its surface like battle plans.

"Damien." He doesn't look surprised by my entrance, though his jaw tightens at my lack of protocol. "I trust you've heard about our...visitors."

"I've heard." I don't sit, preferring to loom over his desk with my hands braced against the polished wood. "And I'm telling you now—Karina doesn't leave this compound."

Hudson's laugh is sharp, humorless. "You forget

yourself, boy. This is still my territory. My pack. My decisions."

"She's mine. Decisions where she's concerned are not yours to question."

"Is she?" His stare pins me, heavy with challenge. "The full moon is still—"

"It's done." The words drop like a blade. "Claimed and recognized by the Moon Goddess herself."

The air tightens between us. I watch my father's face shift—shock hardening into disbelief, then twisting into a hunger that sets my wolf on edge.

"Prove it."

I tug the collar of my shirt down, exposing the raw symbol burning against my skin. It's changed since yesterday—darker, more defined, alive with a faint glow that declares exactly what I've become. For the first time in my life, my father doesn't look unshakable. He looks afraid.

I let the fabric fall back into place, hiding the evidence from his lingering stare. "Is that enough for you?" My voice comes out low, steady. "She's under my protection now. Not yours. Not the pack's. Mine."

He circles his desk with deliberate steps. I can almost see the wheels turning—how this changes his plans, his ambitions, his schemes to use Karina to reclaim Rosewood territory. Always moving pieces into place. But that ends here.

"This is... unexpected," he admits. "But it changes

nothing about our current situation. Lockhart's demanding to see her."

"And you're going to tell him to fuck off."

His laugh cuts sharp as a whip. "You think it's that simple?"

"Make it that simple or lose your only heir and everything that comes with him."

"You insolent child," he snarls.

"Threaten me again," I growl, stepping closer, "and see what happens."

"You forget who you're speaking to."

"No. You forget who you're speaking to. I'm not the boy you sent away to be broken and rebuilt. I'm the Reaper. I've killed for less."

His nostrils flare, catching the shift in my scent—the transformation from son to predator. For a heartbeat, he wavers. Then his Alpha nature rises, rigid and unyielding.

"You would challenge me? In my own territory?"

"If you come for her again, I won't just challenge you. I'll put you down and burn this legacy to the ground."

The study door creaks open behind me, her scent rushing in before her words.

"That won't be necessary."

I turn, breath catching despite the fury in my veins. Karina stands in the doorway, wrapped in one of my black shirts. The fabric hangs loose, but the slip from her shoulder bares the silver mark glowing against her skin.

"I told you to wait in my room," I growl, but she doesn't even glance my way.

"Alpha Hudson." Her stride is steady, her shoulders squared. Authority edges every movement now. "I understand Lockhart is requesting a meeting."

My father inhales sharply, nostrils flaring as her scent fills the room—me woven into her, layered with the sweet musk of a sealed bond. The air hums with it, and my wolf preens with satisfaction even as I fight the urge to drag her behind me.

"Indeed," Hudson says carefully, weighing every word. "Though I fail to see how this concerns you."

"It concerns me because I'm what he wants," Karina replies, moving further into the room despite my silent command to stay back. "And I think it's time we gave it to him."

"No." I move between her and my father, my body forming a barrier she'll have to go through to reach him. "Whatever you're thinking, the answer is fucking no."

"You haven't heard what I'm thinking yet."

"I don't need to hear it. I can feel it." I turn to face her fully, my hands finding her shoulders. "You want to meet with him. To face him down like some kind of alpha challenge."

Her chin lifts, and there it is—that stubborn defiance that makes me want to lock her in a tower and throw away the key. "Maybe that's exactly what this is."

"Over my dead body."

"That can be arranged," my father interjects. "If you continue to defy me in my own territory."

I whirl toward him, my wolf surging so close to the surface that my vision edges with gold. "Try me, old man."

"Stop." Karina's hand finds my arm, her touch immediately calming the beast beneath my skin. "This isn't helping anyone."

"Neither is throwing yourself at Lockhart's mercy like a fucking martyr, Karina."

"Listen to me," she says. "Lockhart wants me. Not you. Not your pack. He wants to use my bloodline to build his empire."

"Which is exactly why you're not going anywhere near him," I snarl, moving to block her path to my father's desk.

She sidesteps me, and for a split second her wolf ripples through the movement—no longer cornered, but alert, sharp, ready. "But he can't have any of those things now, can he?"

My father leans forward, the calculation in him stirring. "To my knowledge, no one has ever rejected such a bond. In theory, you are beyond his reach."

"Don't feed her ideas," I snap, but Karina doesn't so much as glance at me.

"You said it yourself, Damien—he's been watching me for years. Building his fantasy, deciding what I could bring him, the power he could amass through me." She steps closer to Hudson's desk, every instinct in me screaming to pull her back, but I hold still as her defiance burns brighter. "Now imagine his frustration when he realizes all of it is gone. That dream dies here, and he'll want blood for it. Yours. Mine. This pack. Maybe even Bellandis."

My father tilts his head, considering her words with a kind of detached intrigue. "She makes a fair point, son."

"Stay out of this, father." My teeth clench as I step forward, bracing against the tension snapping through the air. "This isn't your conversation. It's between her and me."

"No, it's not, Damien. This isn't just about me. I am a box Lockhart wants to check to secure his power base, and he wants me so desperately, he's willing to enter two different alphas' territories to get me. He's not going to stop." Karina steps forward, her eyes never leaving mine. "Use me as bait. Let Lockhart think he still has a chance. Draw him out and end this once and for all."

"Absolutely fucking not."

"Actually," my father interjects, "that might be worth discussing."

I whirl on him, ready to rip his throat out, but he holds up a hand.

"Think about it, Damien. If Lockhart believes she's available, he'll be less cautious. More vulnerable. We could set a trap that would eliminate this threat permanently."

"And put her directly in harm's way? Have you lost your fucking mind?" I pace the room like a caged predator, unease crawling under my skin. "He'll notice that her scent has changed. Any wolf with half a nose would catch it instantly. Not to mention my mark."

My father leans back in his chair, fingers steepled beneath his chin as if he's already ten steps ahead. "Not necessarily. Not if we're deliberate about where the meeting happens. Neutral ground, so pack law holds. Somewhere dense with other scents—enough to smother what she carries for now. And she's still in her cycle. That alone could be enough to muddy the trail. Long enough for us to draw Lockhart in... and finish this."

"Crimson Howl," Karina says suddenly.

My head snaps toward her.

"Think about it," she continues. "The club will be packed with wolves from different packs. Everyone wears masks. The air is thick with pheromones, alcohol, and sex. If there's anywhere Lockhart's senses might be compromised, it's there."

My father nods slowly, appreciation dawning on his face. "The girl's smarter than she looks."

"Don't call her *girl*," I growl automatically, but my mind is already racing through the possibilities. The club will be crowded. Masks will obscure her identity until the moment of our choosing. The cacophony of scents will make it difficult to isolate the true mate bond unless someone is specifically looking for it.

"I don't like it."

"You don't have to like it," Karina says. "You just have to trust me."

"I trust you. It's everything else I don't trust."

Karina crosses the room to me. She steps into my space, her arms wrapping around my waist, and I instinctively pull her against me, my body recognizing its other half.

"If you want the threat to my safety gone, this is the only way. We have to play on my weaknesses to make this work. Lockhart thinks I am naive, and let's be honest, I am, but we can use that."

Her words sink into me like stones in still water. I hate that she's right. I hate that she's willing to put herself at risk. Most of all, I hate that I can't think of a better alternative.

"It's too risky."

"So, you'd rather hide behind these walls until he storms them. Hurting your pack in his pursuit of me?" She pulls back just enough to look up at me. "We will have the advantage if we do this my way."

My father clears his throat, reminding me of his presence. I've been so focused on Karina that I'd almost forgotten he was there. "She has a point, Damien. If we wait, we're playing defense. This gives us the offense."

"Fine," I relent.

Karina rises on her toes, pressing a soft kiss to my jaw that sends a molten rush surging through my veins.

"Thank you," she speaks against my skin.

"Don't thank me yet," I mutter, already running through the tactical nightmare we're about to walk into.

"You might not survive what I'm going to put you through to prepare for this."

My father moves around his desk, his expression shifting to something I recognize from childhood—the calculating look he wore when planning military campaigns. "I'll contact Anselm. Crimson Howl is still his territory, and we'll need his cooperation to make this work."

"Elias first," I correct. "If his father gets wind of this before I can explain the situation, he might refuse outright. Elias can smooth the way."

"And Lockhart? What do we do about him, considering that he's at your border right now, making demands?"

"Leave Lockhart to me," Hudson remarks. "How long will you need to get the ball rolling on this?"

"A day, maybe a little less."

"I can work with that, and it will be the full moon. Even more enticing for Lockhart." My father nods curtly. "I'll handle Lockhart's people—tell them we're considering their request but need time to discuss terms. That should buy you the time you need."

I shift my weight, already mapping out my next move. One misstep and this whole thing unravels.

Hudson's chair tilts back a fraction, his hands folding loosely on the desk. "If this goes wrong, there's no coming back from it. You know that."

"I know," I reply, steady but measured.

My father rises from his desk, the legs of the chair

sliding back with a muted scrape. He straightens his jacket as if settling invisible armor into place, then crosses the room in even strides.

"Gabriel!" he calls, brushing the doorframe as he passes. "Get the team ready. We're paying our guests at the border a visit."

Damien

I slam the door shut behind us, the sound echoing through my bedroom like a gunshot.

"Come here," I growl, stalking toward Karina as she backs deeper into my room.

She doesn't look afraid—far from it actually.

"Damien—" she starts, but I don't let her finish.

I cross the distance between us in two strides, lifting her against me with hands that tremble from the effort of not being rough. My mouth finds hers, swallowing whatever she was about to say. The kiss is hungry, desperate. A kiss that has nothing to do with pack politics and everything to do with the reckless courage that makes me want to worship her and shake her at the same time.

"You," I declare against her lips, walking her backward until her spine meets the wall, "are the most infuriating woman I've ever met."

Her legs wrap around my waist, ankles locking behind my back as I press her harder against the wall. My hands slide beneath her thighs, supporting her weight as if she's made of air instead of flesh and bone.

"I thought you'd be angrier," she declares, her fingers threading through my hair, tugging just hard enough to make me hiss. "I am angry."

I grind against her, letting her feel exactly how angry —and aroused—I am. The hard length of me presses against her core through the thin barrier of my jeans, drawing a soft gasp from her lips that goes straight to my cock.

"I'm furious," I correct, my mouth moving to her throat. "You want to use yourself as bait. You want to walk into a room with a male who's been hunting you for months, and you think I should smile and nod?"

Her head falls back against the wall, exposing more of her neck to my attention. I drag my teeth along the sensitive skin, not quite biting but close enough to make her shiver.

"But you agreed," she breathes, her hips rolling against mine in a rhythm that makes rational thought nearly impossible.

"Because you're right, and I fucking hate that you're right." I pull back to look at her, my hands tightening on her thighs. "Do you have any idea what it does to me? Knowing you're willing to put yourself in danger?"

"It makes my wolf insane," I continue, one hand sliding up to cup her face. "Makes me want to chain you to this bed so you can never leave my sight again."

Her breath catches, and I feel a rush of fire through our connection that has nothing to do with fear. My mate likes the idea of being at my mercy, completely under my control.

"But that's not what you need, is it?"

"I'm tired of being afraid. Tired of letting others decide my fate."

"Then we do this together." I lean my forehead against hers, breathing in her scent—now permanently mixed with mine in a way that makes my wolf purr with satisfaction. "But when we walk into that club, you follow my lead. No improvising. No heroics."

"I can handle myself. I took self-defense. I got away from you—"

"I know you can." My hands slide up her sides. "That's what terrifies me."

I capture her mouth again, this kiss slower but no less consuming. She tastes like home and danger, like everything I never knew I needed. When I finally pull away, we're both breathing hard.

"I need to make some calls," I say, though every instinct roars at me to scoop her up and take her to the bed instead.

Her fingers tighten in my shirt, preventing me from stepping away. "Wait."

I pause, raising an eyebrow at her.

"This might be the only time we have before everything starts moving," she says, soft but resolute. "A few moments delay won't hurt, will it?"

A laugh nearly escapes me at the absurdity. A few minutes? As if what I want from her could be contained in that.

"You think I can take you against this wall in minutes and be satisfied?" I growl, caging her between my arms, palms braced against the plaster. "That's almost insulting, kitten."

Her breath stutters, pupils blown wide as I lean closer. "I didn't mean—"

"I know exactly what you meant." My lips skim her ear, each word dragging heat over her skin. "You want me before the calls. Before the plan sets fire to everything. Before the world comes crashing down."

She shivers, her silence louder than any denial. "Yes," she breathes at last, sliding her fingers under my shirt to trace the ridges of muscle. "Is that so wrong?"

"No." I catch her wrists, pinning them high above her head in one hand. "But don't expect me to be gentle when you look at me like this."

My free hand trails down her body, tugging the hem of my shirt higher along her frame, the fabric gliding over warm skin until her hip is bare.

"The calls can wait," I rasp. "Everything can wait."

I let her hands go, pulling my shirt over my head in one rough motion. Her gaze drags over me, lingering on the tattoos that brand me as my father's son.

"I love the way you look at me," I admit, fingers working the buttons of the shirt she wears—my shirt. "Like I'm worth wanting instead of worth fearing."

"You are worth wanting." She lays her hands over mine as the fabric parts. "You're mine."

The ferocity in her words rakes through me, my wolf throwing back his head in savage triumph. Button by button, more of her skin is revealed, the traces of my bond standing out against her flesh. By the time the shirt slips from her shoulders, I'm already straining, every nerve alight with the need to have her again.

"Beautiful." My hands skim over her ribs, her waist, the flare of her hips. "Every inch of you."

I lift her again, carrying her the few steps to my bed. This time I'm not gentle as I lay her down, my body covering hers with predatory intent. She arches beneath me, her hands fisting in the sheets as I trail my mouth down her throat, tasting the salt of her skin.

"I can't get enough of you," I growl against her collarbone, my mouth trailing lower, tasting every inch of her. "Hours buried inside you, and I'm still starving for more."

Her response is a breathy moan that vibrates through our connection, doubling the sensation. I feel her pleasure as if it's my own, amplified and reflected until I can't tell where I end and she begins.

My hands map every curve, every hollow, relearning territory I've already discovered but need to possess all over again. When my fingers find the slick warmth between her thighs, she bucks against me, nails biting crescents into my shoulders.

"Please," she gasps, and the sound of her begging makes something savage unfurl in my chest.

I don't make her wait. Can't make her wait. My fingers drive into her wetness while my thumb teases the bundle of nerves that makes her cry out. She's already so responsive, so achingly ready for me.

"Look at me. I want to see every flicker of pleasure when you break for me. Every drop of it is mine."

Her stare meets mine, heavy-lidded, glazed with need. I add another finger, curling them deep as my thumb circles her swollen peak. She clutches at me, slick and tight, the sounds she makes—broken gasps, desperate little cries—driving me to the edge of madness.

"That's it," I rasp, watching her come undone as tension coils tighter and tighter in her body. "Let me feel it. Show me what I do to you."

The connection between us surges with shared sensation, her ecstasy flooding my system until I'm drowning in it. When she finally shatters, sobbing my name as her body convulses around my fingers, I feel her orgasm as if it were my own.

But it's not enough. It will never be enough.

I pull free, ignoring her protest, and fumble with my jeans. Denim scrapes my oversensitive skin as I shove them down and kick them away with too much force.

"I need to be inside you," I growl, settling between her thighs. "Need to feel you grip me."

She nods, reaching for me, guiding me home. The first slide into her makes us both groan. I can feel everything she feels—every nerve ending sparking as I fill her completely. I pause, buried to the hilt, fighting for control as sensation tears through our link. Her body clutches me like a velvet fist, so perfect I can barely think.

"Move," she begs, nails dragging down my back hard enough to draw fire in their wake. "Please, Damien."

I don't need to be asked twice. I pull back slowly, savoring the drag of friction, before driving forward again with enough force to make the headboard slam against the wall. The sound should probably concern me —my father's compound has excellent acoustics—but I'm beyond caring who hears us.

I feel her body's response to every thrust, every shift in angle, every change in rhythm. It's overwhelming, experiencing her pleasure alongside my own until I can't tell where I end and she begins. When I hit that spot deep inside her that makes her back arch off the mattress, I feel the spike of sensation through both our nervous systems simultaneously.

"Fuck," I gasp, my rhythm stuttering as the dual sensations threaten to overwhelm me. "I can feel everything you feel."

Her legs wrap around my waist, heels digging into my lower back as she meets each thrust with desperate urgency. "Don't stop," she pants, her head thrown back against the pillows. "I'm so close—"

I can feel how close she is through our connection—

the tension coiling tighter in her core, the way her inner walls flutter around me. It drives me harder, faster, deeper. It's not enough. Nowhere near enough.

"Turn over," I command.

She blinks up at me, momentarily confused.

I pull out of her, ignoring her whimper of protest, and flip her onto her stomach with hands that shake from restraint. "On your knees."

She complies instantly, rising onto all fours. The sight of her like this—vulnerable, exposed, waiting for me—nearly breaks what little control I have left.

I grab a fistful of her hair, wrapping it around my hand until I can pull her head back, exposing the elegant curve of her throat. Her gasp of surprise turns into a moan of pleasure as I position myself behind her.

"Mine," I growl against her ear as I enter her in one powerful thrust.

The angle is deeper this way. My grip on her hair tightens, keeping her head pulled back as I set a punishing rhythm.

"Yes," she gasps, pushing back against me, meeting each thrust with equal force. "Harder."

I comply, my free hand gripping her hip hard enough to bruise. I can feel the beast inside me taking over, my control slipping with each thrust. I growl against her skin, teeth grazing the curve where her neck meets her shoulder.

"Damien," she moans, my name sounding like a prayer on her lips. "Please—"

My hips snap forward with brutal force, driving into her so deeply I feel her shudder around me. Through our bond, I experience her pleasure layered over mine. A feedback loop of sensation that threatens to drive me insane. I feel everything. Her surrender, her desperation, the way her body stretches to accommodate mine.

"You...feel...so fucking...good," I snarl, each word punched out with a deep, driving stroke. "Gripping me...milking me...taking it all...just like that."

She pushes back against me, taking me deeper, and I nearly lose my mind. My fingers dig into her hip, sure to leave bruises that will bloom purple by morning. Good. I want everyone to see. Want them to know.

"I'm close," she gasps, her inner walls clenching around me in a way that makes my vision blur. "Please, I—"

I don't let her finish the thought. My teeth sink into her shoulder, not breaking skin this time but applying enough pressure to send shockwaves through our shared connection. The sensation explodes between us transcends flesh and blood.

She comes apart beneath me with a cry that echoes off the walls, her body convulsing as her orgasm crashes through both of us simultaneously. I feel it like lightning in my veins—her release triggering mine with devastating intensity. My vision whites out as I empty myself inside her, my hips jerking erratically as wave after wave of pleasure tears through me.

I collapse over her, my chest pressed to her back as we both struggle to breathe.

"Jesus," she pants beneath me, her body still trembling with aftershocks.

I press a kiss to her shoulder, tasting salt and satisfaction on her skin. "I need to call Elias."

"The world can wait five more minutes," she says, turning in my arms until she can face me. Her hair is wild, her lips swollen, and there's a satisfied smirk on her lips that makes my chest tight with something I can't name.

I smooth the tangled strands away from her face, marveling at how she can look so fierce and vulnerable at the same time. "Five minutes," I agree, though we both know it's a lie. With her looking at me like that, I could stay buried in this bed for days.

But the reality of what's coming slams back into me like ice water—Lockhart's people at our borders, the plan already in motion, and the very real possibility that tomorrow night could end with Karina in mortal danger.

My wolf snarls at the thought, pressing hard against my skin, demanding to take control. I force him down, knowing instinct won't win this fight. Strategy will.

"I have to call Elias first," I mutter, pulling away from her warmth with reluctance clawing at my chest. "If Anselm refuses to let us use Crimson Howl, we're back to square one."

Karina pushes upright, the sheet falling to her waist, hair mussed, and my mark gleaming bright on her throat.

Even like this, she radiates defiance. Reckless. Unyielding. Mine.

"Will he agree to it?" she asks.

"Elias will. His father…" I shake my head, scrolling through my contacts. "Anselm doesn't gamble unless the odds are rigged in his favor. This plan has too many cracks for his taste."

I find Elias's number and press call. The line rings three times before he finally answers, his breath rough but steady.

"About fucking time. Please tell me you're not dead."

"Not yet," I say, mouth twisting. "But I might be after the favor I'm about to ask."

"Favor?" His laugh turns into a ragged cough. "Let me guess—you need me to bury a body? Or did you finally decide to run off with your new girl and need a safe house?"

Despite everything, a reluctant smile tugs at me. Only Elias could make a joke with one foot in the grave. It's why we've always worked as friends.

"I need Crimson Howl," I say, going straight for it. "Tomorrow night. And I need your father to sign off."

The silence on the other end stretches long enough that I think the call's dropped. Then Elias exhales, heavy with resignation.

"You want to use my family's club as a trap for Lockhart." Not a question. "That's bold. Even for you."

"Trust me, I wanted to take a more direct approach with me tearing out his throat. This is all Karina's plan."

"And you want me to convince my father to let you potentially destroy his most profitable business if things go sideways? Have you met my father?"

"I need this, Elias." I rarely ask for anything, and he knows it. "Lockhart's people are at my father's borders right now demanding to see Karina. We need neutral ground where we control the variables."

"I'm not saying no. I'm saying it's complicated. The club is neutral territory by design. If we start using it for pack warfare, we lose that status forever."

"This isn't warfare. It's an execution." That's exactly what tomorrow night will be. Lockhart's execution, carefully staged to look like anything but.

"My father will want guarantees," Elias warns. "And he'll want something in return. You know how he operates."

I do know. Anselm never gives anything without expecting twice its value in return. It's how he's built his empire—calculated generosity that always leaves him on top.

"What do you think he'll ask for?"

"Territory, most likely."

"Whatever it takes. I need it, and if you're up for it, I need you too, and the wolves you trust the most at Crimson Howl."

Elias sighs heavily on the other end of the line. "I'll do my best, Dom, but I can't make any promises. My father's pissed about the security breach and the fact that I nearly got my head blown off. Getting him to agree to another potential disaster..." He trails off, then adds, "We might have to do this without his blessing and deal with the consequences later. Wouldn't be the first time we've asked for forgiveness instead of permission."

I glance at Karina, who's watching me with unwavering intensity. She's wrapped the sheet around herself now.

"Just get me access," I tell him. "Your father can bill me for damages afterward. Keep this between you and your father. No one else can know what we're planning. If Lockhart gets even a hint that this is a trap—"

"I know. I'll handle it."

The call ends. I set the phone aside and cross the room to the bed. Karina eases back as I climb in beside her, the sheet shifting between us. "What do we do now?

"We wait until I hear back from Elias," I say, leaning closer, my hand sliding to her hip. "And while we wait..." My smile turns deliberate. "...I can think of better ways to keep busy."

Her sheet slips lower, and whatever plan I had for the day dissolves.

Karina

I stare at my reflection in Damien's mirror, barely recognizing the woman looking back at me. Twenty-four hours ago, I was hiding from my wolf. Now I'm deliberately walking into the den of the man who wants to breed me for my bloodline.

"Everything's set in motion," Damien says, ending the call with Elias. His phone lands on the bed with a dull thud. "Crimson Howl is ours for tonight."

My stomach lurches. "Elias agreed?"

"He secured it, but at a cost. He didn't explain, just said our fathers struck an arrangement."

A chill runs through me. "That sounds ominous."

"With those two, it always is." He steps behind me, broad hands settling on my shoulders, his warmth bleeding through the fabric of my shirt. "Are you certain about this, kitten? There's still time to walk away."

"I'm certain," I answer, though the first attempt falters, thin as paper. I draw in a breath, steadying myself before saying it again, stronger. "I'm certain."

His hands tighten on my shoulders, his thumb tracing the mark that brands me as his. Even through the mirror, I can see the war playing out across his features. The man who wants to protect me battling with the one who knows I need to face this.

"Walk me through it again," I say, needing the repetition to calm my racing thoughts. "Every detail."

Damien's reflection nods grimly. "We arrive separately. You'll go in first with Gabriel—my father insisted on that detail. You'll be wearing the same mask as before."

"I still can't believe you actually agreed to this." My voice comes out sharper than I intend, a mix of disbelief and adrenaline. "I said I'd do it, but I didn't think you'd *let* me."

His jaw tightens, the muscle in his cheek working. "It's not what I want, but it's what has to happen to end Lockhart's hunt."

I blink at him in the mirror. "You're really letting me walk in there alone?"

"This is your plan, Karina," he responds, voice low, almost pained. "And I swore I'd treat you as my equal. If I drag you out now, if I take away your choice, then I'm no better than my father."

I stare at him, searching for some crack in his calm. "You're not going to change your mind when we get there?"

He exhales through his nose. "No. Your plan, as much as it infuriates me, is the right one. Lockhart needs to think you've defied me or are looking for a better option—if he thinks you're unprotected—he'll make a mistake. And when he does, I'll be there to rip out his fucking throat."

I bite my lip, but the fire in my chest is real now. "You're trusting me to do this."

"I'm trusting you," he confirms, meeting my eyes in the glass. The wolf flickers behind his gaze. "I hate it, but you asked me to let you fight, and I'm doing it."

"Thank you."

"Don't thank me yet, kitten. We still have to survive this. Thank me after." He takes a deep breath. "You'll need your mask."

Damien steps away from me and over to his dresser in the far corner of the room. He tugs open a drawer and pulls something out. It's not until he's closer that I realize it's the mask I wore the night we met.

"I thought I lost this when I shifted that night and ran."

"I found it," he shrugs.

"And you kept it?" I fire back.

"At the time, I was trying to hunt you down, kitten. It had your scent on it."

I take the mask from his hands. How could something so simple as wearing this mask brought me to the place I am now? It's ironic, really. A night out to nurse the wounds from a bad breakup brought me into this world. It brought me a mate, and a backstory I never knew existed, no thanks to my parents. There's so much about my life I still don't understand, but maybe after all of this is said and done, Anselm or Hudson will be willing to help fill in those blanks that my parents no longer can.

"Gabriel will escort you to the VIP section," Damien continues. "You'll be visible but protected. Lockhart won't be able to reach you without going through pack security."

"And then?"

"Then we wait. Let him see you, let him think he has a chance. When he makes his move—and he will—we'll be ready."

"What if he doesn't take the bait?"

"Then we improvise."

"That's not very reassuring."

"Nothing about this is reassuring, kitten." His voice is low, almost rough. He steps closer, his hands framing my face with surprising gentleness, thumbs brushing just beneath my eyes. "I can feel it. Your heartbeat, your fear. It's bleeding through the bond like it's my own." His eyes flicker, wolf-bright for a heartbeat. "I hate that I'm sending you in there like this."

He leans in until his forehead nearly touches mine. "But I'll be there. Every second. If anything goes wrong, anything at all, you get out. No heroics. No trying to save the day. You shift and run. Do you understand?"

His words settle deep, the steadiness in his voice anchoring the chaos in my chest. It isn't a command. It's a promise.

I want to argue, to tell him I won't leave him if things fall apart. The words burn on my tongue, sharp and ready. But through the bond I feel it. The tight coil beneath his skin, the dread he's hiding under that calm voice. It presses against my chest, heavy and alive, not mine but his.

And I see it too. In the way his eyes burn, in the way his jaw clenches as if he's holding himself back from pulling me against him and refusing to let me go. The wolf inside him is pacing, furious and afraid, and I can taste it in the back of my throat.

The intensity in his eyes stops me. It's too raw, too honest. Instead of fighting him, I swallow the words and lift my chin. I force a smile, small and wry, trying to lighten the mood even as my stomach twists.

"Don't worry so much. I'll be fine. I took self-defense in high school," I say, forcing a grin. "Pretty sure I still remember how to knee someone where it counts."

Damien doesn't even blink. Not a hint of amusement.

"This isn't a schoolyard bully we're talking about, Karina."

I swallow hard, the smile slipping. My joke hangs awkwardly between us, heavy in the air.

"I know," I say quietly. "I was just trying to make this feel a little less terrifying."

His expression softens slightly as he pulls me against his chest. I breathe in his scent—pine and smoke and something uniquely him—trying to calm my racing heart.

"Nothing about this will be easy, but I need you to understand what we're walking into. These aren't humans with human rules. If Lockhart gets his hands on you, there won't be a chance to use those self-defense moves. He's bigger, faster, and has decades of fighting experience, kitten. So, if it comes down to it. Shift as fast as you can, run, and don't fucking look back."

His warning chills me to the bone, but it's not myself I'm worried about—it's him. The thought of Damien throwing himself into danger for me makes my stomach twist into knots. I shift from the mirror, spinning on my heels to face him, placing my palms against his chest, feeling his heartbeat beneath my fingers.

"What about you? If things go wrong, what's your plan?"

He doesn't answer immediately, and that terrifies me more than anything else.

"Damien," I press, gripping his shirt. "Promise me you won't do anything stupid."

"Define stupid." His attempt at humor falls flat.

"You know exactly what I mean." I pull back to look up at him. "I can feel it through the bond. You're planning something you don't want me to know about."

It's strange how quickly I've come to rely on this connection between us. Just days ago, I was fighting it with everything I had. Now, I can't imagine not feeling his emotions alongside my own, this second heartbeat that tells me things his words don't.

"My priority is keeping you safe," he says, which isn't an answer at all.

I study his face—the hard angles, the stubbled jaw. When did this happen? When did this terrifying man become someone I can't bear the thought of losing?

"When I agreed to be your mate, I didn't do it so you could throw your life away playing hero."

Something flickers across his features—surprise, maybe. Like he wasn't expecting me to push back.

"This isn't about playing hero," he says, but I can feel the lie through our connection. The way his emotions shift, walls slamming up to block me out.

"Don't." I shake my head, stepping back. "Don't shut me out. Not now."

He runs a hand through his hair, frustration radiating off him in waves. "You don't understand—"

"Then make me understand." I cross my arms, channeling every ounce of stubborn determination I possess. "We're supposed to be partners in this, Damien. That means you don't get to make unilateral decisions about our lives."

The silence stretches between us, heavy with unspoken truths. "If Lockhart realizes it's a trap," he says finally, "if things go sideways and there's no other choice...I'll make sure you get out. Whatever it takes. If it's a choice between me or you making it out safely, my choice will always be you, kitten."

"No." The word tears from my throat with such force it surprises us both. "Absolutely not."

He grips my arms, not hard, but enough to make me look at him. His eyes burn like silver caught in moonlight, his wolf right there beneath the surface. "Even if I could find a way to keep breathing without you, my wolf would never allow it. That's not how this bond works. You're not just in my life — you're in my blood, my bones, every breath I take. If you die, so do I. There's no part of me that survives losing you."

He draws a shuddering breath, thumb brushing along my jaw. "I'm not saying this to scare you. I'm saying it because you keep talking about sacrifice like it's an option. It's not. Not for us. The Moon's bond isn't some pretty story. It's a promise written into our souls. True mates don't bury each other. If one falls, the other follows."

His forehead touches mine. "So when you talk about fighting alone, when you think about dying for me, remember this: you'd be killing me too. And I refuse to let that happen. We live together, or we die together. There is no other way."

A sharp knock shatters the fragile quiet between us, jolting me out of Damien's arms. My pulse skips, the bond still humming with the warmth of his touch. He scowls at the interruption but strides to the door.

When it swings open, one of his father's servants stands there, blank-faced, a large shopping bag dangling from her hand.

"The items you requested, Miss Greene," she says, her voice flat as stone, and offers the bag—not to me, but to Damien.

His brow furrows as he takes it, weighing the unexpected bundle before turning back toward me. "What the hell is this?"

"Exactly what I need for tonight," I reply, stepping forward and slipping the handles from his grip before he can argue. "Thank you."

The servant inclines her head once, then disappears silently into the hall. The door shuts, and we're alone again. Damien studies me, suspicion radiating off him as his attention lingers on the bag now hanging from my hand.

"What exactly did you request?"

I clutch the bag to my chest, grabbing the mask as I pass, already backing toward the bathroom. "Don't worry about it. I'll be ready on time."

"Karina." My name becomes a warning on his lips.

"You need to trust me on this," I say, reaching the bathroom door. "I know what I'm doing."

Before he can argue, I slip inside and close the door firmly behind me. I hear his frustrated growl through the wood, but he doesn't follow. I lock the door behind me and dump the contents onto the counter, a thrill of rebellion racing through my veins. Maybe it's stupid.

Maybe it's reckless. But if I'm going to be bait, I need to look the part.

The black mesh top unfolds in my hands, far more revealing than anything I've ever worn. It's exactly what I asked for—strategically placed X's that will barely cover my nipples while leaving the rest of my breasts exposed beneath the sheer material. I slip it over my head, adjusting it in the mirror until it sits just right, the fabric cool against my skin.

Next, I slide on the harness, a set of black straps that cross over my chest and highlight the daring hint of mesh beneath. My fingers tremble as I fumble with the buckles, the cool metal biting into my skin before everything locks into place. The material hugs close, firm but not uncomfortable, a bold reminder of what I'm doing. How the women at Crimson Howl managed to dance in these contraptions without losing their minds, I'll never understand.

I pull on a fitted moto jacket, the smooth texture cool against my skin as it slips over the harness. It hides just enough to keep Damien unaware of what is underneath, at least for now. Adjusting the collar, I can't stop the small, wicked smile that curls my lips at the thought of his reaction when he finds out too late, in a place where stopping me will not be an option.

The pants glide over my hips like liquid, shaping to every curve until I hesitate, startled by the reflection staring back. They sit lower than I would normally dare.

The heels change everything, altering my stance and my stride, shifting me from flight to hunt.

I run my fingers through my hair, leaving it loose in waves that spill over my shoulders. Then comes the final touch: lipstick, a daring red that turns my mouth into a challenge. When I fit the mask into place, soft against my skin, the woman in the mirror is no longer afraid. She is bait, and willing to be.

I take a steadying breath and open the door.

Damien waits in the bedroom, head bent over his phone, broad shoulders tense beneath his jacket. Combat boots, denim, the same lethal calm that makes the air feel thinner around him.

"I'm ready," I say.

His head lifts, and the effect is immediate. The phone drops to his side, forgotten, as his gaze locks on me. His expression hardens, jaw flexing while his focus drags slowly down and back up again. The jacket zipped just enough to tease. The curve of my hips. The red mouth beneath the mask. His entire body goes still, but the space between us hums with something sharp and volatile, caught between fury and hunger.

"What the fuck are you wearing?"

I lift my chin, refusing to back down under his heated stare. "I'm wearing what I need to wear to make this work."

"You're not wearing that. Not a fucking chance."

"I am." I step further into the room, letting the heels announce my determination with each click against the hardwood floor. "This is the whole point, Damien. I need to look the part. I need to look like bait."

"You look like you're offering yourself up on a platter." He stalks toward me, the predator in his movements unmistakable. "That's not the plan."

"The plan is to draw Lockhart out. To make him think I'm available." I stand my ground as he approaches, though my heart hammers against my ribs. "What better way than to look like I'm there for the same reason as everyone else?"

He stops directly in front of me, close enough that I tilt my head back to maintain eye contact. His scowl burns with barely contained fury.

"You're proving my point. This reaction? This is exactly what I need from Lockhart."

Damien's nostrils flare as he inhales sharply. His hands clench at his sides, and I can practically see him counting backwards from ten in his head.

"Take it off."

"No."

"You can be as furious as you want about this later. When we're both safe, you can peel these clothes off me layer by layer. But right now, we need to concentrate on what's coming."

"You're playing with fire," he finally growls, his hand coming up to grip my wrist where it rests against his chest. "If Lockhart so much as breathes in your direction—"

"You'll do your Reaper thing and kill him. That's kind of the point of all this."

He hates this outfit, hates the idea of other wolves seeing me like this. Probably a little more when he fully sees what's under the jacket, but I'll reap the consequences of that later.

"Karina—" he starts, his hands moving to the zipper of my jacket like he's about to pull it down and discover exactly what I'm hiding.

A sharp knock interrupts us. Damien freezes, his fingers still on my zipper, head turning toward the door with a predatory alertness that reminds me of his true nature.

"Miss Greene, it's time."

I swallow hard, reality crashing over me. This is it.

Damien's grip tightens for the briefest second, as if he could hold me back with sheer will alone. His eyes burn with a warning I know he won't voice—not here, not now.

I force my legs to move, every step toward that door echoing louder than it should, like a drumbeat counting down to something I can't escape.

On the other side waits the beginning of the end.

And once I cross that threshold, nothing will ever be the same.

Karina

I can feel her under my skin, scratching and clawing, desperate to break free as the moon calls to her. It's an itch I can't scratch, a burn I can't soothe, and it's getting worse with each passing minute.

"Miss Greene, please," Gabriel says, his hand firmly pressed against the small of my back as he guides me through the unmarked side entrance of Crimson Howl.

The heavy metal door closes behind us with a resounding thud that feels too final for comfort. The scents hit me immediately—sweat, arousal, expensive cologne, and beneath it all, the unmistakable musk of other wolves. My nostrils flare involuntarily, and I fight the urge to bare my teeth.

"This way," Gabriel directs, steering me down a

dimly lit corridor. "Mr. Marek was very specific about the arrangements."

I close my eyes for a moment, trying to center myself despite the sensory overload. Then, before I can second-guess myself, I reach out along that strange, new connection that thrums between Damien and me.

How far away are you?

For a terrifying moment, there's nothing but silence. Then I feel it, a pressure against my consciousness, heavy and intense.

Close. Stay with Gabriel.

"Let's go. We need to be in position before Lockhart arrives," Gabriel grumbles under his breath.

I nod once, my throat too dry to speak as Gabriel's hand guides me forward. The club is pulsing with life around us, but Gabriel deftly navigates us away from the main floor, his movements precise and practiced. I catch glimpses of shadowy figures through doorways—bodies entwined, masks glinting in the low light.

A group ahead of us blocks our path. I shift to move around them, but Gabriel tugs me to the left, subtly changing our course.

I glance up briefly and immediately understand why. Along the far wall, a row of private booths house several alphas. I can smell their dominant pheromones even from here. Gabriel smoothly steers me down a different path, putting several dancing bodies between us and the alphas.

We reach a cordoned-off section marked with a subtle

gold emblem—VIP only. A bouncer twice my size stands guard.

"We're expecting Alpha Lockhart shortly. Make sure he's admitted," Gabriel orders the man standing guard before he pushes me inside.

Inside the VIP section, the room stands empty except for Gabriel and me, the plush couches and private viewing areas eerily silent compared to the throbbing pulse of the main club.

"Sit there," Gabriel instructs, pointing to a black couch positioned directly in front of the one-way glass overlooking the main floor. "Front and center. That's where he wants you."

I hesitate only a moment before obeying, settling into the cool material. The seat faces outward, offering a perfect view of the chaos below while putting me on full display to anyone who enters this private room.

My fingers find the zipper of my jacket and pull it down with a metallic hiss that sounds far too loud in the stillness. I ease it off my shoulders, revealing the harness beneath. Thin black straps cross over my chest, leaving little to the imagination and even less to comfort. I tug one band higher, making sure it conceals the mark at my throat.

Gabriel's sharp inhale breaks the silence. "Jesus Christ," he mutters, snapping his gaze away. "If Lockhart doesn't kill me tonight, Damien sure as hell will for seeing you like this."

"Not before he kills me for wearing it," I reply, trying

for humor and failing. My hands smooth down the straps, the gesture more nervous than I intend. "It'll be fine. At least, it's supposed to be. This is all part of the plan."

Gabriel makes a noncommittal grunt, positioning himself near the entrance where he can monitor both the door and the main floor below. "Plans change when jealous mates see other men looking at what's theirs."

I'm about to respond when that familiar pressure blooms in my mind again, stronger this time. More urgent.

He's here. Lockhart just walked in.

I thought you were coming after Lockhart showed up.

My pulse spikes instantly, and I grip the arm of the couch to keep my hands steady.

I told you I'd keep you safe, kitten. I can't do that if I'm not here. He won't see me coming until it's too late.

Gabriel's phone buzzes, and he glances at it before moving closer to me. He pulls a tiny spray bottle from his pocket, handing it to me. "Heat pheromones. Spray it all over you, and the couch."

I take it from his hand, and press down on the top, spiritizing the liquid onto my wrist. The acrid smell makes me recoil. "This smells like piss."

"Not to males. Now spray it and give me back the bottle once it's empty. We don't have much time."

I do as Gabriel requests, spraying the foul scent all over me, taking extra care to spray my neck. With the remaining two pumps, I spritz the couch before handing him the bottle back."

"It reeks in here," I almost gag.

"That's the point."

I take a deep breath, stowing the growing need to vomit down as much as I can, and shift my weight on the leather couch. The harness straps dig slightly into my skin as I adjust my posture, attempting to channel whatever femme fatale energy I can muster.

Damien's reassuring voice speaks down our bond. *You can do this, kitten. This will all be over soon enough.*

I've never been bait before. Never faced down an alpha who's already proven how dangerous he is. The memory of Lockhart's hands on me, my first time coming to this very club, makes my skin crawl, but I can't let that happen. Tonight is about ending this once and for all.

He's coming up the stairs now.

I swallow hard, my fingers nervously tracing the straps across my collarbone. *Where are you exactly?* I project back, unable to stop myself from scanning the room again.

Close enough to rip his throat out if he tries anything.

Gabriel shifts his stance, one hand casually drifting toward what I suspect is a concealed weapon.

"Showtime," Gabriel mutters under his breath, nodding toward the entrance.

I hear footsteps outside the door and then the

metallic click of the handle turning. My breath catches in my throat as the door swings open.

Thomas Lockhart strides in like he owns the air itself, his broad frame blotting out the doorway. The black mask does little to disguise him. I would know that cruel smirk in a crowd of thousands. His attention lands on me instantly, dragging over every inch of bare skin with a hunger that makes my stomach knot.

"Well, well," he purrs, closing the door with a soft click that feels louder than a gunshot. "Karina Greene. What a pleasant surprise."

I shift deliberately, crossing one leg over the other. His focus follows the motion. "Is it really a surprise," I counter, "when you've been hunting me?"

"Hunting," he repeats with mock disapproval. "Such an ugly word. I prefer...pursuing." He advances a step at a time, deliberate as a stalking predator. "Though I didn't expect to find you here alone. Dressed like that and smelling so divine."

Gabriel shifts subtly at my side, drawing his attention for a fleeting second. Maybe he was right about the pheromones after all.

"Your watchdog can leave," Lockhart says, not even bothering to face him. "We have private matters to discuss."

I force stillness into my body, keep my pulse from betraying me. "He stays."

Lockhart's jaw works, irritation darkening his

features. "So demanding, Karina. All I want to do is talk about our future."

"Future? You presume too much, Thomas. I know who I am now, and with that knowledge, it means I have my pick for a mate."

He laughs, the sound sharp and unpleasant. "So you've decided to ditch the pup for someone with more power." He takes another step toward me, his cologne making my nose itch. "Smart little wolf. He isn't deserving of a female of your worth."

"And let me guess you are?" I roll my eyes intentionally. "Sending your goons to kidnap me isn't exactly how a female of worth, as you called me, should be treated."

Lockhart's smile stretches thin, a flicker of irritation breaking through his arrogance before he reins it back in. "A necessary misunderstanding," he says smoothly. "Soon, you'll understand why I did it. A female like you deserves an alpha who can give her everything she's been denied."

Inside me, my wolf snarls, pacing behind my ribs. She hates this act, hates letting him think he's in control. Through the bond, Damien's presence presses against my awareness like a hand at my back, steadying me. *You're doing fine. He's showing his hand. Just a little longer.*

I angle my body slightly, shifting so the harness cuts a sharper line across my skin. His eyes flick down before he can stop himself, and the bastard's tongue flicks over his lips before he catches it.

"I don't know what story you've told yourself, but you're not impressing me."

He steps closer, closing the space between us until his scent brushes the edge of my nose. My wolf thrashes, claws against my skin, but I stay still. Slowly, deliberately, I drag my palms over the tops of my thighs, up my stomach, across the bare strip of skin above the harness, rubbing warmth into my skin as if trying to comfort myself. In reality, I'm pushing the scent of my heat into the air, letting it bloom around me.

Lockhart inhales sharply, pupils dilating. His smile twists into something darker. "Moon above... you smell incredible," he murmurs. "Do you have any idea what you're doing to me, little wolf?"

I tilt my head, feigning confusion, though my heart is hammering so hard I can feel it in my teeth. "Do tell."

His nostrils flare again as he leans in, voice dropping low and hungry. "Your heat is calling to me. Begging my wolf to breed you. Every breath you take is a promise." His eyes glint like a predator's. "And you think I'm the one not impressing you?"

Lockhart's hand twitches at his side, his wolf pushing to the surface, drawn by the scent. He's seconds away from doing exactly what we need him to do.

"Tell me something, Karina. Did you let him fuck you?"

"Why is that any of your business?" I challenge him.

"Because purging an unwanted pup from your

womb will delay my timeline," he snarls. "Did. You. Fuck. Him?"

I shake my head to prevent myself from retching at the thought. "My future mate will not have to worry about an unwanted pregnancy."

"Good. I didn't take you for the type to whore yourself for protection, but one can never be too careful."

The insult burns through me like acid, but I force a calm smile, channeling every ounce of false bravado I have left.

"Your actions drove me to seek protection, So if I fucked Damien, or Elias, or anyone else willing to stand between me and you, that's on *you*, not me. You left me with no other choice."

His face flashes with fury, and I know I've hit the nerve I was aiming for. Good. He leans closer, his breath hot against my face. "It was you who chose the path we find ourselves on now. You ran from me."

"You tried to kidnap me...twice," I remind him again. "Despite your best efforts to convince me otherwise that particular fact will never change, Thomas."

Lockhart's expression freezes, just for a second, before twisting into something uglier. His nostrils flare, his composure slipping as offense flares like a struck match.

"Careful," he says quietly, the word edged with a growl. "You're treading close to disrespect."

I arch a brow, keeping my tone deliberately light. "I thought we'd already crossed that line."

His hand slams down on the table between us, the sound cracking through the room. Gabriel takes a step forward, but I lift my palm to stop him. "You think this is a game? That you can mock me and walk away unscathed?"

My pulse spikes, but I don't flinch. I let my voice go flat, cutting. "I think you're proving my point, Thomas. You don't understand the word *no*. You don't even understand choice. You think if you hound me long enough, if you flex hard enough, you can force me into your bed and call it a bond."

I shift closer to the edge of the couch, leaning forward so every word lands like a strike. "Let me be very fucking clear, Thomas." My eyes lock on his, unblinking, unafraid. "You will never be my mate. Not in this life. Not in any life. I would rather let my bloodline die with me than ever let you try to benefit from it."

For a heartbeat, he just stares and then something inside him shatters.

His face contorts, all pretense of control gone. "You ungrateful little—" He lunges, faster than I can breathe, his hand shooting out to catch my throat. The impact sends me sprawling back against the couch, his grip hard enough to bruise.

My wolf surges upward, claws raking just beneath my skin.

Lockhart leans in, his voice a snarl. "I'll make you remember your place—"

The lights go out.

Emergency lights flare to life a heartbeat later, flooding the room in pulsing crimson. In that blink of illumination, the energy shifts. Thomas's grip on my throat tightens reflexively as his head jerks toward the door.

"What the fuck—" he starts.

The emergency lights flicker, stutter, then die.

Darkness swallows everything.

A body slams against the door. A gunshot cracks the silence. The muzzle flash sears the room in white light, and for an instant, I see it all. Gabriel crumpling and blood blooming across his chest, a slender figure looming above him, silver mask glinting.

Then blackness again.

My scream sticks in my throat as Thomas yanks me over the couch, his hand like an iron collar.

"Right on time," Thomas hisses against my ear, smug and certain. "Did you really think I'd come alone? Unlike your pathetic protectors, I plan ahead."

"Let me go," I snarl, clawing at his arm. My wolf thrashes inside me, frantic, battering against the cage I keep her in. "Damien!" I cry, his name tearing from my throat, echoing both aloud and through our frayed bond. The connection twists, faint and broken, like static over a ruined radio. Something—or someone—is cutting us off.

The masked figure glides through the shadows, their outline barely distinguishable from the gloom. A thin spill of light from the upstairs windows catches on polished silver where their face should be. "We need to leave."

Thomas's grip on my throat slackens as he turns toward the newcomer. I seize the chance, slamming my elbow into his ribs with all the strength I can summon. His grunt of pain vibrates against my back, though his hold doesn't break.

"Who are you?" The words rasp from my raw throat, every syllable scraping as my eyes strain to pierce the mask. The flickering emergency lights throw jagged shadows across the room, warping everything into something monstrous.

Before I can react, the figure lunges forward with startling speed. I feel a sharp pinch at the side of my neck, followed immediately by a warm, tingling sensation that spreads through my veins like wildfire. My limbs grow heavy within seconds.

"What did you..." My words slur as the room begins to tilt. Thomas finally releases me, and I slump against the couch, unable to command my muscles to fight back.

The figure steps closer. With deliberate slowness, they reach up and remove the mask, revealing a face I've seen before, sitting around the breakfast table.

Saloma Bellandi. Anselm's Luna.

She smiles, slow and merciless, crouching close enough that I can't look away. "We'll make good use of you."

And then, nothing but darkness.

Damien

I feel the moment Lockhart touches her.

My skin burns as if branded, rage exploding through me like wildfire. Across the crowded club floor, through the sea of writhing bodies and flashing lights, I can see him. His fingers gripping my mate's chin, forcing her to look at him. My wolf claws beneath my skin, demanding release, demanding blood.

Mine. Mine. Mine.

She's playing her part perfectly, keeping him distracted, but it's taking everything in me not to tear across this room and rip his fucking throat out with my teeth.

"Easy," Elias mutters beside me, his hand gripping my shoulder. "Stick to the plan."

I shrug him off, my attention never leaving the VIP section where my mate sits half-naked in that fucking harness and mesh shirt. We'd be discussing that later once she's safe and after I'd pried that fucking outfit off of her with my goddamn teeth. The leather straps cross her perfect skin, drawing every male eye in the place, including Lockhart's. His hand moves to her throat now, and I feel my control slipping.

"If he doesn't remove his hand in the next five seconds, I'm going to remove it for him," I growl. "Permanently."

"Two more minutes," Elias says, checking his watch. "That's all we need."

Two minutes might as well be two years. I can feel Karina reaching for me through our bond, her consciousness brushing against mine like a lifeline. Lockhart is talking to her, his words making her bristle through our connection. I want to tear his tongue out along with his hands. The lights flicker—once, twice. Elias tenses beside me.

"That's not supposed to happen," he mutters, scanning the room with sudden alertness.

Before I can respond, the power fails. Emergency lights kick on almost immediately, bathing everything in blood-red. I curse under my breath, instinctively reaching for the knife at my belt. This wasn't part of the plan.

"Elias—"

A gunshot cracks through the air, muffled but unmistakable.

Damien! Her plea rips through our connection—thin, desperate, fading.

I'm already moving, shoving bodies aside as I carve a path toward the VIP section. The emergency lights stutter, then die, plunging the club into chaos. Screams rise from the humans, but I don't need light. My wolf's sight cuts through the black as if it's dusk, every sense sharpened by adrenaline and the need to reach her.

The tether between us falters, growing weaker with every heartbeat. Something's wrong. Terribly wrong.

Karina!

Silence.

A roar tears from my chest, her name ripped free in a sound that shakes the air. Panicked bodies slam against me as the crowd surges for the exits, but I barely register the impacts. My world has shrunk to the void where her presence should be.

"Damien!" Elias shouts somewhere behind me, but I don't slow. Can't. My mate is slipping away, and every second drags her further from my reach.

I reach the VIP entrance, my hands finding the door handle. It's locked. I throw my shoulder against it with enough force to splinter the frame, the door exploding inward with a crash that echoes through the mayhem below.

The stench of blood hits me immediately. Gabriel's blood. I can smell it even before my eyes adjust enough to see his motionless form sprawled near the entrance, liquid pooling beneath him.

"Gabriel!" I drop to my knees beside him, pressing my fingers to his throat. There—weak, but there. A pulse. He's alive, barely.

But the couch where Karina sat is empty. The leather still holds her scent, but it's already fading, mixing with something else. Something medicinal and sharp that makes my wolf snarl in recognition.

Sedative.

"Fuck!" I slam my fist into the floor hard enough to crack the concrete beneath the carpet. They drugged her. That's why I can't feel her.

Elias bursts through the doorway, his phone already at his ear. "Fuck, fuck, fuck! I need a medical team at the VIP section, now. Gabriel's down."

I'm barely listening, my senses working overtime as I try to catch Karina's scent trail. Her perfume, her shampoo, the unique musk that marks her as mine—I search for anything that might tell me which way they took her. But the air is a confusion of smells: Gabriel's blood, spilled alcohol, and overwhelming pheromones.

"Can you tell which way they went?" Elias asks, crouching beside Gabriel and pressing his wadded-up jacket against the wound.

I drop to all fours, my face inches from the carpet as I inhale deeply. There—beneath all of the scents in this room, I catch it. Karina's scent, mixed with Lockhart's, heading toward the back exit. But there's something else. Something that makes my wolf rear back in confusion.

"Saloma," I growl, the name tasting like poison on my tongue.

Elias's head snaps up with disbelief. "What? My stepmother?"

"Her scent is all over this room." I rise to my feet, fury coursing through my veins like molten lead. "She was here with Lockhart. She helped him take Karina."

"That's impossible. Why would my stepmother be here?"

The rage inside me crystallizes into something colder, deadlier. I stare at Elias, my oldest friend, my brother in everything but blood, and for the first time, I see him as a stranger.

"Is it?" I grab him by the throat, slamming him against the wall with enough force to crack the plaster. "Was this your plan all along? Was this what your father wanted in exchange for using his club? My fucking mate?"

Elias's hands claw at my grip. "Damien—I swear—I didn't—"

I tighten my hold, lifting him until his feet barely touch the ground. "Your stepmother's scent is all over this room! She was here with Lockhart. She helped him take Karina!"

"I didn't know," he chokes out, his face reddening from lack of oxygen. "Damien, you have to believe me."

Part of me wants to crush his windpipe, to feel something break beneath my hands since I can't reach the people who truly deserve my wrath. But beneath my fury, I smell his terror that can't be faked.

I release him abruptly, and he collapses to his knees, gasping for air.

"If I find out you knew anything about this," I snarl, looming over him, "I will end your entire bloodline. Starting with you."

Elias wipes blood from his mouth. "Listen to me, Dom. I had no fucking idea Saloma would be involved. This wasn't the deal."

"What deal?" I grab him by his shirt collar, hauling him back to his feet. "What exactly did your father and mine arrange behind my back?"

Elias looks away, jaw clenched tight. "I can't tell you. My father...he bound me to silence."

"Your father bound you?" My laugh cuts sharp and ugly through the tension. "Your Luna helped orchestrate a kidnapping, and you're worried about a fucking command?"

Elias flinches but holds his ground. "It isn't just a command. It's a blood oath. If I break it, I lose everything—my rank, my wolf... maybe even my life."

I shove him back, disgust twisting in my gut. "So, he strikes a bargain with my father that involve Karina, and you can't warn me because you swore an oath like some obedient dog?"

"He was never supposed to touch her!" Elias's voice cracks as his hands tremble, dragging over his shirt to steady himself. "If Saloma's got her fingers in this, that's on her. My father wouldn't risk what he's built with Hudson. It's too valuable."

"What's so valuable?" I snarl, every word vibrating with the promise of violence.

His gaze flicks to Gabriel's bloody form on the floor, then back to me, haunted. "You'll find out soon enough, probably before you kill me. But if you want her alive, focus now. We've only got hours before moonrise, and they'll try to chain her into something she can't escape."

A growl rips out of me, low and feral. "They can't touch her."

"Damien, you don't get it—"

I fist his shirtfront and yank him close. "No, you don't. The tie is already sealed. True. Absolute. The Moon Goddess herself marked it."

Elias freezes, shock etched across his features. "But that's not possible. The full moon isn't until tonight."

"Tell that to the Moon Goddess," I snap, shoving him back. "It's done. Nothing can undo it now."

"Fuck." His complexion drains. "If Lockhart tries to force a bond, it won't matter that she can't consent. The attempt alone could kill her. If another male pushes for a bond while yours is already in place, the competing pull could rip Karina apart from the inside. Her body would reject it violently. Fatally."

"How long do we have?" I ask, already moving toward the door.

"Until moonrise. Maybe three hours." Elias follows me, his footsteps unsteady. "But Dom, if my stepmother helped plan this, she'll have thought of everything. Security, escape routes, backup plans."

I pause at the doorway, my hand gripping the splintered frame hard enough to draw blood from my palm. "Then it's a good thing I don't plan on giving her or Lockhart time to use them."

"You can't just storm their territory alone. It's suicide."

"Watch me." I step over Gabriel's prone form, my wolf pushing closer to the surface with each passing second. The beast wants blood. Wants to hunt. Wants to tear apart everyone who dared touch what's mine.

"Damien, wait!" Elias grabs my arm, his grip desperate. "You need backup. You need a plan."

I turn on him, letting him see the predator that lurks beneath my skin. "The plan is simple. I find my mate. I kill everyone who took her. I bring her home."

"And if you get yourself killed in the process? What happens to her then?"

I don't have an answer that will satisfy him. Truth is, I don't care about the consequences to myself. All that matters is getting to Karina before moonrise.

"They'll take her to neutral ground," I say, my mind racing through possibilities. "Lockhart's not stupid enough to bring her directly to his territory. He knows I'll come after her."

"She could be anywhere by now. And without her consciousness, tracking her will be impossible."

I let out a harsh laugh, reaching into my pocket. "Not as impossible as you might think."

I pull out my phone, swiping past the lock screen and opening an app. The interface loads, revealing a pulsing red dot moving steadily northeast.

"What is that?"

"Insurance." I zoom in on the map, watching the dot's steady movement. "I injected her with a tracker."

"You did what?" Elias stares at me like I've grown a second head. "Does she know you did this?"

I don't give a fuck what he thinks. I knew this plan was dangerous from the beginning. Knew that putting Karina in Lockhart's sights was playing with fire. I hated doing it without her consent—hated the secrecy, the violation of her trust—but the alternative was unthinkable. Allowing her to walk into the wolf's den without a way of finding her was never going to be the plan. Will she be happy about it when she finds out? No. But we can fight about it later when she's safe.

"They're heading north on Route 16," I say, already moving toward the exit.

"Isn't that the road that leads to the Rosewood territory? Lockhart is going to make a show of it, but that territory is huge. It's going to take more than just the two of us to cover it, even with tracking her."

"I don't give a fuck if it's the entire state of California, I'm going after her." I push past Elias, my mind already calculating time and distance. "They've got maybe a fifteen to twenty-minute head start. If we move now, we can catch them before they reach whatever hell-hole Lockhart's taking her to."

"You're going to need help," Elias insists, keeping pace with me as I storm through the club's back hallway. "My father—"

I whirl on him, slamming him against the wall with enough force to make the pipes rattle. "Your father is the last person I want involved in this. Your stepmother helped kidnap my mate. For all I know, he was in on it too."

"He wasn't," Elias chokes out, not even bothering to fight my grip. "I swear on my wolf, Damien. Whatever Saloma's done, she's done on her own."

I search his face for any sign of deception but find only desperation and what looks like genuine shock. My wolf is still screaming for blood, but the tactical part of my brain—the part that earned me the name Reaper—knows he's right. I can't do this alone.

"Fine." I release him, already pulling out my phone again. "But we do this my way."

"Whatever you need," Elias agrees, rubbing his throat. "My pack, my resources, they're yours."

I dial my father's number, my jaw clenched so tight I might crack teeth. Each ring feels like an eternity when every second takes Karina further from me.

"I trust everything is—"

"She's gone." The words tear from my throat like broken glass. "Lockhart took her. With help from Saloma Bellandi."

The silence that follows is deafening. I can almost hear the calculations running through my father's head—the political implications, the power dynamics, the potential fallout.

"Where are you?" he finally asks, his tone shifted to something harder, more focused.

"Crimson Howl. Heading to my car." I push through the back exit, the cold night air hitting my face like a slap. The moon hangs heavy in the sky, not quite full but close enough that my wolf howls beneath my skin. "I've tracked her heading north on Route 16."

"Tracked her how?"

"Does it fucking matter?" I snap, yanking open my car door. Elias slides into the passenger seat beside me, already on his own phone, barking orders to his security team. "They're taking her to Rosewood territory. They are trying to force a mating before moonrise."

Another pause, this one briefer. "They can't."

"Which is exactly why we need to find her before they try." I start the engine, my hands trembling with barely controlled rage. "I'm heading there now."

"Don't." The command lashes across the line, sharp enough to make my wolf bristle. "Wait for backup."

"Like hell." I slam the car into drive, tires screaming as rubber peels against asphalt. "Every second I wait is another second they have to hurt her."

"And every second you charge in blind is another chance you die before you can reach her," my father counters. "Think with your head, not your wolf."

"My head is what got her into this mess." The snarl rips free before I can stop it. I wrench the wheel, taking the corner so hard Elias curses and grabs for the door handle. "I should've trusted my instincts. Should've locked her down where no one could touch her."

"Regret doesn't save lives." Hudson cuts clean through the spiral of guilt. "Focus. How many men does Lockhart have with him?"

I glance at Elias, who's still coordinating with his security team. He holds up three fingers, then shakes his head and makes it five.

"Unknown. At least five, maybe more."

"Then you need an army, not a suicide mission." My father's tone brooks no argument. "I'm mobilizing our forces now. Meet us at the old logging station on Route 16. We'll coordinate from there."

"I'm not waiting—"

"You are." The alpha command hits me. My foot hesitates on the gas pedal for only a second before I press it harder to the floor. "That won't work on me anymore."

"It wasn't an alpha command. It was a father asking his son not to die needlessly when we can save her together."

The sincerity in his voice catches me off guard. Since when does Hudson Marek care about anything beyond his legacy and his pack?

"Twenty minutes," I concede finally, rechecking the tracker. The red dot has slowed, turning off the main highway onto what looks like a service road. "I'll give you twenty minutes to mobilize. Not a second more."

"We'll be there in fifteen." The line goes dead before I can respond.

I toss my phone into Elias's lap, focusing on the road ahead. The speedometer climbs past ninety, the engine roaring as I push it to its limits. Through the windshield, the moon seems to mock me—so close to full, so hungry for what's mine.

The hum of the tires fades into a steady rhythm, a war drum beneath my chest. I can almost feel her, a faint thread tugging at the edges of my instincts, pulling me closer.

Elias clears his throat, but I cut him off before he can speak. "Don't. Not now." Words would only slow me down, and I don't have the luxury of slowing.

The tracker pings again. The red dot is still moving—sluggish, like a wounded animal—or a lure meant to look that way. Either way, I follow.

For a heartbeat, it feels like the whole world holds its breath.

I push the accelerator down, harder. Not for him. Not for the pack. For her.

Whatever waits for me at the end of this road, I'll face it head-on because monsters don't get to take what's mine and walk away.

And tonight, they'll remember why they call me the Reaper.

Karina

I'm drowning in a sea of shadows, my consciousness bobbing like a cork in black water. Up, down, surfacing for seconds before plunging back into inky blackness. The world spins without me, somewhere beyond the thick cotton that's replaced my brain.

"...still out cold. How much did you give her?"

The sound cuts through the fog, muffled and distant. I try to force my eyes open, but my lids may as well be glued shut. My limbs hang useless, heavy as stone, every muscle refusing to respond. Only my wolf stirs, howling beneath my skin, clawing frantically against the chemical cage holding us both prisoner.

Damien?

I grope for the tether between us, finding it faint but

still there. The effort of pushing along that thread stabs through my skull like knives, but I don't stop.

Damien, please...

A jolt runs through my body, something hard beneath me shifting. Not a floor. A seat. The low growl of an engine and the steady vibration under my cheek confirm I'm in a car. My wrists are cinched tight behind me, plastic biting into my skin.

"...almost there. Make the next turn."

Saloma.

My wolf surges at the sound of her, snarling, fighting to burn off the drug in our blood. The fog is thinning. My fingers twitch against the restraints—unyielding, but not unbreakable.

"She's coming around," another voice observes from the front. Lockhart. Heavy, guttural. "Good. I want her awake for what comes next."

Ice floods my veins despite the drug's warm haze. I keep my breathing steady, my body limp, playing unconscious while I gather what information I can. We're moving fast—highway speeds. The dashboard clock glows 11:47 PM when I manage to crack my eyes open the tiniest fraction—less than an hour until moonrise.

"The clearing's just ahead," Saloma declares. "Everything's been prepared according to your specifications."

"Excellent." Lockhart's satisfaction makes my skin crawl. "And the witnesses?"

"Waiting. Though I still think this is unnecessarily theatrical."

"Theater has its place, Saloma. Binding her on her family's ancestral land, it sends a message. The old bloodlines will bow to the new order."

My heart hammers against my ribs, but I force myself to remain still. My wolf surges against the chemical restraints, rage giving her strength. The old bloodlines. He wants to rape me on my family's land. The violation goes deeper than just my body. He's trying to desecrate everything.

Over my dead fucking body.

The car slows, tires crunching over gravel and fallen leaves. Through my barely cracked eyelids, I catch glimpses of towering redwoods blocking out most of the moonlight. We're deep in the forest now, far from any roads I recognize. The perfect place for Lockhart to commit his crimes without witnesses.

"How long until the moon reaches its peak?" Lockhart asks as the engine cuts out.

"Forty-three minutes," Saloma replies, checking what sounds like an expensive watch. "More than enough time for the ritual."

Ritual. The word makes my stomach clench with dread. This isn't just about claiming me—it's about making a statement. A public declaration that Thomas Lockhart has conquered the Rosewood bloodline.

Car doors slam shut, and cold night air rushes in as they open the back door beside me. Lockhart's hands grip my shoulders, dragging me from the seat with no regard for gentleness. I let my body stay limp, my head lolling as he hauls me upright.

"Still playing dead, little wolf?" His breath is hot against my ear. "I can feel your pulse racing." His fingers brush over my throat, lingering on my jugular. "The sedative is wearing off. No need to pretend."

I jerk upright, every muscle tight with loathing. "Go to hell."

He laughs, the sound echoing through the trees around us. "There she is. I was beginning to think Saloma had given you too much."

I test the zip ties again, the plastic digging into my wrists. My muscles still feel leaden, my reactions slow, but the drug is definitely wearing off. My wolf paces beneath my skin, growing stronger with each passing minute.

Lockhart drags me forward into a small clearing. What I see makes my blood run cold.

A stone altar sits in the center, ancient and weathered, its surface stained with what I suspect is centuries of blood. Torches surround it, casting long shadows across the faces of at least a dozen wolves watching me. They're all masked, just like at Crimson Howl, but these masks are different—carved wood depicting various predators, painted with symbols I don't recognize.

"Welcome home, Karina. To the land your mother abandoned."

I struggle against his grip, but my limbs still won't fully cooperate. His grip on my arm tightens as he drags me toward the altar. My feet stumble over exposed roots and stones, my body still fighting the sedative's grip. The surrounding wolves move closer, forming a tighter circle around us, their masks hiding everything but hungry eyes that reflect the torchlight.

I scan the clearing desperately, looking for any escape route. The trees stand like silent sentinels, offering shadows but no salvation. Saloma moves ahead of us, placing something on the altar—a knife, its blade catching the firelight. My heart hammers against my ribs as panic claws up my throat.

"You're insane if you think I'll willingly accept you," I spit, finally finding enough strength to dig my heels into the soft earth. "I'd rather die."

Lockhart laughs, the sound echoing off the ancient trees. "Willing has nothing to do with it. Not when the moon rises." He leans closer, his breath hot against my ear. "Your wolf will recognize my dominance. She'll submit, even if you fight it."

"My wolf despises you as much as I do," I growl, feeling her rage building beneath my skin, burning through the last of the sedative's fog. The moon's pull growing stronger with each passing second.

"She'll submit to me just to ease the ache of your heat cycle. You reek of desperation."

"No, she won't," I spit back, tugging at my restraints.

He jerks me against him, snarling. "Defiance is something I will have to beat out of you once you're my mate, it seems. Too bad for you, I will immensely enjoy doing it."

"You will never have the chance."

Rage surges through me, not just mine, but my wolf's too. She's fully awake now, snarling beneath my skin, her fury burning away the last vestiges of the sedative.

"Your mother should have taught you respect instead of how to hide in human skin. She was so busy teaching you to deny what you are that she forgot to teach you your place."

"My mother saved me from monsters like you," I spit, straining against his grip.

Lockhart's fingers dig deeper into my arm as he yanks me closer to the altar. "Saved you? She squandered you. She squandered *all of you*. She wasted a bloodline that could've produced legends on a beta. On a nobody. She weakened our kind because she was too soft, too blind. She could've bred power. Instead she bred you, and now you are all that left of it."

"Yet you want what I can give you badly enough to force me to mate you," I spit, twisting my face from his grip.

His hand cracks across my face, the slap echoing through the clearing. I taste blood, metallic and warm, as my lip splits under the force of the blow.

"The alphas of her time didn't see her potential, but even as a pup, I did. Your mother could have strengthened our species had she picked the right mate. I won't chance that happening again."

The circle of masked onlookers tightens around us, their collective energy feeding the tension in the clearing.

"You could be the start of a new era, Karina. Strong females bred properly, loyal to the ones who shape them. Do you understand what that means? Every alpha from here to the northern border would pay to have what your blood can create."

"You mean pay you."

"Precisely, little wolf. Through you, and our pups, you will give me what your mother should have given her generation. The ability to create a pack that will rule everything."

"Enough words, Thomas," Saloma interjects. "Every second you waste goading the bitch, you risk being discovered."

Lockhart's jaw tightens, irritation flashing across his face at being interrupted. "You forget your place, Saloma," he says without turning to her.

"I helped you find her," Saloma hisses, stepping closer to Lockhart. "I drugged her. I got her out of that club under the Reaper's nose. And now you dare to speak to me of my place?"

"Your assistance has been noted," Lockhart says coldly to Saloma. "You'll receive what was promised once I've completed the bond."

"Then do it."

"You're denying me my fun, but I see your point." He turns his attention back to me. "The moon is calling, little wolf."

Lockhart drags me by my hair now, the sharp pain drawing a gasp from my lips as he pulls me toward the altar. The stone surface is cold against my back as he shoves me down, my bound arms crushed painfully beneath me.

"Keep her still," he commands, and two masked figures step forward, their hands pinning my shoulders and ankles to the unforgiving stone.

I struggle against their grip, but my drugged muscles are still too weak to overpower them. The moon peeks through the canopy of trees above, its silver light falling across my face. My wolf howls at its touch, surging closer to the surface with each passing second.

Saloma takes a step forward towards me. I bare my teeth at her, letting my wolf rise closer to the surface. "Does Anselm know what his Luna is doing?"

Her laugh is sharp as the blade in her hands. "My husband is an old fool, too blinded by notions of honor. He chose me because I was the only option after I killed his first wife."

My blood turns to ice at her casual admission of murder. This woman standing before me isn't just helping Lockhart. She's a monster in her own right.

"You killed Elias's mother?" I gasp, the pieces falling into place. She was murdered by the woman who replaced her.

Saloma's smile is evil incarnate. "Accidents happen to those who stand in my way. Just as they'll happen to my stepson if necessary. Matthew and Leo are my blood.

They deserve the Bellandi legacy, not that arrogant firstborn."

"That's why you're doing this. He's going to make your son alpha."

She answers with a smile and shrug.

"Begin the ritual," Lockhart orders.

She approaches with the knife, its edge catching moonlight as she raises it. "The old ways require blood. Her blood must anoint the altar."

My wolf surges forward with renewed panic, lending me strength I didn't know I had. I buck against the hands holding me, twisting violently as Saloma brings the blade toward my exposed collarbone.

"Hold her still!" she commands.

The hands on my shoulders tighten painfully, the grip strong enough to bruise. I can feel my power fading as the knife descends. I twist desperately, throwing my head back with all my strength. The movement jerks my neck into the firelight, exposing my throat, as the harness covering my mark breaks under the strain.

Saloma freezes, the knife hovering inches from my skin. Her eyes widen, fixed on a point at the base of my neck.

"Wait," she hisses, leaning closer to inspect whatever has caught her attention. "She's mated."

"Impossible," he snarls, shoving Saloma aside to see for himself. His grip clamps around my jaw, forcing my head to the side until the mark at my throat catches the torchlight.

Saloma stumbles back, her composure cracking. "It's a true mates bond," she gasps, as if speaking it aloud makes it more real.

Lockhart's roar of rage shatters the night, sending birds scattering from the surrounding trees.

"You see?" I laugh, even as the sound tears at my raw throat. "I'm already mated. You can't have me."

His hand connects with my face again, harder this time. I taste fresh blood, but I don't give him the satisfaction of crying out. My wolf howls in triumph inside me —let him see that I'm not his to break.

"This changes nothing," Lockhart snarls, turning to the masked observers whose murmurs have grown louder, more uncertain.

"You can't break a true mate bond. Not without killing them both."

Lockhart's face contorts with fury as he looms over me. "We'll see about that."

He grabs my face, fingers digging into my cheeks as he forces me to look at him. His eyes have already begun to change, amber bleeding into the irises as his wolf pushes forward.

"The ceremony continues," he announces to his followers, though I notice several shifting uncomfortably. "True mate or not, I will have what is mine."

"Thomas, stop. You don't understand what you're dealing with. A true mate bond can't be overwritten. If you try to force a bond over a true mate bond, you'll kill her, taking her bloodline with her." Saloma insists.

"Bleed her, Saloma. Fucking do it."

Saloma hesitates, the knife trembling in her hand. "This isn't what we agreed to. You promised me power, not a bloodbath."

"Do it!" Lockhart roars, his face contorting as his wolf pushes closer to the surface. The moonlight catches his features, highlighting the inhuman rage that transforms them.

"He'll come for me. Damien's already hunting you. And when he finds you there won't be enough left of you to bury."

Lockhart backhands me again, his ring catching my cheekbone. Pain explodes across my face, but I laugh through it, tasting blood and victory.

"Hit me all you want," I taunt, feeling reckless power surge through me as the moon climbs higher. "It won't change what Damien and I have. It won't make me yours."

"Shut up!" he roars, grabbing me by the throat. His fingers press against my windpipe, cutting off my air. "Stop saying his name."

Black spots dance at the edges of my vision as I struggle for breath. My wolf howls in panic, throwing herself against the cage of my ribs. The moon calls to her —to us—stronger than ever before. I feel her clawing for control, desperate to save us both.

"Thomas, stop!" Saloma grabs his arm, trying to pull him away. "You're killing her."

His fingers tighten around my throat, the pressure

building until stars explode in my vision. Through the encroaching darkness, I see several of the masked figures shifting uncomfortably, backing away from what's unfolding.

"I'll take what's mine!" Lockhart roars, his face contorted with rage. "One way or another!"

The world blurs at the edges, oxygen-starved and fading, when his grip suddenly loosens. I gasp desperately, dragging air into my burning lungs as Lockhart's face swims back into focus.

"No," he says, his voice eerily calm. "That's too quick." He turns to Saloma, who's watching with barely concealed horror. "Change of plans."

"Thomas—" she starts, but he cuts her off with a raised hand.

"I want the Reaper to see what becomes of those who take what's mine."

My blood runs cold as the meaning sinks in. He drags me off the altar, his fist tangled cruelly in my hair.

"Find him," he commands one of the masked followers. His grip wrenches my head back, exposing my throat to the moonlight. "I want him to watch as I open her up. I want him to see her blood stain sacred ground."

I fight against him with renewed frenzy, twisting, clawing, anything to break free. His hold only tightens, sharp pain lancing across my scalp and forcing tears to my lashes. My gaze flicks toward the tree line, hunting for the shadow of Damien. Is he there? Has he found me?

"You're making a mistake," Saloma hisses, striding

forward, the sharp edge of panic breaking through her usual composure. "Killing her will bring the wrath of every pack down on us. They'll hunt us to extinction."

"Let them try." Lockhart's laugh has a manic edge that makes my skin crawl. "When I'm done, they'll know better than to challenge me."

I struggle against his grip, feeling my wolf surge closer to the surface as the moonlight bathes the clearing. She's so close now, clawing beneath my skin, demanding release. The zip ties dig into my wrists as I twist, searching for any weakness.

Damien?

The bond flares suddenly—a supernova of rage and relief flooding through me. I gasp, my eyes flying to the trees surrounding us.

"Your executioner is here," I say, unable to contain the smile that spreads across my face despite the blood trickling from my split lip. I laugh, the sound wild and untethered.

A howl splits the night—deep, commanding, and unmistakably alpha. It's followed by another, then another, until the forest rings with them, the sound coming from all directions at once. The masked figures freeze, heads swiveling as they try to locate the source of the threat.

The Reaper has come for me and no one will be spared.

Damien

I step from the shadows, my paws silent against the forest floor. Every muscle in my body tenses at the sight before me. Karina, her pale skin gleaming in the moonlight, Lockhart's filthy hands tangled in her hair. The harness she wore to lure him crosses her exposed skin is now torn and twisted from her struggles. Blood trickles from her split lip, and bruises bloom across her face where he's struck her.

My wolf howls for blood, for vengeance, for the head of the male who dared touch what's mine.

I will tear him apart slowly. I will make him beg for death before I grant it.

Lockhart freezes at the sight of me, shock flickering across his features as he drags Karina tighter against his body like a shield. Even for an alpha, the size of my wolf is daunting—midnight fur bristling, fangs gleaming under the moonlight. The Reaper in this form is the last thing most enemies ever see.

"Impossible," he spits, panic cracking his authority. "You can't be here already."

Karina lifts her chin, battered but unbroken, her focus finding me instantly across the clearing. I feel the bond between us flare alive, her call threading through me.

Shift, kitten. Now.

I shove the command down that tether with every ounce of dominance I possess. The full moon sings above us, tugging at every wolf in earshot. Around the edges of the clearing, my father's forces emerge from the shadows. Their presence is thick as smoke. For once, his obsession with control works in my favor. Tonight, we're aligned.

Understanding sparks in her expression. She knows exactly what I'm demanding, even if the cost terrifies us both.

"Kill him!" Lockhart shrieks, his mask of composure splintering. "Kill them all!"

His followers hesitate. Some step backward, sensing the tide has turned. The wiser ones melt into the tree line.

I prowl forward, each step deliberate, a growl rolling from deep in my chest. Karina never wavers, her battered form alight with something fierce. My focus stays locked on her—not Lockhart, not the traitors—because she's the only reason I came here.

Let your wolf free.

Karina's body locks, every muscle straining as the moon claims her. Lockhart's grip slips when she convulses, a scream ripping free—not agony, but release. Her bones crack and realign, her spine bowing as fur ripples in a silver wave across her skin.

"No!" Lockhart lunges, claws flashing. "I won't let you—"

I'm on him before the threat is finished. Two bounds, and my jaws snap around his wrist. Bone crunches, sinew tears. His roar shakes the night as I wrench him backward, dragging him away from her.

The restraints binding Karina fall in pieces as her body completes its transformation. She lands on four legs, smaller than me but radiant in silver-gray fur that gleams like moonlight.

Mine, my wolf thrums, a fierce satisfaction flooding us both.

Lockhart rips free, leaving shreds of flesh behind. His own shift overtakes him in a mess of snapping bone and ripping skin. When he steadies, he's massive, dark-furred, scar-mapped from countless battles. Rage burns off him like heat from a forge as he charges, jaws wide for my throat. I pivot at the last moment, claws carving deep across his ribs. Blood sprays the ground in an arc as he crashes past.

Across the clearing, Karina turns. Saloma has backed herself against the altar, clutching the ceremonial knife with trembling hands.

She's yours, kitten. Let your wolf free.

Karina's wolf snarls, the sound fierce enough to raise the fur along my spine. She springs. Saloma flails with the blade, slashing empty air as her terror spills over.

"Stay back!" she shrieks, her grip shaking. "I am a Luna! You can't touch me!"

I prowl around Lockhart, cutting off his path to Karina. His chest heaves, flanks streaked with blood, yellow irises burning. More of my father's wolves close in from the tree line, hemming him in. The wound I carved isn't fatal. Not yet. And for everything he's done, I won't settle for less than final.

He feints left, then lunges right, trying to get past me to Karina. I meet him in midair, our bodies colliding with bone-crushing force. My teeth find his shoulder, tearing through muscle and tendon. The taste of his blood fills my mouth, metallic and satisfying.

Behind us, Saloma drops the knife and begins to tear at her clothes. I can smell her desperation as she tries to shift, her body contorting awkwardly as she struggles to call her wolf. It's almost unnatural how slow her transformation is—especially for a Luna who has supposedly lived her entire life in our world like her body seems to resist the change.

Lockhart tears free from my grip, his claws raking across my muzzle as he spins away. Pain flares, but it only fuels my rage. I shake my head, blood spattering the ground, and bare my teeth in what might be called a smile if wolves could smile.

Come on, I think, circling him slowly. Show me what you've got.

I glance over at Karina's wolf, who has Saloma pinned to the ground, claws pressed into her chest. Saloma writhes beneath her, caught mid-shift, her body jerking and twisting in unnatural rhythm. Fur ripples across one arm, recedes from the other. Bones crack, reset, and crack again. Her face flickers between human and wolf, teeth too long for her mouth, fingers half-formed into claws.

It isn't a transformation. It's a fracture.

She's wrong, Damien. She smells wrong.

Fuck. Saloma is a fucking crossbreed. It explains everything. Why she was willing to forsake her protected position and align with Lockhart. She needed her sons to be alpha to protect her and their secret.

I roar down our bond. *Do not kill her. Incapacitant her, but do not fucking kill her. Leave her for Anselm.*

Lockhart must notice my distraction and lunges again, desperation making him sloppy. I duck under his snapping jaws and drive my shoulder into his chest, sending him sprawling. He rolls with the impact, coming up with dirt and leaves clinging to his fur. I lunge at him. My teeth find the soft flesh where his neck meets his shoulder, and I clamp down with every ounce of strength I possess. Lockhart howls—a sound that splits the night and sends birds scattering from the trees. I feel flesh tear, arteries rupture beneath my jaws. His blood floods my mouth, hot and metallic, fueling the rage of my wolf.

I shake my head violently, tearing deeper into his flesh. Lockhart thrashes beneath me, his claws raking desperately at my sides, but I barely feel the pain. All I can focus on is the scent of his fear, the taste of his defeat, and the knowledge that he will never touch my mate again.

With one final, savage twist, I tear away a chunk of his throat. Blood sprays across my muzzle as I release him, stepping back to watch him stumble. He tries to maintain his wolf form, but the damage is too severe. His body convulses, the shift reversing against his will as his wolf retreats to preserve what little life remains.

Where the brown wolf stood moments before, Lockhart now lies in human form, naked and bleeding out on the forest floor. His hands clutch futilely at the gaping wound in his neck, blood seeping between his fingers in rhythmic pulses that grow weaker with each beat of his failing heart.

The shift tears through me, bones grinding as my wolf recedes. The rage doesn't leave—it simmers, a fire under my skin.

Flesh knits, fur vanishes, and I rise in the moonlight, naked and streaked with blood. Lockhart lies crumpled at my feet, chest heaving in ragged bursts. His lips twist into a grotesque smile, crimson bubbling at the corners. "She'll...never...be...safe."

"She's safe from you." My hand clamps around his throat, fingers digging deep as I rip his throat from his body. His thick blood drips down my hand in warm waves. I hold it up for him to see as his eyes glaze, and the forest swallows the silence of his end.

A sharp crack splits the air behind me. I turn in time to see Karina's wolf folding back into human form, her body trembling with the effort. She lands hard on her hands and knees, breath ragged, hair tangled and matted with dirt and blood. Some hers, most not. A few long scratches mar her beautiful skin.

Saloma lies several feet away, half-shifted and barely conscious, one arm twisted unnaturally beneath her. A deep gash runs along her shoulder, pulsing sluggishly but not fatal. Her eyes flicker once, unfocused, before rolling back as her body slumps against the ground.

Karina's gaze locks on the fallen Luna. There's no triumph in her expression.

I crouch low, cupping her face. My thumb wipes a smear of blood away, uncovering the ugly bruise blooming beneath. Fury ignites in me again at what she endured, but I shove it down. Lockhart's corpse is proof enough of justice served.

Karina leans into my touch, her lashes lowering for an instant of stolen peace. "Is it over?"

"Yes." I gather her against me, uncaring of the blood that paints both our bodies. Her skin is cool against mine, her heartbeat a frantic flutter that gradually steadies as I hold her. "It's over."

The forest shifts with the sound of men returning to themselves—bones cracking, fur receding, low groans filling the air as wolves give way to flesh again. Gabriel emerges from the tree line, limping heavily, his chest bound in rough bandages where Saloma's bullet struck.

He looks worn and pale with blood loss, but alive. Relief flickers across his features as his gaze meets mine, and he inclines his head.

"Thank you," she rasps. "For finding me. For coming for me."

I press my lips to Karina's forehead, tasting sweat and salt, copper and iron. "I'll always come for you, kitten. Always."

My father strides toward us. He carries two folded blankets in one hand, his expression hard as stone. Without looking directly at Karina, he extends them. I accept with a curt nod, wrapping one carefully around her shoulders before securing the other around my waist.

"Lockhart's forces have broken," he reports. "The cowards fled into the trees. Those who bent the knee are being held."

"And Saloma?"

"Anselm has been notified."

I can picture it clearly. To discover your Luna conspiring with your enemy, it would be enough to test even Anselm's infamous control.

"Take her," my father orders, flicking his chin toward Saloma's unconscious body. Two of his men step forward, dragging her limp form without ceremony.

"She said she killed Elias's mother."

My father stills, his composure fracturing for the barest instant. A curse slips from between his teeth, low and venomous.

"That's not all, Father." My voice is grim as I tighten

the blanket around Karina, shielding her from both the night and the stares of our pack. "She's a crossbreed."

His head snaps toward me, pale eyes narrowing, nostrils flaring as he inhales sharply, testing the air as though scent might confirm it.

"You're certain?" he demands.

I nod, my arm tightening around Karina's shoulders.

Karina shivers against me, and I pull her closer, wrapping the blanket more securely around her shoulders. Her skin feels like ice, despite the warm night air, as shock sets in now that the immediate danger has passed.

"I need to get her out of here," I tell my father, already scanning the clearing for the quickest path back to the cars.

He nods once, his expression unreadable. "Take her to the compound. I'll handle the cleanup here."

I don't wait for further instructions. With one arm supporting Karina, I guide her away from the altar, away from Lockhart's cooling corpse, away from the nightmare this clearing has become. Her legs tremble with each step, and I can feel her exhaustion through our bond—bone-deep and overwhelming.

"I can carry you," I offer, but she shakes her head.

"I need to walk."

"We'll take it slow."

"Are we going home?"

Home. The word settles something deep in my chest. Soon I'll have Karina back where she belongs—in my bed, in my arms, where I can protect her properly. Where no one can ever touch her again.

"Yes, kitten. We're going home."

I gather Karina closer, her body still trembling against mine. Even now, with Lockhart's blood still wet on my hands, I want more vengeance for what he's done to her.

We pick our way through the forest, following the path back to where I left my car. Each step takes us further from the horror of that clearing.

"I can feel you thinking," she murmurs.

"I was thinking about killing him again," I admit.

Her hand finds mine, fingers intertwining despite the blood that stains them both. "He's gone. That's enough."

But it's not. Not for the wolf in me that demands retribution for every blemish on her skin, every moment of terror she endured. I want to hunt down every wolf who stood in that circle watching, every masked figure who would have witnessed her violation. I want to tear apart the world that dared threaten what's mine.

"How did you find me?"

"I injected you with a tracking device."

Her body stiffens against mine.

"You what?"

"I couldn't risk losing you." The words sound hollow even to my own ears. An excuse, not an explanation. "I knew the plan was dangerous. I knew Lockhart might find a way to take you."

She pulls away slightly, just enough to look up at me. The bruises on her face look worse in this light.

"You put a tracker in me without telling me?"

"Yes." I don't sugarcoat it. Don't try to justify what we both know was a violation of trust. "I did what I needed to do to keep you safe."

"You should have told me. We're supposed to be partners, Damien. Equals."

"I know." I tighten my grip on her hand, afraid she'll pull away completely. "I was wrong not to tell you. But I'm not sorry I did it. Not when it meant the difference between finding you and losing you tonight. The second we're home, I'll remove it if it survived your shift."

She's quiet for a long moment, processing my words. "We'll talk about this when I'm not naked in a forest covered in blood."

I nod, accepting the reprieve she's offering. We both know this conversation isn't over, but she's right—now isn't the time for it.

We reach the cars where one of my father's enforcers waits. He tosses me a set of keys without a word, understanding that I need to be the one driving us home.

I guide Karina to the car, opening the passenger door and helping her inside. Her body feels fragile under my hands, though I know better than anyone how strong she truly is. The shift has exhausted her—especially her first complete transformation after years of suppressing her wolf. I grab a gym bag from the trunk and find a spare t-shirt for her to wear.

"Here," I say, handing it to her. "It's not much, but it's better than a blanket."

She takes it with trembling hands, her eyes downcast. The blood on her skin has begun to dry, cracking like macabre paint as she moves. I want to help her, to clean every trace of this night from her body, but I know better than to push right now. She needs space to process what's happened. She slips it over her and wraps the blanket around her for added warmth. I close the door and head back for the trunk, pulling on a pair of my workout shorts before closing the truck and walking around to the driver's side.

I slide into my seat and start the engine. The heater kicks on, pushing warm air through the vents. Karina huddles against the door, my shirt drowning her slender frame. The silence between us stretches, heavy with everything we're not saying.

The road hums beneath us, the heater filling the car with warmth that still can't quite chase the chill from my skin. I want to say something. Anything. But the words knot in my throat, heavy with everything that's happened tonight. So, I keep driving, letting the silence stretch between us like a fragile thread neither of us dares to break.

Her hand shifts under the blanket, fingers brushing the seat between us—so slight I almost think I imagined it. But I don't.

And for the first time tonight, I let myself believe.

The worst is over.

Karina

I don't know what hurts more—the bruises throbbing across my face, or the truth I can't escape. I was hunted like prey for a bloodline I didn't even know I carried until days ago. That my existence alone is enough to shatter worlds, to tip the balance of power, and spark wars.

I never asked for this. For any of it. And yet wishing it all away feels like another kind of lie. Because in the chaos of these past days, I've unearthed parts of myself I never knew existed...and found someone who feels essential to the marrow of who I am.

Damien.

Losing that connection was like being split open, like having half of my soul torn away. And I realized then that some truths, no matter how terrifying, are worth holding onto.

Because the truth is, no matter how much I wanted to deny it, the tie altered me. It carved itself into the deepest parts of who I am, reshaping everything I thought I knew about strength, about belonging, about myself.

And now I cannot imagine a world without it. Without him.

Maybe that's what terrifies me most. That for the first time in my life, I have something to lose. Not my bloodline. Not the war it threatens to ignite. But Damien. The piece of me I didn't know I was missing until he was here.

The drive back to the Marek compound passes in silence, each mile putting distance between us and the clearing where Damien tore out Lockhart's throat. I can still taste blood in my mouth, can still feel the phantom pressure of Lockhart's fingers around my neck. My wolf paces anxiously beneath my skin, exhausted from her full shift but too restless to settle, her energy feeding the hollow ache still thrumming through me.

When we finally arrive, Damien guides me from the car with a gentleness that feels at odds with the predator I watched tear a man apart an hour ago. His hand on the small of my back is steady, grounding me as we move through the quiet compound. Dawn is still hours away, and the house sleeps around us, unaware of the night's violence.

"Almost there."

My body feels like it belongs to someone else—heavy, foreign, marked by hands that had no right to touch me.

He opens the door to his bedroom and ushers me inside before he closes it. The light flicks on, and I wince at the sudden brightness. My eyes feel swollen, my face tender where Lockhart's hands left their mark. I can still feel him on my skin, the phantom pressure of his fingers around my throat. I lower myself onto the edge of Damien's bed, my legs too weak to keep standing.

From the bathroom comes the sudden rush of water—not the sharp spray of a shower, but the heavy pour of a bath being drawn. The sound is unexpectedly soothing, like rainfall on a metal roof. I didn't even noticed Damien disappearing into the bathroom.

"I thought you might prefer a bath," he says, emerging from the doorway. "The heat will help with the soreness."

I nod, unable to find words. My fingers twist in the blanket still wrapped around my shoulders, anchoring me to something tangible when everything else feels like it might dissolve at any moment.

Damien crouches in front of me, somehow making himself smaller as he looks up into my face.

"You don't have to be strong right now," he says quietly. "Not for me."

Tears blur my vision as I look down at him. This man who killed an alpha to save me, who holds me now like I might shatter if he's not careful enough.

"I was so scared." The words scrape my throat raw. "Not just of Lockhart, but of losing you. Of losing us. When the bond went quiet, I thought—"

"I know." His hands cover mine where they clutch the blanket. "I felt it too. The silence. It nearly drove me insane."

I lean forward, resting my forehead against his. The simple contact sends relief flooding through our connection. A warmth I hadn't realized I was desperately craving.

"The tracker," I say, pulling back enough to face him directly. "I understand why you did it. I hate that you didn't tell me, but I understand."

His jaw tightens. "I violated your trust. I should have—"

"You saved my life." The truth of it settles between us, complicated and messy but undeniable. "We'll figure out the trust part later. Right now, I just need you to help me wash him off my skin."

Damien rises, offering me his hand. "Come on. Let me take care of you."

He leads me into the bathroom, where the soaking tub is already filling with water hot enough to cloud the mirrors. Steam curls through the air, carrying the scent of heat and stone. When he shuts off the faucet, he uncaps a small bottle on the counter and lets a few drops fall into the water. The sharp hiss of oil meeting heat fills the space, and the scent of lavender blooms between us, soft and grounding.

He turns back toward me, ready to help, but I lift a hand to stop him.

"I can manage," I start to say, but he shakes his head.

"Let me. Please."

There's something in his voice—a need that matches my own. He needs to care for me as much as I need to be cared for. To replace Lockhart's violence with his gentleness, his possession with protection.

I nod, letting the blanket fall away. His shirt follows, pooling at my feet. Damien's eyes don't linger on my nakedness. Instead, they catalog every mark, rage flickering behind his careful control.

"I should have killed him slower," he growls, his hands clenching at his sides.

"You killed him. That's what matters."

He helps me into the tub. The hot water engulfs me, and I can't suppress the groan. I sink deeper into the water, letting it rise to my collarbone. The warmth penetrates my aching muscles, drawing out pain I didn't even realize I was holding. Damien kneels beside the tub, rolling up his sleeves before reaching for a washcloth and soap.

"This might sting," he warns, gently lifting my arm from the water.

His touch is reverent as he washes away the dried blood. I watch his face as he works, the muscle ticking in his jaw each time he uncovers another bruise beneath the grime.

"I felt my wolf tonight," I say, breaking the silence. "Really felt her."

"Your wolf was always part of you, kitten. You just needed to stop being afraid of her."

"I'm not afraid anymore." The words surprise me with their certainty. "Not of her. Not of what I am." I pause, studying his face as he rinses soap from my skin. "I'm more afraid of what comes next than my wolf."

"What do you mean?"

"Lockhart's dead, but that doesn't end this. Other alphas will now be aware of my bloodline. They'll want what he wanted."

Damien's hands still in the water. "Let them come," he says quietly, but there's nothing quiet about the promise. "They'll learn what happened to the last alpha who tried to take you."

I reach up, cupping his face with my wet hand. "I don't want you to have to keep killing for me."

"Then they shouldn't keep threatening you." His thumb traces my lower lip, careful of the cut there. "This is what being mated to me means, Karina. I will destroy anyone who tries to harm you. It's not a choice. It's what I am."

The water sloshes as I shift closer to him. "The Reaper."

"Yours," he corrects, turning his face to press a kiss against my palm. "First and always, yours."

The simple declaration makes something bloom in my chest, warm and certain despite everything we've been through tonight. I lean forward, pressing my forehead against his.

"I vow to you, Karina, that I will always keep you safe. My life, my needs, my desires—they all come second to yours. Always."

"Damien—"

"No," he cuts me off gently. "You need to understand what this means. What you mean to me." His hands frame my face, careful of my bruises. "Before you, I existed. I fought. I killed. But I never lived. You've given me something I didn't know I was missing."

Tears blur my vision as his words sink deep into places I've kept guarded for so long. "I can't ask you to put me before everything else."

"You're not asking. I'm choosing." His thumb catches a tear as it falls. "My father sent me away to learn a lesson, but the real lesson came from you. Protection isn't about possession or control. It's about sacrifice. About putting someone else's needs before your own."

I lean into his touch. "I don't want to be your weakness."

A smile touches his lips—small but genuine. "You're not my weakness, kitten. You're my strength." His forehead presses against mine again. "My reason to be better than what I used to be."

The last few days have rewritten everything I thought I knew about love, about strength, about what it means to belong to someone completely.

"I need to tell you something." The words slip out as

I draw in a shaky breath, tilting my head toward him. "When that silence stretched between us, I realized I'd rather die than live in a world without you."

His breath catches. "Karina..."

"I know it's crazy. We've known each other for less than a week. But this feeling, this certainty—it's the first real thing I've ever experienced. The first time I've felt like I'm exactly where I'm supposed to be."

His hands tighten on my face, and I watch something flicker behind his eyes. "Say it again."

"I'd rather die than live without you."

"The other part."

I smile despite the ache in my split lip. "I'm exactly where I'm supposed to be."

He kisses me then, soft and careful around my injuries, but with an intensity that makes my heart race. I taste his relief, his love, his absolute devotion. When he pulls back, his eyes are molten silver.

"I'm going to spend the rest of my life making sure you never doubt that truth," he finishes.

The water has begun to cool around us, but I don't want to leave this moment. Don't want to face whatever comes next beyond this bathroom, beyond the safety of his arms. Here, with steam rising around us and his hands gentle on my skin, the world feels manageable again.

"The water's getting cold," Damien observes, though he makes no move to rush me.

I nod reluctantly. My fingers have started to prune,

and the warmth that felt so soothing minutes ago, now barely penetrates the chill settling into my bones. Exhaustion weighs on me like a physical thing, pressing down until even sitting upright feels like effort.

Damien helps me from the tub, wrapping me in a towel that's been warmed on the heated rack. The simple luxury of it—soft cotton that smells like cedar and safety—almost undoes me completely. I lean into him as he dries my hair with another towel, his movements careful around the tender spots on my scalp where Lockhart's fingers had twisted.

"Better?" he asks, and I realize some of the tension has finally started to leave my shoulders.

"Getting there."

He guides me back into the bedroom before leaving me to head to his closet. He returns with one of his shirts and hands it to me. I slip it on, the fabric soft and oversized, hanging to my thighs like a dress. It carries his scent.

"You should lie down," Damien nearly orders me as he pulls back the covers on his bed. "You need to rest."

I hesitate, suddenly reluctant to be alone with my thoughts. "Where are you going?"

He tucks a strand of damp hair behind my ear, his touch so light it barely registers against my bruised skin. "To get you something to eat. You need to rebuild your strength after the shift."

The thought of food makes my stomach clench with unexpected hunger. I hadn't realized how famished I am until this moment. The shift and everything that came before it burned through my energy reserves completely.

"I'm not sure I can sleep," I admit, even as I sink onto the mattress. The sheets are cool against my skin, and my body practically melts into their softness.

"Try," he requests, pulling the covers over me. "I'll be back before you know it."

I catch his wrist before he can move away. "Don't be long." After everything that's happened tonight, I don't want to pretend I'm stronger than I am.

"Five minutes. I promise."

I want to say more, but exhaustion tugs at me like an undertow. I watch Damien walk toward the door, his movements fluid despite everything we've been through tonight. Just as he reaches for the handle, it swings open without warning.

Damien freezes, his body instantly shifting into a defensive stance. I sit up straighter, adrenaline cutting through my fatigue as my eyes lock on the figure in the doorway.

His father stands there, hand frozen mid-knock, surprise flickering across his usually stoic features. His attention drifts from Damien to me, lingering on my bruised face and damp hair before settling back on his son.

"Father, I was just going to get Karina something to eat."

Hudson's expression remains unreadable as he lowers his hand. "That can wait. We need to talk."

Karina

The sheet slides up to my chin as Hudson enters, my fingers clutching the fabric like armor. Every bruise throbs with new awareness beneath the thin cotton of Damien's borrowed shirt. The air shifts. The intimate warmth between Damien and me evaporating as his father's alpha presence floods the room like winter air through an open door.

"This isn't a good time," Damien replies, not moving from his protective position between me and his father.

"We need to discuss what happened tonight."

Damien's shoulders tense, his posture shifting from protective to confrontational in an instant. "No."

I watch the two alphas square off, father and son locked in a silent battle of wills.

"This isn't optional," Hudson insists. "What happened tonight has consequences that—"

"I said no." Damien takes a step forward, his body blocking Hudson's view of me more completely. "She's been drugged, kidnapped, beaten, and nearly killed. Whatever you need to say can wait until morning."

I should say something. Should tell them I'm fine, that I can handle this conversation. But the truth is, I can't. My body feels like it's made of glass, ready to shatter at the slightest pressure. The mere thought of reliving what happened in that clearing makes my stomach twist with nausea.

Hudson's expression hardens, his focus sliding past Damien to land on me. I straighten as much as I can, clinging to what little dignity remains, though I know exactly what he takes in—a bruised, broken girl wrapped in his son's shirt, curled in his son's bed.

"This cannot wait, Damien. Decisions need to be made right here and now."

Damien looks over his shoulder at me, his eyes asking a silent question. I nod slightly, knowing this conversation is inevitable. As much as I want to hide away from the world right now, his father isn't a man who takes no for an answer.

"Fine," Damien says, stepping aside reluctantly.

Hudson enters the room, closing the door behind him with a soft click that somehow feels final. The air grows heavier with his presence, that unmistakable alpha energy filling the space like a physical thing.

"You have five minutes," Damien tells him, his voice leaving no room for negotiation. "Then you leave, and she rests."

I pull myself up straighter against the headboard. The movement sends pain shooting through my ribs, but I refuse to wince. I won't appear weak in front of this man, no matter how broken I feel inside.

"What happened tonight changes everything," Hudson begins, his attention locked on me rather than his son. "Lockhart's death will create a power vacuum. The alphas who supported him will be looking for someone to blame."

"They can blame me," Damien growls, moving to stand beside the bed. His hand finds mine on top of the covers. "I killed him."

"It's not that simple. Lockhart held a large territory and had no heirs. His pack will fracture, but the territory will be up for grabs. Other alphas will see opportunity where we see justice."

I squeeze Damien's hand, drawing strength from his touch. "What does that mean for us?"

"Our law is simple. Damien killed the heirless Lockhart alpha, and by right, the territory is his."

I stare at Hudson, his words echoing in my head like a bell that won't stop ringing. Territory. Damien's territory now, because he killed to protect me.

"I don't want it," Damien says immediately, his grip on my hand tightening. "I have no interest in ruling Lockhart's pack. I am your heir."

"What you want is irrelevant. The law is clear. You killed an alpha without an heir in defense of your mate. The territory is yours by right of conquest."

My stomach drops as the implications crash over me. "This is my fault."

"No." Damien turns to me. "This is not your fault. None of this is your fault."

But it is, isn't it? If I hadn't been born Rosewood, if my mother hadn't run, if I'd never walked into Crimson Howl—none of this would've happened. Damien wouldn't be stuck ruling land he never wanted, all because he had to save me from a monster chasing my bloodline.

"The pack elders will expect you to accept it within the week," Hudson continues, ignoring our exchange. "If you don't, they'll assume weakness and divide the territory among themselves. That kind of power struggle will destabilize the entire region."

I feel sick. Actually, physically sick. My head spins as I try to process what this means. "So what you're saying is—Damien has to take over Lockhart's territory?"

"Yes," Hudson answers.

My head throbs with each heartbeat, making it hard to focus.

"I'm not leaving her. Not now. Not after what just happened."

Hudson's expression doesn't change. "You won't have to. You'll both go. The territory needs an alpha. You need protection. The solution is obvious." Hudson looks between us. "You'll take command of the territory together."

Damien and I, ruling a territory? Becoming responsible for an entire pack of wolves who just lost their alpha. Wolves who might hate us for killing him.

"She's not ready for that," Damien argues. "She's only just accepted her wolf. She doesn't even know our ways, our politics—"

"Then teach her," Hudson cuts in. "Lockhart's pack is only the beginning, son. You're going to need to bring them to heel to take back the Rosewood territory. Your mother's pack has been without an alpha for decades. The land has been divided, weakened, and left open to predators like Lockhart. With his death, you have a chance to restore what was stolen from your family."

"I never asked for any of this."

"None of us ask for the blood that runs in our veins," Hudson replies, unmoved by my distress. "But we all must answer for it eventually."

The room spins around me as I struggle to process what he's saying. Territories. Packs. Power. It's too much, too fast. Just days ago, I was a normal woman with a normal job, living a normal life. Now I'm expected to help rule a territory I've never even seen?

"You're overwhelming her," Damien growls. "Your five minutes is up."

Hudson ignores him. "You need to understand what's at stake here, Karina. With Lockhart's territory and eventually the Rosewood lands under your control, you'll command one of the largest territories on the west coast. That kind of power doesn't just protect you—it ensures your safety for generations. Not only yours, but your children's safety."

Children.

"I haven't even thought about children." The concept is so foreign it feels like Hudson is speaking another language.

"The future comes whether you're ready or not," Hudson replies, his tone softening just slightly. "Your bloodline is too valuable to leave unprotected. Too many will covet what you represent."

I look up at Damien, searching his face for any sign of what he's thinking.

"We need time," Damien answer resolutely. "Time to heal, time to decide what we want."

"Time is a luxury you don't have," Hudson counters. "Word travels fast in our world. By sunrise, every alpha within five hundred miles will know that Lockhart is dead."

My head pounds harder, exhaustion and stress blurring the edges of my vision. "And if we refuse? If we just...walk away?"

Hudson's expression hardens. "Then you sign your own death warrant. Both of you. Your mother and father ran, and look what happened to them, and to you. Don't make their mistakes."

"That's enough," Damien growls, rising to his full height. "Get out."

For a moment, I think Hudson will refuse. His jaw tightens, his shoulders squaring as father and son face off in a silent battle of dominance. Then his shoulders relax slightly, though his expression remains implacable.

"We'll speak again once your both rested. I expect a decision by then." He turns and walks toward the door, pausing only when his hand reaches the handle. "For what it's worth, your mother would be proud of the woman you've become. Elena never backed down from a fight either."

The door closes behind him with a soft click, leaving Damien and me alone in the sudden quiet. I stare at the space where Hudson stood, my mind reeling from everything he just laid at our feet. Territory. Responsibility. A future I never wanted stretching out before us like an unavoidable path.

"Breathe," Damien says softly, settling back onto the bed beside me. His hand finds mine again, warm and steady against my trembling fingers. "Just breathe."

I try, but each inhale feels like it catches in my chest. "This is insane. We can't rule a territory. I don't know the first thing about being an alpha."

"Neither did I when I first shifted," Damien admits, his thumb tracing circles on the back of my hand. "But you learn. You adapt. You do what needs to be done to protect your pack."

"Your pack," I correct, shaking my head. "I'm not cut out for this, Damien. I've spent my entire adult life running from who I am. How can I suddenly turn around and embrace it? How can I lead a pack when I've barely figured out how to be a wolf myself?"

Damien shifts closer, his body warm against my side.

"You shifted tonight without hesitation when you needed to. You faced down Saloma. You survived Lockhart's torture and came out stronger. That's not the behavior of someone who runs from who they are."

"That was survival. This is..." I gesture helplessly at the air between us. "This is politics. Leadership. Making decisions that affect hundreds of lives."

"And you think I was born knowing how to do those things? I learned by watching my father. By making mistakes. By having someone believe in me even when I didn't believe in myself."

The parallel he's drawing isn't lost on me. I can feel through our bond that he means it—that he believes I'm capable of this impossible thing his father is asking of us. The faith he has in me makes something flutter in my chest, fragile as moth wings.

"What if I make the wrong choice? What if people die because I don't know what I'm doing?"

"Then we learn from it and do better next time." His hand cups my bruised cheek with infinite gentleness. "That's what leadership is, kitten." He pauses before he continues. "I vowed to put your first, Karina, and despite the advantages and protection this would give us, I don't want it unless you do. I meant what I said earlier, you before me. If you want to run, tell me where you want to go, and I'll pack the fucking car."

"Where would we go?" I ask, allowing myself to imagine it for just a moment. "How far would we have to run to escape what I am? What my blood means?"

"Anywhere. Everywhere. I'd take you to the ends of the earth if that's what you wanted."

I search his face for any hint of reluctance, any shadow that suggests he's offering this sacrifice against his nature. But I find only certainty—and something else, something that makes my heart ache with its intensity.

"You'd leave everything behind? Your pack, your position, your father? For me?"

"In a heartbeat."

I believe him. That's the terrifying part. I believe him completely.

And maybe that's why I can't ask.

"We can't run. If your father is right, they'll just keep coming. Other alphas, other packs. They'll hunt us down."

The words taste bitter on my tongue, but I know they're true. Running didn't save my parents. It didn't save me from Lockhart. It only delayed the inevitable while making me weaker, more vulnerable.

"So we stay and fight?"

I close my eyes, trying to imagine myself as an alpha. Leading pack meetings. Making decisions about territory disputes. The image feels foreign, impossible. But then I remember the feeling of my wolf tonight—not cowering, not hiding, but fierce and protective. Ready to kill Saloma for her betrayal.

Maybe that's what leadership is. Not some innate ability to command, but the willingness to do what needs to be done to protect the people you care about.

"I don't know the first thing about ruling a pack," I admit, lifting my head to face him fully. "But if not taking this territory means other innocents will suffer, we don't have a choice. We have to do this."

"Then we do it together," Damien finishes, his hand tightening on mine. "Not because my father demands it, but because it's the right thing to do."

I nod, feeling something settle in my chest—not peace exactly, but resolution. The kind that comes from finally choosing your path instead of having it chosen for you.

"We need to take the territory."

"You're sure?"

"No," I admit with a shaky laugh. "I'm terrified. But I'm sure about us. About this." I gesture between us. "And if we're going to be hunted anyway, I'd rather face it with power than without it."

His smile is small but genuine. "My fierce mate."

"Your terrified mate," I correct, though warmth spreads through me at his words. "Who has absolutely no idea what she's doing."

"We'll figure it out together." He leans down to press a soft kiss to my forehead, careful of my bruises. "One decision at a time."

My stomach chooses that moment to growl loudly, reminding us both that I haven't eaten in hours.

Damien chuckles, the sound rumbling through his chest.

"Right. Food first, conquering territories second."

"That should probably be our pack motto," I say, settling back against the pillows as he rises from the bed. "Practical priorities for practical alphas."

"I like it." He stops at the door, his features gentling, affection flickering in his eyes. "You're already thinking like an alpha. Putting everyone else before yourself."

After he leaves, I sink deeper into the pillows, my body finally beginning to relax now that we've made our decision. The truth of our situation settles over me—not crushing, but substantial. Real. In a matter of days, I'll be responsible for an entire pack of wolves who lost their alpha tonight.

The thought should terrify me more than it does. Instead, I find myself thinking about the masked figures in that clearing. How some of them backed away when they realized what Lockhart was truly planning. How even monsters have lines they won't cross.

Maybe leadership isn't about being fearless. Maybe it's about being afraid and choosing to act anyway.

I close my eyes, letting exhaustion pull me toward sleep. Tomorrow will bring new challenges, new responsibilities I never asked for but can't avoid. But tonight, I'm safe in Damien's bed.

And that's enough for me.

Damien

I stir awake, her scent enveloping me like a familiar embrace. Karina is nestled against my chest, her breath steady and rhythmic, each soft exhale brushing against my exposed skin. The afternoon sun streams through the curtains, casting a warm glow that dances across her bruised skin. Even with the remnants of Lockhart's brutality etched on her, she radiates a beauty that captivates me completely.

Mine.

My wolf rumbles with satisfaction as I trace the curve of her shoulder with my fingertips. The marks from last night have already begun to fade—one of the benefits of her werewolf healing. By tomorrow, they'll be nothing but memories. The physical ones, at least.

I brush a strand of hair from her face, my touch light enough not to wake her. After everything she endured yesterday, she needs rest. The shift, the fight, the decisions we made afterward—all of it has taken a toll.

And yet, I can't stop touching her. Can't stop reassuring myself that she's here, safe in my arms, where nothing can harm her. My fingertips drift along the curve of her spine, memorizing each vertebra through the thin cotton of my borrowed shirt.

She stirs, her body arching into my touch like a cat seeking more. A small sound escapes her throat—half sigh, half moan—and my body responds instantly, hardening against her hip.

"Mmm." The sound slips from her as she shifts closer, still half-asleep. Her lashes lift slowly, eyes hazy before they sharpen on my face. The bruise on her cheekbone has already faded to a yellow smear. My fingers skim over it, memorizing every trace before it vanishes completely.

"How long was I out?"

"Almost fourteen hours." A reluctant smile tugs at my mouth. "You needed it."

She stretches languidly against me, every subtle brush of her body sparking a want I struggle to ignore. My cock aches, but I force my thoughts back to her recovery, not the ache thrumming in my blood. She's still healing. Still fragile.

"Fourteen?" Karina blinks up at me, startled. "What time is it?"

"Just after three." My palm settles on her hip, thumb tracing idle circles against the soft fabric of my shirt draped over her frame. "How do you feel?"

Her eyes fall shut again as she takes inventory of herself, the small furrow between her brows deepening while she measures each ache, each lingering bruise.

"Still sore, but...better." Her stomach growls loudly. "And apparently still hungry."

I can't help but smile. "The shift burns through calories. Your body's trying to replenish what it lost."

"Is that why I feel like I could eat an entire cow? Raw?"

"That's your wolf talking." I tuck a strand of hair behind her ear, marveling at how quickly she's adapting to her nature. "She's closer to the surface now that you've embraced her."

"You're hungry too," she smiles, her hand sliding up my bare chest. "Just not for food."

My breath catches as her fingers trace the contours of my muscles, leaving trails of heat in their wake. She's right—I'm starving, but not in a way that can be satisfied with meat or bread.

"Karina," I warn, capturing her wandering hand. "You're still healing."

"I'm a werewolf, remember? I heal fast." She leans closer, her lips brushing against my jaw. "Besides, I want to replace those memories with better ones."

I understand immediately what she means.

Lockhart's hands on her. His threats. His possession. She wants to erase them with my touch, my love.

"Are you sure?" I ask, even as my resolve weakens with each soft press of her lips against my skin.

She answers by shifting her body until she's straddling me, her thighs bracketing my hips. The thin cotton of my shirt rides up, revealing the curve of her ass and the fact that she's wearing absolutely nothing underneath. The sight nearly undoes me completely.

She answers by grinding her hips against my cock, straining against my shorts. "I need this. Need you. You don't have to be gentle with me. I won't break."

My hands find her hips, steadying her as she rocks against me.

"I need to hear you say it," I growl, the last thread of discipline fraying as her hips move against me. "Tell me exactly what you want, kitten."

She leans down until her lips brush against my ear, her breath hot against my skin. "I want you to make me forget every hand that touched me except yours. I want you to reclaim what's yours."

My restraint shatters. In one fluid motion, I flip her onto her back, caging her beneath me. I capture her mouth with mine, careful of her healing lip but unable to hold back the hunger that's been building since I found her in that clearing. She responds immediately, her body arching up to meet mine, her hands sliding down my back to push at my shorts.

"These. Off. Now," she demands between kisses, her fingers hooking into the waistband.

I oblige, breaking away just long enough to shed the last barrier between us. When I return to her, she's pulled my shirt over her head, leaving her gloriously naked beneath me. I pause, drinking in the sight of her. My breath catches in my throat. Bruises still mark her skin—fading, but visible reminders of what she endured. Yet she's never looked more beautiful to me than she does right now, sprawled across my sheets.

"Damien," she begs, reaching for me. "Don't stop."

I lower myself over her, careful to keep my weight on my forearms as I settle between her thighs. She's warm and wet against my cock, her body ready for me despite everything. The scent of her arousal fills my lungs, making my wolf growl with satisfaction.

"I'll never stop wanting you. Never stop needing you."

Her fingers tangle in my hair, tugging me closer as she lifts her hips, seeking friction. "Then show me."

I trail kisses down her throat, over her collarbone, taking my time despite the urgency building in my blood. Each bruise gets special attention—a gentle press of lips, a whispered promise against her skin. I'm erasing Lockhart's touch with my own.

When I reach her breasts, I pause to look up at her face. Her eyes are heavy-lidded, her bottom lip caught between her teeth as she watches me worship her body. The vulnerability in her expression steals my breath. In this moment, she's offering more than just her body. She's giving me her trust, her faith that I can help her.

"You're so beautiful," I breathe against her skin, reverence lacing every word as I draw one dusky nipple into my mouth. She gasps, her back arching off the bed as I lavish her with slow, gentle attention, my tongue circling the sensitive peak until it hardens beneath my care. Her hands slip into my hair, not just urging but anchoring me there, as if she knows I would worship her forever if given the chance.

I shift my attention to her other breast, giving it the same reverent treatment while my hand slides down her stomach, feeling the quiver of muscles beneath my touch. When I reach the apex of her thighs, I find her slick and ready, her body responding to me in ways that make my cock throb with need.

"Please," she whimpers, her hips lifting to meet my touch as I circle her clit with my thumb. "I need you inside me."

"I need to be inside you too, kitten, but I'm worried about hurting you." I press a kiss to her inner thigh, feeling her tremble beneath my lips. "Your body's still healing."

She sits up, pushing against my shoulders. "Then let me take control."

Before I can respond, she shifts us, rolling me onto my back with surprising strength. She straddles me again, slick warmth hovering just above my cock, teasing us both.

"Like this. Let me show you what I need."

Fuck. The sight of her above me, bruised but unbowed, claiming her own pleasure, is the most erotic thing I've ever seen. My hands grip her thighs as she lowers herself, the head of my cock pressing against her entrance.

"Take what's yours," I growl, fighting the urge to thrust up into that wet, welcoming heat.

She sinks down slowly, her body stretching to accommodate me. A moan escapes her lips as she takes me inch by inch, her eyes locked with mine the entire time. When she's fully seated, she pauses, adjusting to the feeling of being completely filled.

"That's it," I encourage, my voice rough with need. "You feel so fucking good around me, kitten."

Her hands brace against my chest as she begins to move, lifting herself up before sliding back down with agonizing slowness. I groan at the sensation, my fingers digging into the soft flesh of her thighs.

"That's it," I encourage, watching her find her rhythm. "Take what you need."

She moves with growing confidence, her body rising and falling in a hypnotic rhythm that has me fighting to hold myself together. Each downward stroke pulls a small gasp from her lips.

I'm mesmerized by the sight of her. Her palms press against my chest for leverage as she begins to move faster, chasing her release.

"You're mine," I growl, unable to stop the possessive

words that tear from my throat. "Every beautiful inch of you."

"Yours," she agrees. "Only yours."

I slide my hands from her thighs to her hips, helping guide her movements as she rides me.

I can't look away. Karina moves above me like a goddess—strong, unyielding, determined. My hands anchor her hips, guiding her into a rhythm that wrings every ounce of pleasure from us both.

"That's it, kitten," I urge. "Take what you need."

She shifts forward, changing the angle until each stroke draws a sharp gasp from her throat. Her curls fall around us, a dark veil that shuts out the world until there's only her and me. I reach up, cupping her face, my thumb brushing over the bruise on her cheekbone like a vow.

"You're the most beautiful thing I've ever seen."

Her movements falter as she leans into my touch, a shiver running through her body. I can feel her tightening around me, each pulse dragging me closer to the edge. My wolf howls with satisfaction.

I growl, sliding my hand to the back of her neck and hauling her down into a kiss. She moans against my mouth, still riding me, chasing the oblivion only I can give her. I taste her desperation, her need to scrub away the ghosts of last night.

But I want more than her body. I want her soul.

"I love you," I rasp into her kiss, the words ripping

out of me before I can stop them. Raw, undeniable. "I fucking love you, Karina."

The taste of her fuses with the force of the words, searing them into truth. It's not instinct, not compulsion—it's me, stripped bare, offering everything.

She freezes above me, lips parted, breath caught. Shock flashes across her features, halting the rhythm of her body.

"Say it again," she requests.

"I love you," I repeat, my hands framing her face as she continues to move above me, slower now but with more purpose. "I love your strength, your stubbornness, the way you challenge me. I love that you chose me even when every instinct told you to run."

Tears gather in her eyes, but her smile is radiant. "I love you too."

She loves me. My fierce, stubborn, perfect mate loves me back.

I flip us again, needing to be deeper inside her, needing to show her with my body what words can't express. She wraps her legs around my waist as I drive into her, setting a rhythm that has us both gasping.

"Damien," she gasps, her nails digging into my shoulders as I move inside her. The sound of my name on her lips drives me wild, making me thrust deeper, harder. I need to be as close to her as physically possible, need to merge our bodies until there's no space left between us. Her body tightens around me, pulling me deeper with each stroke.

"Give in to me, kitten," I murmur against her ear, rough with need. "Give your greedy fucking cunt what it needs."

She comes with a cry that echoes off the walls, her body arching beneath me as waves of pleasure crash through our connection. I follow her with a growl that sounds more wolf than man.

I drop beside her, breath coming hard as I pull her close. Her pulse pounds against my ribs, echoing the rhythm still racing through me. The bond hums with her calm, her release. My wolf growls low in approval, knowing I've driven out every trace of another's scent.

Karina shifts against me. "I can feel your smugness," she says with a sleepy laugh.

"Good. You should know how satisfied I am." I press a kiss to the top of her head, tasting the salt of her skin. "How completely you've ruined me for anyone else."

"Damien, I swear to the Gods that if you are seriously thinking about anyone else, but me right now—"

I press my finger to her lips. "Shh, kitten. The only female I am thinking about is you, and only you."

"Good," she murmurs, nestling deeper into my arms. "Because I'm not interested in sharing."

I stroke her hair, letting the silky curls slip through my fingers. The wolf in me is utterly content, sated in a way that goes beyond physical pleasure. She's here. She's safe. She's mine.

"How are you feeling?"

"Like I'm exactly where I'm supposed to be." She tilts

her head to look up at me. "I meant what I said, Damien. I love you. It terrifies me how quickly it happened, but I can't deny it."

"Why does it terrify you?"

She's quiet for a moment, her fingers drawing idle patterns on my chest. "Because loving someone means having something to lose. All my life, I've kept people at a distance. Even my ex..." She pauses. "I never let him see all of me. Never told him about my wolf. It was easier that way."

"And now?"

"Now I've handed you every part of me—human and wolf. You know me in ways no one else ever has. That kind of vulnerability is scary."

I tighten my arms around her. "I'll never use it against you. I'd rather die than betray the trust you've placed in me."

She shifts, propping herself up on one elbow to look at me more directly.

"Do you really think we can do this?" she asks. "Run our own territory?"

This isn't just about us anymore. It's about the responsibility we've taken on, the lives that will depend on our decisions.

"I think we can," I say, though I understand her concern. "But I won't lie to you, it won't be easy."

She bites her lower lip, wincing slightly as she aggravates the healing cut there. "It's just...so much, so fast. You're already heir to your father's lands, and now we have Lockhart's territory. And if we try to reclaim my family's lands too..." She shakes her head. "Three territories, Damien."

I sit up, pulling her with me until we're facing each other, the sheets pooled around our waists. My hands find hers, squeezing gently.

"It is daunting," I admit. "But we don't have to do everything at once. Lockhart's territory first. We establish control, and then we can look towards the Rosewood lands."

"What about your own pack?"

I barely contain a chuckle. "My father is too stubborn to die young. We won't need to worry about my pack for many, many years to come. Even then, he'll figure out a way to keep his position as a ghost."

Karina laughs despite herself, the sound light and musical in the afternoon stillness. "A ghostly alpha. That's a terrifying thought."

"He'd probably enjoy it. All the power, none of the responsibility." I trace the curve of her shoulder with my fingertips, marveling at how much of the bruising has already faded. "But that's decades away. Right now, we focus on what's in front of us."

Her expression grows serious again. "What exactly are we walking into with Lockhart's pack? Do we know anything about them?"

I consider how much to tell her, how much truth she can handle right now.

"They're not going to welcome us with open arms," I

admit. "Lockhart ruled through fear and intimidation. His inner circle profited from that system. They're going to see us as threats to their power. and their bottom line."

"And the others? The ones who weren't part of his inner circle?"

"Some will be relieved he's gone. Others will be suspicious of any change." I brush a strand of hair from her face. "Pack loyalty runs deep, kitten. Even when the alpha is a monster, some wolves will defend him out of habit."

"So, we'll have to prove ourselves."

"We will. But not today." I lean forward, pressing a soft kiss to her forehead. "Today, all we need to do is tell my father of our decision and come back to bed. If we only have a week until we takeover those lands, that's seven days that I get you to myself, and I, for damn sure, am going to make sure to soak up every fucking second of that time."

Her smile transforms her entire face, erasing the last shadows of worry. "Seven days of just us?"

"Seven days of me worshipping every inch of your body," I promise, my voice dropping to that rough register that makes her shiver. "Seven days of showing you exactly how much I love you."

She laughs, the sound pure and joyful in a way that makes my chest tight with emotion. "That's quite an ambitious schedule, Mr. Marek."

"I'm very motivated." I capture her lips in a slow, thorough kiss that tastes like promises and forever. Her smile lingers against my mouth, soft and sure, and for the first time in days, there's no trace of fear hiding beneath it. Just her. Just us.

"I never pictured my life ending up here," she admits softly, a smile curving her lips. "But I wouldn't trade it for anything."

"You won't ever have to," I promise, threading my fingers tighter through hers. "It's you and me, kitten. Always. Whatever future we build, we build it together. And in the meantime..." I let my mouth brush hers, teasing, "I fully intend to make good on those plans."

Seven days. Seven lifetimes. It makes no difference. However, much time we're given, I'll spend every second proving my love for her.

And this time, nothing—and no one—will ever come between us.

Damien

I feel hundred eyes on me as I step into the clearing. These wolves, Lockhart's former pack, have gathered for what they believe will be a simple formality. Instead, they're about to witness a challenge that will determine their future.

My future. Our future.

Karina walks beside me. She's dressed for war in black leather pants and a jacket that hugs her curves, her hair pulled back in a tight braid that exposes the mating mark on her neck. Let them all see it. Let them know she's mine, and I am hers.

Three days since we made our decision. Three days of preparation, of strategy, of enjoying each other's bodies like the world might end tomorrow. Because for some of us in this clearing, it just might.

"That's him," someone states from the crowd. "The Reaper."

The name slides off me like water. I've been called worse. I'll be called worse before this day is done. My father taught me that a name is just a weapon others use against you unless you claim it first.

"Damien Marek," a voice calls out, silencing the murmurs that ripple through the gathering. A man steps forward from the front of the crowd—tall, broad-shouldered, with a shock of white-blond hair and eyes so pale they're almost colorless. Frost. Thomas Lockhart's Beta. The man who's been running this pack since his alpha's death. "You have no right to be here. This territory belongs to the Lockhart pack."

I step forward, feeling my father and his enforcers move into position behind me. The Marek pack, standing as witnesses to what is about to unfold. At the edge of the clearing, I spot Elias and his father, Anselm. The Bellandis have come too—though whether to support me or to watch me fail remains to be seen.

"This territory belongs to me by right of conquest," I state. "I killed Thomas Lockhart. The law is clear."

Murmurs ripple through the crowd. Some nod in acknowledgment of pack law, while others bare their teeth in silent challenge. Frost remains unmoved.

"The law is clear when an alpha dies without an heir," he agrees, taking another step toward me. "But

Thomas wasn't without an heir. He named me his successor before his death."

Lies. I can smell the deception on him like rancid meat.

"Lockhart died with my teeth in his throat," I growl, letting my wolf rise closer to the surface. I let my canines lengthen just enough to be visible when I speak. "He had no time to name an heir between his begging and his dying. You are nothing more than an opportunist. A coward who fled into the trees while his alpha bled out."

Frost's face twists with fury, but he doesn't deny it. He can't. Too many witnessed his retreat that night.

"Lockhart would never name you heir anyway," Karina speaks up. "You were just a tool to him. Useful, but disposable."

I feel a surge of pride as several wolves in the crowd shift uncomfortably, recognizing the truth in what she says. Karina may be new to pack politics, but she understands the power of perception.

Frost turns his head toward her, his expression tightening with open contempt. "And who are you to speak of pack matters?"

I take a step forward, my wolf surging with protective rage, but Karina's hand on my arm stops me.

"I am Karina Rosewood," she announces, her voice carrying across the clearing. "Daughter of Elena Rosewood. True mate to Damien Marek. And by right of both blood and conquest, I stand before you as your future Luna."

The name *Rosewood* ripples through the crowd like wildfire. Shock registers in faces both young and weathered. Some of the elders lean forward, recognition dawning as they piece together the lineage they thought long extinguished. Others bristle, lips curling back, unsettled by what her existence means for the balance of power.

Frost is the first to recover. His surprise hardens into contempt. "Rosewood?" His laugh is sharp, humorless. "That line was erased decades ago."

Karina doesn't flinch. "My mother fled to protect me from men like Lockhart. Why do you think he wanted me above all others, when any female here would have bent at the chance to call herself Luna? He hunted me because of my bloodline. He admitted it before he died. His obsession wasn't with me. It was with my mother. He saw me as his property by inheritance."

A stir passes through the pack. From the front, an older woman steps closer. Her white-streaked braid swings against her back, her movements measured but sure. Lines of memory etch her face, but her gaze is steady as it settles on Karina.

"I knew Elena," the woman remarks.

Frost snarls at the woman. "Silence, Mara! This is pack business."

"It is pack business," Mara replies, unflinching under his glare. "And if she truly is Elena's daughter, that changes everything."

I feel Damien shift beside me, his body angling subtly to keep both Frost and the newcomer in his line of sight.

"It changes nothing," Frost snaps, his attention returning to us. "Rosewood or not, you have no claim here. This territory has belonged to the Lockhart pack for generations."

"That ends today," I challenge him. "This transition does not merit bloodshed. I am giving you a choice. Submit or leave."

Frost's laugh is harsh, grating against my ears like claws on stone. "Submit? To a pup who thinks killing one alpha makes him worthy of leading a pack? I've served this territory for fifteen years. I know every border, every threat, every weakness. What do you know besides how to follow orders?"

The challenge hangs in the air between us, heavy with implication. I can feel the pack's attention shift, weighing his words against my presence. Some nod in agreement.

"I know how to protect what's mine. I know the difference between leadership and tyranny. And I know that any wolf who stood by while Lockhart tortured innocents has already proven themselves unfit to lead."

Murmurs ripple through the crowd again. I catch fragments of whispered conversations—wolves recounting memories of Lockhart's cruelties, his excesses, the fear that permeated every aspect of pack life under his rule.

Frost's jaw tightens. "You know nothing of what it

takes to keep a pack alive. To make the hard choices. Thomas may have been harsh, but he kept us strong. Kept us unified."

"He kept you terrified," Karina interjects.

"He kept you isolated," I say evenly. "Fear isn't strength—it's weakness wearing a mask of dominance."

Frost's nostrils flare as the realization hits that he's losing ground.

"Pretty words from someone who's never led anything," he spits. "What happens when neighboring packs test our borders? When food runs short? Will your mate's bloodline feed our young?"

"My mate's bloodline will make sure they have a future worth fighting for," I growl, stepping forward until only a few feet separate us. "Under Lockhart, you were scavengers. Under me, you'll remember what it means to be wolves."

Something in Frost fractures. His composure shatters, gold flooding his eyes as his wolf surges free. Bones pop and twist as the change takes hold. "Then prove it!" he snarls, voice warping as his canines lengthen. "Face me as wolves do. Winner takes all."

The crowd forms a circle around us, their excitement palpable as they scent the coming violence. This is what they understand—not politics or bloodlines, but raw power. The most primal form of pack law.

I begin to strip, handing my clothes to Karina without breaking eye contact with Frost. Her fingers brush mine as she takes them. It steadies something wild in my chest.

"End this quickly," she murmurs, low enough that only I can hear.

I nod once, then let my wolf surge forward. The shift tears through me like lightning—bones cracking, muscles expanding, my human form dissolving into something far more lethal. When I rise on four legs, I'm massive even by alpha standards.

He's smaller than I expected. Lean where I'm broad, built for speed rather than raw power. His white-blond fur makes him look ghostly in the afternoon light filtering through the trees. He circles me slowly, looking for weakness, for an opening.

I don't give him one.

The pack falls silent around us, the only sounds our heavy breathing and the soft pad of paws on forest floor.

Frost lunges first, aiming for my throat in a move that speaks of desperation rather than strategy. I sidestep easily, my larger frame moving with surprising grace. His momentum carries him past me, and I rake my claws across his ribs as he stumbles.

First blood. The metallic scent fills the air, and several wolves in the circle shift restlessly, their wolves eager to witness the outcome.

Frost recovers quickly, wheeling around to face me with bared fangs. Blood drips from his wounded side, but he shows no sign of backing down. If anything, the injury seems to fuel his desperation.

He feints left, then launches himself at my flank. This time, I'm ready for the deception, catching him mid-leap with my jaws. My teeth sink deep into his shoulder, and his howl of pain echoes through the clearing. I shake him once, violently, before releasing him to crash into the circle of watching wolves.

They scatter back, giving us more room as Frost struggles to his feet. His left foreleg trembles with the effort of supporting his weight, but he doesn't submit. Stubborn bastard.

Frost circles me again, more cautiously this time. I almost feel sorry for him. Almost.

He tries a different approach this time, staying low and going for my legs. If he can bring me down, limit my mobility, he might stand a chance. But I've faced faster, more skilled opponents than Frost. I leap over his attack, twisting in midair to land behind him.

Before he can recover, I'm on him, my jaws clamping down on the back of his neck. Not hard enough to kill, not yet, but enough to immobilize him.

Frost struggles beneath me, his body thrashing as he tries to break free. I increase the pressure just enough to make him yelp, to remind him and everyone watching who holds the power here.

The clearing falls silent except for Frost's ragged breathing. The pack's focus presses down on me, heavy and unrelenting, every wolf waiting for my choice. I could end him now—tear out his throat as I did Lockhart's. It would be simple. Final.

But killing Frost won't win me this pack's loyalty. It would only reinforce oppression they've lived under for too long.

I release him suddenly, stepping back as he collapses to the ground. I shift back to human form, my bones cracking and reshaping until I stand on two legs again. Naked, vulnerable, but unquestionably victorious.

"Submit or leave," I repeat my earlier offer.

Frost writhes through the last spasms of his shift, bones cracking as his wolf peels away to leave raw, battered flesh. Blood seeps from the gashes I carved into him, staining the earth beneath his knees. But it isn't the torn skin or the broken pride of his body that truly cripples him. It's the humiliation. The defeat hangs heavy on his shoulders, pressing him lower than any physical blow could.

"I'll never submit to you," he spits, crimson spattering his mouth. His chest heaves as he glares up at me. "You think one fight makes you worthy to lead this pack? You know nothing of us."

Karina moves into my periphery, steady as moonlight, her warmth brushing against me as she presses my clothes into my hands. I don't look away from Frost as I drag on my pants, keeping my body angled between him and my mate. My stance says what words don't: he won't touch her, not again, not ever.

"Then leave. Take what's yours and go. But understand this, if you choose exile, there's no coming back."

Frost scans the gathered wolves, searching for allies.

For anyone willing to stand with him. Most turn their heads away, unwilling to tie their fate to a defeated beta. Only a handful, three, maybe four, shift into place at his back.

"This isn't over," he promises. "The Lockhart legacy won't die with me."

"No," I agree, scanning the faces of my new pack. "It died with that bastard days ago."

Frost staggers to his feet, blood still dripping from his wounds.

"You'll regret this decision," one of them snarls at the remaining pack members. "When the neighboring territories come for you, when winter brings starvation, don't come crawling back to us."

I watch them disappear into the forest, their threats echoing off the trees. Good riddance. A pack is only as strong as its weakest link, and those wolves were already rotting from the inside.

The silence that follows their departure stretches uncomfortably long. Forty-three wolves remain—I count them quickly, cataloging ages, injuries, the way they hold themselves. Most avoid direct eye contact, the ingrained habit of submission to authority still strong. A few, like the older woman who recognized Karina's bloodline, study us with cautious curiosity.

"So," I address the pack. "Here we are."

A murmur ripples through the gathered wolves, uneasy and uncertain. The young male's voice has shattered the silence like a stone through glass, and now every shoulder tilts toward me, waiting. Expectant. Hungry for something beyond submission.

I let my gaze sweep over them—not with dominance, but with purpose. These wolves have been broken, shaped into survivors by Lockhart's cruelty. What they need now isn't another master. It's meaning.

"What happens now?" I echo, letting my voice carry across the clearing. "Now we rebuild. Now we heal. Now we become more than what he made us."

A few lift their heads, hesitant sparks of hope kindling in their eyes.

"Lockhart kept you small so you would always depend on him," I say. "That ends tonight. Every wolf will have a place. Every voice will matter. We will be a pack again—not through fear, but through strength."

Beside me, Karina steps forward, her presence a steadying weight. I focus once more on the young wolf who spoke, meeting the raw, fragile hope in his expression. "It starts with you. With all of you. No more bowing. No more begging for scraps."

I step into the center of the clearing. Karina stands tall at my side, her presence grounding me like bedrock.

An older woman steps forward, her weathered features giving away nothing. "Pretty words. But words don't feed pups or secure borders."

"You're right," I acknowledge, shifting my stance toward her, giving her challenge the respect it demands. "Actions do. So, here's my first action as your alpha. Every wolf in this pack will be evaluated for their skills and strengths. Not to judge, but to understand what we're working with. Every wolf will have a place. Every wolf will have a purpose."

A low rumble moves through the crowd.

"Lockhart hoarded resources," I continue. "Food, medicine, information. Those will be distributed immediately. Tonight, we will celebrate this new beginning. Not as the Lockhart pack, but as the Rosemark pack."

A pause settles over the clearing as they process the name.

"The Rosemark pack," I repeat, letting the words settle. "We honor both our histories while building something new together."

We hadn't discussed this beforehand, but the rightness of it resonates between us. Not the Marek pack extending its reach, not the Lockhart pack under new management, but something entirely fresh.

"Return to your homes. Tend to your families. Tonight, we gather here again to break bread together as a unified pack."

The wolves disperse slowly, many still casting uncertain glances in our direction. Change doesn't come easily after years of oppression. Trust will take time to build, but we've taken the first step.

"Rosemark," Karina murmurs beside me. "You didn't tell me."

I turn to her, drinking in the sight of her proud stance. "It came to me in the moment. Do you like it?"

"I love it." Her fingers find mine, squeezing gently. "A new beginning for all of us."

"For all of us," I echo, bringing her hand to my lips.

Karina leans into me, her warmth grounding the enormity of the moment. Around us, the clearing grows quiet, the last steps fading into the forest until only the quiet rustle of leaves remain.

For the first time in years, I can see leadership not as a burden, but as a promise. The name Rosemark doesn't just bind our lines together—it binds every wolf who calls this pack home. It is carved from the past but aimed toward a future we will shape with our own hands and fangs.

A breeze sweeps through, carrying with it the mingled scents of pine and hope. Life, fragile and enduring. My chest tightens with the fierce need to protect it, to prove that this change was not born of ambition but of love—for Karina, for our wolves, for the generations yet to come.

Karina tilts her head. "Tomorrow will be hard."

"Yes," I admit. "But tonight, we begin again. Together."

She smiles, and it's like the sun breaking through storm clouds. "Then let's make sure they believe it."

EPILOGUE

Karina - Six Months Later

Six months ago, I was a woman who hid from what she was. Now I'm the Luna of the Rosemark territory, and I've learned that power isn't something you're given. It's something you take.

I stand at the window of our study, watching snow gather on the pines that surround our home. The mountains look different in winter.

"The eastern border patrol just reported in," Damien says from his desk, not looking up from the maps spread before him. "No sign of trespassers since we installed the new security system."

I nod, my fingers tracing patterns on the cold glass. "That's the third quiet week in a row. Maybe they're finally getting the message."

"Or they're planning something bigger." His voice carries that edge it always does when we discuss potential threats. Six months as Alpha hasn't softened my Damien's paranoia—if anything, it's sharpened it.

As Damien predicted, the inner circle of Lockhart's pack fought us at every turn during those first brutal weeks. Three challenges for leadership in the first month alone. I still remember the sound of bones breaking as Damien put down the last one—a hulking enforcer named Vance who thought I'd be the weaker target. He learned quickly that being Elena Rosewood's daughter meant I inherited more than just her looks.

The rest of the pack fell into place more easily than we expected.

While Damien and I had agreed for me to assume the role of Luna for this pack to keep the peace with the more outspoken, traditional wolves under our care, I have been training, growing stronger and faster every day. Preparing for the fight ahead for my own pack lands. The lands I would rule as alpha with Damien by my side. We've been workshopping names for a male Luna, but he hasn't liked any of my suggestions. Though Luman is still my favorite. Maybe it will grow on him.

"I'll be ready when they come," I say, turning from the window to face him. The firelight catches on Damien's face, highlighting the new scar that runs along his jawline—a souvenir from the second challenge. I've memorized every inch of that face, every expression, every micro-movement that betrays his thoughts before he speaks to them.

"I know you will. Your combat training with Gabriel is going well. He says you're a natural."

I can't help but smile at that. Gabriel has become one of our most loyal allies. After recovering from Saloma's bullet, he took it upon himself to train me personally. Repayment, he says, for failing to protect me that night at Crimson Howl.

"I'm still not as fast as you," I admit, crossing the room to stand behind him. My hands find his shoulders, feeling the tension coiled there like springs. "But I'm getting stronger every day."

Damien reaches up, his hand covering mine. "You don't need to be as fast as me. You just need to be faster than whoever comes for us next."

There's always someone coming for us. That's the reality we've come to accept. Whether it's remnants of Lockhart's old allies or wolves eyeing our territory, the threats never truly end. They just change shape.

"That's the problem, isn't it?" I say, kneading the muscles at the base of Damien's neck. "There's always someone waiting to test us."

He leans into my touch, a rare moment of vulnerability he shows only when we're alone. "Nature of the beast, kitten. Power attracts challengers."

I've learned this lesson well over these past months. Every decision we make is scrutinized. Every show of strength measured against Lockhart's brutal legacy. The pack doesn't want another tyrant, but they also don't respect weakness. It's a delicate balance we walk daily.

The fire crackles in the hearth, casting dancing shadows across the study walls. Outside, the snow falls heavier now, blanketing our territory in pristine white. Six months in this place, and I'm still adjusting to the brutal mountain winters. My wolf loves it though—she thrives in the cold, finding freedom in the snow-covered forests where we run during full moons.

"Any word from your father?" I ask, my fingers working at the knots in Damien's shoulders. He groans as I hit a particularly tight spot.

"Nothing new. He's still handling the fallout from Saloma's trial."

I suppress a shudder at the mention of her name. After what she did to me—to us—Anselm had no choice but to hold a formal trial. The revelation that his mate was not only a traitor, but a crossbreed had nearly broken him. The once-proud Alpha aged a decade in a matter of weeks.

"And Elias? How is he taking everything?"

Damien leans back into my touch, his eyes closing briefly. "Better than expected. He's stepped up as his father's right hand. The pack respects him more now that he's proven himself."

"Good. He deserves that." I mean it. Despite our rocky start, Elias has become something of a brother to me.

"He's coming by today."

"Did he say why?"

"Just that there's news he'd rather deliver in person."

"That's not ominous at all."

"With Elias, it could be anything from pack politics to his latest romantic conquest," Damien shrugs, but I can feel his tension returning beneath my fingers. "Whatever it is, we'll handle it."

I'm about to respond when our intercom buzzes. The guard's voice crackles through the system, slightly distorted by the snowfall interfering with our communications.

"Alpha, Luna—Elias Bellandi has arrived at the gate. He's alone."

Damien and I exchange a glance. Alone is unusual. Typically, Elias travels with at least one security detail, especially in this weather.

"Send him up," Damien replies, already rising from his chair.

I straighten my sweater and run a hand through my hair, an automatic response to visitors even after months of being Luna. Some habits from my previous life are hard to break.

"Should we be worried?" I ask, moving to stand beside Damien as we wait.

He shrugs, but his body language tells a different story. The easy relaxation from moments ago has vanished, replaced with the coiled readiness I've come to recognize as his default state when facing potential threats.

"Let's hear what he has to say before we decide."

The sound of tires on gravel reaches us even through the thick walls of our home. Moments later, the front door opens and closes, followed by the sound of familiar footsteps approaching the study. A soft knock echoes through the room.

"Come in," Damien calls.

Elias enters, shaking snow from his coat. His usually immaculate appearance is disheveled, blonde hair damp from the storm.

"Christ, it's brutal out there," he says, pulling off his gloves. "The roads are barely passable."

"Which explains why you came alone," I observe, studying his face for clues about what brought him here in such weather.

He nods grimly. "What I have to tell you couldn't wait for better conditions."

My stomach tightens with familiar dread. In our world, news that requires absolute secrecy is rarely good news.

"Sit," Damien gestures toward the leather chairs arranged near the fireplace. "You look like you could use the warmth."

Elias settles into the chair closest to the fire, his hands extended toward the flames. I notice they're trembling slightly—whether from cold or nerves, I can't tell.

"Drink?" I offer, moving toward the bar cart in the corner.

"Please. Something strong."

I pour three glasses of whiskey, the amber liquid catching the firelight as I hand them out. Elias downs his in one gulp, while Damien and I wait with untouched glasses in our hands. He sets the empty tumbler down with a decisive click against the side table.

"Saloma was executed at dawn this morning," Elias blurts out.

The whiskey glass nearly slips from my fingers. I tighten my grip. "Was it...was it quick?"

"No. My father insisted on the old ways. Public. Before the entire pack."

I sink into the chair opposite him, memories flooding back with nauseating clarity.

"Good," Damien says beside me. "She deserved nothing less."

"I don't disagree. Saloma was a grade A bitch, and she reaped what she sowed. But there's more," Elias continues, reaching for the bottle to pour himself another measure, "my stepbrothers have been exiled."

"Both of them?" I lean forward, the whiskey forgotten in my hand. "Matthew and Leo?"

"They're barely adults," Damien interjects. "What did they do to warrant exile? Surely, they weren't involved."

Elias runs a hand through his damp hair, leaving it standing in disheveled spikes. "They knew. About Saloma's plans with Lockhart. Not everything, but enough."

The room suddenly feels colder despite the roaring

fire. I set my glass down before my trembling hands can betray me.

"Old enough to know right from wrong," Damien growls beside me. "Old enough to understand what kidnapping and forced mating means."

I reach for his hand, feeling the tension vibrating through him. "What happens to them now?"

"They've been stripped of the Bellandi name and protection," Elias explains, staring into his whiskey. "Given enough money to start somewhere new but forbidden from contacting anyone in the pack. If they return to our territory..." He trails off, the implication clear.

Death. The punishment for returning from exile is always death.

"Your father's handling of this situation seems...thorough," I say carefully, watching Elias's face. There's more he isn't telling us—I can see it written clearly on his face.

"Thorough doesn't begin to cover it," Elias says, draining his second glass. He shifts in his seat, suddenly finding the fire intensely interesting. "There's something else. Something that concerns both of you, actually."

I exchange a glance with Damien. "What is it?"

Elias fidgets with his empty glass, turning it between his fingers. "My father has...made arrangements."

"Arrangements?"

"For me," Elias clarifies, still not meeting our eyes. "I'm to be mated at the next full moon."

The statement hangs in the air like smoke, unexpected and suffocating. I blink, trying to process what I've just heard.

"Mated?" I repeat, leaning forward. "Considering what your father went through, I would have thought he'd have wanted to wait for the smoke to settle."

"You'd have thought so, but not my father," Elias confirms, "He thinks the family line needs immediate strengthening after a scandal." His bitter laugh holds no humor. "Nothing says 'business as usual' like a traditional mating ceremony, apparently."

Damien sets his untouched whiskey down with deliberate care. "And you're agreeing to this?"

"Do I look like I have a choice?" Elias lifts his head at last, squaring himself to Damien. "My father's word is law."

"Who is she?" Damien asks.

Elias shifts uncomfortably, suddenly finding the contents of his empty glass fascinating. The firelight catches on his profile, highlighting the tension in his jaw.

"That's the thing..." he begins, then stops, running a hand through his hair again. "I don't think you're going to like this part."

"Just tell us," I press, unease crawling up my spine.

Elias takes a deep breath. "It's Bella."

The room temperature seems to drop ten degrees instantly. I feel the shock pulse through our bond before Damien's face even registers the emotion. The glass slips from my fingers, shattering against the hardwood floor with a sharp crack that echoes through the sudden silence. Amber liquid spreads across the wood like spilled blood, but I barely notice. All I can focus on is the way Damien's entire body goes rigid beside me, fury radiating from him in waves so intense I can taste it in the air.

"My own sister," he snarls at Elias, jerking away from my grip. "The sister who was kidnapped and tortured while I was being punished for failing to protect her. And now you want to claim her like a fucking prize?"

I step between them, feeling the tension crackling in the air like electricity before a storm. Elias rises from his chair, hands raised in a placating gesture that only seems to infuriate Damien more.

"I didn't ask for this either," Elias declares. "But I thought you deserved to know—"

"To know what?" Damien cuts him off. "That our fathers have been plotting behind our backs? That my sister is being traded away like property? That my best friend—" his voice breaks slightly on the word "—is going along with it? When were you going to tell me?" Damien demands, his body vibrating with barely contained fury. "After the ceremony? Or were you hoping I'd just accept it once it was done?"

"Damien, let him explain."

"Explain what? How he's going to fuck my traumatized sister because daddy told him to?"

"It's not like that," Elias protests, his own temper flaring. "You think I want this? You think I want to be tied to someone who doesn't choose me?"

"Then don't do it," Damien growls, taking a step closer. "Tell my father and yours to go to hell."

"And watch my pack fall apart?" Elias shakes his head. "Watch my father lose what little respect he has left after the Saloma disaster? I can't do that."

I watch this confrontation unfold, feeling helpless as two of the most important men in my life tear each other apart. The broken glass crunches under my feet as I move closer to them, whiskey seeping into the soles of my slippers.

"There has to be another way," I interject, looking between them. "Some compromise that doesn't involve forcing Bella into a mating she doesn't want."

Elias's laugh is hollow, empty of any real humor. "That's just it," he says, his shoulders slumping as the fight seems to drain out of him. "Bella's already made her choice."

"What do you mean?" Damien demands, taking another step forward.

Elias meets his eyes directly, and I see something there that makes my stomach drop—regret, guilt, and something else I can't quite name.

"She's gone, Damien," he says quietly. "Bella took matters into her own hands. She disappeared last night after hearing about the arrangement."

The silence that follows his words is deafening. I watch as Damien's expression transforms from rage to confusion to something like dread in the span of seconds.

"Gone?" he repeats, the word falling between us like a stone. "What do you mean, gone?"

"She left a note," Elias continues, reaching into his jacket to pull out a folded piece of paper. "For you."

The look on Damien's face as he takes the letter from Elias makes my blood run cold. I've never seen that particular expression before—a mixture of dread, hope, and barely contained rage that makes his hands tremble slightly as he unfolds the paper.

"What does it say?"

Damien's jaw works silently for a moment before he hands me the letter.

"Read it."

I take the paper. The handwriting is elegant but rushed, the ink smudged in places as if written in haste:

Damien,

By the time you read this, I'll be somewhere even Father can't find me. I refuse to be a bargaining chip in a game I never agreed to play.

Don't blame Elias. He's as much a prisoner of duty as I am. But I won't live in another cage, no matter how gilded.

I know it's selfish to run, but for once in my life, I need to be selfish. I need to choose my own path, even if it leads nowhere.

Be happy, brother. You deserve it after everything you've sacrificed.

All my love,
Bella

I stare at the letter until the words blur, then lift my gaze to Elias, whose face is a mask of restrained anguish.

"How long?" I ask, handing the letter back to Damien. His fingers brush mine as he takes it.

"Almost twenty-four hours," Elias says quietly. "We've had search parties out since dawn, but the storm..." He nods toward the window, where snow still falls in thick, relentless sheets. "It's buried any trace of her scent."

Damien folds the letter with slow, deliberate care—movements too precise to hide the turmoil roiling beneath his calm exterior. "She wouldn't have left without a plan," he says. "Bella's too smart for that."

"Smart enough to disable the GPS in her car and leave her phone behind," Elias confirms. "She took cash from her safe—a lot of it—and nothing traceable."

I move to Damien's side, my hand finding his. His skin is ice-cold despite the roaring fire. "We need to find her before someone else does. If word gets out that she is alone and unprotected..."

I don't need to finish the thought. We all know what happens to lone wolves, especially female ones with valuable bloodlines. The same fate that nearly befell me.

"We'll find her."

"And then what? Force her back into a mating she's willing to risk everything to escape?"

The question hangs between us, unanswerable. I know what it means to run from a life you never chose. I spent years hiding from my wolf, from my own nature.

The difference is, Bella is running toward freedom, while I was running from myself.

"We can't force her to come back. Even if we find her, the choice has to be hers."

Elias looks between us, something like relief flickering across his features. "You think she should stay hidden?"

"I think she should have the right to choose," Damien growls, his grip tightening on the letter until the paper crumples.

"My father won't see it that way," Elias says, sinking back into his chair. "He's already sent word to the surrounding packs about the ceremony. The invitations have gone out. If we cancel now…"

"Then we deal with the political fallout," Damien cuts him off. "Your father's reputation isn't worth my sister's happiness. If the wrong people realize what she is…"

He doesn't finish the thought. He doesn't have to.

The silence in the room sharpens until it feels like the air itself might shatter. And in that instant, I know our fight is far from over.

Because Bella isn't just running from duty. She's running straight into danger. And the only people who can protect her are us.

My family's land will have to wait.

THANK YOU!

I have always wanted to write a paranormal book. It probably started during my *True Blood* era, when I spent way too much time arguing with my TV about who deserved Sookie. I was firmly Team Eric with a side of Alcide thirst. And Bill Compton? Absolutely not. Fuck Bill Compton. That brooding vampire ruined more evenings than my Wi-Fi ever has.

To my husband Glen, who not only puts up with me writing about cursed bloodlines and feral soulmates, but also came out of retirement to attend Book Harvest—where he survived questions like, "How many Hail Marys does it take to repent for attending a smutty book signing?" The answer is probably "infinite," but you took it like a champ. You've seen me at my weirdest and still choose to show up, which either means you truly love me or you've just accepted your fate.

Cass and Mads, my chaos cheerleaders. Our Facebook messages are basically unhinged therapy sessions fueled by caffeine, memes, and plot rants. Cass, thank you for always bringing the right kind of feral energy when I start doubting myself. And Mads—look at you, one book closer to getting Luca and Alex. Only three more to go. LOL. You two are the reason my imaginary worlds feel real, and the reason I haven't actually joined a cult of sleep-deprived writers.

Alicia and Rae, my grounding forces. You reminded me to eat, sleep, and occasionally step away from the screen. You cut through my spirals with logic, caffeine, and memes, which is probably the only reason this book exists outside of a Google Doc titled "unholy nonsense."

To my readers, you magnificent weirdos who followed me into the dark. You made this book worth writing. You made me brave enough to try.

And finally, to the stories that haunted me for years. The ones with claws, teeth, and hearts that still beat after death. Thank you for waiting.

This one's for the ones who believe in monsters, the ones who root for the doomed, and the ones who can never pick between Eric or Alcide. But seriously...fuck Bill.

MEET AVELYN

Meet Avelyn Paige, the creative genius behind thrilling romantic suspense and heart-pounding motorcycle club and mafia romance novels that have conquered the Wall Street Journal and USA TODAY bestseller lists. Nestled in a cozy corner of Indiana, she shares her quaint abode with her hubby and a lively bunch of five furballs.

By day, Avelyn transforms into a cancer research superhero, battling in the realm of science. But when the lab coat comes off, the writing cap goes on, and she dives into a world of passion, intrigue, and leather-clad rebels. An unabashed bookworm from the get-go, Avelyn decided to weave her own tales after a plot twist in her life – losing her dad in 2015. Since then, she's been on a wild ride through imagination and hasn't hit the brakes!

Join Avelyn's Reader Group: Avelyn's Angels

Also by Avelyn Paige

Heaven's Rejects MC Series

Heaven Sent

Angels and Ashes

Absolution

Lies and Illusions

Resolution

Bad Luck, Hard Love

The Black Hoods MC

Dark Protector

Dark Secret

Dark Guardian

Dark Desires

Dark Destiny

Dark Redemption

Dark Salvation

Dark Seduction

The Bastard Boilers MC

Property of Azrael

Property of Fox

Voodoo City Queens MC

Devil's Queen

Second Sons Duet

All The Pretty Little Lies

All The Darkest Truths

Standalone

The Reaper's Vow

Hogging The Holidays